S0-AYO-232

100 YEARS

SIMON & SCHUSTER

# BRIGHT OBJECTS

*A Novel*

# RUBY TODD

**SIMON & SCHUSTER**

*New York   London   Toronto   Sydney   New Delhi*

**SIMON &
SCHUSTER**

1230 Avenue of the Americas
New York, NY 10020

This book is a work of fiction. Any references to historical events, real people, or real places are used fictitiously. Other names, characters, places, and events are products of the author's imagination, and any resemblance to actual events or places or persons, living or dead, is entirely coincidental.

While inspired by various real events and places, this story is a work of imagination, with a fictional Australian setting in New South Wales. Beyond peripheral reference to named public figures and historic events, it does not depict any real person, event, organization, or place.

Copyright © 2024 by Ruby Todd

Originally published in Australia in 2024 by Allen & Unwin

All rights reserved, including the right to reproduce this book or portions thereof in any form whatsoever. For information, address Simon & Schuster Subsidiary Rights Department, 1230 Avenue of the Americas, New York, NY 10020.

First Simon & Schuster hardcover edition July 2024

SIMON & SCHUSTER and colophon are registered trademarks of Simon & Schuster, LLC

Simon & Schuster: Celebrating 100 Years of Publishing in 2024

For information about special discounts for bulk purchases, please contact Simon & Schuster Special Sales at 1-866-506-1949 or business@simonandschuster.com.

The Simon & Schuster Speakers Bureau can bring authors to your live event. For more information or to book an event, contact the Simon & Schuster Speakers Bureau at 1-866-248-3049 or visit our website at www.simonspeakers.com.

*Interior design by Carly Loman*

Manufactured in the United States of America

10  9  8  7  6  5  4  3  2  1

Library of Congress Cataloging-in-Publication Data

Names: Todd, Ruby, author.

Title: Bright objects : a novel / Ruby Todd.

Description: First Simon & Schuster hardcover edition. | New York : Simon & Schuster, 2024. | Summary: "A young widow grapples with the arrival of a once-in-a-lifetime comet and its tumultuous consequences, in a debut novel that blends mystery, astronomy, and romance, perfect for fans of Emma Cline's The Girls and Ottessa Moshfegh's Death in Her Hands"—Provided by publisher.

Identifiers: LCCN 2024015400 (print) | LCCN 2024015401 (ebook) | ISBN 9781668053218 (hardcover) | ISBN 9781668053225 (trade paperback) | ISBN 9781668053232 (ebook)

Subjects: LCGFT: Detective and mystery fiction. | Romance fiction. | Novels.

Classification: LCC PR9619.4.T63 B75 2024  (print) | LCC PR9619.4.T63 (ebook) | DDC 823/.92--dc23/eng/20240403

LC record available at https://lccn.loc.gov/2024015400
LC ebook record available at https://lccn.loc.gov/2024015401

ISBN 978-1-6680-5321-8
ISBN 978-1-6680-5323-2 (ebook)

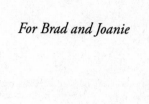

*For Brad and Joanie*

And so people keep asking and wishing to know whether it's a portent or a star.

—SENECA, *On Comets*

In the midst of winter, I finally learned that there was in me an invincible summer.

—ALBERT CAMUS, "Return to Tipasa"

# BRIGHT
# OBJECTS

# DIVINATIONS

Barely an hour before my first death on a warm night in January 1995—when I blacked out in a crumpled Toyota south of a town called Jericho—a bright object was sighted somewhere in the constellation of Virgo, the sign of the maiden, not far from a star named Porrima, after the Roman goddess of prophecy.

When I died for the second time, in August 1997, inside the floral bedroom of a country house as Chopin's *Nocturnes* played, the same object, visible to the world for months by then—the talk of backyard barbecues and press junkets in both hemispheres—had reached its maximum apparent magnitude of minus three, the moment of its greatest brightness as viewed from Earth, before it began to retreat from our inner solar system and slowly disappear.

What happened in between is the story I will tell, a story that took place under the eye of a comet, the last great comet of that millennium: the Comet St. John.

When I close my eyes and peer as dreamers do into the mind's darkness, I can still see it—a streak of light suspended in motion, brighter than Sirius, brighter even than Jupiter. It was forty-four light-seconds from our planet on the night of my second death, when I found myself being borne out of the house, the voices of paramedics in my ears like insects chirring, the blue-red headlights bruising the dark. It was the last thing I saw, there above the ghost gum trees before the van door shut and, with it, my brain: a torch-star with tails, white and blue-green; a winged creature in flight.

I wonder sometimes about the last time it was seen, appearing much the same to the eyes of the pharaohs and Assyrians as it had to mine—

gorgeous and strange, a question. What other lives were altered by its course? What events understood only in the shadow of its passing?

It was not until the end that I saw St. John for what it was, a sign of destruction and strange rebirth, and then all that had occurred seemed obvious somehow; inevitable as the looping line of its course. But the truth it would reveal within my own small life was there from the start, when we were all blind, when the comet still hid in the dark skies above our heads—a nucleus of white fire, streaming its tails of dust and ion, and sodium-blue, those compounds we all came from.

# DARK SKIES

I.

SOME MIGHT HAVE THOUGHT IT UNHEALTHY FOR A NEW WIDOW TO begin work in a funeral home, especially the same one that just months before had sent off her husband in a premium rosewood casket. But Jericho was a small town, and I was suited to the business. I grew fond of the ritual chores, the somber quiet, the tight-lipped atmosphere of wood polish and plush carpet and heavy drapes. I enjoyed the feeling of marshaling the stricken troops to church, and the soothing sound of a casket closing. I knew the tone to take with the bereaved, knew how to slide around details as if by way of a network of delicate balustrades, to deflect death. But neither was I afraid of allowing the Reaper into the reception room as I served tea to those customers I liked best, who announced themselves with a look that was naked and steely at once, who wanted no part in a pantomime.

The work tired my body and stilled my brain, and offered at least some prospect of sleep at the end of the day. I often had the sense of moving through water, and imagined that if I could just accumulate enough days behind me as mindlessly as possible, I might at last look up to find I had gained distance from the horizon of all that had happened, and see the approach of some kind of shore.

I can still hear the voice of Clarence Bell, the director of Bell Funerals, bemoaning in his soft Midlands accent that another customer was late with their deposit, or intent on printing their own order of service booklets, or bringing their own roses. As soon as I appeared at reception in the mornings he would approach in his ambling wide-paced way, diminutive in his overlarge gray suit, and begin shaking his head a few steps from me, emitting little puffs of indignant disbelief as he spoke, half under his breath, as though obliged to relate a string of dirty jokes.

Clarence had a drawn, adenoidal look. His sharp dark eyes would dart around as if searching for escape, and sometimes if I spoke too suddenly, he would jump with the nervous quickness of a cornered marsupial. By the end of any service he always appeared deflated some-how, like he had puffed out too much air, at last resigned to facts which despite being routine appeared to wound him afresh each day.

I knew the morning debrief was over when Clarence drew out a handkerchief from his trouser pocket, lowered his face into it and, with an equine flurry, blew his nose. I had learned early on that my role in this exchange was as a passive witness, and that after nodding and sighing a few times myself in sympathy, I should prepare his coffee with-out rejoinder or delay, which he would receive in his office in grateful silence. From my station behind the tall mahogany reception desk, I would then commence my review of the day's appointments, peering out every so often through the shop windows at the wide Victorian-era street just waking up, and measure my smile for the first customer, as Clarence had instructed: sincere yet restrained, with a touch of thought-ful gravity.

That summer, Bell Funerals had been asked to oversee the grand-est service in the recent memory of our town, and we were all feeling the pressure. Joseph Evans, the fifty-five-year-old eldest son of a once-prominent pastoralist family, and a man of exacting tastes in matters of ceremony, wanted a stately farewell for his mother, a farewell worthy of the woman she had been. Patricia Evans—who had died suddenly after a battle with vascular dementia—was remembered locally as a no-nonsense, capable woman who, despite her affluence and acumen in business, had cared more for others than she had for herself. Widowed in her prime, she had run the ancestral farm and raised her sons alone, while supporting numerous charitable causes and becoming revered for the pumpkin scones she baked for the Country Women's Association.

In the days between Patricia's death and her funeral, Joseph often turned up unannounced, asking for Clarence at reception, with a note-book in hand. He was by turns meditative and tense, but always polite, with a patrician voice and a taste for twill trousers paired with Crafts-man boots, as might be expected of a genteel stockman, albeit one with a ponytail.

Because the time we had to plan the event was in no way relative to its grandeur—which seemed set to rival the send-off of King George VI—it was surprising how often Joseph would lapse unprompted into rumi-nations about floral symbolism or the transmigration of souls, just at the point when he needed to finalize his choice of rose spray or casket. At times when he spoke, his palms would float upward, like a saint presiding over a scene in which Clarence and I were the fallen.

I had seen it before of course, and it was natural, this seizing of the dead one's funeral—with all its potential intricacy and pomp, to plan and to stage—as a means of sublimating the freshness of grief. Dead bodies can only be held in cool storage for so long, and it's terrible, really, how quickly a service must be held. For grief is a kind of rational madness, and new grief an alien planet, and it is not therapeutic for all in its exile to be faced with the finer decisions of commemorative slide-shows and casket sateens. The funeral of Patricia Evans, it was clear, was not just a means of distraction for Joseph, but an event burdened with the significance of a final gesture, a monument to his love and grief.

On the January afternoon I'll mark as the beginning—although as always there were other beginnings, casting their cells into this one and declaring themselves only later—Joseph arrived for his first appoint-ment an hour early, with a furtive-looking young brunette in tow. He stood at reception in a white oxford shirt and chinos, with what ap-peared to be a shark's tooth on a cord around his throat, wearing a look of patient expectation. When, at the sound of the bell, I emerged from the storeroom, he summoned a smile and with a rueful sigh glanced at my name tag.

"Ah, hello, Sylvia," he said, his voice mellifluous and warm, as though I were an old friend. His large eyes were almost a true cornflower blue, more striking for the fact that his skin—owing to the shock of loss, I supposed—had acquired a grayish pallor. As his gaze ranged around the room and the noonday sun lit his silver-blond ponytail, I noticed that even in obvious grief, his face had a childlike openness, as though the wonders and torments of life were still striking him as new.

"You're a picture—like something out of a noir film, at this old desk," he said a little nostalgically, before introducing himself and noting that he'd spoken with Clarence on the phone.

Patricia had been dead for only forty-eight hours, but as Joseph began explaining when Clarence appeared, it was especially important to decide on musical arrangements. Due to his appreciation for Clarence's professional input, Joseph had invited his friend Zara, a trained soprano, to trial some recessional songs during their meeting in his office, and had taken the liberty of arriving early, to ensure there was time enough afterward to discuss the flowers.

Even before Joseph's interruption, the day had been destined for chaos. Clarence had already held three consults with newly bereaved families without a break, workmen were laying new carpet in the Serenity Chapel, and I had just returned, clammy and flushed, after finding myself in a broken-down hearse among the wheat fields out of town, with the new apprentice and a casketed corpse due for post-funeral delivery at the local crematorium. Having coordinated a solution that involved hitching a ride back to Bell's with a truck driver and delivering the corpse in the company van without a moment to spare, I'd then had to soothe the nerves of Clarence's daughter, Tania, our mortician. She was red-faced with agitation at a delayed order of cavity fluid, despite having spent the morning in the tranquility of a cool mortuary basement with no one alive to harass or detain her.

I was still catching my breath at reception when the stranger appeared.

The sun streamed through the window, heedless of my attempt to shield it with one hand as I sat slumped over the accounts. For a moment

I closed my eyes, seeking refuge from somewhere deep in my brain, and instead finding the first diffuse throbs of a migraine. Down the hall in Clarence's office, Zara had cycled through an eclectic selection already—"Ave Maria," "Somewhere over the Rainbow," "You Belong to Me"—and was just commencing Bocelli's rousing aria "Time to Say Goodbye." Her voice vibrated through the rooms like a pealing bell; I could feel it in my skull.

The stranger must have been standing there for some time before I opened my eyes, and saw him appraising me in a sharp way, as if I were a kind of equation. He looked a little like a rancher from some other place and time in his chambray shirt and old pointed boots. I apologized at once, straightening in my chair and gesturing behind me toward the source of the voice now nearing its crescendo.

"I mustn't have heard the door," I said, forcing my face into a deferential smile. "How can I help?"

His face was raised in a quizzical look now, the kind that precedes a question, and for an instant I felt his eyes register the scar below my right eye.

"I was hoping for some information," was all he said, his accent American, his shoulders shrugging in a way that seemed nervous and involuntary. I was nodding now, and setting out pamphlets in a fan shape to face him: *Saying Goodbye: Resources for the Grieving*; *A Life Remembered: Memorial Options*; *Bell Funerals: A Gentle Touch*. I came out to stand by the side of the desk, unfolding the pamphlets and pointing at photos as I spoke.

"We can assist with all stages of the service, from the planning to the day itself. We can accommodate all styles, small or large, religious or secular. Our aim is always for the day to unfold just as the family has envisioned."

Closer now, he peered in the direction my hands moved; here to a stock photo of sympathy lilies, there to a detail shot of the Serenity Chapel's altar window, depicting the neutral vision of a tree with sprawling branches. From somewhere in the fibers of his shirt I could smell woodsmoke, tobacco, and something herbal. For an instant I felt light-headed, standing beside him as Zara sang her final soaring note, and I stopped speaking.

The moment seemed to stretch under the force of her voice, which held us within it, like airborne creatures waiting for release. At last there was silence. I took a breath and looked at the visitor, who was already looking at me. I supposed he was still reeling from the shock of new grief, which often ties the tongue and makes one slow.

"I'm sorry you've found yourself here," I said, to ease him. "We rarely have the pleasure of meeting people for happy reasons. Did you want to take a seat by the lounge, and look these over? Or, if you feel ready, I could take you through our selection of caskets and coffins."

At this he gave a noncommittal nod, not looking quite at me, and I wondered who it was he had lost. By this point, I'd usually been told. Perhaps some relative had forced him to come here too early, when naming the loved one in the grammar of the past tense was a new violence. I led him to the windowless display room behind reception, which itself had the aspect of a crypt or vault. I often ventured there between appointments for a few minutes of insulated silence in the glow of the downlights. It had beige walls and plush maroon carpet, a tone rather close to the color of dried blood.

I paused at the pedestal of false carnations, and tried to smile as I swept my hand behind me in a way I hoped was not too saleswoman-like. Stacked two by two in alcoves set into the walls were various vessels, stained or painted, accented with silver or gold, upholstered in different fabrics. The topmost caskets, at eye level, were the premium split-lid hardwoods. To show the comfort of their interiors, Clarence kept the head sections of their lids open. Each was lined with ruched velvet, satin, or crepe, and each had a pillow and matching throw draped over the lower lid, like a quilt just turned down for the night. When I walked down the aisle of the room, I would sometimes imagine I were aboard a train from another century, the alcoves like sleeper cabins with ornately carved bunk beds. Now and then I'd even feel a frisson of anticipation, as if I were settling into my snug quarters for a peaceful transcontinental journey.

I paused at the Polished Oak Classic, a popular midrange design with rounded corners and a navy velvet interior. "Just point out any model you'd like to look at further," I offered, my voice seeming too loud in the silence.

The stranger peered with me into the vacant space, where a small white pillow lay.

I gestured to the inner lid. "Some family members decide to have an image printed or embroidered here, something of significance to their loved one, such as a photo, symbol, or insignia. In this design, there's also a drawer for keepsakes."

I didn't look at him, but felt his intent stare, and wondered whether, like me, he was imagining a figure nestled inside the casket, their head resting right there on the pillow. "We have many models, as you can see, and also a range of vaults, urns, and memorial plaques," I continued, feeling suddenly like a parrot.

I turned to face the man, and gave a sigh I hoped sounded sympathetic. "It might also be that you're still in shock. This isn't a decision you have to make straightaway, of course."

He nodded furtively, and as he peered around I saw him draw a great breath. "They're very ornate," he said at last.

I smiled. "These topmost ones are, but we also have simpler models, traditional coffins which are very serviceable."

When I gestured to the lower displays, and asked whether anything caught his eye, I saw in his face a flash of amusement, which passed as quickly as it had appeared. Just as I felt irritation and curiosity rising in equal measure and considered posing the bald question of why exactly he was here, I heard Clarence calling, and invited the man to peruse the displays at his leisure while I stepped away.

Clarence sighed when he saw me in the hall, and reached out to grip an ornamental pillar. From behind us I could hear the sound of voices and clinking teacups.

"They're on a break," he said, his eyes darting upward as if some saint had blessed him. "Look, I don't think I'm going to make my appointment at the livery stables, Sylvia. You'll need to go in my stead—the owner will be away from tomorrow so we need to see him today. It's to inspect the horse-drawn hearse Joseph wants for the procession."

He handed me a business card, blew his nose, and stood peering at the floor between us, breathing as if winded. It seemed the carpet work was exacerbating his allergies.

"I didn't know you had an appointment this afternoon, Clarence," I said. "You didn't put it in the book. How will I get there? All the cars are tied up, and you know I walk to work."

At this he laughed bitterly, shaking his head. "Well, of course! Honestly, Sylvia, can this day get any worse?" He sighed. "A taxi is out of the question, the fare to Allandale would be astronomical. Oh, please try to sort something out!"

When I turned around, dreading the prospect of walking home through the heat to collect my own car, I was surprised to see the stranger standing there a few yards away with his hands in his pockets. "I wanted to thank you for the info," he said, smiling frankly for a moment before glancing down at his boots.

I nodded, feeling faint, resting my eyes for a moment on a square of carpet and wondering whether the air inside was really as warm as it seemed. I saw the man's feet shift.

"I could give you a lift. If you like."

This struck me as an extraordinary proposition from a stranger who hadn't yet even volunteered his name. But I was so tired suddenly. For a moment I tried to measure the man, testing his effect on my instincts. He looked guileless and almost shy now as I appraised him, standing there holding his keys and pretending to notice the decorative molding on the ceiling. I saw that his nose was a little sunburned, and his eyes when he looked back at me were on the green side of blue. Perhaps in my tiredness I stared at him for an instant too long, as by the time I smiled and thanked him, I'd inexplicably formed the image of his profile as belonging to a soldier on a Roman coin. As he held the door open and I walked into the bright day, I hardly cared, suddenly, whether he was really some gentleman killer with a preference for funeral attendants.

We rarely guess the significance of crucial moments in life while they are happening. For so much of the time we are steering blind. Retrospect reveals the most seemingly minor decisions to have been a crossroads, dividing one life from another. Strange, now, to think that the chaos of that day—Clarence's peevishness and the heat, the lack of cars, the need to inspect a horse-drawn hearse for an overblown funeral—combined to make me reckless enough to ride several kilometers out of town with a stranger. Had I not, I feel sure I'd never have seen him again, and life—unless I'm entirely deceived about the nature of free will—would have followed a different course.

"This really is too kind of you," I said when I was installed in the passenger seat of his green Holden.

He smiled as he turned the ignition key and reversed, his eyes on the rearview mirror.

"Your boss sounded stressed. Besides, I'm off work today."

His voice hadn't lost its grave, tentative quality, but he seemed a little easier suddenly. I'd wondered whether to ask if he wanted to discuss service options further—it seemed unprofessional not to at least conclude the consultation and it was a way to pass the time—but I felt he might withdraw again if I did.

Instead, I asked about his accent. He said it was from Arizona. His family was from a farming town near the Grand Canyon. I pictured that red, yawning place, and asked how it was that he came to be here, in another farming town in a different hemisphere, and he said it was for work. He had a slow way of talking, seeming to measure his words so as not to waste them. For a moment we said nothing, but the silence wasn't unpleasant. I watched him drive, one-handed and leaning back, without a spare movement.

"Do you like your job?" he asked suddenly as we were rounding the corner of the Rising Sun Hotel, a bluestone Victorian built during the gold rush.

I told him it occupied me, and that if I could be useful to devastated people, it was enough.

"It seems ridiculous we haven't exchanged names," I said at last, looking at him. "I'm Sylvia, as you probably heard."

He told me his name was Theo, and I asked him what his work involved. He was a researcher, he said, at the observatory not far from town. I knew the place, a huddle of buildings and telescope domes on a mountain in the nearby national park, an area known for its volcanic rock formations and dark skies.

"You're an astronomer?"

He gave a hesitant nod, as if astronomy were one remove from bootlegging or insider trading.

"How fascinating," I replied. "I suppose you know about the upcoming comet . . . ?"

For months now, and with increasing frequency, Comet St. John—ancient, rare, and huge—had been a presence in the local and international papers. Articles detailed its notable characteristics, its latest whereabouts as it journeyed toward us, how much time had passed since its previous visit, and what it was we could expect when it arrived, as if it were an international celebrity on tour. Editors made a sport of punning headlines—HOLY COMETS, HERE COMES ST. JOHN; CLOSE ENCOUNTERS OF THE COMET KIND; ST. JOHN, PATRON SAINT OF THE SKIES.

Theo nodded, scratching his nose. We were out of town now, coasting through fields of dry grasses, passing the boulder-like shapes of sheep in the distance, old windmills barely moving, and the lone, stricken figures of gum trees reaching into the hot blue sky. My window was half-open to the rushing air, and sometimes the shriek of a crow or cockatoo would sear through the silence like a curse.

He glanced over, scanning my face. "Yes, I know about it," he said with a sigh, looking back ahead. He might have been speaking of some notable local criminal, a near-mythical figure any thinking person in these parts was apprised of, a stealthy outlaw known to steal women and sheep and gold, who had never once been caught. "I discovered it," he said abruptly. "St. John is my last name. Theo St. John."

In the silence that followed, I heard the rush of air through my window. Then, as if of its own accord, my head began to nod, and I heard myself make an affirming noise, because I didn't quite know what to think or say. While he drove on with his gaze ahead, seeming not to expect an answer, I felt the stirring of synapses in some region of my brain, the region still primed to look for meaning in happenstance, and, suddenly light-headed, closed my eyes.

Just that morning on my way to work, I had looked up at the sign-board outside Our Lady of Perpetual Help on High Street, and noticed a new message below the one the young reverend, known for his efforts to attract new recruits with humor, had chosen for that week, which happened to be, LOOKING FOR A SIGN? HERE IT IS. Below this now in spidery capitals were the words, THE NAME OF THE STAR WAS BITTER—REV. 8:11, and finally, HEED ST. JOHN!

Perhaps because I had been vulnerable to certain kinds of fatalism that summer, I'd felt neither pity nor mirth upon reading those words, but rather a cold kind of recognition, which anticipated disaster as inevitable if not deserved—although on what scale, I couldn't tell.

If news of the approaching comet had exposed these tendencies in me, I was not alone. Like the indicator dye used by doctors to reveal disturbances in the body, the comet seemed to be revealing us all to ourselves and to each other, in our various registers of fear, hope, and hubris, like clusters of divergent cells within the same host. And it was growing worse. Even in that moment, there in the car, I could sense it in myself, the dark dilation of fear, unfurling questions without answers, and the feeling of somehow being marked.

Because I wasn't sure how much time had passed and I felt the need to break the silence, I glanced at Theo's inscrutable face, and spoke. "How amazing, to have discovered a comet. Its pending arrival has made quite a stir."

Without looking at me he nodded, and I saw the side of his mouth twitch in grim recognition. "Yes. That can happen with comets."

I waited for more, but he only stared ahead. Through the passenger window now I could smell cow dung, hay, and dry earth. Looking out at the passing fields, I considered how, while much had been made of the town's proximity to the observatory where an internationally significant comet had been found, precious little was known of the person who found it. As we lurched around a bend and I wondered whether the atmosphere between us had grown strange, I recalled references in the papers to the American researcher who had given the comet its name, but these references had always been vague. Some in town had formed the picture of a beleaguered recluse, shying away from the glare, and routinely declining to drop quotable sound bites to the reporters who approached him, a picture that I supposed might be true.

Now he was driving me to see an antique hearse. Despite my assumption that as a scientist he would have given no credence to the dark excitement and dread the comet was inspiring in some quarters, neither had he taken the opportunity to speak against it, to soothe nerves and undermine fearmongers with the tonic of calm, dispassionate scientific proofs. In fact, sitting there beside him, it occurred to me that nothing in his demeanor, when he spoke of the comet, disproved the notion that it really was a portent of doom. As I reminded myself, Theo was, of course, for reasons he hadn't yet shared, living in grief, which as I well knew lent its shade to everything.

I looked at him and smiled.

Seeing me, he nodded rather stiffly. "Almost there."

Perhaps, I thought, it was the intrusions on his privacy caused by the comet that he most resented. Perhaps he shared the ambivalence of some artists about the consequences of success—as soon as their creations gained any public appreciation, those creations ceased to really live for the artist, and instead became a threat to the inner work needed to unearth fresh material. Leaning back, I tried to imagine what it might feel like to search the skies each night for new life, and one day to find it, an object unknown to human records, reborn with your name. Such searching could, I supposed, lead one into a kind of madness— contemplating each day the infinity of space, from the confines of a human body on Earth. I had thought so even as a child, when I had watched the skies on camping trips with my father, sitting on the car roof beneath the Southern Cross with our star maps, taking turns to peer up through a portable telescope which, I now recalled with some regret, I had given a younger cousin years ago, less out of goodwill than because looking at it reminded me too much of those times.

I looked back at Theo to find him gazing gravely ahead at the wide dirt road unrolling before us, his back suddenly rigid, both hands now gripping the wheel. I wondered whether I had spoken out of turn or upset him somehow, and remembered how short-tempered the grieving can be, so I kept quiet, closing my eyes to the breeze on my face.

But then he began to speak, almost as if to himself, while staring out at the road. "It hasn't been here for four thousand two hundred and seven years. Its nucleus is eight times the size of Halley's. It's going to be"—he said, pausing suddenly—"very bright."

Before he could go on, I felt the car slowing and realized we had arrived. Beyond a line of willows and eucalypts I could see stables and sheds and a weatherboard house, and nearer to us, a pair of Clydesdale horses, white and brown, chewing hay and swishing their tails. A sign staked into the ground announced PRESTIGE LIVERY STABLES. I looked over at Theo and asked whether he wanted to come in, but he shook his head.

"I can wait," he said, raising a folded copy of the *Sydney Morning Herald* like a flag.

The stable owner was a ruddy-faced man of about sixty in jeans and a polo shirt, who strode out of the office with half an apple in hand. When I explained I was visiting on behalf of Bell Funerals, he hurled the apple into the scrub behind us and in a deep smoker's voice told me to follow him. The hearse was one of several other carriages in a large barn behind the house. In one swift movement he pulled away the drop cloth covering it and there it appeared, a magician's trick, a funeral carriage from another century, all glass and black lacquer with brass lamps, like something out of a romance of knights and maidens.

"It takes two of our drays," he was saying, "four in pairs if preferred, and you can choose between white, black, or bay. We want them to match, of course. Some clients like a little regalia for the horses—an ostrich plume looks very noble."

As he spoke, detailing how the driver would hold the reins from the box seat, dressed in a black cape and top hat, I had to smile at the theater of it all.

"Everything goes over very well, as a send-off gesture," he concluded. "The guests enjoy it. Something to talk about afterward, over tea and all that."

Following him into the office to collect some pricing pamphlets, I wondered how many caskets the hearse had seen, how many dignified processions with no one left alive now to remember them.

I had only been twenty minutes, but the sun had lowered in the sky when I returned to the car. Theo was sitting on the grass, leaning against one of the wheels with the newspaper on his knees. When he saw me at the gate he stared for a long moment without blinking, as if recalling who I was, before drawing himself up, getting into the car, and starting the engine. When we were strapped in, he gave me a sideways glance. "All sorted?"

I nodded. He smiled thinly and resumed biting his lower lip. I wondered whether he was thinking about the person who had died, the arrangements that had to be made, as waves of grief broke without relief. I felt somehow that this person was a woman, someone he had brought with him or met here, and that her death had been untimely, sudden. Perhaps there had been no goodbye.

I rested my head back and looked out at the fields speeding away, the orange sun on the horizon sinking down, and felt the lure of sleep like a dark lake I couldn't enter. Soon, I thought, he would drop me back at the office, and judging from his reticence so far, might not approach us again. I decided to press him further on the comet, as the chance might not come again. I knew discussing it had upset him, but I didn't understand why, and suddenly I didn't care.

I spoke at once into the silence, peering at him from the edge of my eye and feeling strangely breathless. "It will be here soon, won't it—the comet?"

His lips parted, but no sound came.

"I mean, I know it's here already, above us," I went on. "But when will it be visible, to the naked eye?"

"In nine days. Look up at the sky, in the late night next Sunday," he said. "You'll see it. Everyone will see it. And it will appear earlier, higher and brighter by the day, the closer we get to its greatest magnitude in August."

At the strange charge of his voice, I felt electricity race through me.

"Do you like living here?" I heard him ask suddenly, as we turned back onto the highway. "Were you born in this town?"

I shrugged, inclined to speak plainly. "This place is as good as anywhere. Moving would suppose an agreement with the future, a drive for change that doesn't concern me anymore." I levered up the window, as the breeze was cooler now, and looked back at him. "My husband was born here," I added, wondering whether he might share some aspect of his own life in return.

"I think I know what you mean about the future," he said at last, not looking at me.

I waited for him to go on, but he said nothing more, and I was tired, and increasingly aware of the dull, shooting pain in my spine that always seemed to worsen when I sat for long periods. I closed my eyes and imagined the comet in the darkness of my mind, like an exploding star, a star we were traveling toward as surely as it was traveling toward us, in one rare, inescapable, magnetic movement, a movement that would never be repeated as long as we were alive.

When we arrived back, I turned to Theo in my seat, figuring he wouldn't be coming in, and thanked him for his kindness. I smiled, and on impulse reached out my hand, noticing the marble patterns in his eyes as his cool palm gripped mine.

He looked at me directly then, and returned my smile. "Good luck with the fancy funeral," he said.

I stepped out and watched him drive away. I felt sure, then, that I would not see him again.

Before leaving, I walked over to the window and peered at the street, where people had begun to arrive for dinner orders of fish and chips and Chinese noodles from the shops across the road. There was still light in the sky, and a pale crescent moon. On an impulse that I chose not to interrogate, I drew out a sheet of the thick fibrous letterhead we used for sympathy notes to clients, and wrote with a nice black ink pen.

*Dear Theo,*
    *Thank you again for the lift. And I'm sorry for your loss.*
*With best wishes,*
*Sylvia*

I stared for a moment at the liquid darkness of the ink seeping into the paper, and the luxuriant loops of my cursive. It looked florid, almost immodest somehow. On impulse I grabbed the pen again and wrote a postscript below my name, a line from a book of proverbs I had never forgotten: *Memory sustains man in the world of life.*

Along my route home I dropped the stamped envelope, addressed to Theo care of the observatory, in a postbox, and resolved to think no more of the comet or its discoverer. This would be something of a task, I knew, as the date St. John would show itself in the sky was the same one I'd long had marked in my diary, the date by which I'd given myself permission to finally leave this planet.

## 2.

WHEN I WASN'T WORKING OVERTIME ON A SATURDAY OR SUNDAY funeral, the weekend was a treacherous gulf that had to be crossed. I had a certain routine—my physiotherapy appointment, my grocery run, the library, the laundry—but there were always those spaces in between when I was alone with myself in the house, and certain objects would begin to peer back at me with imperious indifference, and I would hear the sound of my own shallow breathing. Sometimes as I tried to read, or clutched a cup of tea and watched the steam, or stared at the frantic images of the TV news on mute, I would feel a faint breeze on my neck, or hear the bedroom door behind me release itself an inch, with the soft glottal sound of an opening mouth.

Time passed differently at home. I would check the clock and marvel at its glacial pace. I imagined that time was abiding other laws, laws known only to the house and its particular magnetic field, and the atmosphere of the rooms I had to move through was a thick fog I could feel but never see. Often I just kept still.

The Friday evening after I met the reticent astronomer was like all Friday nights. Walking toward the house, its shades drawn behind the cypress pine at the end of the court, I sensed in it a kind of forlorn resignation, a knowledge that its fate rested with mine. Inside, I hoisted up my tabby cat, Lionel, and held his warm body to my chest as we ventured down the hall and into the living room.

Like a night nurse, I did my rounds. I turned on the main lights and the radio, hearing its low drone enter the silence. I poured Lionel's half cup of dry food and my glass of wine. I wandered in my socks to the bathroom, and looked at the poster I'd stuck over the sink to hide the mirror, a seventeenth-century still life by Willem Kalf, depicting the remains of a luxurious meal abandoned in haste. Strewn on a table among a gold pitcher and crystal glass was a torn hunk of bread, an open pomegranate, a lemon, and a swathe of white cloth, all glinting in the half-light. Once my eyes had traveled twice over the shapes and shadows of the painting, I opened the drawer below the sink and traced the tops of my pill jars with a finger before raising one to my ear. Like an hourglass I turned it upside down and back upright again, hearing the sound of the pale blue ovals rotating, the soft exploding sound of popping candy, until I felt a tightness in my chest from holding my breath, and put the jars away.

There was always a time in the hours after dinner when I would begin to feel as if the atmosphere in the house were taking on the thickness of water. I would imagine us sinking together toward the ocean floor. I would feel a pressure against my limbs as I moved muscle and bone through space. These were my shipwrecked hours, the hours I lived in the shadow of sleep, which watched me like a god overhead, invisible and uncompromising. My longing for sleep was like a repulsive force; the more I looked for it, the further away it drew. So I courted it by stealth, and didn't look for it at all.

Often, I would raise my cello from its corner in the study and draw it close, the body of a friend grown mute. The cello had been my father's, and when I played it, I remembered him. As an adolescent I had, for some time, considered relinquishing speech altogether in favor of the cello, and to some extent it had always felt like my true voice. It had spoken from the time I first learned to slide the bow at certain angles like a tongue as I pressed and plucked the strings, drawing out a sound that vibrated radially from my sternum.

Next, I would read, propped up on pillows in the living room as Lionel purred on the arm of the couch, serene as a sphinx. I favored nonfiction hardbacks with lots of color plates, so that when my eyes tired I could just look at the pictures, like a child. The subjects varied—I'd recently leafed through books on fractal geometry in nature, illuminated manuscripts, and the first *Titanic* salvage mission. Because sleep would infiltrate my reading in waves without fully pulling me under, those hours would acquire a surreal, dreamlike quality. Certain images would return to me during the day, like memories of moments I'd lived: the microscopic patterns of a fern; perturbed-looking saints peering out like goblins from inside gilded script; the blue vision of a ship collapsed at the bottom of the North Atlantic.

That Friday, I pulled the cello close and began with a sequence of scales and arpeggios to warm up my fingers. After an aria or two, I felt us traveling further than before, as if the force of the sound and the motion of the bow, drawing oar-like over the strings, were causing us to gain speed, revealing dimensions of our course that had long been hidden. I felt that if we continued we might finally arrive at the place we had been pointed toward, a place that even from a great distance radiated a dark vibrancy my body remembered. When at last my arms grew too heavy and my back began to ache, I had to stop, and in the sudden silence the walls of the room seemed to contract.

Repositioned on the couch, I began reading a folio-sized complete reproduction of the Bayeux Tapestry. Why not take the opportunity to redress my ignorance of the Norman conquest of England? I was amazed to find that it did read like a story in pictures, from Harold Godwinson's departure for Normandy in 1064 to his death only two years later as king of England in the Battle of Hastings, amid flying arrows and the bodies of men and horses. This phase of the night was meant to deliver me to the next: the phase of repose, when either in bed or right there on the couch I would finally surrender to gravity and exhaustion, permit myself to close my eyes and await the obliteration of sleep. But just as my eyelids were growing heavy at the death and funeral procession of King Edward, I turned the page to the coronation of Harold, and there it was, right there in the sky above the crown of the new king—a comet.

A huddle of elongated men to the left of the scene pointed toward it, tense with trepidation at the sight of the strange star, blazing forward like a rocket in the direction of all that was to come—William's wrath, the warships, the attack. For a long time I stared at that shape, embroidered nine hundred years ago by unknown hands and appearing to me that night of all nights, and wondered what, if anything, it meant, and felt a strange adrenaline in my heart.

I closed my eyes, but sleep didn't come. Instead, I was visited by images of the night I couldn't forget, the night two years ago on Horseshoe Road that seemed always to be waiting behind my eyelids for those quiet moments when I was too weak to look away.

I felt myself, mute and resigned, hurtling backward through time, returned to the driver's seat, my hands light on the wheel, laughing about the undercooked experimental jazz that had preceded the symphony performance my husband, Christopher, and I had attended in Sydney a few nights before. There he was beside me, his warm, open face seized with laughter, his shoulders shaking in the Freddie Mercury shirt I'd bought him for Christmas. He was jiggling himself around wildly in an impression of the jazz act's frontman, who had seemed to appeal to the audience with rousing hand gestures and dramatic expressions more than he'd played violin.

Christopher had arranged a brief vacation in the city for my thirtieth birthday, and that Wednesday night we were driving back, returning a day earlier than expected due to a legal case he had to finalize. It was later than we'd planned—already Thursday morning when we approached Horseshoe Road—but Wednesday had been my birthday, and over pizza and tiramisu in Darling Harbour, we'd lost track of time. Neither of us wanted what had been a perfect day to end. I recalled how, as we'd chattered and the sun shone outside, I'd gazed now and then through the glass behind Christopher, where a living statue—dressed and painted in the silver garb of an angel with enormous wings—smiled sweetly at passersby despite the temperature, collecting coins in a feathered cup at her feet.

We were almost home, now. It was a winding two-lane stretch of road where rock wallabies sometimes came bounding, and darkness had fallen. I was trying to stay alert, but I was tired and hungry and could already feel the hot rain of the shower on my skin. Christopher kept making me laugh; now he was imitating the falsetto disco track the jazz act had played using a distortion pedal. As we approached a sharp bend to the left, he mentioned making grilled cheese on toast at home, and groaned about a client he had to see that afternoon, a grazier contesting a ruling over a boundary line. I was only half listening. There was a rusted old Mitsubishi Sigma in front of us that had stopped, its headlights still beaming forward, and I was about to steer around it.

Later I'd learn that the driver of the Sigma, Danny Ward, a twenty-two-year-old assistant at the local video store, had been driving back from a late-night *Star Trek* memorabilia swap meet when he noticed, as was often the case, that his engine was overheating. He had stopped the car to let it cool off, and was eating an apple as I approached.

I wonder often about the course my life might have taken, had Danny Ward not been driving an unroadworthy car, had the swap meet not taken place that Wednesday night, or had Darling Harbour been met with storm clouds instead of sunshine in the afternoon. Any one of those elements reversed might have been enough to divert the particular physics of what was about to happen, the collision of objects and lives in space and time, the instant disappearance of certain futures in favor of others, as we each were moved like pawns in a game of celestial chess, toward that bend in the road under that dark country sky.

I diverted to the right lane to overtake Danny; in just a few seconds we would have been back in the left lane and coasting toward home. But the dark sedan that suddenly appeared from around the bend was moving fast; its oncoming headlights had blended with Danny's and there was no time. It hit us from my side, spinning our Toyota like a tin can so we were nosed up to the Sigma, as the dark car skidded off toward the right lane's bushland verge.

The thought slid across my mind that it hadn't been so bad. A single jolt, some mangled metal and spinning wheels and perhaps some whiplash, and thankfully our car didn't seem about to catch fire. Dizzy, I looked through my smashed window, smelling gas and rubber, while wondering whether the other car was okay and finding that I couldn't properly turn my head. Then I began speaking in tones of relief to Christopher, twisting my shoulders around to face him, but hardly seeing him, because by then I was blinking away what I realized was blood, dripping down from above my right brow and below my right eye, while strange rays of pain broke out in my skull and neck and along my spine.

He was leaning back in his seat—in shock, I supposed. It was only when I refocused and reached over to touch him, and then bent forward to face his wide unblinking eyes, that I knew, in the ancient reptilian part of myself, he was dead.

I remember thinking, then, that this was the point I should begin screaming—the only reasonable response when nothing practical, no emergency maneuver or words of appeal could change what in an instant had become fact. But I couldn't speak. I heard a voice now, a young shrill male voice calling. The other driver, I thought, a person I wanted to kill in cold blood, cleanly and quickly with a sharp knife like a pig, right there on the road before anyone else arrived and before the glaze of shock wore off and made my body useless. But I couldn't get out of the car. And I saw it was just Danny, the witness, approaching now, a blond spectacled boy with plump legs in shorts, his hair like a halo in the headlights, and I began to cry, because he was contaminating the scene before I was ready, and because he wasn't the image of the devil I wanted, a devil I could kill.

That was when I closed my eyes and began to bang my head against the wheel, hard blunt blows I could barely feel, knowing I was the one who should have died, until at last there was darkness.

Finally, there on the couch in my empty house, sleep took me, but it was not peaceful.

Every Saturday morning since the accident, I'd visited Christopher's mother, Sandy, at her house a few streets over from my own, always bringing with me some offering of good cheer. Now, carrying a bag of currant buns in one hand and a bunch of chrysanthemums in the other, I walked the familiar route, with my half dream from the night before still fresh like a bruise.

Sandy was a retired midwife, with dyed russet-red hair, a way of exclaiming in wonderment at ordinary things, and a taste for free-flowing dresses and skirts in shades of fuchsia, mauve, and emerald green. Jericho was her hometown, and when Christopher's father, a carpenter from Queensland who liked to drink, eventually took a one-way flight back to Brisbane when their son was still a baby, she had stayed to raise him alone. We would sit over tea and treats, on her porch when the day was fine, and review the week as Terry, her half-blind sixteen-year-old Shih Tzu, sat panting in her lap, collecting crumbs.

I had never expected Sandy's friendship. The first time I'd seen her after the accident was in the hospital, just hours after the doctors had jump-started my heart. My head injuries from the collision—not helped by those I'd self-inflicted—had caused me to lose consciousness before the ambulance arrived. Then, just after I was wheeled into Emergency, for the first time in my life but not the last, I had died.

My death had spanned one and a half minutes. Yet when I woke to that beeping room in my narrow bed, I remembered everything. I wept to find I'd been revived from oblivion, and implored the doctors to return me there with some chemical salve, only to find myself being mildly sedated. When Sandy appeared, red-eyed and dazed and absently clutching a bag of toiletries she'd bought me from the hospital pharmacy, I began to sob.

I sounded out the words "I'm sorry" like a beggar's hollow prayer, certain she would never forgive me for being at the wheel that night, for not swerving in time, for being the one who survived. But she sat on the edge of my bed, shook her head, and told me to stop. "This isn't your fault," she said, reaching out to grip my hand, as light from the window crept over us and together, we cried.

Two years later, I was still trying to believe her.

\* \* \*

Sandy opened the door in a bright pink shift patterned with dozens of swooping green parrots, and as I followed her down the hall, she spoke of her latest consult with a psychic medium she'd met through her craft group, a retired oncology nurse who claimed to be in communication with Christopher. Once I learned that her fees were nominal and her communications with Christopher were routinely of a pleasant, reassuring kind, I'd felt grateful, as since seeing her, Sandy had been diversifying her former diet of dry crackers and fruit, opening the door in clothes she hadn't slept in, and speaking in a more modulated voice.

As she made tea, I paused for a moment to cast my eye over the framed black-and-white photograph at the end of the hall, which showed a young girl in a garden early in the century, holding out her hand to greet the spry figure of a winged gnome. The girl was Elsie Cottingley, one of two English cousins whose staged photos in 1917 provoked real debate about the existence of fairies and other such creatures.

The photo always made me smile, partly because to me the gnome, like the creatures in the other images, looked exactly like what it was—a cutout illustration held in place with hatpins, captured in soft focus and lacking the natural shadows of a three-dimensional being. But the cousins' hoax, which fooled Arthur Conan Doyle, also reminded me how just like children, most of us, probing deep enough, would be pleased to meet with proof of fairies and gnomes and an animate universe that returned our gaze, and I supposed that the way Sandy wore this desire more openly than most was one of the reasons why I loved her.

Following Sandy, I took the buns and a dish of butter to the wrought-iron table outside, where the porch chimes, attached to a glass bluebird in flight, rang out in the breeze. She set down the tea tray and sank into the chair opposite mine with a dreamy smile, before lifting Terry onto her lap. As she filled our cups, I could smell a new perfume, something sweet and floral she had probably bought at her favored local store, which specialized in Victorian nightgowns, cologne, and fairy figurines. Because I'd taken to buying her a new figurine each birthday and Christmas, I was now able to look at Sandy's hall table and measure my years here in fairies.

"I know you won't believe it," she was saying now of the medium, while restraining Terry's head from the bun on her plate. "But if you could have seen her, Sylvia—it was really like someone else was in the room. She told me that Christopher still has a way of seeing the comedy in life, even now!"

I looked into my tea, nodding. I imagined Christopher in his ethereal form, appearing at the medium's summons in her living room to make jokes that were somehow so inimitable that she could convey to his mother that it was really, undoubtedly him hovering there, impish and happy in his afterlife. I asked Sandy what kind of jokes he made.

"Well, he apparently asked her to tell me he'd realized it was true that he'd inherited my father's habit for puns. Now, having 'passed the time' with Dad up there, he could see what I meant!"

She looked at me brightly as I tried to smile. "You know," she said, between bites, "he mentioned Terry, too. Said I was still overfeeding him." She directed the rest of her words to Terry on her lap. "And that was before I told her about you, wasn't it?"

I nodded and ventured a remark on the sunshine, before she suddenly dusted the crumbs off her hands and began to speak of the comet, while in her eyes I noticed a strange gleam.

"Have you heard what they're saying in the papers about the comet? It's going to be huge, apparently, much bigger than Halley, and never to return. We'll be able to see it without a telescope soon. They say it will be quite beautiful . . ."

In a habit that had become ritual, Sandy and I headed out after morning tea to visit Christopher. I felt St. John hiding somewhere above our heads as we walked with the flowers to the cemetery on the outskirts of town, stopping here and there as Terry's nose led him along scent trails too vivid for us to fathom. I'd wanted to have Christopher cremated, and to keep his ashes by my bed in a cloisonné urn that I'd look at and speak to now and then, as if his spirit were somehow intact inside it. But I'd let Sandy decide, and she had wanted him buried in one of Clarence Bell's premium caskets in the same plot as his grandparents and great-aunts and -uncles, none of whom had arrived there before the age of eighty-five.

We knelt as we always did to collect last week's flowers, and Sandy lit a tea light candle on the headstone. We watched the flame dart in the breeze as the pines rustled and the magpies called. While Sandy arranged the flowers in the holder I looked up at the broad wings of the Victorian angel a few plots beyond, recalling the living angel I'd seen during my last lunch with Christopher, an apparition I'd taken then as a blessing. This angel's face was raised to the sky in an expression that was either serene or anguished, depending on the angle, owing to her missing nose and eroded eyes.

Eventually, Sandy shook her head and pressed her palm to the tombstone, just beneath his name, and gave me a withering look. "Nearly two years now," she said. "Two years and no conviction."

We walked more slowly on the way back than we had on the way there, each haunted by the shadow of a figure who had never been caught, the driver of the dark car who, before the chaos of other cars stopping and the police and ambulance and paramedics, had managed to speed away, absorbed into the night like a stone in a lake.

Comets tend to inspire grandiose thoughts in people, and I was no exception. Reading, in the hours that followed, about comets through history while lying on my couch, I wondered whether this was how King Harold, Claudius, and Nero's wife, Claudia Octavia, had felt, when their own impending deaths were each marked—or so they might have supposed—by a torch of light in the sky. I drew out my two-year diary and felt that the strange coincidence of the comet's apparition date did not make my decision easier. There it was, next Sunday the twelfth, the anniversary of the accident, the day I'd circled in green ink months ago on a night when I'd felt I couldn't continue.

The fact that it fell on a Sunday this year felt right, being the week's end and a word that had always impressed me as having a toll-like, sunken sound. I'd made a bargain with myself to press on until that evening, but that evening had lived in my mind ever since as a limit, beyond which I didn't have to travel if an early night with my blue pills still felt to me like redemption. Then, just as the light had fallen and the comet had announced itself in the sky, I'd leave Lionel on some pretense with Sandy, write a note of apology to her and Clarence and the few others with whom I was still in touch, and retire to bed for my final rest.

Just eight days remained.

# 3.

MONDAY WAS THICK WITH HEAT. ALL MORNING I WALKED THROUGH the rooms of the office lightly, as if I had overnight lost some mineral density that was inessential now. In the Serenity Chapel, I parted the drapes and opened the windows, watching the sun on the carpet and feeling as though my head were hollow. Despite Jericho's small size, Bell's funeral business flowed regularly from the wider district, and I was spot-cleaning the chairs for our first service of the day when Clarence appeared before me with a peevish head wobble, and asked why I hadn't yet closed the windows.

"You know the air-conditioning has to work harder in this wing, Sylvia," he said, bringing his hands to his hips. "Do you want the corpse to cook?"

There was something voluptuous about the way I found myself able to deflect anger before it reached me, that morning, as Clarence grumbled about disorder at the cathedral booked for Patricia Evans's funeral, and bemoaned Joseph's indecision over caskets and horse-drawn hearses. Everything impressed me as a trifle, an absurd diversion that could no longer touch me now that my final week was underway. So I smiled at Clarence, closed the windows and made for the hall, thinking of the upcoming hours which were mine to spend in silence with the new computerized accounts system no one else understood.

As I descended the stairs en route to check on Tania, I wondered whether my muscles and bones were renegotiating their contract with gravity, in response to my mind's altered contract with life. I was beginning to feel almost limp, as if I had been let go, as if I were falling at a pace so steady that this falling was possible to forget.

At the entrance to the basement I tried to shrug off this airborne feeling, and composed my mouth into a smile. Inside the main room, Tania was bent over the sink in her gum boots and violet scrubs, mixing something in a jar. On the stereo, Joni Mitchell was singing "Come in from the Cold," while beneath a sheet on the mortuary table, an embalmed Patricia Evans reposed with a strangely wistful expression. Hunched over the sink, Tania continued to mix the contents of the jar, in a languid way that suggested she had lost sight of whatever practical aim the mixing was meant to serve.

For a moment I stood mindlessly watching her as Joni continued to sing about different kinds of prison. Tania nearly dropped the jar when she suddenly turned and saw me, and I pointed to the stereo, which she promptly switched off.

"Sorry," I said. "We can hear it upstairs."

She gave a tired nod, and flipped up the plastic visor of her safety helmet.

"I didn't realize we were open already. I've been here a while. Joseph's finally ready to view her, so we're freshening Patricia up."

She glanced at Joseph's mother with a private, indulgent look, the kind exchanged by spouses after an argument has been settled. Watching, I wondered whether the increasing amount of time that Tania spent in the basement, which didn't coincide with any rise in custom, had to do with the husband whose blunt, gruff voice I had occasionally encountered on the phone.

She sighed now, and with a practiced resolve began applying cream to Patricia's face. I knew her restful look owed more to Tania's skill with suture thread than to the peace of death. Since joining Bell Funerals, I had learned that we tend to leave Earth with our mouths open, as if to pose a final question. When I first saw a corpse before suturing, its open mouth seemed to suggest the exit wound of life itself.

"There we are," Tania said presently, in the strange self-soothing voice I knew she used when alone, drawing back to rest a hand on one hip. For a moment we both looked down, and as I took in Patricia's extraordinary stillness and noticed my mind's tendency to imagine her suddenly fixing a glazed eye on us, or flexing her chill fingers until she was immobile and animate at once, I wondered how Tania bore it.

"We're almost out of eye caps, Sylvia," she said finally, drawing down her visor. "It would be great if you ordered a few more boxes today."

I said I'd add them to my list, and calmly wished her well.

I imagined my new serenity like a pale blue vapor, enfolding us all. Under its neutralizing influence I pictured Clarence's nervous system, a frayed red circuit of false alarms, growing quiet. I imagined Tania, too, at peace within its amniotic embrace, no longer holding her breath or muttering to herself in tones of rising panic over the shortfalls of sluicing equipment or the facial expressions of corpses downstairs.

Stopping for water in the lunchroom, its beige walls featuring a watercolor of a sailboat in mid-ocean, I remembered an afternoon with Christopher during our honeymoon in Canada. We had hired bikes to ride around Stanley Park in Vancouver. It was autumn, and as I followed behind him, inhaling the bright, damp air that smelled of mulch and fir needles and cedar and brine, I almost had the feeling of leaving my body behind. We glided for miles, looking out at the boats along the marina, at the woodlands and the views of English Bay from the seawall, and I felt giddy and free of thought.

Now and then, Christopher would look back and grin, and call out to me, pointing at things he didn't want me to miss seeing—a squirrel, a distant eagle, a luminous cloud. Halfway through, we stopped to sit on a bench along the seawall, and watched a passenger ship grow closer before turning from the bay.

"Fair winds and a following sea," Christopher said, in a dreamy voice, and I asked what he meant.

"It's a naval toast. My uncle used to say it," he explained, smiling. "The wind's been behind us this whole time."

We had spoken, then, of other things—the prospect of pizza for dinner, our pending departure, but my memory wouldn't offer up the words to me now. I hadn't known, then, how I would long to relive

even those lines, cast so casually between us, in view of so many years
ahead. As we kept riding and the light began to fade, the world seemed
wide and generous, and perhaps this, I had thought, was now how life
would be. The lightness I felt then was different from how I felt now, I
saw, poised by the door regarding my shadow on the carpet. It was not
a feeling I could imagine experiencing again. The airborne sensation I
felt now contained no element of joy, no aspect of hope for the future.
It was just the feeling of having nothing left.

When the doorbell sounded in the late afternoon and I looked up from
the accounts to see who was there, I had to squint through the sunlight
glaring from the windows. I recognized the boots first, and then the
face. I set down my pen. Theo St. John had returned. He was taller
than I remembered, and paused some paces away, regarding me with a
concern I couldn't place. Offering my professional smile, I waited for
him to speak.

"Hi," he said, and after pausing for a moment longer than a breath,
added, "Thanks for the note."

I smiled, embarrassed suddenly by a gesture that seemed excessive.
Even though I was trying not to look at him too directly, I noticed that
sometimes, as now, warmth broke through his reserve and inscrutability,
at the corners of his eyes and mouth. "Also," he said, shifting on his
feet, "thanks for the tour and information the other day. I wanted to
let you know that I won't be needing to see the chapel, though." He
looked at me for a long moment, but I couldn't read his expression. "I
have relatives taking over the planning," he said finally.

"Oh, of course," I replied, registering a dull, falling feeling that
seemed divorced from my logical mind.

He nodded and for a moment looked into his hands as though surprised they were empty, and I knew that in a moment he would leave.

"How are you finding the heat?" I asked abruptly, nodding behind
him toward the window.

He looked at me sidelong for a moment, frowning. "I've never much liked it, really," he said finally. "I prefer spring."

With a half smile and a nod, he turned for the door, and I spoke to the blue-and-white checkerboard of his shirt back. "I hope you don't mind my asking, but I wonder whether you'd mind showing me the comet sometime soon, at the observatory?"

He was facing me now with a look that made me question whether there wasn't some tide or troop advancing from behind my shoulder.

"It's just that I haven't been able to stop thinking about it," I said, and stopped, hearing the words and wondering why they sounded indecent somehow.

He ran a hand over his face and blinked at me for a moment. "Yes," he said. There was a pause as he gazed at the floor between us, before looking up. "I can show you tomorrow night, if you like, or rather, very early Wednesday morning when it'll be visible, if you're up to it."

When I nodded, he told me to meet him at the observatory's main entrance at 1:30 a.m. He left at once, without a farewell.

Before leaving work, as I folded order of service leaflets and tucked memorial keepsake cards into mini envelopes, I shrugged off embarrassment at my own temerity. Because of it, I would see St. John with my own eyes much sooner than Sunday. I had begun to feel that when I did see it, something that was indiscernible now would be revealed to me, and I didn't want to wait. As I thought about the comet and watched the clock, strangely restless to be alone with my thoughts, I scanned the road for dark cars. One, two, three, I counted as they passed in shades of black and navy and dark gray, their drivers mute shadows in the windows. Eventually they all merged together in my mind. This counting was a useless habit, a rosary to measure time as it disappeared.

That evening, shortly after I arrived home with a container of chow mein, which I'd begun to eat with a comet book from the library spread before me, the phone rang and I jumped. It was Vince Chen, a senior constable in the local police force and a school friend of Christopher's. He always greeted me the same way now, his soft voice rising on "Hi" and falling on "Sylvia," a greeting which acknowledged in its very pitch that anything he could go on to say would be meager, the piecemeal work of salvage after the fact.

As I held the receiver, I heard him take a long breath. "Sylvia," he said again. "They're closing Christopher's case."

I looked at the spear of carrot on my fork and set it down. My eyes traveled over the black-and-white photograph of the page in front of me, showing Halley's Comet racing through the sky in 1910. There was insufficient evidence to proceed on any of the leads, Vince was explaining now. "You know it, I know it, the detective senior constable knows it." He sighed. "There's nothing more to investigate, at present, anyway."

"Nothing more to investigate," I echoed, waiting for the words to make sense.

"I'm sorry, Sylvia. The case can be reopened if a new lead comes to light."

I rested on the edge of the couch. I felt shaky and bloodless, panting there.

"But no one will be searching," I said.

Through the receiver I could hear the high-pitched hysterical sounds of children's television, and somewhere, the clatter of plates being set down. I saw Vince, tired and stooped at the kitchen bench in his shirt-sleeves, mouthing at the kids to be quiet, while his wife, Donna, her hair in a French twist, served dinner wearing her tunic from the hair salon.

"Well," I said finally, "it's best I heard it from you. You're good to me, Vince."

"You know I want it solved."

For a while we breathed into the silence.

"Look after yourself, Sylvia. I'm here if you need me. Come by some night—Donna would love to see you."

I made a muffled noise. My tongue felt thick. Eventually I heard the line cut out.

I pictured Sergeant Angus Blair, Vince's boss, seated at a table somewhere in town, smiling beside his purse-lipped wife with her bobbed helmet of hair and their plump little daughter who shared his upturned nose. I thought of scanning the windows of restaurants until I found them, and taking a table nearby just to see if he would dare to look at me. But I was a sniper without a gun, playing war games with myself.

It wasn't that I was mad, or desperate for any random person to blame. In a late-night call just weeks after the accident, Vince himself had mentioned Sergeant Angus Blair, whose breath had supposedly been known to smell of whisky more than once while on duty and whose unmarked black patrol car, a Ford sedan, had been found crashed into a tree near his home less than an hour after the accident that killed Christopher. The morning after that phone call, I had stood in the display yard of a dealership in the next town, looking squarely at the same model, my whole body cold, and felt sure it was the same car I had seen coming for us that night.

Standing there gripping my elbows with a black heart as traffic on the highway hissed by, I mouthed Angus's name and felt all my rage and despair converge around it, gaining the dignity of clarity and direction. Had the culprit not been a prominent policeman, there would have been no need or recourse for conspiracy, and he or she would surely by now have been found. As it was, with Vince's help, I had to guard against the perversion of justice for Christopher, by the very people meant to deliver it.

For a while I walked around the house, keeping my shoulders straight and my face composed, noticing the light fade outside and trying to feel my bare soles on the cool floor, trying to picture my mind as an open space, trying to breathe. I attempted to conjure the blue vapor, and the lightness I had felt earlier, the surrender that precedes many kinds of departure. But I did not feel light or serene. Those feelings seemed to belong to a stranger, or else to a delirious version of myself. Instead, I felt rage, pure and ugly at once. The case was closed. The coward who killed Christopher had acquitted himself. Angus had won. I stood rigid in the living room, my pulse in my ears, my body like a wick on fire, and waited for darkness to fall.

When the sky was black but for the moon and stars, I went for a drive. With a fast heart I coasted through the leafy, wide streets west of the town center, where jacarandas stood in shadow and figures moved behind bright front windows. I slowed down when I reached the stretch of houses I knew best, with the name that stuck in my throat: Jubilee Street. At the end of the road I let the engine idle, a sound like hunger in the silence. Directly opposite, behind the casuarina pine was the pale brick house, wide and set low to the ground amid shrubbery, as if trying to hide. The windows were unlit. They were either in the rooms at the back or not at home.

I don't know how long I sat there in the car watching the house, waiting for them to return. I stared at the dark windows as though they were eyes looking back at me, and thought of the freedom Angus could now be sure of, thought of his happy life, until my chest felt tight and I had to lean on the wheel. All the way home I felt the sky pressing down on my head. When I finally collapsed on the couch with an aching jaw and my stomach in knots, I stared at the ceiling and told myself it was the last time.

In my previous life, I had never taken notice of cars. But Christopher was able to price and date every make and model of any vehicle I ever pointed out in our time together. It became a game, a trick he owed to the same kind of childhood obsession I'd had with prehistoric fauna and ladies' gloves, which despite being short-lived, impressed facts in the brain with singular precision. "What's that?" I'd ask as we drove, and, squinting, he'd immediately announce, "An '84 Nissan Skyline," or, "A '75 Valiant Charger," as though knowing these things at a glance was the same as describing the weather. I'd say, "How much?" and he'd say something like: "New, in today's money? Forty-two, give or take. Now? Probably fifteen, depending on the Ks. Those Chargers had dodgy brakes, though." And I'd laugh, having never seen him take any interest in cars otherwise.

Now I spoke into the silence. "Don't worry, darling," I breathed. Sometimes I would speak to him like this, aloud or in my mind. When I closed my eyes, I could feel my body in motion along the path of the reserve we used to visit on weekends. I could smell the fresh, nitrous rot of leaves and earth, but I couldn't see him. He was there, though, I could hear him, loping beside me half a pace behind, patient and calm, listening. "There's something I'm not seeing," I said, peering at the lunar surface of the ceiling. "But I'm going to get him, Chris."

# 4.

DURING THE WEEKS AND MONTHS AFTER THE ACCIDENT, WHEN I WAS still wearing the spinal brace, fashioned like a metal corset, that held my torso compressed and rigid like an arthropod's exoskeleton, Vince and I would snatch time from lunch to meet at the deserted laundromat near the police station. There, in an atmosphere of damp and ammonia and soap flake dust, he would show me copies of classified records and we would look for conclusive evidence of corruption, some small but deadly inconsistency or lie with which we could mount our case. The first time, we stood over the lid of a rusted dryer where Vince had spread out the report on Angus's crash, and scanned the grainy handwriting of Senior Sergeant Douglas.

"Okay," said Vince, running his finger down the page. "So, Douglas arrives at the scene at 2:35 a.m., and claims to have tested Angus for drugs and alcohol right away. Angus reads negative, or so Douglas says."

Looking over his shoulder, I read out the accident description: "Sergeant Blair's Ford sedan patrol car (Jericho fleet no. eight) was traveling west down Jubilee Street before swerving onto the curb and colliding with a street tree on the corner of Kent Road."

"Look," said Vince, stabbing the bottom of the page. "Here are Angus's excuses for negligent driving: 'disorientation from a dizzy spell,' supposedly caused by ACE inhibitor medication for high blood pressure."

The report closed with a vagueness we found curious. "Sergeant Blair has received injuries," Douglas wrote, before noting Angus's transportation via ambulance to the Western District Hospital.

At our next meeting, Vince produced an expenses memo in the same handwriting, confirming that on the day of the crash, Angus's patrol car had been towed to the regular police mechanic for damage inspection and immediate repair.

"Interesting," he said, waving the memo in the air like a flag, "interesting that the senior sergeant who filed the crash report, and who oversees the car fleet, isn't just a colleague, but also a known personal friend of the driver."

We sat on the bench by the soap flake dispenser and a yellowed pile of *New Idea* magazines, asking questions as we sipped bitter coffee from the milk bar next door and stared at the peeling aquamarine walls. Angus was the only one we referred to by first name, less to divest him of the authority of his title than to mark him as an intimate, a person we held in mind, who had entered our dreams.

"How is it not suspect?" I asked. "Angus's car crashes shortly after a hit-and-run accident just five kilometers away in the same small town, and the local senior sergeant, his close friend, happens to be the one to appear on the scene, in the predawn hours, to file the report."

"And to breathalyze him," Vince said, "and record the result." He sighed and set down his cup. "I'd say Angus called Douglas, to make sure he was the one who attended."

"You really think they might be close enough that Douglas lied for him?"

Vince shrugged, and squinted at a magazine on the floor, showing Julia Roberts grinning in a ball gown. Some bored miscreant with a Sharpie had filled in her front teeth.

"It happens," he said. "They went through the academy together. Their wives are friends."

"Well," I said, leaning back, "whether it was duplicity or negligence, what takes the cake is the same senior sergeant thinking it unnecessary to have the car examined to rule out evidence of an earlier impact."

"Yes," said Vince, cracking his knuckles. "Instead, he sends it to the panel shop that same day, where any evidence would have likely been erased. It was that decision that put me on alert. The question is, what can we do about it?"

As a lower-ranking officer who wasn't even assigned to Christopher's case, and without conclusive evidence of conspiracy, Vince's powers were limited. Being his family's main breadwinner, he also needed to avoid marking himself as the enemy of those higher up, whom he feared might view suspicion of one of their own as tantamount to treason, or else as a threat to their own reputations. There was, after all, an ongoing Royal Commission investigation into corruption and worse within the state's police force at large, and everyone was on edge. But in the weeks that followed, Vince did succeed in attracting the attention of the main detective on the case, a thin, hard-edged young man called Watts, to the coincidence of Angus's car crashing so soon after the nearby hit-and-run. Such a crash, Watts conceded, could conceivably have been manufactured by the hit-and-run driver, to cover up damage and injuries from the earlier impact. He agreed that without being able to discount this possibility by checking the vehicle in its post-crash condition, further investigation was warranted, "if only to avoid any outward impression of police corruption," he had said.

But in the end, this further investigation consisted of little more than a polite cup of tea with Angus's wife, who would by then have had ample time to rehearse a credible statement. Having obtained this statement about Angus's whereabouts before his collision with the tree, Watts could now tick off her name and file away the report. "He's ambitious," Vince said of Watts, when I asked for his opinion. "He'd want the case off his books, for sure. It's not high profile enough, and who knows whether he hasn't been nudged not to look too hard."

We were unsurprised to learn, upon reading the report, that Angus's wife had provided him with an alibi for the time of the hit-and-run, shortly before 1:30 a.m. on that Thursday morning in January 1995. I imagined her facing Watts with a beleaguered smile over her cup of tea, a tray of biscuits between them at the kitchen table, the clean, quiet rooms of her house at noon holding themselves discreetly, as if attesting to the inherent rectitude of the lives lived there. Through the report I heard her voice, saw her deliver her lines with an earnest poise, now and then shot through with a quaver of frailty, as, under the table, her fingers spun the wedding ring on her left hand.

"Wednesday was Angus's day off, and Sally was still on school break, so we were all at home," she said, when asked of her family's activities on the day and night leading up to her husband's predawn crash. "It was a peaceful afternoon—I was in and out doing the washing, weeding the garden, chatting for a while with my sister Debra on the phone, and Angus watched *My Girl 2* with Sally on the couch before dozing off. He wasn't feeling himself," she continued, pausing to take a sip, as Watts nodded and wrote on his pad. "It was his new medication, making him queasy and sleepy, I suppose. And he went to bed early that night. He was there beside me the whole time, right until his alarm sounded, and he didn't leave for the station until 1:50 a.m."

With a vexed look into her cup, she explained that Angus had felt well enough upon waking to leave for the early shift, despite his symptoms the previous day.

When Watts pointed out the fact that Angus had neither been rostered nor called in to work for that early shift, she nodded and sighed.

"That's true," she said. "He got his weeks mixed up. It happens. And as I said, he wasn't feeling himself."

Whatever the reason was for Angus's predawn excursion, we doubted Mrs. Blair's claims about his departure time, and suspected that what she'd have said about this night, when at home with her husband and in the absence of a note-taking detective, might have been quite different. For no reason we could understand, Watts's report contained zero reference to the fact that, of only two possible routes from Angus's house to the Jericho Police Station, one involved the stretch of road where the hit-and-run occurred.

In the end, Angus was never even an official suspect, and it was difficult not to believe that his friends had simply closed ranks around him.

To shield Sandy from the poisons of rage and obsession that had infected me, I told her only enough about my suspicions regarding Angus to feel I wasn't deceiving her. After a while, she stopped asking if I had anything new to report, and at first I assumed it was because she trusted that if there was a way to achieve justice, Vince and I would find it. But as the months wore on, I wondered whether she simply had a greater instinct for self-protection than I did. I wondered, too, whether she was more resigned than me to the fact that no conviction would bring Christopher back. And I supposed she shrank from the version of me that was summoned at any mention of the case—the gritted teeth, the rigid shoulders, and hard, bitter voice. I had seen it in her eyes.

A month after we read the report—when Vince started to loosen his hold of the case and winter had begun, and a lackluster appeal to the public for leads had yielded only dead ends—I finally came face-to-face with Angus. I'd been called in for an additional interview, and because Watts was away on the afternoon it was scheduled, Angus was, to my dismay, the one appointed to meet with me. He seemed composed enough as he arrived in the foyer, offering a cursory smile and his hand. I looked without blinking into his pale blue eyes, and watched as they darted around. His palm was warm and dry, and perhaps I held it for a little too long, as he cleared his throat when I released it. Briefly he wiped at his mouth and offered me coffee in a tight voice, which I refused, before he led me into the small, dim back room I knew well, with its beige laminate table and vinyl chairs, and view of the car park with its one lonely gum tree.

"So," he said in his deep, resonant voice, sitting opposite me under the window, his hands clasped together on the desk, "we're here to go over some of the details of what you remember. Just answer as best you can."

As he spoke I watched the tree above his head, its stretching branches, its leaves wavering in the breeze. They seemed to move as if in slow motion, like reflections on water.

"I'd like you to think back to the night of the accident. Take your time. What did the other car, the car that hit yours, look like?"

I stared at his large pink hands on the table, frozen there like some side-crawling crustacean, and felt a rising heat. "We've been over this," I said quietly. "Why are you asking again?"

He tried to smile. "Generally, key details like these are worth revisiting, as a safeguard. Memory is fallible, and sometimes new insights emerge with time, especially in the case of traumatic events."

"Well, the facts of the car are the same," I said, peering at the thick gold wedding band constricting one of his hairy knuckles. "As I've stated, it was a dark sedan, and in daylight could only have been one of three shades: black, navy, or dark gray."

He took a deep breath in and out of his nose, and glanced at the legal pad by his hands. I noticed the tender pink dome of his head, like a crop circle in the field of his hair.

Looking back at me, he pursed his lips in an imitation smile, and explained how at this point, we had to consider the possibility that the investigation had thus far been unsuccessful precisely because it had been focused on the wrong shade of car.

But his words bled together in my mind until they were only sound, and as I looked at the gum leaves through the window I tried to measure the tone and cadence of that sound, to deduce how much of it was sincere. Finally I met his gaze.

"I trust you've also reconfirmed Danny's recollection?"

At his false, mollifying look, I spoke again. "Let me guess, our sole witness still remembers nothing!"

As Angus began to speak about the many variables that determine a person's recollection of a crime, I marveled at how, despite having had a box seat to the accident from his position meters away by the road, Danny claimed to recollect nothing more of the driver or the car than a blur that merged with the night. I recalled how, after vaguely calling out to me just after the crash, he had stood there in the glare of our headlights, open-mouthed and expressionless, before I finally lost consciousness, only to learn later that he'd restarted his car and disappeared as soon as a truck driver stopped to radio for an ambulance.

I recalled, too, how when I was only a few weeks out of hospital,

I had seen him driving a shiny new Subaru, the kind I doubted his video store wages would pay for. Now, as the hairs on my neck stood to attention, I pictured Angus, days after the accident, slipping Danny an envelope, shaking his hand on a job well done, and still, nearly two years later, reminding him of their understanding.

Dimly, I sensed Angus had finished speaking, and when I looked at him, I saw his palms were open in that old gesture of the diplomat. Suddenly, I felt breathless.

"Well," I said, unable to keep the sneer from my voice, "I'm not changing my statement, as much as you might like me to."

He glanced at me with his chin raised then, and while his expression was inscrutable, I saw the flint in his eyes.

"I know what I saw, and I'll bet Danny saw it, too," I said, standing and, suddenly faint, lurching toward the door. When I reached it, I turned back to see him still sitting there, peering at me narrowly with his lips parted for speech. "A dark sedan," I said. "Rather like your patrol car."

I left before he could speak. As I wandered away in the cold air, the image that remained was of Angus's gaze, which throughout the interview would fix on me for only seconds before sliding away.

For all the time that had passed since, that memory of Angus had been a scab to pick, a maze of dark potential to retrace. But now, with the landmass of my own end in sight and the whole world veiled in blue shadows, it seemed like one more dim window in a lonely city I was leaving, a city that had beaten me.

# 5.

FROM MY CHAIR AT RECEPTION ON TUESDAY, I PHONED OUR FLORAL supplier about a huge rose and lisianthus wreath for Joseph, while staring through the window at the clouds, like a traveler anticipating the end of a journey. I ate my lunch in the botanical gardens. Under the shade of a huge elm, I watched the dark reflections of branches on the ground, felt the dry grass beneath my palms, and listened to the breathing leaves. As I walked past Jericho Memorial Hall on my way back—trying to disregard a dark surge in my chest at the apparition of Christopher and me in our wedding attire, passing lightly through the old double doors—I noticed a series of A3 posters. They were stuck at hasty angles in a row along the rear wall. The text, which seemed to lack certain necessary information, announced itself in a multicolored, psychedelic font, and was phrased in the manner of a deranged telegraph.

MEETING! the posters exclaimed. ARE YOU BEING TOLD THE TRUTH?!? CONCERNED CITIZENS DISCUSS THE COMET. THIS FRIDAY 6 P.M. MEETING ROOM 2 DON'T BE CAUGHT OUT. IMPORTANT INFORMATION DISCLOSED ABOUT COMET. NO TIME TO WAIT! COMING SOON.

Whether what was "coming soon" was the comet itself, the meeting about the comet, or a movie about the comet—which, for all I knew, these posters might have been promoting—was a question that detained me for some time as I stood there. Also undisclosed were details about who exactly was holding the meeting, the nature of their interest in the comet, and on what grounds they were claiming to know more than anyone else. My suspicion was that the grounds were divine, but regardless, I made a mental note of the time. If there was anything I was sure of, it was that I would not blithely allow any comet-related intelligence-sharing to happen without first installing myself as a witness. By then, I thought, walking back to the office at a clip and savoring the breeze on my neck, I could be the one with facts to share, thanks to my private viewing with the comet's discoverer taking place in a few hours' time.

In reality, when I closed my eyes and thought of the comet in the darkness of my mind, it always seemed to defy my understanding, like a mirror that could reflect anything. But somewhere in my body, in the cells where primitive convictions are stored, I also felt a strange hope. It was there as I waited at the traffic lights, a radiance behind my eyes. My hope was that, if nothing else, the comet, like the celestial equivalent of a Rorschach inkblot, might cause me to face proof of a truth I had on some level long known, but been unable to see—allowing me to square my earthly affairs, before I left, with a level of peace and grace I might not otherwise find in time.

When I rounded the corner of High Street and Station Road, where the coral-colored shop front of Starz Video stood, I was already running late to return to the office, but I stopped to scan the shop's sunburst signs of two-for-one new release offers, and peered through the windows, only to find myself looking at the pallid profile of Danny Ward.

I hadn't seen him there since I'd rented *Pride and Prejudice* for a popcorn night with Sandy months ago, and had supposed he'd quit. For a moment I watched him in profile, slumped over a comic at the desk, with a lollipop stick dangling freely from his mouth and wearing the insouciant look of a bored child. Without prevaricating, I walked inside. Upon seeing me, he dropped the lollipop into the mug by his hand, and blinked at me in a placid, watchful way.

"Hello, Danny," I said, as he nodded and clasped his hands together over the comic, which showed Batman scaling a tall building in Gotham, while a pretty woman stood crying on a ledge above.

"Looking for something?" he asked in his soft, lisping voice. The edges of his small, bow-shaped mouth were stained green.

"I haven't seen you for a while," I said. "Have you been away?"

He shrugged. "Done some work for my dad for a bit."

I nodded, recalling that his father ran an orchard out of town, and resolved to question him while I could. My fear was that he would lie and I wouldn't be able to tell, but I had to ask.

"Danny, you saw how my husband, Christopher, died. You know I just want justice. Are you sure you can't remember anything at all about the car that hit us, or the driver?"

His expression remained blank, and before he could respond, I spoke again in a lowered voice. "If you were bribed to say nothing, I'll understand." But I knew when the words came out that they weren't true.

I watched his eyes blink and shift, appraising me. It was impossible to read his face.

"Like I told the cops, it was dark," he said, shrugging so casually that I imagined my hands around his pale young neck. "Besides, it happened so fast, y'know?" He raised his palms a few inches in the air.

I frowned, wanting to shake him. "It wasn't that dark, Danny. There were three sets of headlights. Look, I know that sometimes police can be intimidating, but you're the only eyewitness; you must share what you know!"

I watched his eyes regarding mine, and believed I saw in them a flash of dark resolve, which passed as he nudged the lollipop back inside his cheek as if to mark the end of our exchange.

"I know nothing," he said from the side of his mouth, slumping into position again over his comic, clearly waiting for me to leave.

Cold heat began to prick my skin, then, and I felt faint. In my mind I envisioned Angus again, grinning smugly, patting Danny on the back, asking how he liked his new wheels. I wondered whether threats of some kind had further mitigated the risk of his breaking the deal. To steady myself, I reached for the counter's edge, thinking about what I could, in turn, offer and threaten. I could offer money, but how much? And what could I threaten, other than raw violence, considering I had no proof of his deception or payoff? And if I didn't trust what he told me now, how could I trust what he might tell me under the influence of my own bribery and blackmail? For an instant I closed my eyes, and when I reopened them, another customer had arrived, a silver-haired man paused in the shop doorway, peering at me with concern. As I straightened and looked back at Danny, I realized that his black T-shirt was styled in what seemed like the same rainbow font as in the comet posters down the road. KC, it read, the letters set inside an equal-sided triangle that seemed to glint.

Suddenly breathless and unable to think, I steered myself outside without looking back, and stood panting against the wall of the bank next door, waiting for my heart to slow as an elderly woman with a dachshund at the ATM regarded me as though I were a thief. The feeling of Danny knowing something crucial that he wouldn't share was like something viral and alive in my organs, and I didn't understand why the comet seemed to find me everywhere, like an urgent hieroglyph from a language I couldn't speak.

Back at work, as I sat processing invoices from our casket supplier, I remembered how I had been thinking about the movements of celestial satellites, if not comets, the evening I first met Christopher, years ago.

It was midwinter in Sydney, and I was standing behind the loans desk of the inner-city library where I'd worked throughout the best part of a psychology degree I'd lost the appetite to finish. It was a midweek evening, apparently quiet, but the street outside was bright beneath a full moon, so I was on guard.

Like ancient Romans, many nurses, and some police officers, I had come to anticipate a rise in erratic behavior on full moons, whether due to the operations of tidal force or something more difficult to measure. Screaming toddlers, raving adults, handbag theft, and aggressive disputes about overdue fines were not uncommon, and occasionally there would be scuffles or accidents in the nightclub strip outside for which either police or paramedics had to be called.

Still, I felt cautiously optimistic as I surveyed the handful of patrons browsing the shelves. Only a short while remained before closing, and not far from my desk, Bert, a regular patron who spent hours creating elaborate crayon drawings of collectible cars, seemed content at his table. Chronologically, he was about forty-five, but mentally he was much younger. In between drawings, he would deliver rambling monologues about the latest changes to processes he was planning to implement in his imaginary role as library manager.

I was on my way back from the bathroom when I heard Bert scream. He'd been teetering on his chair's rear legs, and had now fallen backward onto the carpet. He lay there like an overturned beetle, arms and legs flailing, and then he began to wail. It was only possible to disregard how comical he looked because of how volatile he became when his ego was bruised, and I was worried he'd hurt his head. Racing over, I tried to soothe him, checking he was okay and setting him upright again. Meanwhile, now that he had the benefit of an audience, his sobs of outrage and indignation grew louder and more insistent.

"The chair broke," he cried, before pointing out, between sobs, the bruise that was supposedly forming on his right elbow. As he sniffled and took a tissue from the box I brought him, he waggled his finger and suggested that something would have to be done to protect the public.

"What are you looking at?" he yelled suddenly at a woman who had shown the audacity to glance over at him from the fiction shelves, and as I rebuked him for rudeness, I wondered how to prevent his sour mood from spiraling. I knew from experience that if I didn't distract him successfully, he would cause disruptions all night.

Patting his shoulder, I stood over his drawing of the electric-blue car he'd been copying from *Classic Muscle Cars Volume 2*, and made an approving noise. "This is looking great. If you finish it tonight, we'll be able to pin it up with the others in the staff room."

Bert gave me a sullen look, rubbing his elbow and muttering something unintelligible about meeting with the real library manager. Then, as if he'd gathered fresh strength, his wails began again, piercing my temples. "My arm's broken!" he cried, although I was sure this wasn't true.

That was when I saw the man I would marry turn toward us from an adjacent table, where he had been discreetly pretending to be able to read amid the noise. To me, Christopher was just a stranger in a double-breasted coat, who might have been about to complain. Instead, he looked brightly at Bert in distress.

"Is that an XV Falcon?" he asked, leaning toward the drawing. "My dad used to have one of those. Good picture."

Bert continued to sniff and rub at his elbow, but peered curiously at Christopher. "Thanks," he said.

"Looks like you've only got the tires left to finish," Christopher said with a wink.

For a moment, Christopher and I shared a conspiratorial look, and as I felt the color rising in my cheeks, I told myself I was being ridiculous. The poor man just wanted to restore the peace. I nodded at him in thanks on my way back to the desk, as a queue had formed—the librarian on duty was a retiring person who preferred shelving to serving the public, and at times like these I couldn't blame her.

When I looked up from the desk and saw Christopher again, we were half an hour from closing. He waited while I finished scanning romance paperbacks for a septuagenarian who refused to read anything without a racy cover. As I waved her goodbye, I noticed the look of pleasant inquiry on his face.

"Hello again," he nodded, setting down a pile of nonfiction books as I registered the warm, candid tone of his voice and smiled, trying to think of something clever to say.

"Thanks for your help earlier," I said instead, taking his library card and noting from his member record that he was twenty-eight, and had only joined the previous week.

"No problem. I was just worried he was going to hurl the chair through the wall or something."

"Well," I said, a little dryly, as I begin to scan his books, "I thought your assessment of the drawing was very kind."

"To be honest, I think it looked more like a Mack Truck than a Falcon, but that's just between us."

I smiled. "I didn't think it was too bad—you haven't seen me draw. Crayons can be tricky."

He laughed, and I forced myself to look at him directly. "So, do you often perform hostage negotiations?"

"Not exactly," he said, grinning, "but I felt for the guy. I forgot where I parked my car earlier and would have loved to have a tantrum myself."

I smiled, and noticed the titles as I scanned: *Competitive Advantage: Creating and Sustaining Superior Performance*; *Shout!: The True Story of the Beatles*; *Contact* by Carl Sagan.

"Maybe we should normalize public tantrums for all ages—equal opportunity for all," I said, looking up. "Although, then every day would be like a full moon, if tonight's any indication."

He smiled at me more directly this time, but said nothing, and when I resumed scanning, I worried that I'd held his gaze for too long. To deflect my anxiety, I rested my eyes on the books that remained— *Winning Strategies for Small Business*; *Reduce Your Stress Now*; *Guitar Chords for Dummies*—each barcode met my scanning wand with a beep that seemed rudely abrupt. When the last one—*Unlimited Power: The New Science of Personal Achievement* by Tony Robbins—wouldn't read, I looked up again and apologized. It took a strange kind of concentration to type in the barcode manually, while he watched.

When I set it down on the pile, he pointed at it with a comical wink. "That one's for a friend."

I smiled. "Of course. You'll have to let me know if it works. Right now I don't even feel powerful enough to face my final statistics unit."

He nodded as the docket printer began to splutter.

"I will," he replied, before I tore off his loans receipt and held it out, and regarded his bright, expectant face, the sharp eyes, the cheeks that seemed flushed with health and good humor.

"Might see you next week," he said, taking the receipt and books, and raising his free hand in a salute before turning for the doors.

When he left, it was as if some invisible auric field had collapsed, leaving the atmosphere gray and slack. Standing in the vacuum Christopher had left behind was the woman from the fiction shelves, holding a Maeve Binchy and looking at me incredulously.

I told myself afterward that I was too romantic about chance encounters, too keen for the altered lens they give ordinary life. But for a few days, in idle moments, I recalled the cheerful yet contained tone of his voice, its hints of mirth and hesitation, and the way his eyes had brightened before he turned away. Finally I decided that I had mistaken friendliness for flirtation, in someone so unknown to me that he might as well have been my own mind's projection. By the time he reappeared during my next shift, I had begun to believe I didn't care, but knew this for the lie it was when he suggested we exchange numbers and meet for a drink that weekend. A wild feeling flew through my chest when I said yes.

Fourteen months later, we were married.

At home after work and dinner and a long spell of reading, having resolved to defer my anxieties about Danny for the evening, I stood in front of my open wardrobe, running my hand over dresses I hadn't worn in years. I held them against my body to see how they felt, as if each were a vessel designed to deliver me to a different place. Eventually I stepped into a cotton tea dress I had bought at a Sydney flea market the summer I was twenty-two. Its skirt flared from the waist and ended at the knee in the fifties style.

The dress was more appropriate for the warm air than my polyester trousers and blouse, but I felt naked wearing it. Without thinking I walked to the bathroom and peeled back a corner of the Kalf poster to reveal a wedge of silver mirror. I looked at the reflection of the red and yellow roses of the dress, and as my gaze traveled upward, met with one of my own eyes, the one without the scar below it. The eye looked wary and intent, and when I pitched forward I could glimpse my whole head, peering, inside the pupil. I hadn't seen myself for weeks, not since my last unintended glance in the bathroom mirror at work, and for a moment as I stared, I felt the eye belonged to someone else, like a grave maiden aunt whom I vaguely resembled.

I had taped up the poster a week after the accident, when I returned from hospital, because perhaps if I couldn't see myself, my bruised face, my ghoulish expression, I would only have to partially exist. It was enough to see my face reflected in the faces of the neighbors who dropped off casseroles. I didn't want to watch myself age without Christopher, didn't want to watch time express itself in my features, like some tragic Nosferatu, alone and tired of life but condemned to survive, even though I was the one who should have died. Besides, I thought, humans had lived for millennia without silvered-glass mirrors, perhaps for the better, and I preferred looking at sliced pomegranate when I washed my hands. So the poster remained.

I put on some sandals and brushed back my hair, checking how it looked in sections, as revealed by the single triangle of exposed mirror, before pressing the poster back in place with a feeling of relief. Lionel looked at me as I stood in the hall with my bag, as if to say he could see through my games. I had the same stirrings in my stomach as one might have in preparing to meet a foreign dignitary who had the final verdict in a matter of freedom or exile.

# 6.

DRIVING IN SILENCE THROUGH EMPTY PREDAWN STREETS TOWARD the ranges west of town, I felt my mind grow as wide and still as the dark sky above, which seemed to press closer the further I drove. I heard the rumble of the engine, the tick of the indicators, and the air of my own breath like sounds on a deserted stage, and told myself that with each mile I was reaching closer to certainty, and the grim peace of knowing exactly how and why my release from life was possible. Then I thought of Sandy, oblivious to my plans, and felt a drift of ice within me.

After winding my way up the road slowly in the dark toward the summit of Black Mountain, I reached the main entrance. The boom gates were shut, the surrounding area deserted but for me and a miniature model of Mercury. I pulled onto the shoulder and parked. Emerging from the car, I could hear only the movement of leaves in the bushland beyond. Above me, the waning moon was just a shard amid the stars. For a moment, I peered up close at the signboard that shared facts about the moonless planet, where mass and time follow other laws. On Mercury, I learned, my body would weigh only a third of its weight on Earth, yet a single day there would span over fourteen hundred hours here. Only minutes had passed when, hearing the rumble of a car from behind, I turned to see the boom gates opening. Through the driver's window, Theo nodded in greeting and told me to hop in.

"I'll give you the grand tour, if you like," he said with a half smile as we coasted off up the mountain and I began to glimpse the various structures of the observatory through the scrubland. Here and there, Theo pointed them out. A nondescript visitors' center, service buildings from the seventies, and white domes of various sizes, luminous in the night, lay scattered around us like a Cycladic village among eucalypts. In the glow of the headlights, I made out a picture board that allowed visitors to position their faces inside a blazing meteor in space, and, outside the university service buildings, a sign that said, QUIET PLEASE! ASTRONOMERS SLEEPING.

From all sides, the mountain summit on which the structures were built sheered away into forested darkness, and I had the sense of having reached an island, whose remoteness only drew the bright sky closer.

"I'm up here," Theo said finally, as we circled back past the visitors' center, and up a narrow track that led to the gazebo-sized observatory dome where he worked, mostly alone, he told me, in alternation with another survey astronomer.

"Welcome," he said, as we exited the car and I saw that the rear of the dome was positioned near the mountain's edge. Wandering over, I peered down at the shadowy slopes of wattle, heath, and eucalyptus, and past those, to the jagged forms of the trachyte mountains beyond.

"Not a bad office view, from any direction," I said, turning back to Theo as he nodded and motioned for me to follow him inside, where I found myself in a spartan igloo-like space, centered around a mounted blue telescope half a meter in diameter and several meters in length. The telescope was angled toward the dome's apex, an oblong of which was open to the stars. As I looked, a thought passed by like another object above, the thought of my own boldness in asking him to grant me a private night viewing.

"It's already in position," I heard him say suddenly, as he raised himself onto a nearby stepladder and brought his eye to the lens of the finderscope, a small secondary telescope attached to the main one. Theo nodded, and jumped down from the ladder. "The viewing's good tonight. Clear skies."

For a moment, I stood there clutching my bag, wondering why he was watching me. I felt strangely awake in the dim light of the stars, and found myself, quite without inhibition, searching his eyes as if for proof of something, the nature of which my conscious mind was not apprised.

When I realized he was simply waiting for me to approach the lens, I felt my cheeks begin to burn, and, setting down my bag, propelled myself forward. But I moved slowly, as if thwarted by some opposite force, and regarded the lens from a distance before I brought my eye to it.

I felt like one summoned to at last face a final truth, and suddenly I didn't feel ready. I felt, somehow, that I should prepare myself by closing my eyes for a moment or making a plea, but I only took a long breath, before stepping onto the ladder myself and bringing my right eye to the lens. What I saw was a star larger than all the others, a sphere of white fire casting its rays into the darkness like a second sun. As I looked, I heard Theo speaking.

"It's just crossed into Libra," he said. "It's finally speeding up."

When I asked what he meant, he explained that celestial bodies are slower the farther they are from the sun. "When I found it two years ago," he said, "it was one-and-a-half-billion kilometers away, near the orbital plane of Saturn, so for a long time it seemed to barely move. Now that the comet's entering our inner solar system and heading toward the sun, its apparent motion is increasing, and as its ice sublimates into gas and dust it will grow tails."

His words seemed far away as I looked at St. John. But after a moment I felt him at my side, and then the comet was just a blur of refracted light in my eyes. Perched on the ladder peering through the lens, I held my breath, suddenly aware only of his nearness, his shape at the edge of my vision, his faint smell of tobacco and some kind of peppermint soap or cologne. Frozen there like an animal in shock, I had to command myself to move, and when I stepped back from the lens, unable to quite look at him, he adjusted the telescope's focus with a remote control and gestured for me to look again, as though nothing was wrong.

The comet was smaller now, a bright patch to the left of the constellation. I tried to make out the scales of justice, which my father had shown me when I was a child, but couldn't quite connect the lines between the stars, and wondered why my cheeks were burning. Vague names returned to me of other star groups and objects, their names haunted by the myths and characters of human history: Hercules, Hydra, Titania, Andromeda, Ptolemy's Cluster, Berenice's Hair. As I looked again at the comet, trying to refocus, I imagined it growing larger and reaching closer, a star of Bethlehem hurtling toward me, and when I closed my eyes I could see its brightness still, a brightness that reminded me of the light I had seen approaching in my mind the night I died, before a series of electric jolts forced my heart to restart and returned me to my broken body in a loud fluorescent room. I realized, then, that Theo was speaking again, his voice strange and distant as if suddenly recalling a dream of the future.

"Eventually it will move into Scorpius, then Ophiuchus, then Sagittarius, hugging the ecliptic until it dips south into Microscopium later this year for its perihelion—the point when the comet will reach closest to the sun, and shine brightest. It will be quite a show."

I turned around. He was sitting behind me on one of two swivel chairs, looking not at me or the sky but at some arbitrary point along the wall behind me. He spoke again as if to himself, and as I watched him through the gloom, noticing his wide, unblinking eyes and his frown, I saw him as a figure from myth, an oracle delivering a riddle.

"That will be in winter," he said softly, "when right at the zenith for New South Wales, the comet will reach an apparent magnitude that could be as great as minus three. By then it will share its brightness with southern Europe and much of the US, before finally heading east toward Cetus and slowly leaving us for latitudes further north."

I stood and moved to the empty chair beside him. For a while we sat side by side, looking up at the dome's open window of sky like lovers in an open-air cinema. The air had cooled, and I could smell the eucalyptus of the forest beyond. I felt briefly as if I had landed on another planet, resembling Earth but discretely different from the reality I knew.

"I understand what the expression 'falling star' means now," I said into the silence, and forced myself to look at him through the gloom. "It really does look like it's falling."

He smiled. "That expression refers to meteors and meteorites, but I know what you mean," he said, before offering me a coffee.

Caffeine at night hardly helped my insomnia, but because I didn't yet feel ready to leave, I accepted, and followed him out of the dome into the small demountable control room beside it, where my eyes had to adjust to the electric light. Below the window, a row of computers glowed on a desk, while in the corner a bar fridge and refreshments trolley stood beside a sofa. As the kettle boiled and the light bulb buzzed, we stood facing each other.

"I hope the plans for the funeral are going smoothly?" I asked, to fill the silence as he spooned coffee into a plunger.

"Yes, fine," he said in a cool voice, and I felt a stab of regret for having asked, alongside, if I was honest, irritation that he wouldn't trust me with the barest detail when I was, professionally and personally, a worthy audience.

I was grateful when, as we returned with the mugs to sit beside each other in the dome, he changed the topic and asked how long I'd lived in town.

"A few years. I was in the city, before." As I spoke between sips, I felt his eyes graze my face, returning more than once to the scar that I could never quite conceal.

I was inclined to be frank, to throw his own stiff evasion into relief and measure the effect. "Two and a half years ago I followed my husband here to begin a new life. He wanted to be close to his mother and have his own legal practice and raise our future kids in the fresh air. But when he died suddenly, I was left behind. It's a new life, just not the one I planned."

He looked down into his mug for a while, and for a moment I imagined him as a large seabird retreating into the refuge of its feathers. "I'm very sorry," he said abruptly, and to change the topic I asked what his main work at the observatory involved. He said he surveyed the southern skies for near-Earth objects like asteroids, which might pose a potential threat of impact with our planet. He had been brought over to assist after having worked on the sister program in Arizona. Suddenly, as we sat there, I had a vision of him as a kind of celestial lighthouse keeper, stationed as he was during unsociable hours in a white building, scanning for wayward objects in an effort to avert disaster.

I asked him, now, whether I was right in thinking asteroids were akin to small planets. He nodded and said that some even had their own moons.

"Actually," he said, turning toward me with a smile, "somewhere up there in the main asteroid belt between Jupiter and Mars is a dark, spinning rock that shares your name."

I laughed, and asked if I could see it.

"We can try," he said, rising to grab the remote control to adjust the telescope's position further north. After a moment he peered into the finderscope.

"We're still in Libra," he said, waving me over. "In the center of the lens, you'll see the star of Gamma Librae, an orange giant star at the left of Libra's measuring scales," he explained as I looked. "From this distance, asteroids look much like stars. Left of Gamma Librae you can make out Sylvia just beginning to appear, over the eastern horizon. Do you see?"

I nodded, glimpsing a hazy glow not nearly as bright as the star.

"She's more remote than the stars," he said, "even though they might look the same distance away."

"Ah," I replied, with a hint of teasing humor, "is that so?"

With my eye still at the lens, I heard him release a breath, the kind that attends a hesitant smile. As I peered at my namesake's dim light among the other lights in the vast darkness, I thought how wondrous it was that in a sky so crowded, anyone had ever been able to find a single object twice before the invention of star maps and telescopes.

Despite the visions I had seen, no great answer seemed forthcoming in my mind as to what to do about Angus, how to grant myself absolution over Christopher, or how to say goodbye to life before Sunday night. Realizing this, I wondered whether it was time to leave.

It was then, with my eye still pressed to the lens, that there came the sudden sound of a great thunderclap in the distance, and closer in, a popping sound like gunshots, and through the glass there passed a radiance as if the sky were alight. I jerked away from the lens and screamed, wondering whether a war had begun, or else whether some vagrant asteroid Theo had missed had made impact with our sphere of the central west.

As adrenaline flooded through me, and my heart issued its dark throbs throughout my body, I tried to breathe. The dome was undamaged, and my limbs intact, and I was being held against a comforting pressure which I realized was Theo.

"It's okay," he said. "It's just fireworks. You're okay."

When I inhaled again, I recognized the faint smell of sulphur, and heard the familiar fizz and crackle. I was steady now, and when I straightened on my feet I felt him draw away, and an image came to me of two minor planets nearing eclipse before retreating into their own inevitable orbits. For a few seconds in his wake I felt myself surrounded by a strange, static haze. My body remembered the warmth and solidity of being harbored by another body, even if my mind had for a time forgotten it.

I followed him through the door now, to the grass outside where we stood before the last explosions half a kilometer away, where flares and sparks and pinwheels of orange and white light whined and banged like grenades, igniting the trees in the forest beyond and dispersing through the sky in shards which hovered before falling. Now and then a hoot or manic shriek erupted with the lights from the vicinity of the forest, and at one point in the momentary daybreak of an eruption, I saw spindly hooded figures streaking through the eucalypts, like trickster spirits from myth.

"Local kids," Theo muttered beside me, without taking his eyes from the sky. "It happened a few months ago. They come out to get high in the forest."

The display seemed more violent than beautiful after the silence of the stars, and when finally the last bursts ended and the world again grew dark, I could hear us breathing in faint gasps, as if finding ourselves the lone survivors of some rogue attack. When he asked whether I was alright and I nodded, turning to face him, I saw him frown and step closer. Suddenly he loomed over me like a shade tree, squinting at the scar below my eye as though it were a strange star, and seemingly without forethought reached out as if to touch it. For an instant his fingers hovered above my skin, as if he were about to bless me, and then his hand dropped back to his side.

"You must have cut yourself against the lens," he said, followed by something I didn't quite hear, about antiseptic.

So much is possible only in darkness. I remember how the half-meter of space between us disappeared then, as something in my brain blotted out and I reached out to him. My hands landed on his shoulders, and I felt the clean rough cotton of his shirt, and he became still. For a moment we stood there as if about to dance, while the breeze stirred our clothes and I felt, through the fabric, the warmth of his skin beneath my palms.

Through the darkness I looked at him, and as shame pricked my body and something soft seemed to collapse in my chest, I realized that what I saw in his face was fear. Gently, he made to turn for the door, and as he did, I dropped my hands. I didn't move from the path, or raise my head to watch as he walked inside with slow, scraping steps. I stood there beneath the sky, waiting for my heart to slow, feeling swallowed by something I couldn't name.

The light inside the control room seemed terribly bright when I entered, after collecting my bag. I found Theo stooped over the computer. Upon hearing me he turned around, holding up a first-aid kit like a shield and not quite looking at me. I tried to smile, as though there was nothing to discuss, and watched as he drew out and handed me an antiseptic swab and a strip of prepackaged gauze, as if these things were capable of treating not just a surface cut but also the deeper ailment that might cause someone to grab hold of a stranger without provocation in the dark.

"Thanks," I said. "I'll patch myself up at home."

He nodded, desperate, I was sure, to be alone.

"Thank you for the viewing." Careful to keep my voice even, I re-adjusted my bag. "I won't forget it."

"You're welcome," he said, tucking his hands in his trouser pockets.

"And I'm sorry," I added, from over my shoulder when I'd reached the door, before walking back into the dark morning, ignoring his offer to drive me back.

# 7.

AT FIRST, CONSIDERING THERE REMAINED JUST FOUR DAYS UNTIL MY appointment with oblivion, I wondered whether I might simply forget what had happened with Theo. Perhaps this once, I thought, I could skip the cross-examinations, the plea hearings in my mind. But forgoing such an opportunity for self-recrimination was against my nature, and so in the end, like a ship's figurehead in bad weather, I faced it open-armed.

After all, if there was anyone with whom I wanted to find a measure of peace before departing, it was my own self. So in the sleepless hours after leaving the observatory and through the gray tasks of Wednesday, I carried out the rituals of a private tribunal. My concern was not with the fact of my own humiliation, which was ordinary enough, but with how I had found myself making advances on a stranger so suddenly, and what it meant. It hadn't yet been two years since Christopher's death. Was I really so flimsy, so inconstant as to forget him so soon? I had betrayed him, I felt. I had betrayed, too, my image of myself.

I was ejected from my thoughts when Joseph arrived bleary-eyed in the late morning to tour the showroom for the second time. Clarence, having reached the end of his patience despite his reverence for the Evans family name, had instructed me to press upon Joseph the urgency of confirming his choice of casket, but he didn't seem in a decisive mood. As I led him once again through the displays, he moved in his linen short-sleeve shirt and beige moleskins with a languid hesitation.

"It just feels so soon," he said, looking drawn as we paused by a premium steel model, powder-coated in pastel blue with a pink satin interior. "So soon," he went on, as if to himself, "to make decisions about an event of such magnitude."

He looked at me then, his blue eyes wide and imploring. "I fear I'm beginning to forget her already, Sylvia—her voice, her smile. I keep asking myself what service she would have wanted, but since she died there's been a fog in my mind."

For an instant he took a labored breath, before turning to me with a pained smile and regarding me with what seemed a strange kind of knowing, as though peering behind my eyes. I caught myself hoping he might be about to deliver some diagnosis or absolution, that would free me.

"You're a sympathetic, discreet sort of soul, Sylvia, someone who's suffered herself, I can tell. That's why I can speak like this to you." He sighed before turning to absently run a hand over the lip of the steel casket, and as he resumed talking, I found myself lulled by the lilting resonance of his voice. "I sense that those in my circle expect me to take this quite smoothly, for one reason or another," he went on, growing rigid now as he gazed into the casket's interior. "Well, I'm failing. My mother was eighty-seven but losing her has been a shock. I've dreaded her death all my life."

As he tried to face me again with a forbearing smile, I recalled Tania mentioning that Patricia's death had left Joseph, a lifelong bachelor, alone on the family farm and the sole remaining Evans in town, his younger brother having lived abroad for years. Now at the sight of him standing there, I wondered whether to reach for his hand. Instead, I patted his arm, a gesture he met with an uneasy nod.

"I'm sorry, Joseph," I said. "We don't want to rush you. But it may help to know that funerals are almost always planned and held in the midst of shock, when mourning's barely even begun. It's a regrettable consequence of how quickly our loved ones must be buried or cremated. No one's ever ready."

He nodded. "Yes, that's what Clarence said." Glancing at me, his mouth twitched in a faint smile. "I rather prefer the style of the ancient Egyptian elites, don't you? Taking months, building monuments—rituals that grant a little space. I suppose that wouldn't do, though, in our expedient society. Anyway, my preference is for burial. But I still can't bear to think of her in the ground."

I watched him stand before me as if paralyzed, and was surprised to hear myself speaking of Christopher. "When my husband died, I found it helped to imagine myself walking a tightrope, moving forward one step at a time without ever peering too far ahead. Easier said than done, I know."

At this, he smiled and nodded, recognizing my offering for the intimacy it was, before affecting a tone of valiant resolve. "Well, my mother was a classy dame, Sylvia," he said, motioning now to the steel casket beside us. "No disrespect, but this one's like some tarted-up Cadillac."

"Don't tell Clarence, but I have to agree with you," I said, as we kept walking and he allowed himself a half laugh, before finally deciding on the Mahogany Statesman Half-Lid model, and two horses with ostrich plumes for the hearse.

To reward me for my victory with Joseph, Clarence sent me on an extended lunch break. In the beer garden of the Rising Sun Hotel, I ate a focaccia while a pair of middle-aged women in floral dresses conferred about the comet between mouthfuls of Caesar salad.

"Did you see the comet biscuits at the bakery?"

"Yeah, it's all a bit mad, isn't it?"

"My friend from the bowls club says it's not unusual when comets appear. Apparently, when Halley's Comet came back in 1910, people went nuts—buying gas masks and oxygen bottles, blocking their keyholes, all because they thought Halley was bringing some kind of acid to Earth!" She shook her head. "Some were selling comet protection pills, some were sending postcards about the end of the world, a few did themselves in, and the rest were having a party—banquets, climbing the Eiffel Tower, chartering balloons."

"That's people for you."

"Yeah. But when the comet was meant to show itself, the weather was mostly cloudy. They could barely see it! So, even back then, folks were acting strange."

Leaving the pair to deliberate over their plans for a comet-viewing potluck party on Sunday, I wandered on a whim into the nearby National Geographic shop. But I was unprepared for just how prescient the woman's words would prove in the scene I found there. On the shop floor before a despairing sales assistant, two respectable-looking men in their forties were squabbling over the last remaining amateur telescope.

The first man, ginger-haired in a polo shirt, was holding the box to his chest as though it were a child, while the other, burly and red-faced in cargo shorts, tried to wrest it from his rival's grip. "I'm warning you," the first said, releasing one hand momentarily to adjust his glasses, "shove off!"

The burly one appealed to the sales assistant, a young man with a buzz cut: "Like I told you, I'd set the telescope aside while I grabbed some night-vision goggles, and now this bugger's filched it!"

"It was unattended," claimed the other. "I promised my wife I'd buy a telescope, and it's not my fault if you've missed out!"

As passersby trailed in behind me to gawk, the sales assistant raised his hands and offered to sell the burly man the display telescope at a discount, to which he grudgingly agreed. Even as I watched their absurd behavior, I wondered why I'd lacked the foresight to buy my own telescope in time, so that I, too, might magnify my view of the comet at even greater brilliance than its plain-sight apparition.

For a moment along High Street, with the women's chatter about Halley in my head, I imagined us all assailed by an invisible signal, a wave of nervous illness, a panic—brought on as if broadcast by the invisible rays of a body in the sky. First, there would be a feeling upon waking of somehow being pinned, a heaviness about the limbs, and an instinct to look over your shoulder, to hide, to measure your sins. Then, among some, driven too far by their apprehension of a cosmic pressure, a preemptive strike—the decision to at once restore control, and surrender, by hurling themselves into the void at a time of their choosing. I pictured a procession of coffins, presided over by Tania, wringing her hands and looking on in open-mouthed horror. Until one day, the shadow passed, the work of narrative shaping began, and neighbors clicked their tongues at the delusions of people, as though they had never themselves lain awake in the night, peering through the crack between logical reality and oblivion.

Later, as I dusted the casket showroom and ferried cups of tea to Clarence, I thought of picking up the phone and calling my mother—just dialing the number and speaking the words into the receiver, and waiting like a child with a shell to her ear, listening for an inscrutable sound. I tried to summon her voice, which for years had always seemed so far away. I remembered her hesitant pauses, her veiled impatience, the way my questions would fold into themselves.

What would I even say? "Hello, Mother, I know it's been a while but as I'm planning to end my life this Sunday, I'm hoping for some advice about how to absolve myself of an unintended romantic indiscretion that occurred last night with an astronomer I barely know." I let out a bitter laugh as I spot-vacuumed the casket linings. My mother was hardly the right person to ask about honoring dead loved ones, or atoning for betraying them. I thought about calling one of my old friends, many of whom I hadn't seen since Christopher's funeral, and who were now busy in Sydney with small children, but the notion felt strange; I felt remote, like an object that had spun too far away. I thought of appearing at Vince's door to speak with Donna, but remembered how she had looked at me months ago when I saw her in the fresh produce section of the local supermarket, the way her eyes had wanted to slide away, the smile, too long delayed, that appeared on her face like a twitch as she held her bag of plums and asked how I was, and the way her words had hung there.

So instead, I wandered alone in my mind down a long hall full of monsters, trying to discover, as in the Egyptian judgment, how the scales fell; how, in the end, my own heart might be measured. And I did it all as my body, in this earthly dimension, arranged our new delivery of office flowers, posted invoices, and collected from the printer's the thick cream keepsake cards for Patricia Evans's funeral, on which was written a verse from the order of service booklets for King George's funeral in 1952. It was a verse from none other than St. John: *I am the resurrection and the life, saith the Lord: he that believeth in me, though he were dead, yet shall he live . . .*

No great revelations were forthcoming, and when I finally left the office that afternoon, walking out into a street that was still bright, with my bag on one shoulder and my arms strangely limp by my sides, I was desperate to be alone. The airborne feeling had returned, and with it a vertiginous kind of dread, to which the only answer seemed surrender. As I walked to the cemetery, carrying, in the time-honored fashion of those with guilty hearts, fresh flowers, my mind grew blank, and the sound of my own footsteps seemed loud, and I felt the air around my empty hands.

When I arrived, the cicadas were out, filling the air with the thrumming of their tymbals, looking for mates in the few weeks left before they died. I knelt on the dry grass before Christopher's headstone, and rested my palm for a while on the cool granite. I looked at the gold Victorian lettering I had chosen. *Christopher Knight*, it said. *Beloved husband, son, nephew, and friend. 1963–1995.* I had intended to have a quotation below it, some line from secular scripture, but everything that seemed right had been used so often it had lost its power, and so nothing more was written.

Lately I'd wondered whether a certain passage from the Song of Solomon wasn't in fact the best choice for an epitaph, despite its fame and our agnosticism. I imagined it carved there in uncompromising cursive, the words of God to the Israelites in disgrace: *Vengeance is Mine; I will repay; In due time their foot will slip; for their day of disaster is near, and their doom is coming quickly.* Not the tender affirmation I would have liked, but consoling in its way. It was a promise of sorts, and not only to Christopher and myself. It wasn't unthinkable that his killer might one day pass by his stone and read it, in the reckoning that would surely come, even if I wasn't around to see it.

*   *   *

As I sat, listening to the cicadas and feeling the air turn softly around my bare arms, I closed my eyes to clear my mind, and suddenly saw the image of my mother as she had appeared years ago on a summer afternoon like this one.

She was waiting by the gate of our house and watching me as I approached, with a white, pinched look. I was twelve, walking home after the last bell, along the sunlit path in the shade of plane trees. I had just graduated primary school. My nylon backpack thunked with books, the breeze stirred my dress, and as the sounds of voices and slowing cars receded in my ears, I thought about how I would never return to that sprawling brick building or that tan bark and concrete yard, with its tall peppercorns and silver monkey bars and ruthless, arcane traditions. I felt winded, as though I had escaped a version of myself just in time. As I walked I could smell chlorophyll in the air, the ripe green atmosphere that soon would mingle with the smells of chlorine and suntan lotion and hot chips at the local pool, with its shadowed grandstand and carnival bunting and strange resonance of sound.

When I saw my mother standing there at the gate like a sentinel, I slowed down, knowing something had happened to divide this day from the rest. After I reached her, she drew me close and kissed my head, and I heard her take a shaky breath. I followed her inside to the kitchen table where we sat together, and she scanned my face and brushed back my hair and rested one arm around me like a shield. Her voice when she spoke sounded shaky and thin.

"Your dad died today, my darling," she said. "I'm so sorry. It was very sudden."

Her arm around me drew tight, and I felt myself keel toward her, my body now heavy and stupid. With my cheek on her shoulder I peered at her free hand pressed flat on the table as if to steady us, and heard myself asking in a thick voice what had happened. As she spoke I closed my eyes, wishing I could will us into another dimension.

"I came home for lunch and found him collapsed beneath his cello,"

I heard her say. "It was a blood clot in his brain. He died on the way to the hospital."

Her shoulder rose and fell beneath my cheek as she breathed, and I looked at the loose, thatched weave of the linen threads in her blouse, which was a pale shade of peach. I noticed the clock above the sink poised at five to four; noticed, too, the mugs hanging off their hooks, the blue pitcher of pink hydrangeas, the framed Royal Hall concert poster of the young Beatles with open mouths, ready to sing. Everything looked frozen and suspect.

At some point I asked where he was, and she said he was in the part of the hospital where people who have died wait for their families to arrange their funerals. I pictured him there, in a dormitory row of other pale people on trolleys, checking his watch and looking glum like a passenger at a station.

"The paramedics . . . ," my mother said after a silence, "the paramedics told me he didn't suffer."

I said nothing, but wondered how they could have known such a thing for sure. My ear was growing hot against her shoulder, my neck beginning to ache as we sat braced there, entwined like figs. As I listened to our breathing I thought of how soft and prone a body is, and how condemned.

Eventually it grew dim and we switched on the lights, and my mother ordered a pizza we didn't eat. While she made calls on the bedroom phone, I sat cross-legged on the floor of my father's study, at the foot of the empty ladder-back chair. The cello stood poised on its end pin, its neck leaning against the study wall, and as I looked at it, I became aware of the silence, its voluptuous negative quality, like a voice that had paused.

With closed eyes, I reached for my memory of that morning, before he collapsed and, as I learned later, the network of arteries in his frontal lobe silently imploded. Just ten hours earlier, he had been sitting there in that chair, in his old gray T-shirt and track pants, holding the neck of the cello with one hand and a piece of toast in the other, as he peered at the sheet music on the stand. It was a Friday, his day off from teaching, and he was practicing for an upcoming performance with the quartet he had played with since university.

Before rushing out for school, I had stopped in the doorway to wave, and when he looked up he grinned, and raised the hand holding the toast in a victory gesture.

"Last day, Sylvie!" he cheered. "Tonight, we celebrate!"

I had nodded, hardly looking back as I raced for the door and the first deep notes of Brahms's Cello Sonata No. 1 floated down the hall.

I pictured him there in the chair now, drawing the bow, his eyes closed as he frowned and raised his eyebrows and turned his head as if in conversation, I would always think, with the spirit that lived inside the instrument.

Later, when my mother was in bed and I couldn't sleep, I wandered to the kitchen for a glass of milk and, standing in the spaceship light of the open fridge, saw the ingredients for my favorite dinner, corn fritters. I pictured him, earlier that day, strolling easily down the supermarket aisles, dropping things into a basket, smiling at the cashier on his way out, blind to the waste of a half hour that, with the mercy of some warning, could have been spent with my mother and me. My eyes slid past the ears of corn, the parsley, and sour cream, witnesses to his final hours that couldn't speak.

In the hall, the old canvas tent and gas stove and folding chairs were piled in readiness, alongside our old four-and-a-half-inch Dobsonian telescope and dog-eared *Guide to the Southern Night Sky*. We had planned to set off the next afternoon on a camping trip, to survey the summer constellations for five nights from the roof of the Corolla. Next to the telescope was a supermarket bag of supplies. Kneeling on the floor in a kind of trance, I lifted each thing out and looked at it, and each thing seemed new and strange, possessed of a mute knowledge that I couldn't intuit.

When they were all assembled before me on the floorboards, they seemed like creatures in a tribal ritual, awaiting instruction: a bag of crisps, tins of tomato soup, some apples, a hand of still-green bananas,

Désirée potatoes, a shaker of salt. But I was as blind and mute as they were. The whole world seemed suddenly to consist only of such creatures, human and natural, living and inanimate, that had simply happened here on this planet to exist for a while and then disappear, for no reason that any of us knew.

The breeze had picked up in the cemetery, and briefly I saw myself as if from without, hunched immobilized over the stone like a disheveled life-sized sculpture. It was darker now, and my lower spine was aching. When I rose to my feet I found they had grown numb. As a means of dimming the lights on my thoughts and my pain, I tried to focus on external things—the crunch of the pebble path leading out, the orange tinge of the sky, and the almost invisible moon. I watched my feet, and pressed away the visions that were hovering, visions of my mother's swift second marriage.

I remembered how, between my father's death and his replacement in Ed Walker, a blue-eyed architect from her office, I had watched my mother leave for another coast. She spoke of my father less and less, as if he had simply been a visitor who was now returned, as planned, to his own remote hemisphere. That my father lived now only in the past tense was a fact she had naturally accepted. There was—at least that I observed—no bargaining with God, and no anger; her mourning did not pass through stages, take on different tones, or evolve. It was as if, in the immediate aftermath, she passed through an interval of pressure, a new atmosphere to which her lungs needed to adjust, and she slowed down, spoke less, slept more. But then she was returned to herself, having metabolized the fact of my father's departure from our lives. She was alive; he was not. It was no one's fault, and no staged misery or deprivation on her part would restore him.

Within five months she had regained almost entirely her native good cheer, her bright cheeks, her birdlike quickness and animation, darting through the competing tasks of each day as if they were the squares of a game to be played on one foot. And then there was Ed, with his cool, slippery voice and strange remoteness, fully installed in my father's place within two years. I could not forgive her.

At home, after feeding Lionel, bathing, and mindlessly performing a round of resistance band exercises to support my fractured spine, I sat on the couch in my pajamas with the lights off. The last lorikeets were shrieking through the evening sky. As I watched them, I felt a strange pinching in the muscles of my heart. Some months ago, I had convinced myself that this pinching constituted the early stages of a heart attack, and more out of curiosity than concern visited a young female doctor who failed to conceal her condescending amusement at my self-diagnosis. The sensation was just panic, she said, and would pass.

The same sensation had visited me at fourteen, on the morning of my mother's second wedding. I saw her now as she had appeared then, triumphant in the doorway and backlit by the sun, clutching her bouquet of baby's breath in both hands like a grenade. I felt my body there on the couch give way, felt myself back inside that fraught pubescent frame, clad in white stockings and a floral polyester party dress, sitting on a bench and picking mindlessly at a thumbnail that was already bleeding.

We were in a small white chapel on an artists' estate in the hills, that had grown forlorn since the sixties but retained its whimsical neo-Tudor cottages and green fields. It was early spring, and the air outside held the sharp, green smell of earth and vegetation and recent rain. In the moments before she appeared, I stared ahead at the stained glass window behind the altar, which showed St. Matthew in red robes, holding a lamb on one shoulder as he looked beyond me with mystic resignation. As guests murmured and shuffled in their seats, I remained still, focused on the halo that hovered like a noonday sun over St. Matthew's head, and the blue sky behind him, and his delicate toes, long as fingers, poised on the earth.

I'm sure I was the last to turn, when the first notes of Pachelbel's Canon sounded from the speakers and my mother arrived in the light of the doorway. I watched her face as she moved forward in her knee-length sixties-style dress. There was coyness in her smile and a jauntiness in her step, as if this whole show was quite amusing, but as the music continued her eyes grew watchful, her smile more reserved. Almost everyone on her side of the aisle had been at my father's funeral two years before, in another chapel, listening to other music and other speeches, their eyes directed not at a bride in white but at a white coffin under carnations.

I had made a speech that afternoon, composed as a letter to my father, which detailed an abridged list of all the things for which I loved him (his good cheer, his homemade dill pickles, his explanations of the stars, his ability to braid my hair in thirty seconds, his impression of Miss Snyder, my caustic schoolteacher) and all the ways I would keep his memory alive (placing his photo in each room, learning to play his cello, sitting by his grave with my lunch every Sunday). I was not making a speech today.

My dress had a high lace collar, which was causing my throat to itch. As I tried to unbutton it, the music finally stopped and the chapel entered into silence. My mother had now arrived at the altar beside Ed, who, standing there with rigidly correct posture in his beige suit, looked as unmoved as a customer in a queue. Presiding over them was a grizzled celebrant resembling Santa in a purple cloak. As I looked down at my shiny black Mary Janes, I wondered whether my father could see us somehow, and if he could, what he might have to say. As they began to speak, in the warm, mirthful tones of people whose happiness is being witnessed, my skin grew clammy, and I returned my eyes to St. Matthew so that I wouldn't have to see as well as hear them.

Now and then their voices faded from my focus and became a background gibberish, but when my mother spoke her final vows, I heard her clearly, heard her tender, frank voice, saying she would take Ed, from this day forward, for better or worse, in sickness and in health, to love and cherish until death did them part. "I do," she said, her bright voice verging on laughter. I turned the words over in my mind, like the spheres of a Chinese puzzle ball that don't align. I couldn't understand how, having said such words once, they could ever be said again.

*  *  *

I switched on the TV news. Protesters were marching in Belgrade. As Lionel jumped onto my lap and began to knead my stomach, the footage switched to preparations for Elvis's sixty-second birthday. An impersonator in a gold jumpsuit stood on the lawns at Graceland, dabbing at his eye amid a crowd.

At our own wedding, between dinner and dessert, Christopher and I had danced to Elvis. No one was rising up to start the party, so when "A Little Less Conversation" began, Christopher dragged me from my chair and we made fools of ourselves while our guests laughed. My chest felt tight again. I remembered everything.

We had married in the botanical gardens on a gray-skied afternoon in September. He wore in his buttonhole a red anemone that drooped on its stem, and forgot to put on the new shoes he had bought for the service. Before our vows, as we stood under the arbor of ivy and the guests were seated, I looked down to see his old brown brogues nosing out from under the trouser hems of his navy suit, and felt exasperation even as he grinned at me.

I was more annoyed still with myself—having failed to buy the right bra for my dress, I felt uncomfortable, and was breathless from last-minute decorations at Memorial Hall next door where the reception was being held—the space seemed too large for the tables, there weren't quite enough flowers, and I was distracted by the ugly internal cladding the council had installed along the rear wall to avoid noise complaints. Then, when I had returned to the gardens and everyone was seated and the Kath Bloom folk song that was my cue sounded from the stereo, I found myself walking down the aisle too quickly, so that I had to stand sheepishly by the celebrant for nearly two minutes while the song ended.

Waiting there, I thought of how it was all happening too fast for me to be truly present and alive to each moment that was passing, in a day that, despite feeling like a rehearsal, could never be repeated. Opposite me, Christopher in his old shoes stood tall, bearing his chest forward like a contented parrot, beaming.

To defy what I viewed as sexist tradition, I spoke my vows first. I told him how I loved his steadfastness and calm, his good heart, his sunny disposition, and I told him about how long the years had felt, waiting for him to arrive in my life, that evening in the library, with the motivational self-help books he saw me sneer at as I scanned them.

When I finished my speech, his face looked blotchy and stunned, and before he could speak he had to blink and swallow for a while. When he began to read out his own speech, from the stack of index cards he held out at arm's length as if to catch his reflection, he often had to pause, blinking, breathing deeply, smiling at his own strain. Now and then between the words, his head would shake a little in emphasis or disbelief, as he looked at me with wide eyes from under his newsboy cap.

"In summary, Sylvia," he said, "you are utterly enchanting. You will always have me, and I hope you will always want me."

At some point, the celebrant bound our hands together with the red velvet ribbon I had bought from Lincraft the week before, and the guests clapped. I kissed him, and found I had left a flagrant red mark on his lip and cheek which could not be wiped off. Just as someone in an adjacent property set off the whine and throttle of a serious lawn mower, Christopher and I held hands and walked through the tunnel formed by the standing bodies of our guests. Rose petals fell on our heads and camera shutters clicked like crickets, while we moved through laughing, thinking of our future.

"Do you promise," the celebrant had asked, "to love, cherish, and honor him, in sickness and in health, for better and for worse, forsaking all others, and holding only to him, forevermore?"

Lying in the dark that night with an empty stomach and my hands in fists, I tried to peer inside myself, to find the mechanism that had sprung so suddenly to betray us both, so that, like a surgeon, I could know and name it, and then cut it away.

δ.

I KEPT SEEING A SWEEPING AERIAL VIEW OF TOWN, LIKE SOMETHING by Pieter Bruegel the Elder, in which we all appeared as peasants from the Northern Renaissance looking up with open mouths while competing visions of the comet from my books shot through the skies above our heads. Overnight I'd dreamed I was a soldier in Nero's Rome, tasked with implementing the emperor's orders to kill all potential challengers to his rule, lest they be emboldened by the ill omen of a comet that had been visible for some time in the sky.

At work, even as I stirred my tea and flicked through an old P&O cruise brochure someone had left on the lunchroom table, I felt removed from my own century, and it was hard to shake the sense of being marked by murder. When I dared to peer at myself for an instant in the bathroom mirror, the face that stared back looked sallow and alarmed.

Feeling faint, I pressed on, setting up the trestles while listening to the radio. As I wrangled with the trestle struts on my knees, a woman with a loud, nasal voice quizzed a paranormal researcher and a member of Australian Skeptics about a crop circle that had appeared overnight in a canola field near Jericho. The central design, the researcher explained, was a star composed of two tetrahedrons, symbolizing spiritual ascension. One of many mysteries concerning crop circles, he went on, was the number of visitors around the world who reported feeling strange magnetic energies when standing inside them, prompting everything from headaches to wound healing.

"Who or what creates these designs, and why?" he asked merrily, but was cut off by the skeptic before he could array any possibilities.

"Humans do, for the thrill," she said hoarsely. "Two watercolorists from Wiltshire have admitted as much, and even shared their methods with the press."

The researcher, clearly familiar with this line of defense, began to object, but I didn't get to hear him. As I lifted the second trestle, I accidentally lost hold of the folded legs, which swung down on my shin, and I howled.

Despite everything, I was starving. After dry-swallowing some Panadol from the chemist, I stood in line at the bakery, trying to regulate my breathing and disregard the barking of other customers for their sausage rolls and potato-top pies. I couldn't help noticing that the comet biscuits they had begun selling—streaming star-form gingerbreads, with white icing and silver dragées—had been replaced by crumbs: SOLD OUT! MORE SOON, read the sign. Because I felt like a mollusk without its shell, I ate my lukewarm quiche while hiding behind the newspapers. They were full of the predictions and suppositions of various observers, qualified and otherwise, concerning the comet that would be visible from Sunday.

As I read, the voices of the commentators merged in my mind like a flock of twittering birds; excited, impatient, plucky. I was reminded of the circus surrounding royal births—the professional watchers, the spokespeople, the public, and the press, all wanting to fill the void before the new creature's first appearance, all betraying the fundamental impatience of human beings.

*It's still uncertain just how bright St. John will be,* one voice said, *but all the signs are pointing to its being one of the brightest comets of the century.*

*I would be cautious of grand predictions as to St. John's brightness,* said another. *To become a truly great comet, St. John's magnitude would need to rise rapidly indeed, before visibility is impaired by its orbital movement toward the sun.*

*The comet's position on the horizon will generally be low.*

*At its expected magnitude, St. John's coma and tail should gleam against the southern stars.*

*We can only guess currently as to how long its tail might grow, but given available evidence, it could be quite glorious.*

*The tail could be up to three degrees long.*

*The comet will drag a gorgeous tail of at least eight degrees.*

*On an axis such as this, we can hope for a tail length of five degrees at most. Whether this length is visible depends of course on optimum evening viewing conditions—low fog, for instance, and a moon that is close to new.*

*At its closest sweep with the sun, St. John will boast a brilliant dust tail of up to thirty-five degrees.*

*Mr. Theo St. John, the Black Mountain Observatory astronomer who discovered the comet, has been contacted for comment.*

For a moment I closed my eyes, noting a greasy aftertaste from the quiche and trying not to think of Theo. I heard the fly-strip curtain slap as customers entered and left, cups and saucers clinking, voices rising and falling like the absurd soundtrack of a dream. And in the dark of my mind I saw a speck of light, a magnetic center, a vanishing point growing closer. It tempted superstition to discover that the first naked-eye appearance of a historic comet would coincide with my planned appointment with oblivion, on the anniversary of Christopher's death. But it struck me as rather self-aggrandizing to synchronize one's end with the arrival of a comet, not least because of the great figures through history whose deaths had been linked to them.

The incident with King Harold was not isolated—the comet that followed Caesar's death was widely viewed as the expression of his eternal soul, and according to my reading, the list of others said to have met their various ends under the light of comets was long. It included Agrippa, Augustus, Vespasian, Cicero, Empress Octavia the Younger, Emperor Wu of Han, and Demetrius Soter, king of Syria. And while Nero's demise came by his own hand, it was not before the portent of at least one comet had overseen his extermination of two wives, the philosopher Seneca, and various others. This century, Mark Twain had correctly predicted his own demise with the return of Halley's Comet in 1910, which in May of that year, just a fortnight after its closest approach to Earth, had also been linked to the death of King Edward VII.

Given the scope and antiquity of this phenomenon, I was unsurprised to find it referenced in a verse from Shakespeare:

*When beggars die, there are no comets seen;*
*The heavens themselves blaze forth the death of princes.*

I thought myself closer to a beggar than a prince.

I was on my way back to the office, thinking about Joseph's brief for his mother's memorial slideshow and raising my eyes to a sky tense with rain, when I heard a laugh that made me turn. There, several meters away on the veranda of the Empress Hotel, was Angus in plain clothes, holding a beer and nodding in wry agreement at something his companion had just said. It was only when his companion, who was wearing a baseball cap, turned his face away from the shadow of the awning that I saw it was Danny. For a moment I stood on the street with my bag, squinting at them, feeling as though the storm clouds must have been forming for me alone.

Angus was shrugging now, Danny gesticulating in response. I imagined a comic strip caption above them: A MUTUALLY AGREEABLE DEAL. Perhaps their deal had graded into friendship—they seemed to be having a fine old time. I imagined racing toward them, scaling the veranda railing, smashing their schooners over their brutish heads. I had to hold my breath so as not to scream right there on the street, and was forced to steer myself back to the office against my every instinct, like a machine locked into the wrong gear.

Desperate to escape my own thoughts that evening, I arrived home with fried rice and a bottle of merlot, and picnicked on the living room floor in front of a dramatized documentary about the life and death of Mary, Queen of Scots. After its final scenes of her brutal and botched beheading, I sat on the couch considering the fact that despite all the reasons that existed to suspect Angus, the case had been closed, and meanwhile he and Danny were enjoying beers at the pub. Feeling winded, I began on the bottle of port from Christopher's last birthday, and sought distraction in the still-unanswered question of why I had made advances on a virtual stranger two nights ago.

Leaning back, I raised my glass to one eye and peered, as I had peered through the telescope that night to see the comet. The glass, part of a Turkish tea set that Christopher had given me one birthday, was indigo blue, and through it, the living room grew distorted and strange, a cool-blooded landscape. The answer, I supposed, still looking through the blue, was neither new nor an adequate excuse—loneliness and grief, combined, and the seeming comfort of a living body in the absence of one who will not return. In short, what I viewed as the coward's way out, the route my own mother took, casting another into the shape left behind, to start over, to forget.

Outside, it was finally dark. The air through the window smelled of moss and stone. For a moment as I closed my eyes, I felt the rush of years that had dissolved when Christopher died, the years we would have lived together, a scale of time that seemed wild to me now, but which we had believed in as people believe in God. Images passed through my mind, then, like the flashes that precede sleep—images of places we might have been, moments from life the lens would catch—Christopher and me in hiking boots, shrouded against the heat of a vast red desert, or holding gelato cones in a narrow, sunlit street. At some point I could see myself against pillows, looking fevered and stunned, holding to my chest a small, rosy form, and then, both of us grown older, smiling candidly at beaches and parks, our hands resting easily on the shoulders of small people whose faces I couldn't quite see. I recalled now the memorial slideshows I compiled for elderly widows and widowers, the way their photos would evoke the wide reaches of decades together, and thought of how, with the gift of time, a lover's face became a double exposure, an image in which the past and present were equally alive. But I would never see Christopher old: this fact occurred to me afresh; I felt it like a dropped weight in the darkness of my organs.

Not the cello, nor any book would help me tonight. Instead, I went to bed. Lionel leapt onto the pillow, pushing his head into my shoulder as I lay in the gloom, drinking intermittently with one eye on the dim mauve sky through the window. Eventually I lay on my side, and for a moment I saw Christopher asleep there next to me as though he had never left. I watched him as I had often watched him, his broad peaceful face, his eyelids that never quite closed. If I peered up at him from the level of his chin, he would always seem to look back at me with the glazed, nocturnal eyes of a seer. But the image didn't last. More and more, I was finding myself having to close my eyes and strain for the moments of vividness my memory held, as if for fish in a deep lake.

Finally I stood up out of bed and pulled out his old mustard sweater from the wardrobe, wrapping it around my neck like a scarf and inhaling its fibers. Early on I had been sure this sweater had the best imprint of his smell, a clean, sweet smell, which I had never quite been able to break down into discrete parts. Now all I could detect was the mustiness of wool, and the sweetness of the port on my own breath.

Standing by the window, I looked out at the stars, and thought finally about the laws of balance in space and matter, and alternative forms of justice. I thought of my dead husband, my ruined life, my fractured spine: crimes for which no one, it seemed, would be called to pay. Then I reached into the wardrobe for a light jacket, slipped it over my pajamas, and walked out to the car, feeling the arrival of clarity at last.

There was nothing left to fear.

In the dark and the quiet of the streets at night, the air felt alert and permeable, as if with the fading of daylight all things had lost a layer of skin. I felt better in motion, surveying the stillness of houses and trees as I drove. For a while I imagined I was the commander of a stealth military vehicle, gaining on the enemy while the world slept, making good time. When I arrived at Jubilee Street, just as it had begun to rain, I parked a hundred meters down from the pale brick house and closed my eyes, gathering strength.

It was 8:30 p.m., late enough, I hoped, for Angus's daughter to be in bed. Ideally, I wanted to catch him alone, but I knew this was unlikely, unless he suddenly appeared to deposit a bag of rubbish or smoke a secret cigarette. He and his wife were probably drinking wine now, watching television, conferring about the events of the week, although I imagined that Angus's avoidance of a conviction for manslaughter was a fact they largely left aside.

It was a wild, plunging feeling, the feeling of having nothing left to lose. I felt the adrenaline of rage in my chest like a pointed tool. Without thinking further, I climbed out and strode through the rain to the door, where for a moment I faced my own reflection in the large brass number 27 bolted there. My expression was calm, if grim, and resolute, as droplets rolled down my hair. For an instant I inhaled the rich smell of earth from the garden beds behind me.

When I knocked, the door opened almost at once. Angus stood before me holding a beer, wearing a gray tracksuit that lent him the look of an overgrown and grizzled toddler. He peered at me with an unyielding expression and sighed. My eyes traveled to his polka-dot socks. I had been ready to deliver venom, in the form of an indictment so rousing that even in the face of his selfishness and lies, I might have extracted a glimmer of truth or remorse, and in doing so find myself somehow relieved. But standing there before him, aware that no oratory miracle could change the reality of Christopher's body deep in the cold ground, I felt empty and sober.

"There is a price to be paid, Angus," I said simply. "My husband is dead. Please tell the truth."

For a moment he closed his eyes and pressed his lips into a line, and his expression reminded me of the strange plaster casts I had seen of convicts after they were hanged.

"I'm sorry your husband's dead," he said, looking at me now with his sly, reddened, narrow eyes. "And I'm sorry the case hasn't been solved. But I didn't do it, and you can't keep turning up at my house."

I heard the clomp of heels, then, and his wife behind him, who immediately made a hooting noise and started shaking her head. She reminded me of a turkey. "Get out!" she shrieked. "Get out!"

I wished, then, that I were some kind of shaman or witch, possessed with the power to utter a real incantation or curse. But as the door closed and I heard Angus trying to calm her, I only yelled that it was nice to see him enjoying a pint with Danny today, and I would see them both in Hell.

Panting and winded and feeling there was nothing more to do than turn back for home, I stood for a moment and looked at the blond wood door, which returned my gaze as surely as a face, defiant and prim. To the right of the door was a shiny brass coach lamp on a sconce. Baring my teeth like an animal about to snarl and possessed of an energy from elsewhere, I curled my fist around the lamp's neck, ripped it clean off the wall, and holding it like a club, barely able to see, hurled it twice into the door as its glass smashed.

When Angus reappeared, his face flushed and his nostrils flaring, I began to scream. "You absolute bastard! I hope you enjoy your peaceful life!"

He was looming over me on the step now, and suddenly I felt my wrist nearly crushed by the pressure of his grip. He held me rigid and close, like the brute he was, and breathed into my ear. "This is a serious game you're playing, you mad little bitch," he said. "If you keep on, I'll make you regret it. You don't want me as an enemy. Now, fuck off."

He pushed me, then, with such force that I skinned my knee on the wet paving as the door slammed. As a final gesture, even though it nearly made me gag, I dredged up a gob of spit and lobbed it at the porch. As I limped out of his yard I saw that I had attracted a small audience of neighbors, standing slack-jawed under porches like scarecrows in robes. I felt like spitting at them all.

\* \* \*

When I arrived home, I was shaking, and noticed that my right palm was smeared with blood. For a while as I swabbed it clean, I sat with Lionel in front of a TV travel special about the best resorts and sight-seeing tours in Queensland. The presenter had a grating, nasal voice and each scene seemed to end with her posing in a pool with a martini. Just as she was chatting with a tour guide in the Daintree rainforest, and I was considering the fact that the Daintree was just one place among all the others that I was now sure to never visit, I heard the phone ring.

It was Vince.

"What were you thinking, confronting Angus at his house? My God, Sylvia—you broke his porch lamp and used it as a weapon!"

"I want Angus to confess," I said, hoping the slur in my voice didn't make my words sound any less true. "I want the law and the town to acknowledge that the emperor has no clothes and is a murderer to boot. I want justice for Christopher, without further delay."

I heard Vince sigh.

"He wants to file a report, and I think he will."

"I don't care."

"You will in the morning."

I nearly told him that there was little that could touch me when I would be beyond this world by Sunday evening, but my tongue was slow, and I just heard my own breathing.

"What's going on with you?" he asked finally. "I'm coming over."

Fifteen minutes later, Vince appeared at my door, dangling his keys in one hand and looking bleary in a T-shirt and jeans. At the sight of my hand, which I'd bandaged, he shook his head.

"Come on," he said. "Let's get out of here."

He drove us to the deserted Chinese restaurant on High Street, where we were shown to a table just before the kitchen closed. We sat beneath paper lanterns that glowed like red suns. He ordered a huge bowl of dumplings, and I ordered spring rolls despite not being hungry. When the waiter left, he rested his chin on his fist.

"Angus said he's going to seek a court order to prevent you from coming within twenty meters of his property. Even if you mount a good defense, the order will probably be granted, because of his connections and also because there were witnesses to your display." He leaned back and looked at me for a moment without blinking. "I'm worried about you, Sylvia."

"Don't be," I said, in a voice that sounded off pitch and thin. "Don't worry, Vince. Everything will be okay."

I could tell he didn't believe me, and I didn't blame him. I was quite drunk, and lying, after all.

He frowned. "You're not thinking of doing anything else silly, are you?"

In the pause that followed, I tried to look incredulous. "I didn't get what I wanted from Angus, but I'm not going to try it again."

He looked at his hands on the table. "Well, it doesn't have to be the end of the world, this court order. You just need to obey it. It'll lapse in a year. Obviously it would be good meanwhile to send him a written apology, and a check for the damage."

I nodded as our food was delivered, and looked at the pale glutinous forms of Vince's dumplings floating in broth, the gleaming cigars of the spring rolls on my plate. Vince bent over the dumplings, eating rapidly. He had a family to attend to, and out of concern that I was eventually going to land myself in prison, had sacrificed his evening. I watched the intent bobbing shape of his head, the cropped black hair of his crown beginning to prematurely thin.

He looked up, reaching for his water glass and scanning my face. I smiled, dipping one of the spring rolls in the bowl of soy sauce and taking a bite. As I chewed mechanically, I looked out at the quiet street, the wide road, the glinting windows of shop fronts, a solitary figure here and there strolling by in the shadows with a dog or bag of shopping, moving slowly as if stricken by some truth. There was so much to remember, to understand and record, but even my bones felt brittle. For an instant I closed my eyes, feeling the urgency of certain resolutions and final rites like a rushing breeze passing on.

I glanced back at him. "We've failed, haven't we?"

In the silence while he peered at his hands on the table, I thought of his role in Christopher's life, long before I appeared. They had been playmates sharing crayons in kindergarten, scab-kneed allies at school, co-conspirators wheeling on bikes throughout the yawning summers of small-town adolescence, and best men at each other's weddings. I had first met Vince six years ago, when on weekends he still wore a baseball cap backward, and was just losing the jaunty R&B stride he had cultivated to impress girls at fifteen. Now it occurred to me that I was likely seeing him for the last time, and my throat felt tight.

"We don't know that yet," he said finally, in a defeated voice. He wiped his mouth on a napkin and sighed. "These things can turn on a dime. Who's to say we don't receive a phone tip next week, or uncover some new clue we'd missed?"

I only looked at him, feeling giddy from my drinking and too heavy for my own skeleton.

"I saw Angus drinking with Danny at the pub today, carefree and laughing. Angus has his freedom, and Danny has his car—what's not to celebrate?"

Vince, who had heard all this before, shook his head. "You know their being in cahoots is just a theory; we have no hard proof."

"Exactly. That was their plan."

He squinted at me now, leaning forward. "Don't you ask yourself what Chris would have wanted? It wouldn't have been this. You're destroying yourself to get a conviction that won't bring him back."

"It's not about what he would have wanted," I said. "It's about what he deserves."

I pushed away my plate and tried to smile as we sat there beneath the lanterns. I wanted to face him in a final way, to thank him for his love and kindness, but knew that if I did, I would begin to cry.

Outside my house a short while later, he kissed my cheek and I thanked him for dropping by, and then he was gone.

I felt bad about causing trouble for Vince, who had always looked out for me. But I was glad to have seen him once more before time ran out. On TV, the travel special was ending. The presenter was poised grinning at the top of an enormous theme park waterslide, about to ricochet like a bullet around its steep turns, and as I switched off the screen I thought of the idiocy of existence.

Later, as I lay in bed, I thought of Angus's wife. I imagined her lying, as I was, in darkness. I wondered about the degree to which her anger was sparked by fear. I wondered how well she knew her husband.

# 9.

2 DAYS TILL COMET! GET YOUR SNAX!

On High Street at lunchtime the next day, with my bandaged hand like a stiff white paw, I blinked stupidly at the newsagent's A-frames, thinking of how the countdown to the comet's plain-sight appearance also measured the time I had left. Alongside entreating punters to prepare for St. John, the headlines announced the next $20 Million Lotto Jackpot above the image of a white-sand beach. Forcing myself to dismiss the vision of a last swim in the Pacific before Sunday, I resumed walking to the Safeway around the corner, while the preschooler being pushed in front of me held a pink balloon floating limply from a string. The supermarket was busier than usual, and the sounds of chatter, car doors slamming, and Top 20 pop ballads from inside bathed me in a dull panic.

It was only after collecting Lionel's cat litter that I realized what was wrong. In certain sections, the aisles were nearly bare. Now, as I paid attention, I saw more than one staff member looking harried, or speaking in tones of apology to a customer, and when I reached the sardines, there were only two tins left. In the shelves reserved for pasta, canned tomatoes, flour, and all manner of product tinned and dry, I encountered hastily Blu-Tacked signs: DUE TO INCREASED DEMAND, WE ARE CURRENTLY EXPERIENCING SUPPLY SHORTAGES.

After work, the air was warm and still, the streets quick with people and cars. There was, I saw now in the world outside myself, an electric charge, the kind of charge I was aware of as a child before Christmas, when everyone draws with an edge of panic toward the same magnetic limit. Today was the date of the comet meeting at Memorial Hall, and I was glad for an excuse to delay being alone. Like most public meetings, I supposed it would be a forum for tea and biscuits and the release of pent-up emotion among strangers—although this meeting was not about inappropriate development or too many trucks, but instead about a celestial body in the sky.

There was no escaping it. When I reached the corner, I saw that the window display in Sweet Mementos, Sandy's favorite shop, had changed. Hanging now in front of the teddies and fairies was a mass of glittering festoon lights and a line of silver bunting which spelled out the phrase STARSTRUCK! Below this was a sign in Edwardian script: BESPOKE KEEPSAKES OF A ONCE-IN-4000+-YEAR EVENT! WHILE STOCKS LAST! I cast an eye over the cabinet displays, smiling despite myself. There were bone china cups emblazoned with the comet, souvenir tea towels, comet-shaped stars of silver wire, and comet-shaped moonstone brooches made by a local artist.

As I walked on, I noticed an ABC news van parked on the other side of the road outside Our Lady of Perpetual Help. A woman in heels and a navy suit stood on the curb before a cameraman, holding a mic in one hand and smoothing back her lacquered hair with the other. Crossing the road, I joined the other gawkers loitering by the van. It was only now that I noticed the reverend's new signboard message, which the camera was poised to capture:

HEAVENS ABOVE

THERE'S A STAR IN TOWN

THERE'S NOTHING TO FEAR

SO ENJOY THE COUNTDOWN

It lodged in my head like a riddle as the news reporter swept out her hand and began to speak.

"Here in the town of Jericho," she said, "the mood is feverish in view of the impending arrival of a very special visitor in the skies late this Sunday night—Comet St. John, discovered by an astronomer from nearby Black Mountain Observatory."

As the woman continued, I sat down on the low bluestone fence of the church and peered up at the white clouds coasting by, feeling empty rather than feverish, while her voice echoed in my head.

"Unlike Comet Halley," she was saying now, "which returns to us every seventy-six years, Comet St. John has not visited our solar system for over four thousand years. While viewing conditions during Halley's last appearance in 1986 were generally disappointing, St. John, with a nucleus eight times the size of Halley's, is set to stage a spectacular show. In fact, sky-watchers around the world are saying this comet will not only be one of the brightest in recorded history, but also perhaps the most widely and enduringly visible, on a global scale. In New South Wales, the comet at its closest will appear at the celestial zenith, or directly overhead—meaning that perhaps the best place to see it on Earth will be right here, in the unusually dark skies of the Jericho region . . ."

Half a dozen people of various ages were clustered outside the hall when I approached, all murmuring and holding paper cups. Meeting Room 2, accessed through a narrow corridor to the side of the heritage main hall, was the size of a large classroom and, with only one small window, had the feeling of a bunker. Even with the window and two fluorescent tube lights, one of which flickered every few seconds, the room was darker than the daylight outside, and its old carpet smelled of stale wool.

When my eyes adjusted, I peered over at the small stage, empty but for an overhead projector, glowing screen, chair, and microphone. In the front row of chairs sat several people dressed in black T-shirts, holding their spines erect and looking ahead at the stage as if for a cue. From my vantage point by the refreshments station near the door, I could only see the backs of their heads, but figured they might be bored local teens jacked up on pills and doomsday fantasies. Several couples and lone rangers like me lounged listlessly in the other rows, or stood beside the urn jiggling tea bags in cups or munching on the Starburst sweets and fun-sized Milky Way bars on offer.

As I settled into a middle row, a man entered the stage from a side

room, carrying a folder which he placed on the chair. Despite his ponytail and thoughtful swagger, it took me a second to register that it
was Joseph, and even as I did, my mind arrived at no firm conclusion
about what it meant.

When he took a transparency from the folder and lowered it onto
the projector box, the black-and-white image of a starry sky appeared.
Facing us there from behind the microphone with a wry smile, he
waited for us to stop shifting in our seats. Most would not have caught
the flicker of trepidation that crossed his face, in the moment before he
spoke with a poise that induced a sudden stillness in us all.

"Hello, Jericho," he said. "I'm Joseph Evans, and I'm glad you're here."
With a thoughtful smile, he peered up at the screen of stars.

"For those with eyes to see," he began, "the signs are always there."

Falling silent, he looked out at us unblinkingly, and I watched his
hands lift upward as if to collect rain.

"'The stars,' said Plotinus," he continued gravely, "'reveal themselves
like letters perpetually being inscribed on the heavens.'"

As he replaced the first slide, I realized how apt his voice was for the
stage, rising and falling in volume and pitch as a pastor's might do in
sermon. The screen now showed an intricate six-pointed star, inside a
scalloped mandala pattern.

"In other words," he went on, "the universe is inscribed with
symbol—an idea as true today as it was in the third century. If we've
forgotten, we need only look up at the night sky to remember." With
a frank smile, he nodded at the screen. "Or down below, at the canola
fields a few Ks southwest of this very town, where just days ago this star
formation appeared."

He raised his arms, as I realized I was looking at the aerial image of
the crop circle mentioned on the radio.

"In this hexagram symbol, we can read the sacred geometry understood by Plato to encode the cosmos."

While he paused for dramatic effect, I peered at the crop circle,
blazing golden like a sun. It looked to me suddenly like a cipher from

another dimension, arrived to betray the grayness of our modern world. As Joseph spoke on, my mind summoned the fact of the hoaxers from Wiltshire and others like them, toiling before dawn with ropes and planks, to bend wheat and barley so precisely and at such scale that their patterns were visible from the air. But the star form in the canola field looked too wild, too sublime to have been made by humans, and I wanted to hope it hadn't been.

Now Joseph was relating all the corresponding patterns supposedly present within the crop circle's star, found in forms as diverse as snowflakes, electrons, and diffracted sunbeams, and for a second I imagined myself within a diaphanous prism, merging with the brightness.

"'The wise man is the man who in any one thing can read another,'" he went on. "In this star, we can also read the Jewish Star of David, the Anahata symbol of the heart chakra, and the Shatkona symbol of Hinduism, representing divine union."

The next slide showed two drawings I'd already seen, of comets as crude star shapes with streaming tails, like the biscuits at the bakery. One, from the *Nuremberg Chronicle*, depicted Halley's appearance in AD 684. The other presented the sixteenth-century Aztec ruler, Montezuma II, standing on the roof of a building as if about to jump into the path of a comet blazing before him, one of several portents said to have preceded the Spanish conquest of Mesoamerica and Montezuma's own death.

"This is another kind of star, the kind that brings us together here tonight," Joseph said. "Comets were 'broom stars' to the Chinese. To the Greeks and Romans they were bearded stars, long-haired stars; stars classed by their similarity to all kinds of shapes on Earth—arrows, swords, discs, horns, torches, even horses."

He set down an observatory image of Comet St. John that had been released to the press. It was a white streak in a dark sky that indeed looked like a fire torch hurled into the heavens.

"Throughout history," he continued, "humans have heeded the appearance of comets as signs of something momentous to come—the death of a ruler, the end of a kingdom, the shock of war or natural disaster. A comet oversaw the Black Death in 1347, and Halley's last appearance was bookended by the tragedies of the space shuttle *Challenger*, and Chernobyl."

I leaned back, unsure why he had paused when there were so many other examples to list. He slipped his hands in his pockets now and offered us a thoughtful frown, while I recalled the men fighting over the telescope, the shortages at the supermarket, and the fact of our own time in history, at the tail end of a millennium that began with the Bronze Age.

"But as much as comets have been aligned throughout history with death and disaster," he went on suddenly, "so are they believed to have played a part in the creation of life, by bringing traces of the organic matter they're made of to the early Earth."

As he spoke on, his voice became mellow and slow, as if he were surprised by the conclusion he was forming. Peering around, I noticed that the audience had mostly remained watchful and still, although here and there I could spy a tagalong spouse, hunched forward in a pose of polite forbearance.

"It's been speculated, not least in art," he was saying now with a radiant urgency, "that the star under which Jesus was born, the star of Bethlehem, was in fact a comet. What's more, Edison first lit up Wall Street against the backdrop of the Great Comet of 1882. And in 1910, the year of Halley's return, China criminalized slavery. So, I put it to you—perhaps it's wiser to view comets the way we do the Tower card in the tarot, which symbolizes the crisis that so often precedes creation, revolution, and release."

In the pause that followed, presumably intended as a moment of reflection, I heard someone behind me clear their throat.

"Or," came a man's voice, "we could embrace the eighteenth-century discovery that comets are simply bright objects visiting our celestial neighborhood."

I recognized the deep timbre of that voice, its blend of shrewdness and restraint, before I turned around and saw the speaker, but even so I was surprised to find Theo sitting there in the audience, looking stoic. The cold heat of shame pricked my skin, just being near him.

"We could accept," he continued, "that comets are physical phenomena of ice and gas and soot and vapor, which far from portending future events on Earth, can themselves be predicted by us, with science. *I* put it to *you*—we can enjoy comets, we can learn from them, and we can also let them pass without fear or primitive superstition!"

Joseph was smiling. In the pause, he began to nod. "Thanks for your candor," he said. "Look, I'm no enemy of science. I just don't accept it as a reason to dismiss possibilities and truths that are immaterial, and can't easily be measured."

He sat down and offered a thoughtful shrug in Theo's direction. "Why do you feel our positions are mutually exclusive? Why does mainstream science insist on divesting our cosmos of its inherent intelligence and meaning, just because we don't yet understand how it all works?"

"Because," Theo replied, "there's no rational scientific basis for the idea that a comet in the sky—or Neptune or Mars—has any connection to events on Earth. Peddling those ideas harks back to the Dark Ages, when we also believed in witches and the Devil and treated fever with leeches."

Joseph peered back, quizzical and a little sad. "Well," he began, "the idea of there being an intrinsic correspondence between different orders of reality—mind and matter, the terrestrial and the celestial—this idea isn't dismissed by all of science. Quantum entanglement supports it, although Einstein dismissed that theory as 'spooky.' I suppose you dismiss it, too?"

There was a pause, and like the rest of the audience, I turned again in my chair toward Theo, awaiting his response.

"I'm not here to debate quantum mechanics," he said wearily. "My objection is to your magical thinking about comets. It's the twentieth century. If you don't want to listen to me, listen to Maupertuis, who said it all in 1742: 'These stars, after having been the world's terror for a long time, have suddenly become discredited, so that they are able to cause no more than a cold in the head.'"

It was the most animated I'd seen him, although now in silence he appeared deflated, leaning back limply in his chair and, for a rather long moment, looking right at me. Everyone, myself included, now turned back to regard Joseph.

Far from looking perturbed or flustered, his face expressed an expansive patience. "In this forum I simply offer my own thoughts, and I'm glad you've shared yours. If we can agree on nothing else, we can perhaps agree on this: comets always inspire impassioned responses."

With a sense of resolve, he rose from his chair and projected a new image. It showed a strange computer-generated mandala, with a center of colored crisscrossing lines like a cat's cradle.

"This is the astrological chart of St. John's discovery two years ago," he began, as Theo emitted a loud groan. "If you look closely at the aspects highlighted in blue, you'll see another star . . ."

As Joseph spoke on, I turned my gaze to the clouds through the window, conscious of Theo's position behind me like a force field. Whatever Theo said, I could understand the need to believe in a numinous order of existence, an order beyond mundane physical reality, that might explain and redeem the fact of finding ourselves landed here, like the amnesiac survivors of some celestial shipwreck. In the same instant, I confronted my own longing to believe, which pulsed inside me like a heart, and which I supposed Theo might not understand. The clouds, charged with light, were moving, and as I tracked them I couldn't help but imagine that through them somehow, the universe was gazing back at me quite urgently, insistent that I understand a simple truth that would soon change everything.

Finally Joseph took a breath and directed a thoughtful smile to the floor, and in the pause I saw Theo lurch from his seat and stalk out.

"Jung," Joseph announced, "believed that what we blithely call coincidence is more often the meaningful expression of the cosmic interconnectedness of all things, and an example of the way the universe is always speaking to us in signs. It's our choice whether to heed or ignore them."

As he continued I looked toward the door, wondering whether to go after Theo. But why, I asked myself, would his agitation be soothed by a woman whose unwanted advances had recently soured his evening?

"My *suggestion* to you," Joseph said now, "is that St. John is visiting us for a reason. It is up to each of us to meet it at the level of awareness it demands, which is a level beyond the register of fear. My *invitation* to you, finally, is to join me and my colleagues at no cost late this Sunday evening at our meditation school on Bakers Road. There, we will lead you on a transcendental journey within your own internal cosmos, and, together, attune ourselves to the frequencies and potentials of the comet that will at last be visible above us. The evening will conclude with bamboo flute music and an Ayurvedic feast. Thank you for listening. I'll now take questions."

It was strange to see Joseph bear himself with such radiant assurance after our encounters at the office, and if I could still discern hints of the exhaustion and grief that existed behind his public façade, I must have been the only one. As he peered out at us in search of raised hands, I considered staying, but felt adrenaline springing from a wily holdout in myself that wanted to know whether Theo was still nearby.

On my way out, I found Joseph's friend Zara, the soprano, and none other than Danny flanking the doors holding flyers, both wearing the same black KC T-shirts that recalled the album art for Pink Floyd's *The Dark Side of the Moon*. From Zara I took one and smiled, before exchanging a stony look with Danny as I left. Even though I had my own journey planned for Sunday night, I was curious about Joseph's classes, and wondered whether a meditation group might help Sandy to get out of the house more.

KINGDOM COME MEDITATION SCHOOL: DISCOVER INNER SPACE, the flyer said. Kingdom Come—that, I realized, was the meaning of the T-shirts. I wondered what Joseph's apparently business-minded,

scone-baking mother had made of her son's pursuit of spiritual enlight-
enment. Considering the fact that the meditation session on Sunday
night was happening after her funeral during the day, I supposed that
for Joseph it would also serve as a means of honoring her.

As I rounded the corner for home, mulling over the religiosity of the
school's name and how to reconcile the notion of meditation with what
I knew of Danny, I saw Theo, and couldn't help but wonder whether
he'd been waiting for me. He was sitting on a picnic table at the edge
of the gardens, dragging on a cigarette. The wind had picked up, and I
stood on the road for too long, tucking back my hair. He saw me before
I'd decided what to do, and without expression, held up his hand.

"What's happened to you?" he asked, looking at my bandage as I
walked over.

I shrugged, and said I'd cut myself on a porch lamp.

His guarded look dropped away. "How did you do that?"

I couldn't be bothered lying. "By smashing it against a door," I replied, as he nodded slowly and we each looked to the clouds, and I saw
him smile from the edge of my eye.

"So," he said after a moment, "what do you make of the New Age
priest?"

I shrugged. "You really gave him a serve."

He squinted at the road. "It's always risky, with comets. When you
find one, prophets appear. People are just so credulous."

I sat down, grateful that we seemed to have slid around Tuesday
night, and mentioned that Joseph was a client who'd just lost his mother.
"Besides, it's understandable, isn't it—the instinct to believe that sudden
visions in the sky have meaning?"

He shrugged and peered at his boots on the seat. "It's certainly predictable."

When I suggested that Joseph, at least, seemed to be trying to move
curiosity about the comet away from fear, he stubbed out his cigarette
and asked how the talk had ended. I explained the invitation to the
meditation school, and he nodded.

"Yup, it was a sales pitch." He met my stare with a look of gloomy amusement. "In 1773, there was a panic in Paris about a comet supposedly due to impact Earth. Even though astronomers refuted the rumors, the charlatans who went about selling tickets to Paradise still got paid."

He shook his head. "People were primed by then. Only months before, an unknown prophet had been making house calls."

"House calls?"

He nodded. In return for food and lodgings, he explained, this prophet had evangelized about the cometary destruction to come if people didn't repent and atone. By the time he was questioned by authorities, the man was enjoying a degree of renown, and claimed that as an envoy of God Himself, he'd answer only to the king.

"So what if Joseph's spin is more positive?" he asked finally. "If the history of comets tells us anything, it's that where there's potential for panic, there's a vacuum to be filled and a profit to be made."

As we sat there, regarding the orange sky as the trees shuddered around us, I thought of how strange it was to see him so candid. Beside him in silence while the wind rippled our clothes, I admitted to myself that not even Theo's cynicism could dim my curiosity about the comet and all that concerned it, including Joseph, who was certainly the most interesting funeral client I'd yet encountered.

"Well," I said at last, not wanting to go, but eager to avoid another awkward parting, "it's getting blustery. I might leave you to your evening."

A glum half smile passed over Theo's face as he rose to follow me, but we didn't get far. From a glade of trees a few meters away came a screeching sound. Moving closer, we saw a crow pecking at a smaller bird collapsed beneath a Victoria palm. While he shooed off the crow, I crouched over the smaller bird. It looked like a noisy miner, on the verge of death. The wind had grown so strong that with each gust, he was nearly blown off the ground, and he lay now surrounded by his own feathers. I had nothing with which to shield him, but couldn't imagine just walking on.

"I'll sit for a while. You can go," I told Theo, but he stayed.

Together we knelt there watching the bird being ruffled by the wind, waiting for him to die. His glimmering black eye flew open and shut.

"Perhaps we should find some kind of box," I said.

Theo nodded, and said he could check the trunk of his car. It felt like he was away for a long time, as I sat there growing chilled while the wind worsened, and the bird's eye kept opening. Eventually I stood to move my feet, and thought that I must have looked strange there, stamping around under the palm as daylight faded and everything shook. When I looked back a few seconds later to find the bird wasn't there, I thought something was wrong with my vision, but I could only see his feathers. I didn't want to think the wind might have lifted him away like some airborne seed, right at the moment of death. When Theo returned with what looked like a chip tray from the general store, I was still searching.

"Maybe he flew away," he said, as I frowned and shook my head.

"Look," he added a moment later, standing directly under the palm and craning his neck. "He's right there. He must have flown up."

When I moved closer, I saw the bird perched on a lower branch, sheltered by the fronds, gazing past us with a stoic indifference.

"He must have just been gathering strength," he said. "At least we warned off the crow."

I nodded, feeling foolish, but grateful the bird was alive. I looked at Theo under the shadow of the tree for a fraction too long, thinking of how swiftly his expressions changed, and how it might feel to rest my head just for a moment on his shoulder.

"It's going to rain," he said finally, raising an eye to the sky, which was alive now with the strange, electric light that so often precedes thunder.

Together we walked to the road, and there exchanged half-comic shrugs, the shrugs of people who have nothing to say. I thought we were about to wave and walk off in opposite directions, until he peered again at the sky and offered to drive me home. It was only a few minutes away, but I was glad to escape the wind.

As he wove through the back streets following my directions, I watched the clouds, which had turned amber.

"I guess you won't be attending the meditation on Sunday," I said archly, when we reached my house.

He gave me an incredulous look as I stepped out. "Are you?"

I shook my head. "Not in this life," I said, and thanked him for the lift.

He waved and I watched his car coast away. I should have thanked him for staying to watch the bird, I thought when I arrived inside. I reasoned that, in fact, I might have told him anything at all, something wild, even—exactly what, I wasn't sure—but why not, if I'd not be around long enough to regret the consequences? In the hall, just as the thunder began, I picked up Lionel and felt his warmth, his small quick heart under my palm as we watched each other. Setting out his sardines, I realized that I'd assumed the nearness of oblivion might, by now, have at least lent me courage. I thought of the bird, facing fate calmly. I thought of Joseph, radiant in his conviction that the universe speaks to us, that no coincidence is random, no wound or sacrifice wasted, and wondered what the bird might have signaled to him.

Saturday, my birthday, passed in a slow, formless wave. After sleeping in, I played "Clair de Lune" on the cello with my eyes closed, contemplating the fact that I was now thirty-two. The phone rang a few times, but I carried on playing. I heard the secret in the melody, feeling myself nearing a final shore, a landform which I had in fact been pointed toward all along, on whose ground the strangeness of life would at last make sense, but of course I never reached it.

Before getting dressed, I phoned the trust that oversaw the town cemetery. With the help of my credit card and a receptionist whose motherly voice reminded me of my favorite high school history teacher, I reserved the grave site adjacent to Christopher's. I'd meant to do it for some time. As I told customers, much peace can be gained by exercising our powers of choice while we're still alive.

In the late morning I visited Sandy, who was delighted with my impromptu gift of two new fairies for her collection.

"You're a sly one, giving gifts on your own birthday," she said, patting my cheek and depositing in my lap a gift of her own: a fuchsia kiss-lock purse on a bright gold chain, and a bottle of Elizabeth Arden cologne I would never use. I could barely read the card, with its message about brighter days ahead.

Together we visited Christopher's grave and laid down new flowers, expensive white roses I had bought from the florist instead of the grocer. Later, over tea and comet biscuits on the porch, I handed her the meditation flyer and told her about the Memorial Hall meeting.

"Oh, Sylvia," she said, gazing out at the garden, "I just love the idea that the comet could actually be a sign of good things to come!"

After hugging Sandy more tightly than usual and saying goodbye, I returned my library books about shipwrecks and fractal geometry and comets. I paid an overdue rates bill at the post office and smiled at the clerk, who never smiled at me. At home I cleaned. I scrubbed two years of grime from the windows and floors, cleared out the fridge and cupboards, discarded my old papers and rattiest clothes, and changed the linens, all with an eye on the few rare things I owned that might please certain people—a vintage brocade jacket Donna might like; Venetian glass beads for Sandy—which I parceled in old Christmas paper and labeled with their names.

During one of my trips back from the bins, I found the chamber music that had been playing on the radio replaced by a presentation cataloguing the criminal genius of the still-unidentified Zodiac Killer. "Zodiac," as he called himself—everyone seemed sure it was a he—had terrorized Northern California in the late sixties and taunted the San Francisco Police Department with regular correspondence. Killing people, he crowed, "is even better than getting your rocks off with a girl." Zodiac claimed responsibility for thirty-seven murders and threatened more, the presenter explained, not only for the fun of it, but also so that he would amass a good number of slaves for his afterlife in Paradise.

He was, I thought, as I bagged up my decent clothes for the local Red Cross, just one example of how brazenly a person could flout justice in this world. It was not unlikely that Zodiac was, right then, enjoying a peaceful old age somewhere, replete with cruise vacations and family barbecues and even comet-viewing potlucks, the chemicals of rage and violence having subsided along with his youth, years before.

Warmed by a tumbler of the whisky I had always used in Christopher's favorite chocolate cake, I hurled open his side of the wardrobe. Without allowing myself to pause too long over anything, not even his wedding suit, I began to pile his clothes into bags, so that no one else, least of all Sandy, would have to do it when I was gone. Once his wardrobe was reduced to a stale cavern of negative space, I felt I was looking at my own mind's reflection. For a moment I crouched inside the space and inhaled, but I still couldn't locate his smell.

Unable to go on any longer, I sank into the couch and stroked Lionel as he kneaded my lap and fixed me with his otherworldly green eyes, telling myself he would be happy with Sandy and Terry, and wondering what, if anything, I should say to my mother in my final note. Then the parrots outside began to shriek, and I closed my eyes, thinking of the moment I'd heard described by Tibetan Buddhists, when consciousness collects itself in a single drop at the heart, and the radiance of death dawns before the next incarnation. It was an idea I longed to believe. I pictured Christopher's body, silent in the dark ground a few kilometers away. I pictured my father, long absorbed by the earth, whose grave in Sydney I'd not see again.

Everything, as I sat there, seemed terribly sharp—the parrots' cries, the vibrations of Lionel purring, the undulating branches of the jacaranda outside. As the light faded around us and the house closed in, I tried to shake the feeling of the surrounding walls and objects watching in strange expectation, as if waiting for me to comprehend something they had always known.

# 10.

IN THE MORNING, SUNLIGHT BOUNCED OFF THE PEAR-CUT DIAMOND of my engagement ring, forming the star shapes of which Joseph spoke. My hands seemed separate from the part of me that watched them, and the diamond's luminescence seemed to belong to another dimension.

I'd woken with the dawn, light-headed, as if my consciousness were already cleaving away from my flesh. In the bathroom before one corner of the mirror, I concealed my under-eye shadows, rouged a bloom into my cheeks, and arranged at my nape a braided bun, as though I were my own mortician. I peered up close at one of my eyes, owl-like and stunned in the glass, and thought of how it had all arrived: the anniversary, the comet, the end.

On my way to prepare for the Evans service in the afternoon, I passed a man pruning his camellias in the company of a radio. "If you've just joined us, folks," the presenter barked, "we're here with a space-themed soundtrack, leading up to St. John's arrival tonight!" As Elton John's "Rocket Man" began, I thought of the comet brightening above us, almost feeling it waiting in some hemisphere of my brain, waiting to deliver the burst of light, the chemical combustion that so often precedes darkness.

I was unprepared for the scene that met me in the office. At reception, Clarence and Tania were conferring in tones of disaster. Just hours before it was due to take place, Joseph had called off his mother's funeral. I dropped my bag and stood to attention as Clarence gritted his teeth and threw up his hands.

"Our client won't see reason," he said. "In any case, he's waiting to speak with you, Sylvia."

Moments later in the polished gloom of Clarence's office, I faced Joseph. He stood by the window with his hands in his pockets, and met me with an apologetic smile.

"I hope Clarence will recover. Naturally, I don't expect any refunds."

I asked him what had happened, and followed his eye as he glanced through the window at the laneway, the shop rooftops, the blue sky.

"I got lost in the planning," he said, turning back to me. "And in the process, I lost sight of her. My mother was not an extroverted person, despite her activities in the district, and she wasn't extravagant, either. Most of her dearest friends and relatives are already dead. And she wasn't a Catholic in any true sense. She wouldn't have wanted the funeral we've planned."

"Okay," I said, realizing that there was no changing his mind.

His face looked ashen in the light of the window. "I want to bury her at home, on the farm. I'm applying for permission from the council. When it comes through, we can have the service there."

I frowned. "Joseph, this would be highly unusual. Your application could easily be refused, and we'd have to retain your mother in refrigeration until we find out."

"Well," he said, "I want to try."

I stood there thinking of the cathedral we had booked being filled with flowers even as we spoke. I thought of the priest, the caterers, the horse-drawn-hearse driver, and the guests, all preparing for an event that had already receded like a tide.

"I thought I'd cope better with losing her," he went on, his voice quavering. "I thought my belief in the continuation of consciousness would make it easier to be without her, in the here and now."

"Doesn't it?" I asked. Something about his face, and the feeling in my own chest made me ask.

"Compared to total materialism, yes. But there's still the loss, still the fact of being left behind."

As I lowered myself into the guest chair and faced him, I watched him peer back at the sky through the window, and wondered whether he was thinking of the comet. Then I heard my own voice break the silence.

"Two years ago, after my husband died in an accident, I wanted to die, too, and in hospital afterward, I almost did." I explained how, when the doctors succeeded in jump-starting my heart and returning me violently to consciousness, I longed to return to the place I had been—a strange region of golden silence, a far-reaching void, swirling with light like the visions I'd seen in documentaries of distant nebulae.

"I can only say that it didn't feel like a dream," I went on, "even if that's what it was. I saw no people, no landscapes. I heard no voices. There was just the light, more real than the light in the sky right now, and the feeling of a homecoming I still can't understand."

He nodded and smiled, as I recalled how time had seemed to stretch, in the one and a half minutes during which my heart had stopped and I had hung somewhere between life and death. "You experienced one of the mysteries," he said. "I've heard similar accounts. How beautiful it sounds." He sighed. "Some would say you caught your glimpse of God, the oneness we all return to."

For a moment I looked at the solid fact of my sensible buckled shoes, wondering what Theo would think. It was odd to speak of my experience aloud. I'd barely shared the details with Sandy. And yet it was suddenly easy to be honest in this way with Joseph, a near stranger.

"Perhaps it's why you found us—I saw you in the audience on Friday," he said, watching me. "Eventually, in certain states of meditation, we can learn to find our way back to that place."

When I asked him whether he knew this from experience, he nodded.

"I've come close. Perhaps nearly as close as a person can go, while still grounded by the body in all its weight and limitation."

After a moment spent in silence, peering at the sky and then at each other, he turned to me with a smile that creased the edges of his eyes, but when he spoke his voice was rueful: "We all find our way home, eventually. Death is just another beginning—we'd both do well to remember that."

His words reached me like an electric charge. "What if we don't want to wait?" were the words on my lips, but I said nothing, aware of how far I had crossed the professional line, and conscious of my colleagues waiting for help with emergency cancellations, even as I figured that those things hardly mattered anymore. For a moment in my chair, it was as though the fabric of time wavered. I was suspended again between two worlds. In the presence of Joseph's awareness and with St. John invisibly near, I felt the strange pressure of an understanding just out of reach, like a traveler in the desert glimpsing water. For some without faith, and for mongrels like me, I supposed it would always be like this—a bereft and stumbling feeling, grasping now and then in the dark, but always returning to the conclusion that nothing about being here, alive in the world, would ever quite make sense.

I left work a few hours later, assailed by the vertigo of reaching a moment that had been marked for so long as the future. Joseph's words still echoed in my head. I felt the details of the day recording themselves on my skin: the sun on my hands as I walked, the rasp of my shoe soles on the pavement, the manic cackle of kookaburras above. I noticed the light glittering at the edges of my eyes, the distant mauve hills in the west, the blue sky.

There was a strange edge to the streets. Cars sped by in all directions. The few pedestrians I saw scurried along with resolute faces, carrying bags of groceries. No one lingered anywhere except on their own front porches, holding a beer or a hose or a small child distractedly, looking out at the horizon, waiting.

As I entered the house, I felt my ship making its silent crossing into a hemisphere from which I'd not return. It was disconcerting to realize there was still so much to do. I hadn't yet written my note, or nominated my beneficiaries, or taken Lionel to Sandy's, or destroyed the forms of ID that might be valuable to thieves. But there were hours of daylight left before the comet came in the deep night, and I resolved to be as ready as one should be for a long-awaited guest.

To begin, I set up Satie's "Gymnopédies" on the stereo—it was neither too despairing nor too upbeat, but rather offered an atmosphere of controlled resignation, in which there was a kind of peace. After gathering up my identity documents and purse, I sat on the couch with Lionel and lined up my driver's licence, Medicare card, passport, and birth certificate on the coffee table. I looked at the salient facts of my birth: the date and time, the town and doctor, the father and mother. She had been twenty-nine when she delivered me into the world, three years younger than I was now. I wondered what she was doing presently— something briskly efficient, I imagined, such as finalizing plans for next week's dinners, or power walking for cardiovascular health, or imbibing the news via radio while also vacuuming the living room.

Opening my passport, I faced the image of myself from four years ago taken in the frantic few weeks before my wedding, perhaps on the same day I finally decided, with a friend's help, on a hairpiece rather than a veil. In the photo, I was wearing cherry lipstick, although my hair was messy. Peering at it, I saw a woman who was accustomed to presenting as calm and assured, a woman who had imagined the broad lines of her life were now settled.

Without indulging myself further, I scrawled down all the crucial numbers on a notepad. Then I took to everything with scissors, satisfied in the knowledge that I was denying some opportunist the chance to sell my afterlife to the highest bidder. As I swept the fragments into a bag, I thought of an article I'd once read about the last-meal choices of death row inmates in America—fried chicken and various kinds of sweet pie had featured prominently, although there was also much variation.

What had surprised me was how few had forgone the choice at all, or intuited that they might not be hungry in the hours before their electrocution. Perhaps what the last meal really offered, I thought, was the chance to assert a degree of control in the most abject of circumstances. Perhaps it was, beyond this, a chance for self-expression—a kind of culinary last testament. My last meal, it seemed clear, was going to be the lukewarm porridge I'd had for breakfast. I certainly wasn't hungry now.

At the kitchen table, I sat down with a pen and an old sheaf of letter stationery, which was bordered by magenta-colored roses. It was, I felt, more romantic in style than was appropriate, but it beat the alternative of a tear-off note sheet. Because it felt overzealous to itemize every person whom the note was to serve, I did away with a salutation.

"Because I find myself now at the limit of what I can reasonably stand," I began, "I am freeing myself of all contracts." After a moment's pause, I went on:

*I am making good on a promise to myself. Don't think I haven't tried. Don't think your efforts have been wasted. All the help that might have redeemed me has been offered. This is my choice. I am sorry.*

*To the practicalities. The house will need to be sold, and its proceeds distributed to my mother-in-law, Sandra (Sandy) Knight. The funds remaining in my bank account, after the costs of the funeral and house sale are deducted, are to be donated to the Cat Protection Society. As for my body—I wish to be buried in the plot next to my husband, which has already been reserved, with a matching photography-free headstone inscribed in Optimus Princeps font. I have no wishes regarding the funeral other than for it to be simple, with a closed coffin. To spare my colleagues at Bell Funerals of the duty, please appoint Dewitt Brothers Memorials instead. (Tell them when they try to overcharge on goods and services that I had an aversion to embalming, and expressly asked for the economy coffin.)*

*I ask that this note serve as my will.*

*Sandy, I am sorry. Please take care of my darling Lionel; I hope Terry won't mind.*

*Yours,*
*Sylvia Knight*

Having signed the letter, I set it down beside a bank statement and the note detailing my important numbers. It was early evening, now. The late sunlight streamed in and cast shadows. The shape of the jacaranda wavered over my arms. My pulse ticked like a clock. As I watched Lionel sitting in a patch of sun at my feet, I felt like a passenger with a ticket, playing for time. I picked him up and met his emerald eyes, his uncompromising stare. I couldn't imagine how to say goodbye. It was time to take him to Sandy's, to make up some excuse about having to go away for a few days, in a brief hallway interaction that she would, in her mind's eye, be condemned to puzzle over for years—but my body was just so tired, my limbs so heavy.

I thought I'd rest for a few hours, since there was a while yet to go. Commentators were predicting that the comet would be easily visible to the naked eye from a little before 2 a.m., when it would appear about ten degrees due east over the horizon, not far from Mars to the northwest. Lying on my bed in the half-light, I tried to picture my mind as a still surface, but it felt more like a cave of inert gases, slowly entering the atmosphere outside me. I could hear the sounds of women's heels and rushing cars and hooting voices on the street outside, couples and families journeying to nearby houses, obeying the reverend's directive to enjoy the countdown. It was as if a new year were about to begin, but then, as Joseph noted, beginnings and endings are always closely tied.

From what sounded like a few streets away now came the sound of a young man screaming. It pierced my skull and passed through it, along with his speeding car and its low, throbbing music. I just wanted to sleep for a while, to blot out the world and be lucid for the night. But I felt myself set against the edge of everything: the edge of words, the edge of my own flesh, the edge of time; and running from sternum to stomach, I had the feeling of falling from the inside. I did drift off eventually, because when I noticed the room again, the sky through the shutters was dark, and I remembered that I had dreamed. In the dream, I had found myself returned to the Gap, a lookout I often visited while living in Sydney before meeting Christopher. I sometimes woke early on my days off, and walked all the way from Surry Hills to Watsons Bay, where I'd stand on the sandstone cliff and rest my eyes on the Tasman Sea. I'd watch the waterbirds, think about the *Dunbar*, a ship wrecked there in 1857, imagine the paradise Australia must have been before the First Fleet arrived with their axes and guns, and wonder what to do with my life. In the dream, I had stood right on the edge, ready to jump, and raised my arms like a diver, but had hesitated despite feeling no fear when I looked down at the rocks one hundred meters below, where, for some reason, Joseph stood in a white robe, watching me.

Now as I lay in bed looking at the darkness through the window, I remembered how on one autumn morning, a weekday, I'd arrived at the Gap earlier than usual to find no one around but for a scrawny-looking man in a windbreaker and jeans, perched perilously close to the cliff's edge. I saw him from behind, sitting cross-legged while the wind ruffled his hair. To get there, he must have hopped over the fence that separated onlookers from the sheer fall of the cliff. I remembered noticing the straightness of his spine, as though he was meditating, or else simply waiting for something to arrive.

What bothered me was his nearness to the edge, and how still he was. I didn't want to surprise him, but I knew I needed to approach him somehow. Walking up to the fence on his left side, I coughed softly, and when he didn't turn around, I asked if he was okay.

He glanced back at me with a bleary, stricken look, and I saw that he was older than I'd imagined, late thirties perhaps, and his eyes were red-rimmed. Without looking at me directly, he gave a shifty nod, and then I heard him say something I couldn't discern over the wind. I cupped my hand to my ear, and he spoke again, more loudly: "Things have just been hard. I'm tired, you know?" For a moment he looked as though he was about to laugh. A universe of platitudes entered my head: *It happens*; *I've been there*; *Life can bring us all down sometimes.*

"What's been hard?" I was kneeling now on the other side of the fence, so as to hear him better, while he addressed his words to the sea.

"Wife left me. Hate my job. Just can't be bothered anymore."

"If you really want to do it," I said, peering at the rocks below us, "I can't stop you. But maybe you could hear me out first."

Looking at me furtively, he drew his knees to his chest. I told him that I, too, more than once, had looked out longingly at the water, as though simply to step beyond the rock, to jump, to fall, would release me that same instant from my body, from the laws of gravity and life, and allow me to merge with something larger.

"But it's only when you jump," I said, "that you know for sure whether you really want to fall, and by then there's no returning; and there are those seconds before things go dark when you're very much alive, when you're simply falling and waiting for velocity and surface tension to break you."

He said nothing, so I went on. "And then, you'll never know whether things might have become better. You'll never know who else you might have loved."

He looked at me directly then, with eyes more alert than before. The sun was higher in the sky now, and joggers and dog walkers had begun to appear on the track. I told him that it was no longer the time to act on his plan, if he wanted to avoid leaving behind more than one traumatized witness. "Step over to my side," I said finally, "and have coffee with me. What's another day?"

After looking at me for a moment and surveying another jogger about to pass, he hopped over the fence and followed me to a nearby café where he told me about his wife, his problems with drinking, his repetitive job at a car parts factory, and I told him about how I hadn't seen my family in three years, and managed my own dark moods by spending time in places where trees outnumbered people. We parted with a hug. I gave him my number, but he never called.

Now Lionel leapt onto my nightstand, tripping over my water glass, and I saw from the clock that it was almost time. My limbs still felt thick, my head foggy as I rose and walked down the hall. By the laundry I paused to take a breath. I noticed Lionel's toy basket and told myself I'd have to pack his favorite plaything when we left for Sandy's, a glove with tiny mice dangling from each finger. Finally I steered myself forward into the living room, and at once my mouth opened like a fairground clown's, because at last it was there in the sky outside, a white flame amid the stars, a firework falling to Earth: the comet, bigger and brighter than I'd dreamed.

Without conscious effort I felt myself being carried through the doors and into the dark garden, where I sank to my knees and craned my neck. I watched the comet as my hands clutched at the cool grass. I watched it as if its light could impart something more to me than wonder, as if it could grant me absolution for the night I was at the wheel when my husband died, or permission to hope that if I stayed alive, it wouldn't always feel like this.

I thought of Joseph, suggesting that St. John was here to test us. I thought of Sandy, abandoning *Better Homes and Gardens* to greet the comet out on her veranda, imagining it was a sign of hope rather than disaster. I thought of Angus, feeling lighter upon hearing I had died, and of Vince, charging himself unfairly with a double failure. I saw Theo, sitting silently in the dark somewhere, staring at the burning tip of his cigarette beneath his namesake in the sky, thinking of prophets and perhaps of the woman he had loved. I saw the bird in the palm tree, waiting out the wind.

Finally I thought of my father, who, but for a network of arteries in his brain, might have been beside me now, sharing the light of an extraterrestrial wanderer that hadn't visited since around the time the last mammoths went extinct, more than two thousand years before Christ. I tried to picture it, the same flaring creature passing by, a bird in flight, its wings of gas and dust blazing blue-green and white, over a planet yet to see the collapse of the Bronze Age, the birth of Babylon, the date of the biblical flood, or the beginning of recorded history. I wanted to know what he would have said. I wanted to share a toast with him, a wink at the fact of finding ourselves alive on this planet in the universe, in this place, during this millisecond of cosmic time.

From next door, I heard cheering and glasses clinking, and the voices of children, awake despite the hour. "That's a big star, Daddy," one of them said breathlessly, and then, with a note of humor, "I hope it doesn't fall into our yard!" Further off in the distance, some very drunk people cried out like banshees before descending into laughter. Not everyone was having a spiritual experience.

Somewhere nearby, I imagined the women from the pub and a gaggle of friends, standing with their shandies in hand, passing around binoculars with a variable zoom and peering up with open mouths between forkfuls of potato salad. Not far away on Bakers Road, I saw another group, sitting on floor cushions in a circle outside, chanting perhaps, as tea lights in lanterns flickered, incense smoke unfurled into the sky, and they each trained their vision inward, to see through the eye inside. As Lionel came to brush by me, I wondered how we might appear through the eye of a comet, making its icy passage through our galaxy, in a journey whose time span couldn't tally with the dimensions of our human lives.

I imagined it peering down, noting once more the ocean swirls of our plankton blooms, the white peaks of the Himalayas, the snaking Amazon, the Grand Canyon, the luminescent Great Barrier Reef, the Pyramids.

I imagined it squinting at what was new: the lights of our cities at night, the greenhouses of Almería, the Kennecott Copper Mine. I closed my eyes and felt the fact of my small body on the grass, the reaches of my mind, which seemed at that moment to contain the whole blue marble of our planet, spinning in the darkness of space around our burning star.

I imagined jumping over the edge. I imagined flailing in the far reaches of some shadow place, returning to dark matter or else to nothing at all. I imagined missing the world, the moment I jumped—the dawn, the smell of rain, the galahs at dusk, the motion of swimming, my heart beating—and knowing for those final seconds that it was too late to return.

When I edged inside and adjusted to the electric light, the house seemed false and distant from me, as if colluding in another reality. I saw the prim neatness of everything, the parcels and bags labeled and waiting, the letter on the table. In the bathroom I tore off the Kalf poster and faced myself. I looked flushed and alert, like someone overcoming a fever. I took out my pill jars, gathered them in the fold of my T-shirt, and set them down one by one on the kitchen table like I was a bartender serving shots. The pills made a clicking sound as I sat down and poured them out into a mound of tiny blue bullets.

As I watched them, I recalled a paper I'd once read for a unit on adult psychopathology. Because only a fraction of suicidal people follow through with an attempt, the authors noted, more research was needed to understand what made the difference. It was, the paper suggested, likely to do with the degree to which life experience lowered a person's fear of death, and raised their tolerance for pain, until the natural mechanism that would otherwise bar the way to self-annihilation was, like a dam wall, blown away.

I looked at Lionel in the next chair, calmly anticipating my decision. I thought of Joseph, suggesting that death was just another beginning, while I registered at last, insistent as a pulse, the fact that I wasn't finished with this life yet. Through the window, the comet watched me pointedly. The pact I had made with myself all those months ago, that had made it possible to continue, now revealed itself as an empty wager, a ruse, a sleight of hand. I was still wired to survive.

The truth of it crystallized as I sat there, following with my eyes the twin lines of the comet's tails, feeling the horizon of my life pushing back into the distance. It wasn't permission to die that I needed but rather permission to live a larger life, while I waited for Angus to slip, while I drew on deeper seams of patience, while I played the long game.

\* \* \*

It was only ten minutes later that the doorbell rang, sounding so shrill and loud to my ears that I jumped. I had no clue who might be calling so late. Silently I walked down the hall, peered through the spy hole, and opened the door to find Theo standing there. I blinked at him, vaguely conscious of the old summer robe I was wearing, and the scent of the jasmine growing by the fence.

"I'm sorry," he said, "I figured you'd still be up."

Mutely I nodded and stood aside for him to enter.

"I just wanted to talk with you," he added, as I closed the door and smelled the alcohol on his breath.

"Okay," I said, waving him through the hall. "Can I get you anything?"

He shook his head. "So, you've seen it?" he asked, when we reached the living room. He nodded toward the backyard.

I tried to smile. "Yes. It's bright already, like you said."

He seemed a little out of breath, but his face was colorless. I realized that for him, as for me, the comet's appearance might have thrown certain truths into relief—the fact of being here in this place and time, rather than elsewhere; the fact of being alive when others were dead; the question of why. He was, perhaps, as alone as I was. I was glad, if surprised, that he felt he could turn to me.

He was twisting his fingers now, and nodding as if to himself.

"Why don't you sit down?" I offered, motioning to the couch. "I was just going to make some mint tea."

He nodded, but didn't sit. He stood facing the French doors, looking out at the sky.

Perhaps, I thought, setting the kettle to boil, he was regretting having come. I knew how it felt to reel back in certain words you'd been ready to say, when speech lends new sharpness to each grief it names.

"I remember it was like being assailed by a double wave, early on," I said, placing tea bags into cups. "Grief and shock in equal measure. Has it been one of those days?"

When I looked up, I saw he had wandered closer. He was standing by the dining table, with one eye on the letter and pills. He glanced at me with a curious, vexed look, and nodded vaguely before casting his gaze about the wider room. The kettle clicked off. In a kind of trance, I poured the water for our tea. Facing him from behind the kitchen bench as the steam rose, I saw it all again through his eyes, the evidence of my own planned erasure, each shape now piercing and distinct—the jumbo packing bags lined up against the side wall, the labeled boxes and parcels stacked under the window, and the final clues on the table, which I'd not had the foresight to discard.

He looked lost as I carried the cups to the coffee table.

"You've caught me at a strange time," I said. "I've been getting my thoughts in order. I'm feeling better now."

We sat down beside each other. I handed him his cup and saw him frown.

"Anyway," I added, looking away, "you can believe me when I say that I know how bad it gets."

He cleared his throat and nodded. "I was thinking earlier of the bird, from Friday," he said finally, in a strange, distant voice. "I was thinking of how we're all at the mercy of the wind, in the end." He peered into his tea. "You didn't want to let it die alone, even though it was miserable to wait."

I shrugged and turned to face him. "It wasn't that bad—you kept me company. Besides, don't you find storms energizing, in a way?"

He looked at me sidelong for a moment, and said he wasn't sure.

I set down my cup and sighed. "What was it that you wanted to talk about?"

I heard my voice as if from far away as I leaned back, feeling dazed and alert at once, like someone who had nearly drowned. It was strange to have to appear steady and unfazed at such a time, and I wondered whether I should bother trying, whether Theo would mind. It is often a comfort to encounter the madness of others, when you find yourself arrived at your own limits.

Theo did not appear comforted when I met his stare, but rather, pained.

"You're a good person, Sylvia," he said softly, turning around to face me. His eyes searched mine. He laid a hand on my shoulder and gave it a brief, bolstering squeeze. It felt strange to be touched. For a moment I imagined us perched not on a couch but on a crude raft floating out to sea, our eyes fixed on an endless horizon, a world in which sky and water merged, a world in which everything was blue. He had never before looked at me for so long. I could see my face in his pupils. It felt like a dare.

"You deserve to be happy," he said, lowering his eyes to somewhere beyond my shoulder as we sat there, waiting for someone or something, it seemed, and then as if checking for trip wire, I reached out to touch his hair. For a second he closed his eyes, and then he looked at me gravely, before his eyes darted away and he seemed for an instant to freeze. I lowered my hand but didn't move. I sat there inclined toward him, watching his face, feeling the beat of my blood and the nerves in my skin, trying to comprehend him, until I heard him take a sudden breath and he moved toward me, and his lips found mine, and his arms reached around to hold me, and we didn't speak.

# CLOSER

# 11.

The gold sun rose over my garden with rays so bright I had to squint. Watching from my porch steps, I felt the light lift me with it to a place of calm where everything was clear. When I closed my eyes, I felt the world outside within me, and all my unfinished business: Angus and Danny, Joseph's grief, an astronomer I had kissed. I saw Christopher with his open, smiling face, waiting for me somewhere, and felt at last that I had the capacity to hold it all, as a charioteer holds many reins and drives forward all the same.

It was strange to enter a day, a week, which had been meant to surpass me. Preparing for work, I felt light-headed and suspended, like a planet in eclipse. I moved through space, but my mind was still. I showered in a trance, letting the water sear my skin. When I faced myself, naked and flushed in the unobscured mirror, it was as though a layer of gauze had been peeled away.

The kiss had happened and I felt alive. That was a fact I could not discount. When we broke apart we stared mutely at each other. I didn't want to speak; I had nothing to say. He looked dazed, until his eyes began to range around the room again and he finally said that he had to go. He brought his hand to my hair in a single stroke and then, without another word, he walked down the hall and out the door. It was a strange deliverance to the other side of that night. I wasn't sure what it meant.

I walked to work beneath the blue sky, while magpies cawed, and I noticed the vivid pink of the crepe myrtles in bloom along my street. A river inside me had split in two: that's how it seemed. There was the long river I'd keep following, the river that led to truth and justice and open ocean. And there was the new stream, a tributary running in parallel and merging, finally, with the same source. From this I would draw the patience and oxygen required to reach the end. Such was my new bargain.

For a minute I hung back from High Street, under the shade of a willow on the corner as cars coasted by. I wanted to retrace the end of Sunday night, to see its shape before it faded, in case there was something I'd missed. I closed my eyes and peered into the dark. The kiss had occupied a moment which in retrospect seemed without duration; how many seconds or minutes it had lasted I didn't know. I only remembered how beneath him I experienced a kind of collapse, a yielding in which my mind gave way and a dark radiance entered the space behind my eyes, abandoning me to breath, touch, and the shock of my own quick heart.

What last night had taught me was that I had reached my own limits, in living only to avenge Christopher's death and lift the veil on what had happened two years ago on Horseshoe Road. If I had chosen to live, and if I hoped to find the patience and resolve to achieve justice for Christopher, however long it took, then I needed a new plan; I needed space to breathe. There were greater evils than two souls in grief, consoling each other.

Briefly I recalled my mother, looking at me once through tears after an argument, telling me I was sanctimonious, reductive in my views about her marriage to Ed, as if unaware of how totally she had used it to erase my father. It was, I had told her, the ultimate expression of the violent efficiency with which she approached all tasks in life. My situation with Theo was hardly the same, I told myself as I walked on. No one would ever replace Christopher.

The hours at work, filled with routine appointments and accounting, passed without incident, and I retained a feeling of suspension in my mind. "Well, the comet's in plain sight now and the world remains the same. Now perhaps this damn town will calm down," said Clarence when I delivered his coffee, but I was certain that for myself at least, the world was different. Once or twice at the desk I imagined having seen a shadow flit by the door, and looked up as if Theo might be standing there with something to say, some solution to the riddle he had become.

In the afternoon I dropped by to see Sandy. She had called reception at lunchtime to invite me over for lemonade scones, and I was glad to see her without the specter of my impending departure hovering over us. She was dressed more festively than usual, in a fuchsia caftan with a jeweled clasp in her hair, and I wondered whether the comet's apparition had also made its mark on her. She winked as she ferried jam from the fridge to the table.

"So—last night! Wasn't it spectacular, the comet?" She looked at me with wide eyes as she set down the tray and plates. I split open a scone and buttered it, nodding.

"I rang but you mustn't have heard the phone," she said, handing me a spoon for the jam.

"Sorry," I said, wondering absurdly whether she'd called while I'd been resting, writing my suicide note, or kissing the comet's discoverer, and had to quell an instinct to laugh. "I drifted off for a while," I added, hating my duplicity.

As Terry yapped, she lifted him onto her knees. "Well," she said, stroking his ears, "I was just wondering about that meditation session on Bakers Road."

"Oh?" I smiled, finding it easy to imagine her in the lotus position on a prayer mat, under Joseph's serene gaze.

"I didn't go," she said. "But it sounds rather fun."

As Sandy spooned jam onto a scone, I cast my mind back to the flyer that had advertised regular twice-weekly sessions. I recalled what Joseph had said yesterday about how, in meditation, a person might find their way back to the region of light I'd entered, the night I died. And I thought of Danny sitting prone and pliable in Joseph's circle, an arm's length away from any student who might wish to keep him close.

"Terry and I watched the comet on the porch, instead," Sandy was saying between bites. "He had a rawhide and I had a sherry," she laughed, before peering at a point beyond my shoulder and speaking softly. "Watching it, I couldn't help but think of Christopher. Where *is* he?"

From his perch in Sandy's lap, Terry panted at me, his eyes shining and intent, as the wind chimes outside began to sound and I resolved to steer forward with my new plan.

"Why don't we attend the next meditation, Sandy? There's another on Thursday night."

Our upcoming appointment at Joseph's school gave me a new point of focus as the days passed and the sun blazed and I stared down the late evenings on the porch steps, knowing the comet was soon to dawn and wondering where Theo was. When we arrived together at Bakers Road at 7:30 on Thursday night, Sandy parked her car alongside a dozen others, in a wide drive shaded by eucalypts and scattered with rusting farm machinery. The property appeared to span many acres, with two main buildings—a handsome old colonial farmhouse a few hundred meters in the distance, beyond huddles of grazing sheep, and a newer house nearer the road.

This house was built on stilts, in the manner of a large forest cabin made of unpainted pine left to weather. Hanging from a pole above the apex of the roof was a faded flag painted with the same KC insignia as the T-shirts. The whole effect was of an oversized clubhouse, or a sprawling clipper ship without sails. People were still arriving as we ascended the stairs and entered a large room filled with mirrors, potted Kentia palms, and Tibetan prayer flags. Joseph sat cross-legged on a bolster cushion on the floor beneath a window, with his eyes closed and his hands nested together. A dozen men and women of various ages sat in the same way, forming a circle, but my eyes fixed on Danny, shoulders slouched, looking glum and distinctly unenlightened in his fluorescent-green shirt.

No one spoke, and the handful of others arriving with us each silently took a vacant cushion and settled down as if for a vigil. I would have felt less fraudulent doing the same had there been a dead body in the center of the circle, instead of a rose in a vase. I felt silly and pious, sitting there, while beside me, Zara siphoned air in great gusts through her nostrils. When the sound of footsteps through the door faded and we had sat for a minute in silence, I heard Joseph's voice.

"This is a rose from my mother's garden."

I opened my eyes. He was staring at the rose, which lolled on its stem in an old porcelain vase and threw a shadow on the wooden floor. It was deep pink, almost fully open, and flagrant in the way of all roses.

"Welcome to the new faces," he said, smiling faintly at me. "Together, and yet alone tonight, we are going to travel. We're going to travel while sitting still."

He scanned our circle with an expansive gaze, before letting out a wistful sigh. "To reach the region of inner space, it's useful to have a guide. There are many guides, many maps, all of them leading to the same place. Tonight we have this rose. Let us regard it for a while."

As he lapsed into silence, we all began to stare. The rose was still lit by the late sun. My eyes traced the petals clustered around the hidden pistil, following the gradations of color, the veined green leaves hanging from the stem. Even if I had little idea of what Joseph was talking about, it was pleasant to have a benign point on which to fix my attention, and strangely calming to be told what to do. Still, my mind flickered. I saw the bouquet I had made on the morning of my wedding. I remembered pulling pink roses from the florist's bucket, adding white carnations, red anemones, Queen Anne's lace, and binding it with twine.

"In naming the world," Joseph began suddenly, "language lulls us into illusion. We imagine that the name 'rose' and the ideas it summons—beauty, romance, decoration—are congruent with this singular thing before us here. We imagine that we know it, while also believing ourselves to be separate from it. Forget this. Watch the rose until it becomes strange, until it begins to watch you. Then close your eyes, and see it in your mind."

As I tried and failed to picture the rose, I listened to the sound of my breathing merge with the sound of a dozen others breathing, and beyond us, outside, the sound of gum leaves in the breeze, lorikeets shrieking, and now and then a car rushing by, while my spine radiated its dull ache and I grew drowsy. If there was peace or revelation to be found in the darkness of my mind, the rose didn't reveal it.

I wasn't sure how long passed before Joseph sounded the low ring of a singing bowl and invited us to bow with pressed palms, but by the time we began to rise from the floor and congregate around Zara, who was ladling dandelion tea from a pot into cups, the light outside had dimmed.

After receiving our cups, I led Sandy over to where Joseph was conferring with a somber, drawn-looking young man in a singlet and fisherman's pants.

Upon seeing us, Joseph brightened. "Ah, Sylvia, I'm so glad you've come—and you've brought a friend," he said, smiling and extending his hand to us each in turn as I introduced Sandy. "It might seem strange, to spend an hour focused on a rose," he said brightly. "The rose is just a conduit, though, a way of training our attention."

For a moment he paused, as Zara brought him a cup before sailing back to the table, where everyone else was still crowded. Now he inclined his head toward the window behind us, where the comet's light wasn't yet visible. "And soon our conduit will be much grander," he said. "But you should know that our school stresses the importance of experience over faith. Inner space is a realm we all must experience for ourselves, and in our own time."

Meanwhile, both Sandy and the young man had wandered over to the table, to partake in the murmuring of pleasantries over tea. Before I could excuse myself and join them, Joseph took a deep breath and squinted at me. There seemed a directness to his stare that was naked and somehow wild, although I supposed it could simply have been an effect of his unusually large blue eyes.

He frowned, and spoke in the tone of someone realizing an obvious truth: "You have suffered, Sylvia." He continued to search my face before beginning to nod. "Yes, it's a good thing you're here."

His voice and face seemed to radiate tenderness, concern, and what seemed like recognition as he stood facing me, and I wasn't sure what to say or do. Then he frowned again and drew from the pocket of his linen jacket a deck of cards. While watching me he held them in his palms before pulling one out. "Ah," he said with a smile, glancing at the card and turning it toward me.

THE STAR, it read. It showed a naked woman kneeling by a pool, pouring out the contents of two jugs—one into the water, one onto the land. Behind her was a bird in a tree, and above, a bright star amid smaller satellites.

"This is a woman of courage and strength, in the midst of healing," he said. "The star above her points the way, but its light is within her already." He held the card out for me to take. "Keep it," he said, smiling. "The tarot speaks in riddles, but it's not without a sense of humor, and sometimes it's literal. I doubt the significance of St. John's visit has been lost on you."

Before I could speak he squeezed my shoulder, and I felt myself released from our exchange. I stood there blinking, holding my cup in one hand and the card in the other. Even as I pondered his presumption in telling my fortune, I felt myself yielding to the solace of his claim to the truth.

Joseph turned to the group now and clapped his hands. "Thank you, everyone," he said. "Before you leave tonight I have an announcement to make." He smiled as we fell silent. "To celebrate the point of the comet's perihelion, its closest, brightest brush with our planet, we'll be holding a festival right here on the property in early August, during the new moon in Leo, making for excellent viewing conditions. There will be much to organize but, for now, mark it in your diaries. It will be an unmissable occasion."

Danny, looking alert for once, emitted a loud "Yes!" and held out his cup to Zara for a refill. "Will there be hot dogs?" he asked, to no response. Everyone was wide-eyed, smiling, asking questions. Sandy asked what the plan was if it rained. A slight woman in a cheesecloth

dress wanted to know whether out-of-towners would be invited because
her aunt from Sydney missed out on seeing Halley in 1986. A large
mustachioed guy in shorts and tennis socks, who had introduced himself to me warmly as Roy, asked about the entertainment. "My cousin's
in a metal band," he added hopefully. When Danny piped up again, it
was to ask whether there would be fireworks.

"Why would there be fireworks, Danny?" Joseph scoffed. "We'll
be viewing the last great comet of this millennium, at its maximum
brightness, from the best vantage point on Earth! No backyard explosive
could beat that."

Their voices began to form a buoyant, probing sound that washed
over me as I looked at the woman on the tarot card, while Joseph assumed an indulgent tone and refused to say more.

"Nothing's final yet," he said. "We'll speak further this weekend."

For a while I sipped my tea, waiting for Sandy to conclude her conversation with Zara about the royal history of Shih Tzus. Danny stood a
few paces away, blithely unconcerned by my presence despite my stare,
jabbering to the student in fisherman's pants about the US space shuttle
*Atlantis*, that had apparently just arrived at the Russian space station in
low earth orbit above China.

"Those astronauts have to deal with sixteen sunrises and sunsets a
day!" said Roy, ambling over as he peeled open a Curly Wurly.

"I've heard they keep rats," said Danny, his eyes huge and focused.

"Rats would be the least of my worries," said Zara, sidling up. "How
do they know what time it is up there, anyway?"

"And I've heard they have to be strapped into their space toilets,"
Danny added, to no one in particular.

As Danny went on to note how the astronauts marked their letters
with a special stamp, a silver-haired woman in purple turned to me with
an apologetic look, and asked how I had found my first session. While
I confessed my inexperience with meditation, and she explained how
Joseph's classes had helped her manage the panic attacks induced by her
divorce, Danny's voice grew tense.

"I've tried to access their signal through the ham radio," he said, "but I haven't gotten through yet."

Before leaving, we all nudged notes and coins into the "Donations" box by the tea station, like a congregation giving alms.

So I wouldn't have to discuss it with Sandy, I tucked the tarot card into my trouser pocket. She was merry and inquiring as she drove us home.

"Well?" she asked, peering at me. "Did you have a good time? I think Joseph is so interesting! And isn't it exciting, that he's planning a comet festival in winter?"

Yes, I told her, it had been an interesting experience. As she drove, I looked at her from the edge of my eye, noticing how straight she sat, and how the movements of her face and limbs seemed possessed of a new alertness and poise, as though supported by internal springs.

"So," she asked now, "will you attend this weekend?"

I watched the silver fairy dangling from the chain that hung around the rearview mirror. The fairy swung to and fro, with her wings and arms outspread, as though struggling to land.

"Why not?" I replied, and smiled.

When she dropped me home, I kissed her cheek and told her that I'd see her soon.

She nodded brightly, speaking in singsong through the window before coasting away. "This is good for us, Sylvia!"

A cynic like Theo would say it was a cute trick, I thought as I prepared for bed, to pull a card for a new recruit and offer a few words on her fate. It was like sending a child home with a keepsake from the fair. And just like a child, I pinned it on the hallway wall, so I could look at it as I walked by, at once a prayer I didn't know how to answer, and a reminder of my own longing to believe the things that Joseph said.

For once sleep took me swiftly, like a dark tide. I dreamed of roses— monstrously large with huge thorns, that seemed to watch me as I walked among them, while the comet overhead filled the sky with a light so bright that I shielded my eyes, and it seared a fault line through the earth right where I stood.

# 12.

It was only when I opened the front door for air the next morning that I found the note, wedged against the hallway skirting board. It was scrawled on the back of a business card for a local plumber, and the words were written in a hard-pressed, looping hand:

> *Sylvia,*
> *Sorry I missed you. Do you want to call me?*
> *Theo*

Below this was a number. I realized he must have dropped by the night before, while I was at Bakers Road, trying to be transported by a rose.

All morning, at work, I wondered why he had waited so long to see me, and what it was he wanted to say, but it wasn't until lunchtime that I had time to dial the number. The voice on the other end sounded muffled and wary.

"It's Sylvia," I said, watching the street as I held the receiver. "I found your message."

"Hi," he said, and paused. "Sylvia, I'm sorry I haven't been in touch."

I watched a man in a Hawaiian shirt walk by the office window with a panting Alsatian. The fact was, I didn't want to care that Theo hadn't been in touch since the night we'd kissed. I didn't want to feel a current run through me at the sound of him speaking my name. But neither did I want to tell him that I thought his vanishing act was okay.

"I hope you've been alright?" he asked now, and I felt myself bristle.

"I've been perfectly fine," I said coolly, before realizing that his question was more likely in reference to the evidence he'd seen of my state of mind on Sunday night, than to his lack of contact since.

For an instant in the silence that followed, I found myself listening to his breathing in the way I'd sometimes held my ear to the earth as a child, as though doing so might yield some secret understanding.

"Did you want to go for a walk today, after work?" he asked now.

After a breath, I agreed, but my voice when I spoke sounded wary. He volunteered nothing about his reasons for wanting to see me, and I didn't ask. I felt it was a mystery I'd prefer to solve in person.

"I'll drop by your office at 5:30," he said, in a soft, sober voice, the kind of voice one uses to confirm a business appointment. Before I could say goodbye, I found myself listening to the disconnect tone.

As I moved through the day's tasks and confronted my essential ignorance about Theo and the mechanisms that drove him as a human being, I saw that trying to decode his intentions was foolish. So I tried to set aside all thought of him. I polished the caskets until I could see in their lacquer my own reflection, and slipped the question of what the afternoon might hold into a place out of sight, as though it were an experiment whose results I shouldn't influence, which in a way, it was.

I thought he had forgotten, or else decided not to come, when 5:30 arrived and I locked up, but then I saw him leaning against the solicitor's office next door, staring down at his boots with a blank expression. It wasn't until I was almost standing in front of him that he looked up, as if surprised.

"How was work?" he asked, stepping out from the shadow of the awning to face me.

"Fine," I said, trying to keep my expression pleasant but also inscrutable, lest he think I expected any reprise of Sunday night.

He nodded and slid his hands into his pockets, before gesturing behind me to the west. "Thought we could take a stroll up the canyon track," he said.

It was strange to sit beside him in his car as we made the short drive to the base of the canyon, an eruption of sandstone inside the national park that surrounded the observatory. He sat almost rigidly in his seat, looking ahead, as I pressed my palms together in my lap and watched his hands on the wheel and wondered what was happening. It was a relief to feel the wind on my face when he lowered the windows, and its rushing eased our silence until he glanced at me and spoke.

"I've been wondering how you are," he said, and peered back at the road. On the horizon, the rocky peaks of the mountains rose up, nudging the clouds.

"That's very nice of you," I said in a tinny voice.

He looked over and I heard a faint sigh.

"So, you're feeling better?"

"Yes, Theo, I'm fine," I said, fixing my eyes on the mountains. "Why is it that you care?"

Even though I instantly regretted asking the question, having failed in my attempt at a breezy tone, I still wanted to know the answer.

"I'm sorry it took me a few days to be in touch," he said finally. "I'm sorry about everything, actually."

His jaw tensed as we turned into the car park.

"Why are you sorry?" I asked, when the engine had faded into silence.

He shook his head in a hopeless motion. "It wasn't great timing," he said in a low voice, as if to himself, before glancing at me. "I'd had a bit to drink, and wasn't really thinking."

I slid out of the car and shut the door with a slam. When he stood up on the other side, I offered a brisk smile and tried to dispel my irritation. The sky was still blue, and I had just spotted from the side of my eye what looked like a rare turquoise parrot, and he was just a confused man, newly bereaved.

"You needn't take me on a walk," I said, "to tell me you regret the kiss." For an instant as he looked on, I squinted at the sky and inhaled the smell of eucalyptus, before shaking off my work blazer and throwing it in the car. "But seeing as we're here," I said, "I wouldn't mind a stroll.

I destroyed my driver's licence the other night so it might be a while till I can get back here."

At this he made a sudden expulsive sound, apparently an involuntary laugh, and together we set off up the track. We were crossing the canyon's dry creek bed when he spoke again, a few paces ahead. I was watching his loping gait, the sure tread of his feet from rock to rock.

"You should know you've misunderstood me. I was trying to explain."

"Okay, explain then," I said, as the valley between the sandstone cliffs widened into a glade of red stringybark and pinkwood.

"I was worried I took advantage of the state you were in," he continued without looking back. "I suppose I was in a bit of a state, too."

"Yes," I said after a pause. "I thought you were. But you never seem to want to talk about it. And I'm not a child, you know."

He nodded without turning around, and we kept walking, as magpies and parrots called and our shoes crunched along the path and I tried to intuit what he was thinking.

"It's all so fresh for you," I said eventually. "I know all about the self-recrimination. You feel guilty just for surviving, let alone kissing a virtual stranger."

For a while he said nothing, and I watched the steady motion of his back.

"So, you're doing better?" he asked finally, glancing back with a probing look.

"Yes, I think so. For now, at least."

The light had grown rosy now and I stopped to look up at the steep, ancient rock, which glowed between the eucalypts. When I glanced back at Theo a few meters ahead, I saw that he had stopped, too, and was watching me.

"I never know what you're thinking," I said.

"I'm thinking that I'd like to have met you at a different time."

I smiled and waited, but he said nothing more. I resumed walking while he kept still. When I reached him I paused, still hearing his words in the air.

"Well, you didn't," I said, and met his eyes with a shrug. "But I'm here if you need a friend."

The words echoed like a false verdict. We stood parallel to each other on the track, poised to keep moving but frozen, as though some invisible line lay ahead that we dared not cross. When he returned my stare with his sharp, grave look I felt all the molecules I was made of pay attention.

It was a wild feeling, a feeling I had forgotten. My right arm and hand, hanging inches from his own left side, seemed suddenly charged. I thought for a moment that he might reach out, and I knew I wanted to lose myself again, to feel as alive as I had felt on Sunday night, to merge with someone else, someone who understood. When he looked back ahead and resumed walking amid the soft, collapsing sound of mulch underfoot, I wondered whether he'd somehow heard my thoughts, and I felt something fall in my chest.

After a time of walking uphill through the scrub in silence, we reached the summit lookout, a mountain peak from which we could see the other jagged domes in the range around us, above the canyon we had left behind, and the wide forest plains of the park. We stood peering out at it all, catching our breath.

"I thought you might like the view," he said after a pause. "Sometimes I trek up here to watch the clouds."

"It's beautiful," I said, peering out beyond the distant peaks to the curved horizon.

He looked at me and smiled. "We're standing on ancient lava. These peaks are all volcanic."

For a while we stood in silence. I tried to imagine what the landscape might have looked like all those millions of years ago, when magma welled up from vents in the Earth's mantle, exploding ash and molten lava, while giant wombats and marsupial lions still roamed the wilderness. Beyond the furthest mountains, I could glimpse the patchwork of fields and pastures west of town.

Without thinking, I pointed to it. "I can almost see the farm of Joseph, your favorite prophet."

"Oh," he said. "I didn't take him for a farmer."

I shrugged. "I don't think he is, really."

He looked at me now with a curious frown. "How do you know where he lives, anyway?"

"I attended one of his sessions last night. I thought my mother-in-law might enjoy it, and I could do with some relaxation."

He nodded grimly.

"What's the problem?" I asked. "It was completely innocuous—we spent an hour staring in silence at a rose."

He sighed and looked at me as though I were planning to take on some rogue warlord and his militia, rather than instruction for inner peace.

"I think you should stay away, Sylvia," he said, and turned to begin the walk down. "That guy gives me the creeps."

"If that's all you have to go on," I replied, following behind, "how is it different from the superstition you detest?"

I received no answer, and after a time, we stopped on the track to watch a swamp wallaby bounding through the trees.

"Well," I said, when we resumed walking, "I guess you'll want to avoid the comet festival in August."

He threw me an incredulous look. "Comet festival?"

I nodded. "It's Joseph's idea. You don't have to go."

"No, I have a feeling I'll be busy elsewhere, especially if chanting and panpipes are involved."

As we walked in silence to the car park, I wondered at his heaviness of spirit generally where the comet was concerned, the great comet he discovered, and which had offered me such sustenance. When I asked him whether it hadn't been gratifying, to see the comet he had found appear in our own skies, he said that it was complicated.

"Sometimes, the search is sweeter than the prize," he added, and I didn't press him further.

Falling a few paces behind him, I wondered whether the woman he'd lost had been with him when he found the comet. Perhaps she, too, had loved watching the skies. Perhaps she had also been an astronomer. I imagined an evening two summers ago, a moment of mounting excitement as a patch of unknown brightness was spotted through the lens, checked and rechecked in the maps of the constellations to disprove the impossible fact that this object was new and unnamed. I imagined shrieks of delight, thudding hearts, a warm embrace, as at a birth. I imagined an object once signifying wonder and success, that in a passage of two years had come to stand for the cold distance of space, the horrors of infinity, and everything on Earth that was no longer. The comet was perhaps a sign not just of her death, but also of his own, in the way that all children signal death for their parents. The comet would live on for centuries beyond him, carrying his name for as long as the records of our present civilization lasted.

I was so lost in thought that when we reached his car, Theo had to call out to me before I walked past it. He caught my eye with a warm, wondering smile. "Where were you?" he asked.

I only shrugged, a little sheepish, thinking that it was how he'd looked at me rather than his words that seemed to sear me, in a way I couldn't control.

For a moment before we drove off, I found myself holding my breath, and noticed that he seemed to be paused at the wheel, as if about to say something he quickly thought better of.

Along the road back to town, we began to speak of other things—his homesickness for Arizona and newly divorced older sister; my abandoned psychology degree and exchange year in Italy as a teenager. But all the while I had the sense we were speaking in code, sliding over the surface of things. I felt as though I were being put through a test for a subject I hadn't studied, whose rules I didn't understand, and between our words I registered how ordinary details seemed suddenly insistent and distinct: the rumble of the engine, his square hands on the wheel, the stripe of sunlight across my lap.

When we pulled up at my house, I turned to face him and we exchanged a smile, but he glanced away before I did. "Thanks for the

walk," I said, grabbing my bag and blazer as he nodded and said it had
been good to see me, his hands still on the wheel, the engine idling.
For a moment, I remained seated. Like a gambler, I watched him avoid
my eye, until he looked back and I noticed that his gaze seemed fervent
and alive, and I followed the mad instinct that told me to run my hand
down his cheek. As I did, he caught my hand and in a movement that
seemed born of the same mute instinct as my own, turned it palm up,
to trace his finger over the lines Joseph might have said foretold my fate.

It felt like a rite, a sign of the cross, and I shivered. From the rise
and fall of his chest, I knew he was breathing fast, but just as he leaned
toward me, still holding my hand, I saw the light in his eyes dim, and
he hung his head, like a priest who could not be tempted.

"I'm sorry, Sylvia," he said, drawing away. "I can't."

He didn't look back as I crawled out and shut the door, or as I stood
on the street, turning away as if in modesty and lumbering forward to
grip my gate. I watched his profile speeding away in the window, recalling the image of the Roman soldier I'd imagined when we'd first met.

I felt, then, like an explorer who had made land on a continent that
had until now been submerged, a continent rumored of but never seen,
risen again from the deep—for long enough to let me reach the shore,
notice the glinting light, the wild green hinterland, long enough to let
me know it as a place both strange and familiar—before the tide took
it back and left me to catch my breath, still marked by its atmosphere.

I found distraction at Bakers Road that Saturday night with Sandy. The
circle was larger this time, and as people arrived to take their places,
Joseph sat in the same way as before, in silence with closed eyes, while
I noticed that in the late light, his pallor looked almost blue, as though
he were a statue of Shiva in some ornamental garden.

"Tonight we continue our preliminary work of training our spiritual
senses," he began. "Notice, in the center of our circle, a tiny seed."

It was only now that I saw it, a tiny dark pellet on the pinewood
floor.

"Notice its shape, its color," he continued as we stared. "What might be its texture, were you to touch it?"

An age seemed to pass as we sat there, silently contemplating the seed, and my eyes wandered inevitably to Danny. He gazed morosely at the floor and refused to look back at me. Behind him, the ghost gum trees stood against a sky that was still blue. Sitting there, I resolved that if I could watch him with patience for long enough, I'd learn how to force his hand.

"When planted in soil and nourished by water and light, this seed will yield a sunflower," Joseph said. "This singular life-form is already energetically encoded within the seed, and yet it is invisible. Once planted, and in time, the invisible will become visible. Consider this. Close your eyes and envision, in your mind, what the seed will become."

His voice continued on in the darkness behind my eyes, guiding me to see the root penetrating the soil, the green shoot pushing up to find light, and the first leaves unfurling, and then to see the new bud, and at last the blooming flower, offering itself to the bees, and finally the petals turning brown, the head drooping, and the flower returning to the earth, leaving its own seeds behind. But as he spoke, my mind kept returning to the feeling of Theo tracing the lines of my palm, and the image of him speeding away as I stood winded at my gate.

"Do you see the sunflower?" Joseph asked, and I sensed him scanning our faces with a radiant smile. "Do you see how the full expression of this very seed already exists? Do not discount what you can't physically observe."

Finally, when we had all opened our eyes again and Joseph had observed a lengthy pause, he pressed his hands together and spoke in a low, fervent voice. "The universe exists within each of us," he said, peering around our circle. "We belong not just to Earth, but also to the cosmos, to the world of stars—the world of comets. But to recognize our oneness with creation, as Plotinus said, we must close our eyes to see anew."

As we joined him in bowing our heads to the floor, I caught myself imagining Theo looking on in horror, and tried to push the thought of him away.

As soon as the singing bowl chimed and the food began arriving—ferried from the kitchen by other students and set on a low table surrounded by scatter cushions—everyone began to speak of the festival.

"What's going to happen, Joseph?" asked a woman with red corkscrew curls, as she knelt on a cushion and ladled potato curry onto a plate.

"Can't you tell us, now?" asked Roy, his brown eyes wide and his hulking frame appearing almost dainty in his cross-legged position.

As others gathered around the table and began to press the same case, Joseph, who was still standing, raised his hands and nodded. "Yes, we'll discuss the preliminaries. The festival will commence here on the property on the first Sunday in August. By then the comet will be nearest the sun, so we'll be seeing it at its brightest."

He lowered himself onto a cushion now and swept out his arms. "There will be music, meditation, and food stalls. Also guest speakers and telescopes. The whole town and beyond will be invited."

He nodded to Zara, while she smiled and shuffled over to kneel beside him with a notepad and pen.

"Zara will oversee the organizing committee. We're seeking volunteers for food preparation and event setup first. Does anyone have carpentry skills? We'll need to build a stage . . ."

Everyone began to speak and to add their names to various lists, including Sandy, who was suddenly eager to make industrial quantities of savory scones. The room seemed to fill with a manic hum, while I sat motionless, noticing how much I liked the idea of an official farewell to the comet, orchestrated by someone who seemed to share my own sense of its significance, a significance that I would never be able to argue scientifically, or explain to a man like Theo. I barely understood it myself, not, at least, on the level of language.

Despite the noise around me as I sat there, I realized a new feeling possessed me, an altered equation between my body and gravity. There was, for that moment at least, a stillness to my spine, and a strange calm in my heart.

When I arrived home and brought in the mail that had recently accumulated in my letter box, the feeling remained. Whatever the means, I thought, Joseph's exercises seemed to offer a refuge from the lower registers of my mind. I considered this as I sorted the mail on the couch with Lionel. Among bank statements and bills and a local handyman's offer to tidy my front yard was an official-looking envelope which I opened without thinking.

Having unfolded the document inside, I blinked stupidly before comprehending the words. "Apprehended Personal Violence Order—Sylvia Knight," it read. Below this was a list of commandments about what I could no longer do "to Angus Blair and family," including assault, threaten, stalk, intimidate, or otherwise harass them. After this was a list of actions that could be taken against me, should I breach these conditions, including imprisonment, being fined, and being charged with additional offenses. The order concluded by instructing me to take my firearms and weapons to the police.

For a moment I imagined dropping Angus's porch lamp on his desk at the station. "Your lamp, sir," I imagined saying, with a bow like a figure from Dickens. "This is the only weapon I have to surrender," I heard myself add, "seeing as how my tongue is attached to my body, and will be required in the process of deposing you legally, however long that takes, now that I've decided to survive." I saw his face grow red as he stared, his hands furl into fists on his desk, and felt my stomach twinge with bile.

But right now I didn't want to think of Angus. Behind my eyes I pushed him away, watched him fall through the floor and keep falling, as through the darkness of an endless well.

I leaned back, let go of the letter and tried to see, in his place, the sunflower reaching upward, opening itself to the sky while below, in the blind soil, its roots dug in.

## 13.

THE LAST DAYS OF JANUARY WASHED AWAY, AND I LOOKED ON HALF-dazed to find myself still standing at the end of a month I'd thought would swallow me. Between work shifts, I unpacked the bags and boxes I'd used to set aside my life, sent a check for the porch lamp and damages to Angus via Vince, and applied to various authorities to restore the forms of identification I had destroyed.

Outside, the light took on a glaring edge, the lawns grew brown, and sometimes at noon when I braved the heat, High Street would be mine alone, as though all the world were hiding after news of some imminent attack. When the thick, dry air was still, and cicadas hummed in the trees, and the sky above was an unmarked blue, I felt a pressure in my blood, a sense that my body knew something my mind did not, something the day was waiting to reveal.

As for Joseph's meditation sessions, whether or not he was right about the eternal nature of the soul, I was always interested in what he had to say, and since starting to attend I'd been sleeping better and drinking less. Over the next fortnight, I found that Thursday and Saturday evenings at Bakers Road began to structure my week, like a fine thread spun from the inside. And at every session, I tracked Danny, certain that in time his mask would slip, if I didn't deduce a way to trap him first. Meanwhile, from midnight until sunrise the comet looked down over Jericho, and Patricia Evans remained in Bell's mortuary refrigerator.

From Theo, I heard nothing.

I first noticed the change in Joseph at the beginning of February. Not long after, when the rose reappeared, I knew there was something wrong.

It was a Thursday night. We were sitting on the floor in our usual horseshoe around him, while he tapped just above the point between his brows and reminded us to focus on breathing through the third eye. This was an exercise we'd been working on for a while, a fundamental means, he said, of accessing the gateway to the inner realms of existence, the realms which, he was fond of noting, we must each experience for ourselves in order to know.

"Focus on this point with your inner vision," he was saying now, with none of his usual levity. "Train your breath through it, without expectation."

I peered at him through one half-closed eye. He had lost weight, and his face had a drawn, somber look as he sat there, clasping his hands in his lap. Initially, I'd assumed the change in him was due to the ongoing stress of pursuing government bureaucrats for permission to bury his mother at home, a process that was taking longer than we had hoped. I knew it could hardly be helping his grief process to know his mother still lay in icy repose inside our mortuary, and as Clarence reiterated at every opportunity, the permission we'd sought from the health authority to keep her there was soon to expire. Added to this, Joseph was planning the festival, which had now expanded to encompass a drumming circle and a hot-air balloon.

But looking at him now, I wondered whether he wasn't unwell in some other way, because in whatever light I saw him these days, his complexion appeared rather blue, like a person bloodless and half-frozen. No one had breathed a word of the change in class, but I couldn't have been the only one to notice, and I had no idea what it meant.

It felt like hours before he finally invited us to open our eyes and attend to the object at hand in the center of our circle—another pink rose in a vase, only this one drooped on its stem, its petals limp and withered and starting to brown.

"Here is the same rose we saw some weeks ago, in full bloom," he said in a grave, low voice. As he looked at us, I noticed how only one edge of his mouth lifted, making for a grimace instead of a smile. "This rose will wither and die, as all organic forms must," he added, and for a few seconds he was quiet, looking at the flower. "It is, essentially, already dead," he went on, "although its petals and leaves are yet to return to the earth." He sniffed. "But its pollen will have been spread by bees, butterflies, and the wind, seeding new plants."

Just as Joseph took a breath and seemed about to continue, he paused and cast a narrow look at Danny, who sat a few cushions away from me, wearing a Pearl Jam T-shirt and picking absently at a thumbnail. Some instinct caused Danny to glance at me before he looked back at Joseph, and I offered him the same expression I always did, stony and uncompromising. Before my gaze, something in him seemed to shrink, and I allowed myself a private smile—he was learning that I was always watching him.

"And what does this suggest to you, Danny?" Joseph asked.

Danny scratched his ear and let his mouth hang slack for a while. "Uh, that there'll be other roses," he offered, with the flatness of a child reciting a rote-learned prayer.

"Well, yes," said Joseph, sighing. "But it also suggests, doesn't it, that no single rose ever really disappears? Beings seem to exist only in the interval between physical birth and death. But this is an illusion of the external senses, which can't discern the spirit hidden in all things, the spirit which exists before birth and beyond death, and which transforms as readily as the petals of a rose like this, just not in a manner we can see." For a moment he spread out his arms. "Even when we know this truth, it is easy to forget it, in this technicolor, collective dream of the physical plane. It's very convincing, is it not?"

He fell silent now, and dropped his arms.

"We'll end here, tonight," he said finally. "I'm quite tired."

The mood around the tea table was subdued. Joseph had disappeared through the corridor while we were all still sitting on the floor, and some students, including Danny, left early. Sandy, treating Joseph's metaphor quite literally, was undeterred, taking the opportunity to share with

Zara and Roy her understanding of the crossbreeding process responsible for modern hybrid tea roses, such as the "Brigadoon" and "Double Delight" varieties now thriving in her own front garden.

"Repeat bloomers, both of them," she was saying between sips. "A dash of Epsom salts and a good deadheading in the spring, those are my secrets."

As I half listened to a pair of women discuss signage for the festival and the grounding properties of obsidian, Joseph appeared beside me. He regarded me with unsmiling resolve, and asked if we might speak.

Moments later, in a sparse office off the corridor, I found myself standing with him before a window, looking out over the paddocks as the light faded and the sheep beyond cried out like crows.

"It's been nice to have you with us, Sylvia," he said, shifting to face me and clasping his hands. "I hope you're finding the sessions of benefit."

"Yes," I said, smiling but unable to hide my concern. "And how have you been, Joseph? Any updates on your application?"

He nodded. "The reason I wanted to have a word with you is not a happy one," he replied softly, before turning back to the window. "I'm afraid that I've received a rejection notice."

I watched his shoulders stiffen as he explained, in a voice now tight with rage, the verdict of the geotechnical report he had commissioned at the council's instruction. The report, he said, had revealed that burial of human remains on the farm carried a risk of groundwater contamination.

"That's what they say, anyway," he concluded.

I heard his voice catch, and peered down at my socks on the seagrass matting while he recovered. When I offered my commiserations, he smiled thinly.

"Now, I'm assessing my options."

"Okay," I said, concerned he was hinting at some kind of appeal, when we were already running out of time. But looking at him, I was unsure it was the right moment to suggest he accept defeat and move on. "Well, I'm here to help," I offered, hoping this might draw him out.

But he had returned his attention to the sky.

"You know," he said suddenly, "ever since it appeared, I've been sharing my thoughts with the comet. Perhaps in doing so, I'll sooner learn what it's here to teach us." He glanced back at me with a wry look, despite his mood. "I find it's rather a good listener."

I smiled, and confessed that, in a way, I supposed I'd been doing something similar.

"And why should we not? It's an ancient instinct, to address the heavens, the moon, and stars. Modernity, Sylvia, has so much to answer for."

After a long pause, he sighed and turned back to the window. "I just so wanted her here with me, at home." Suddenly he pointed at a spot through the glass, and his voice took on a wistful, pondering tone. "I'm building her a shrine in the back paddock, over there."

I was still digesting this news when he thanked me for listening in a tone of closure, and for a moment before I left we stood there, breathing in the resinous smell of pinewood paneling while the sheep bleated and the sun sank down and, somewhere in the east, the comet prepared itself to brighten into a flame above the horizon.

That night, I dreamed of Joseph. He was beckoning to me from his position in the clouds, long-haired and robed with a pious, indulgent look, in the manner of kitsch devotional paintings. No matter how high I jumped, I couldn't reach him, but I watched as he threw down the silver cutout shapes of stars.

In the morning, I faced Tania in the basement as the embalming tank, mimicking the rhythm of a human heartbeat, pumped bright pink fluid into the veins of a middle-aged male corpse with mermaid tattoos. As the fluid entered via a catheter into the carotid artery, the blood was flushed out, swirling like paint down the drain of the mortuary table and into the wider tributaries of the municipal sewerage system.

"Jesus Christ," said Tania, hearing of Joseph's reaction to his rejected application, and his plans for a shrine. Rolling her eyes, she sipped the coffee I'd brought her. For a moment we were silent as the fridge hummed.

"Look, Sylvia," she said finally, "that poor woman can't remain in cold storage a minute longer; she's not Lenin! And you know Clarence is fretting. You'll have to get Joseph to accept a compromise."

I only nodded, and didn't bother to suggest that an intervention of this nature might fall within the remit of Clarence himself. After all, I was the only one Joseph ever listened to.

# 14.

*UNIDENTIFIED OBJECT TAILS ST. JOHN*: THIS WAS THE HEADLINE THAT met me on the front page of the regional newspaper, just days after my conversation with Joseph. Below it was an image of the comet that soon branded itself behind my eyes. The image was grainy, but the largest of its shapes was clear—the flaring form of the comet, with its bright center and two tails extending into the darkness of space. Northeast of St. John was the object in question—a glowing sphere smaller than the comet and larger than the surrounding stars, which seemed, upon inspection, to be tilted and ringed, in the manner of the planet Saturn. The newspaper had pointed to the shape with a crude red arrow.

A short time later, while Tania drove the mortuary van down the highway for a pickup and held her face in its resting position of tense expectation, I reclined in the passenger seat and read aloud from the copy I'd bought.

"'Opinion is divided,'" I began, "'over the unidentified object present in the above telescopic photo taken by an amateur astronomer. The photo, first shared yesterday with national paranormal radio show *Other Worlds FM*, has caused a storm in chat rooms on the Web, with certain quarters—not least a cultural studies professor from Slovakia—suggesting the luminous object is a spaceship traveling in concert with the comet toward Earth, for reasons yet unknown.'"

Tania let out a dry laugh. "It's clearly not driven by intelligent life, if Earth's their destination of choice."

As we entered the Western Hospital's loading zone, I read on: "'*When I saw it, I began to pray*, said the photographer, who fears the object could be confirmation the comet is an omen of crisis as we approach the new millennium. The photo has drawn interest from international groups such as ET Truth, which proposes the comet's companion spacecraft is merely an early bird in an upcoming mass landing of interplanetary visitors from the remote star systems of Alpha Centauri and Andromeda.'"

Tania made a scoffing sound. "Why don't they get on with it, then?" she asked, pulling in to park and noting that she wouldn't half mind being abducted by aliens.

The article's conclusion echoed in my head as we wheeled out the mortuary trolley and made for the back entrance:

> Astronomers, meanwhile, suggest that in fact, the object is itself a star, distorted by misaligned astro-mapping software. Theo St. John, the eponymous discoverer of Comet St. John, has been contacted for comment.

As theories about the photo spread, I met with Joseph at his house and at the office. Having failed in his appeals to the council and aware that Patricia's time in our fridge had run out, he'd grimly accepted the need to plan a service swiftly, but as we discussed the details I discerned in his eyes and voice the faint delirium of a person whose contract with sleep has been broken. There was certainly no evidence, where his late mother was concerned, of the Zen-like detachment I had sensed in his meditation sessions, a fact which depressed me to observe, and his skin was now decidedly blue-gray, as though tinged with metal. I had to keep myself from staring incredulously, but he seemed oblivious to his transformation.

Even in grief, he was exceptional—never had I encountered a client whose moods shifted so dramatically between meetings, like a region under wild atmospheric pressures.

"It's time to make a decision: burial or cremation?" I told him at our first meeting in the soft light of Bell's client room. I'd expected a challenge, but his eyes were dim, his shoulders slumped.

Sighing, I reached out to tap his hand. "How about proceeding with the service at the farm with your mother in her casket, and cremating her afterward? That way, you can hold her ashes at home, or even at the shrine."

After a pause, his eyes flickered into focus. "Yes, Sylvia," he said. "Yes, of course!"

Frowning now, he nodded to himself, like an inventor on the verge of a solution that I, for one, couldn't comprehend. Peering at his hands on the table, he spoke again in a soft tone of revelation. "She's just a body, now."

The following day, I called to remind him of our need for Patricia's rest clothes, and found he could barely speak. His sudden pauses and drawn-out vowels mirrored those of a stroke victim, and when he dropped off the outfit at the office hours later, he moved with palpable effort, as if being opposed by some invisible force. Even his breathing was altered—he panted lightly, as though emerging from a fever.

"Here they are," he said simply with a nod, after I greeted him at the desk and took the bag of clothes he set down. His face was slack, his hair a mess, and before I could say anything more he had turned away and shuffled back out onto the street.

Arriving at Bakers Road for our last meeting before the funeral, I was ready with my pocket list of crisis support services, but he seemed transformed.

"Sylvia, thank you for coming," he said with a deferential smile upon opening the door in paint-stained overalls, before asking serenely if I'd like some tea.

I shook my head, rendered dumb with surprise, while he led me briskly down the corridor and waved me into his office, where we sat facing each other at a sunlit table. It was only after setting out sample funeral stationery and a brochure about floral tribute options that I noticed the images along the wall behind Joseph.

"Oh yes," I heard him say as I peered, "it will have to be roses."

He was browsing the floral brochure, unaware of me surveying his wall from the side of my eye. All manner of images were now pinned there that hadn't existed the week before, among them an arcane-looking diagram of a tree with numbered branches, and a poster of the body's chakras visible as colored discs, like a secret rainbow-colored spine.

But the images arresting me were of the comet—clippings from the newspapers, printouts from the Web, all showing at different scales and resolutions the photo of the unidentified object behind St. John. One image, a detail of the object, was blown up so large that it looked like nothing but a cloud of dust or vapor. Beside this was a headshot of Joseph's mother in a mulberry blouse and pearls, regarding the camera with an expression of shrewd good cheer.

Radiant with new resolve, he began to raise the finer points of his vision for the service at the farm by the shrine.

When the day came, there was no horse-drawn hearse, no Catholic cathedral. Instead, Zara crooned Jo Stafford's greatest hits, accompanied by a mandolinist in the hay-scented air, while guests traipsed through kangaroo grass to arrive in the blazing sun of Joseph's back paddock. To either side of the congregation, straw bales lay like golden corks, and sheep stood clustered below the small, solitary clouds, their heads inclined toward us, watchful and still. Clarence and I stood by, proffering booklets to the mourners as they took their places on several dozen spindle-back chairs, while Joseph stood barefoot before them at a rose altar by the portable bier, like a blue Jesus in his white linen shirt and pants.

Behind Joseph was the structure he had been building, which was less a shrine than a small garden pavilion of white wooden beams around which vines might be trained. His bearing and expression would not have been incongruous in a father who was about to give away his betrothed daughter. Briefly, I closed my eyes. Beneath the music came the sounds of crickets, of grass bending to the breeze, and of the old windmill beyond the rise, whining.

As the guests settled, Zara, positioned beside the mandolinist to Joseph's left and wearing a blue lace dress, commenced "Ave Maria" while currawongs called. Her voice wavered and swelled, while Patricia's lacquered casket, like a Venetian gondola on the water, was borne through the grass on the shoulders of Joseph and several conventional-looking male relatives, who had surely never before seen a service like this.

Once the casket was set down on the bier below a spray of tribute roses, Joseph took a breath, peered up at the sky, and at last began to speak.

"My mother, Patricia Marie Evans," he began, "having departed the physical body that tied her to Earth, has now returned to the stars."

He cast his wide, unblinking eyes over us as his face lifted slowly into a smile. "But that doesn't mean she's not here. This morning I was painting the final beam in this structure behind me, telling myself once more to be strong, when out of nowhere, a small yellow butterfly landed on my hand."

He paused to glance at the casket. "Those in spirit send us these signs. They don't want to be mourned. And they don't want to return. Because in physical death, they have reawakened to that radiant reality which we, stranded here, forget the moment we're born."

Lifting his palms, he spoke now to the sky. "In passing beyond the material plane, the soul recalls that this life, with all its space-time limitations and grasping indignities, is the true dream. My mother has reunited with the universal spirit and cosmic source of all things."

He pressed his hands together and regarded us again as a cockatoo shrieked overhead. "Who are we to regret a beloved soul's homecoming? Friends, there is nothing to mourn."

As Zara began the recessional song, her voice flutelike and unfurling toward the chorus of "Dancing Queen," the casket was again borne up onto the shoulders of Joseph and the others. Clarence, in his top hat and tails, led them down the aisle of guests and out toward the road, where our hearse waited, as everyone else, including the mandolinist and Zara, still singing, trailed behind, and I had the vision of a congregation from another age, appealing to the harvest gods for mercy.

We were now within the full swell of the chorus, the high, vaulting notes of ABBA transformed into a transcendent elegy, which seemed to mobilize and distill the emotion that had thus far gathered, ushering it, and us, out of the funeral and into the wide sunlit day, and I thought of Saint Paul's letter to Timothy: *For I am already being poured out like a drink offering, and the time for my departure is near.* As the song ended and we arrived at the back door of the hearse, Clarence met my eye with a look of horror, and I realized that my face was glazed with tears.

It was only then, when I peered over Clarence's shoulder at the passing crowd, that I saw Angus, paused mid-stride in his suit a few meters away with his eyes fixed on me. I returned his stare without blinking, watching his nostrils flare, his lips part grimly as if for speech. I squinted at those lips, flagrant and full and designed to sneer.

"Always good to see you, Angus," I called out, swiping at my eyes before slamming the hearse's door shut.

As he narrowed his eyes, I could see the threat of violence run through him, like the ripple of a muscle, but I stood tall, and with a pinched mouth he turned away.

After Clarence and I had delivered Patricia to the crematorium, I walked from the office through the afternoon heat back toward the cemetery, trying to vanquish the image of Angus and still hearing the calm, ponderous tone of Joseph's voice in my ears. I didn't understand how Joseph's serenity had been so swiftly restored, or on what grounds his beliefs were really built. The explanation was surely more subtle, more complex than willful self-delusion, but short of asking him, I didn't know how to discover it. To distract myself, I turned on my Walkman to listen to the radio, but it was no use. The host was discussing the comet photo.

"It's caused quite a stir, hasn't it?" he was saying. "Now, it's important to note that some astronomers are suggesting the object is in fact just a star, but not everyone agrees, do they?"

"No, that's right," said the guest. "And I guess I'm one of the dissenters—because I was one of the young witnesses to the 1966

Westall High School sighting in Victoria, and I tell you, no government cover-up, no claptrap about military maneuvers using strange craft, has been able to erase the truth of what we saw that day—flying saucers, that's what—strange, speedy, silver objects made by no earthly engineer. So I'm not so quick to believe official reports that dismiss these things. And I'll tell you this much for free: the object in the photo sure looks like the ones I saw that day in 1966 . . ."

It felt like a trick of celestial timing, when minutes later as I passed the football field, I looked up to see the scoreboard transformed with white spray paint. E.T. LAND HERE, it said in huge letters, and I smiled, while sensing that this directive was perhaps not quite the joke it seemed.

When I finally passed through the cemetery's avenue of elms, I removed my headphones, wondering what Theo thought of the object behind St. John. Presumably he agreed it was a star, and for this reason was declining to dignify other theories with a response, but in view of the noise those theories were generating, his silence surprised me.

It was only when I rounded the path into the cemetery's western corner that I broke from my thoughts and looked up, and noticed the figure of a man in the distance, the man I couldn't escape, standing directly under the poplar that shaded Christopher's grave. Squinting, I paused on the path. He had already turned away. I took a deep breath and held still, fighting the urge to run toward him. As he retreated through the trees en route for the northern exit, I measured again his height, his frame, his slow, sure walk, and knew beyond doubt it was Angus.

There was nothing I could do.

15.

COME MARCH, WHEN THE COMET WAS RISING A LITTLE EARLIER each night, I began to fear I was losing my mind. Summer was over, but the dry heat remained, and at times I felt we were all captive within the mouth of a creature yet to exhale. Although newspaper coverage about the question of St. John's companion object had subsided, an atmosphere of hopeful conspiracy persisted in town. In a span of weeks, the bakery had begun selling UFO-shaped gingerbreads, the nearby Theatre Royal had commenced a run of space-themed double features, and a late-night local radio show had aired a two-episode special about the claims of several supposed eyewitnesses to strange lights in the region's skies.

But no one I knew seemed as preoccupied by the topic as Joseph. During the spontaneous lectures that now followed his meditations, I was beginning to feel myself cleaving in two. There was the rational self holding steady, anxiously scanning a bereaved former client for signs of collapse, and the shadow self who still recalled a bright realm glimpsed while clinically dead two years before, who wanted desperately to believe there was more than this: bodies bound to a continental crust, seeing out our time before necrosis, alone in space on a planet formed by accident. In those moments, I would recall my blue pills waiting quietly to transport me, and Joseph's words about death being another beginning.

I wasn't the only one who was wobbling. Sandy was in raptures over Joseph, and I knew why. With shining eyes, she would reflect over tea about the eternal soul, about consciousness preceding matter, about dying just being a release.

"Think about it, Sylvia," she said one afternoon, "if Joseph's right, if our bodies really are just vessels grounding us in the physical dimension, then Christopher's still alive in spirit somewhere, even if we can't see him." Looking in a dazed way at her plate, she had quoted Joseph saying that in reality, it was easier to die than to be born. "And imagine if we really come back," she went on, "if reincarnation is real! Imagine Christopher being reborn somewhere, as someone else's child. It might already have happened!"

In moments like these, I would try to say something moderate and rational, like, "Those are a lot of ideas, Sandy. I can see you're inspired," or, "I'd love to believe those things. But it's hard to know what's true, isn't it?"

But my voice always sounded hollow, as all the while, a beady-eyed part of me held out, performing secret sums, longing to place all my bets on the same roulette wheel of quantum possibility. Like many in Jericho and beyond, I was learning that there is a point beyond which we are all superstitious.

When I heard Sandy's horn outside, one Thursday evening in early March, I considered begging off attending Bakers Road altogether. A documentary had just begun about a group of Peruvian archaeologists, racing against time to excavate as many Incan mummies as possible from beneath the streets of a settlement outside Lima, before the graveyard was destroyed by development. It was a gripping escape from arguments about whether the St. John Comet was being tailed by a spacecraft. At the same time, I wondered whether Joseph might have finally exhausted what there was to say about the telescopic photo, and regained a firmer footing on Earth—even though doing so might require that he face his grief over his mother's death. It was with this hope in mind, and the desire for a meditation that restored my sleep, that I left the house and rode off with Sandy again.

Little had changed. After instructing us to breathe for over an hour through the chakra points along our inner spines, Joseph was on his feet holding forth again about the object of unknown origin. Several students, I noticed, made their apologies soon after Zara brought out the tea trolley, and were furtively making for the door even as Joseph spoke. I looked at Sandy to assess whether this might be a possibility for us, but saw her settled resolutely on a cushion with a cup of tea, next to Roy and Danny, who were frowning in concentration at whatever it was Joseph was saying. Figuring it would be at least a half hour until my escape, I poured myself a tea.

"It's just like the crop circles," Roy was saying now. "According to the powers that be, if there's one hoax, they're all hoaxes." He made a wiping gesture with his hands and shrugged.

"The burden of proof," said Joseph, nodding gravely, "is always on those who dare to allow for possibilities beyond those accepted by the philosophy of the day—the phenomenon of meteorites falling from the sky, the fact of Jupiter's moons, an Earth that isn't flat . . ."

As he raised the question of whether the comet and whatever was behind it were in fact signs, sent to us by a cosmic intelligence seeking to awaken us to the true nature of reality, I felt myself growing dizzy and drowsy at once. In the glow of the late, low sun, his skin looked less blue-gray than silver, and I had a sudden vision of him as the Tin Man in *The Wizard of Oz*, with an upside-down funnel on his head spouting smoke. Now, even when I saw him amid the banality of High Street at noon, he looked like a figure from myth. The blue of his skin was thrown into further relief by his pale hair, lending him an otherworldly effect, as though he existed a measure apart, like a god who walked among us, or else a fool with uncanny powers, and I wondered whether this effect didn't also render him more persuasive in class.

After availing myself of the library's medical encyclopedias, I'd finally learned that his condition was called argyria, and was usually the result of self-administering colloidal silver for months or years as a holistic remedy. It was not a condition that could be reversed, but it wasn't fatal, either. According to my reading, it was a slow alchemy that turned a person blue. Over time, as silver ions accumulated in the body, they corroded into silver salt which entered the blood, before finally reacting to sunlight on the photographic surface of the skin. Joseph's heart, liver, and lungs were likely now also blue.

At times in class, I wondered what the silver had been supposed to cure, and whether its benefits had been worth its mark. I wondered whether he had largely renounced mirrors, as I had until recently. But there was little to be done about the mirror of the human eye. I imagined this was the worst part—the eyes of others. I imagined that, outside of class, adults turned into children when he passed, gawking stupidly, as I did when he wasn't watching. Yet it was his imperviousness to this very attention that lent him his strength of presence, his bearing of dignity under pressure, and his aura of existing at a register above the rest.

Now in class as he spoke on, I was aware of only the sound of his voice, its rise and fall; the meaning of the words seemed to escape me entirely. I looked around and felt that the room was moving, like the cabin of a ship. Sandy, when I glanced at her, seemed deeply relaxed, as though still in meditation, gazing up at him credulously as though he were an icon in a church, and I wondered whether somehow he was sending us all subliminally into a collective trance. In a dim corner of my mind, I heard myself question whether I should ask Vince what he knew of Joseph's background, but felt traitorous somehow, entertaining suspicion about a man who, I knew better than most, was coping as best he could in the midst of grief and in doing so, trying in his own way to help others find some kind of self-understanding and peace.

Danny, for one, seemed alert and was speaking now, counting off points on his fingers with a sense of urgency, and yet I observed him as though from underwater, wondering, as I always did, how to break him.

On the way home, when I felt a little better, I tried to ask Sandy whether she felt the same, and she gave me a dreamy look and said she was fine, and wasn't it marvelous to think that we might all be playing our part in raising the planet's vibrational frequency?

"Oh, you poor love," she added, looking at me again and touching her free hand to my cheek. "You should check in with a doctor about your antidepressants—they can have strange side effects, sometimes—although Joseph might say you're experiencing some kind of third eye activation."

To escape my brain and the question of what reality I had found myself inhabiting, I went to bed early, only to lie awake in the dark for hours, thinking. The fact was, it wasn't only those on the lunatic fringe who were questioning official interpretations of the object in the telescopic photo. Besides the Slovakian cultural studies professor—a maverick known to court media attention—an otherwise respectable American professor in atmospheric physics had also cast doubt on whether the photo had been deliberately or accidentally distorted. While it was true that this professor was the president of a major UFO citizen-research body with chapters in forty-three countries, he was also an international expert on clouds. And he had been quoted in a recent weekend edition of the *Sydney Morning Herald*. It was the kind of human-interest article people like to puzzle over while eating their toast, and I'd obtained my own copy after seeing it pinned on Joseph's office wall.

With a sigh, I switched on the light and reached for it on my nightstand. HEAD IN THE CLOUDS: WEATHER SCIENTIST CLAIMS UFOS ARE REAL, read the title. Below it, the professor peered out of a thumbnail photo with nonplussed sagacity, wearing horn-rimmed glasses and a checked twill suit. In his view, most commentary surrounding the photo represented "yet another example of the way the cynical scientific establishment stifles open and considered research into the possibility of UFOs, in the true spirit of objective inquiry."

Despite the article's derisive title, the professor appeared to entertain the extraterrestrial hypothesis simply because he judged competing hypotheses as inadequate, given his lifelong study of the case histories. Lying there, I asked myself whether it was fair to call this an unreasonable position.

*   *   *

When I surfaced at three in the morning with a desperate thirst, I wandered into the kitchen for water, and found Lionel regarding me from the French doors with a knowing look. He meowed and pawed his cat door, which I locked at night so he couldn't hunt or get into fights. I let him out and stood on the porch, sipping from my glass, inhaling the cool, loamy smell of the dark garden, and listening to the poplar leaves above make their secret, breath-like sound, as Lionel's bell tinkled through the flower beds.

I felt no sudden shock, or sense of revelation, when I peered up at the comet high above the horizon and saw a sharp, distant white light behind it, like no star or satellite I'd ever seen. The light was blinking at irregular intervals, seemingly moving at speed, and for an instant I thought I saw a blue-green flash, as one eyewitness on the radio had described. Feeling unsteady again, I gripped my glass and looked down at my bare feet, the fact of them there against the decking, which Christopher never got around to refinishing, and which was peeling now, revealing the raw timber beneath. Even the decking looked vivid as I peered at it through the half-light from the living room. It was as if I could see every detail: the tenting paint, the wood grain, the microscopic particles, and it was the same when I inspected my open hand—I saw the blue and purple of my capillaries through the semitranslucent skin, the loops and whorls of my finger pads, the map of lines on my palm forming rivers and tributaries.

When I raised my eyes again to the sky, I searched for the blinking light in vain. The comet seemed to look back at me with regal disinterest, and apart from the fixed glow of a thousand stars, it now appeared there was nothing to be seen.

On Friday morning, I called in sick, and sat on the couch beside Lionel with the blinds drawn, watching reruns of *A Country Practice*. I was still thirsty, and strangely breathless, and felt the bone-deep bruising that follows insomnia, but the world seemed steadier—newly dull, even—

an impression the show I was watching helped to solidify. Dr. Simon was entreating a possum to drink from a bottle, when the phone rang. It was Vince, asking if he could meet me for lunch without saying why.

He sounded distracted and harried, so I didn't ask for details. I told him I couldn't be seen on High Street, but would make him scrambled eggs if he dropped by. Vaguely I wondered at his reasons for calling—we hadn't spoken in a fortnight, so I thought he might simply be checking up on me. I couldn't help wondering whether it was something to do with Angus—but unless I'd committed some trespass in a semi-somnolent state, I hadn't ventured near Jubilee Street since smashing his lamp.

When I met Vince at the door a few hours later, he reflected me back to myself in his heavy sigh and sharp, appraising eyes.

"You got the flu or something?" he asked, as I waved him into the hall and explained that I simply wasn't sleeping again.

He nodded as we entered the living room, and I asked him how work was going.

"It's been worse," he said, setting his keys on the dining table.

"You and Donna must be due for a vacation, surely?" I asked from the stove, where I began cooking the eggs.

"Yep," he said, sitting down. "We'll try to get down the coast for Christmas, this year."

I nodded and slid some bread into the toaster. "Better late than never," I said, and regarded him rubbing his hands over his face, as if to relieve pressure.

When I arrived with our plates, he gave me a wary smile, and I tried to disregard the tightness in my chest.

"How about all this comet mania, eh?" he said, biting into a piece of toast. "Actually, you've been attending the Evans property, haven't you? It's Joseph who's behind the festival, right?"

I nodded and explained that his meditation school had been a distraction.

"That's good, Sylv," he said, leaning forward on his elbows.

As we ate, a magpie cawed somewhere, and Lionel flounced past on his way outside.

Finally Vince set down his fork. "Look, I don't want this to spin you out, and I shouldn't really be telling you, but I wanted you to know there's been a development."

Before I could speak, he raised his hands. "Nothing's been solved, Sylvia. And this might not lead to much, okay?"

I only nodded, holding my own hands in fists and waiting for deliverance.

"A few weeks ago," he began, "I was going over some of the photos of the collision site, and in one of them, I noticed a black cable running across the road, about a hundred meters back. When I realized it was a traffic counter, I checked with Roads and Traffic and they told me it belonged to the council. Well, long story short, they released the data. Turns out it's given us some pretty firm details—speed, axle combos, distance between vehicles. But the best thing is, it's given us a clear window of time—we know now that your car, Danny's, and the other driver's were the only vehicles in that vicinity for a forty-minute period."

"Okay, so what does that mean for the investigation? Can you confirm the make of the other driver's car? Can you connect it to Angus?"

He shook his head and explained that because all three cars were standard sedans, the axle info didn't narrow anything down. "But with the time window," he added, "we can at least expand our search for CCTV footage from gas stations right up and down the highway. It's a long shot, but based on exact timings from the counter, we could potentially link any vehicle, shown anywhere along that road, back to the collision."

When I asked what this meant for Angus, he shrugged and said that while the data had given us nothing conclusive so far, neither had it ruled out Angus as a potential suspect.

"The data supports what we already knew about there being plenty of time between the hit-and-run and Angus's crash into the tree on Jubilee Street," he said. "But we still don't have any footage of his car in the vicinity."

"Yet."

He gave a pointed shrug. "Just don't get your hopes up. The old footage from the BP at the intersection with Sturt Road is useless, as you know—nothing but a lone truck refueling for that whole period and a limited view of the highway. We're chasing up a few additional gas stations now, but remember this was two years ago. Most CCTV gets wiped after a month or two. We'd need to be lucky."

I sighed and looked at my uneaten eggs. "Thanks for telling me."

He ran a hand through his hair. "Maybe I shouldn't have. I don't want to stir you up again."

I nodded as he checked his watch.

"You know I worry about you," he added, before taking in a forkful of eggs. "How are those meditations going, anyway? Donna's always saying I should do more to relax." He rolled his eyes good-naturedly. "But you said you're still not sleeping?"

His words arrived as if from a distance, and for a moment I didn't speak. I was watching my hands on the table, the table Christopher and I had bought years ago from a secondhand store in Surry Hills. If we had stayed in Sydney, I thought, if I had simply asked to delay our move for another few years in order to finish my studies, Christopher would still be here, and I would know nothing of Angus Blair.

It was only when Vince pressed his warm hand over mine and spoke my name that I began to breathe again. When I looked up, he repeated his question in a loud, careful voice, like a doctor checking for concussion.

"Well," I said, pushing away my plate and trying to focus, "when I first started attending Joseph's meditations, my sleep improved. It's just over the last few weeks that I've gone backward." I shook my head. "Joseph has become a bit manic. I don't think he's well."

Vince leaned back. "Really? Mania doesn't tend to inspire relaxation."

"No," I said. "Oh, it's a lot of things. His mother just died. And he's fixated on the UFO conspiracy around that comet photo that was in the papers recently, do you remember?"

"Oh yeah, the comet's alien companions?" Vince grinned, dusting toast crumbs from his fingers.

I nodded. "I'm worried about him. I'm worried about all of us, actually. Sandy idolizes him, and she's been acting a bit spacey. As for me, I thought the meditations would have a grounding effect, but now I'm not sure."

When he asked what I meant, I shrugged and peered out through the window behind him to the bright clouds.

"After the last few sessions, I've felt quite dizzy. And I've been seeing things. Last night, I thought I saw what looked like a UFO near the comet, just like in the reports on the radio. I've been telling myself it was just because I was tired, but now I don't know."

He looked bemused. "It's no good you've been feeling dizzy. But couldn't that just be from all the deep breathing? And tiredness can play all sorts of tricks—I know that much from overnight shifts. Besides, how do you know that whatever you saw wasn't a satellite or jet? They can look pretty weird in a dark sky."

Before I could reply, his radio sounded, recalling all units to the station.

"Gotta go," he said, grabbing his keys.

A moment later I faced him at the door, promising to be in touch. It was a sudden instinct that caused me to grab his shoulder, just before he turned for the gate.

"Vince," I said, as he paused to regard me. "Do you know anything about Joseph's background?"

He took a long breath, thinking. "Not much. But I do know Patricia's brother was mixed up with the Comancheros. He ended up doing time for a shooting in Sydney."

I frowned. "Who are the Comancheros?"

"Bikie gang," he said, jangling his keys before darting me a shrewd smile. "I heard the judge was light on him. I always thought Patricia might have had a hand in that."

Registering these details, I felt uneasy in a way I couldn't pinpoint, and asked him what he meant.

He shrugged. "She was a powerful lady."

I wanted to talk more, but knew Vince had to leave, so I asked for what I wanted. "Do you think you could run a check on Joseph for me?"

He squinted for a moment. "That's a tall order. You think he's involved in something shady?"

"Probably not," I said, "but if he has a record, I want to know about it."

# 16.

With the New Philharmonia Orchestra playing Holst's "Neptune" on the tape deck, I drove alone to Joseph's Saturday-night meditation, and tried to let the harps and flutes soothe me. As the wheat fields passed, I listened to the steely part of me that said I needed to gather my wits. I was worried about Sandy, who seemed at risk of floating on Joseph's tide too far out to sea, and I wanted to use the development in Christopher's case to scare Danny.

Regarding the light I'd seen in the sky on Thursday night, I'd been trying not to think of it, and when I did, I reminded myself of all the explanations that seemed more likely than my own madness—the fact that I'd not been sleeping, the highly suggestive nature of my romantic imagination, the extent of my immersion during recent days in talk about spaceships. But the truth was, I was also worried for myself, and when I witnessed Joseph's rhetoric ascend to new heights shortly after the session began, I knew something had to change.

"Let's start," Joseph said, when we were all seated, "by discussing the possibility of biblical references to UFOs by the prophet Ezekiel."

As he spoke, I watched Sandy's face. She sat sandwiched between Zara and Roy in her tangerine caftan, looking up at Joseph with an intent, wondering gaze, a gaze that seemed to betray neither doubt nor hesitation. It was then that I realized my dilemma was not necessarily so simple as whether to leave Joseph's school or remain, if Sandy was to keep attending without me to bring her back to ground.

But who was I to bring anyone back to ground? As I poured myself a tea during the break, I felt dazed, yet compelled myself to speak with Danny all the same. He was making his way back from the bathroom, so I cornered him before he could return to the group. He stiffened as I faced him.

"How are you, Danny?" I asked, forcing myself to take on a considerate tone.

"Fine," he nodded, fixing me with his shifty, bovine stare and stepping forward to make for the refreshments table, before I clamped my hand on his arm.

"Look," I said, "I can't say much, but you should know we're on the brink of a breakthrough with the case."

Without blinking I watched his eyes, those pupils that had reflected the truth of what happened on Horseshoe Road that night. "Now would be a wise time to go on the record about what you saw, Danny—the law will look upon you more favorably if you do it now."

He only scowled, so I spoke again. "After all, you wouldn't want anything to stop you making it to the festival, would you?"

"Piss off," he said, and pushed past me as I stood there, deflated, imagining myself wrestling him to the ground.

After my interlude with Danny, I listened to Joseph transition from Ezekiel to the flying objects he'd discovered in Hieronymus Bosch's sixteenth-century painting, *Triptych of the Temptation of St. Anthony*, and rage gave way to fatigue. I imagined myself floating up like one of the bizarre objects in the painting, like Saint Anthony himself, until I was high enough to gain perspective on the wonder and devastation below, high enough to know for certain what was true and urgent and what was not.

For a while I watched Joseph gesticulating at a reproduction of the painting in an art book, pointing and shaking his head and bearing an odd, distant smile, as we peered at the burning city, the stricken saint, the devils in disguise, and I saw that he was not well. Some students, aside from Sandy, were still listening with rapt attention, but others were clearing their plates, rubbing at their eyes, waiting for release. A few looked to be on the verge of sleep. One new recruit, hoping to find relief from night terrors, held her mug tightly in both hands, looking lost as Joseph tapped at the naked woman in the painting's right panel, and noted how she signified the earthly temptations which Saint Anthony had found the spiritual strength to withstand.

It was in the pause that followed, as Joseph gazed at the painting and gathered his words, that a young woman rose to leave for the back door. She made hardly a sound, but he heard her all the same, and his response was immediate.

"Where are you going?" he asked in a cool, imperious voice, as we all turned to see her standing by the door with her bag, looking embarrassed.

"I just need an early night," she said. "'Bye, everyone."

As she left, I watched his eyes narrow.

"Not everyone's ready to truly open their mind," Roy said suddenly, shaking his head.

"She never even wears her Kingdom Come T-shirt," Danny added.

I peered over at Sandy, who looked puzzled before training her gaze on Joseph.

He presented us now with a philosophical sigh. "At a certain point, we come to realize that the most essential truths in life are a matter of faith."

As he smiled serenely, clasped his hands together, and began to speak again, I realized that his voice had undergone a subtle change. It was deeper, more formal, and carried a more distinct oratory quality—I felt more than ever that we were watching a performance.

"When we wait for materialist science to satisfy its standards of proof before allowing ourselves to believe extraordinary things, we turn from our own souls' knowing. And as we wait, the world grows smaller."

While he continued, I sat down against the wall and felt a warmth fill my chest. Light-headed again, I listened to him from behind the darkness of my closed eyes.

Just as it took centuries for modern science to evolve from natural philosophy, he was explaining now, so were we still waiting for it to recognize what some quantum physicists already knew and what we in our hearts could feel—that the supposed divide between the physical and spiritual, the external and internal in our reality was no true divide at all.

"And in a universe as animate and vast as this," he said breathlessly, "on a planet whose odds of being are so scientifically unlikely, who are we to deny the possibility that we're not alone here?"

Behind my eyelids, I saw planets spinning, Joseph pointing heavenward, and Theo—who still haunted my mind every night when I saw the comet—looking on darkly, as the flying fish and tiny devils from the painting coasted over a desert landscape of windmills and bonfires. Amid it all I sensed Joseph's rapture and his despair. His present condition, it seemed to me then, was little more than a longing to prove the real illusion was the one that said we were only this—only organic forms waiting to expire, accidents of nature appearing and disappearing without reason or design in an indifferent universe, and that was a longing I could understand.

I wasn't sure how much time passed before I heard his voice again and opened my eyes.

"Raise your hands," he said, bringing his own right hand up as though for an oath in court, before pressing it over his heart. I watched as most of the room mirrored his gesture, like weary soldiers summoning strength, while I kept my hands in my lap.

"As above, so below," said Joseph, shooting a cool glance at me. "For those with eyes to see, the signs are always there . . ."

Just as the ancients knew, he explained, the laws of cosmic synchronicity dictated that the movements of the heavens were mirrored in events here on Earth. The discovery of St. John, and its companion object in our own skies, was no different, although exactly what it heralded was not yet certain.

"But make no mistake," he continued, regarding us with his alarmed blue eyes, "it's no coincidence that our comet happens to have been discovered by and named after a man who bears the same name as the prophet who wrote the book of Revelation, who warned of terrible things occurring after a great star fell from heaven."

In the silence that followed, no one moved, and I remembered the graffiti at Our Lady of Perpetual Help, long since removed, that referenced a biblical "bitter star" from Revelation.

"Let St. John's apparition at this late time in our millennium not be in vain," he said finally, in a loud, trembling voice.

I watched what happened next as through dreaming, while Joseph explained that he would close the session with a call-and-response, and directed us to repeat after him a series of lines that echoed in my head for days afterward:

Our eyes are open.
We pledge our allegiance to our own souls' truth, throughout
    all dimensions.
We heed St. John's arrival.

It was with great effort that I rose to my feet in the pause that followed, overtaken as I was with vertigo and shock and a swooning tiredness. Faces and sounds seemed to blur around me, and it was only in obedience to a steely inner voice that I waved to Sandy and forced myself outside without delay, still holding the cup containing the dregs of the tea I'd been drinking that night and each night I'd entered a dreamlike state. It was a connection I'd only made in the final minutes of Joseph's speech, when I noticed how the students who looked most dazed were, like me, holding teacups, like mournful Victorians nodding off. Zara, Danny, Roy, and several others, who on this occasion hadn't been drinking the tea, had still appeared alert. Danny, who seemed to enjoy the lectures far more than the meditations, had again listened with a focus I'd never imagined he possessed, his posture rigid with anticipation, nodding slowly every few minutes as though receiving instruction from a general about an imminent maneuver. Roy had been taking notes on a legal pad while munching loudly on a nut bar.

I shouldn't have driven anywhere of course, and yet I did, with the night air rushing through the windows, under the light of the rising comet, straight to Vince's door.

Donna met me in her robe with her hair in rollers, and observed me for what seemed like a long moment on the porch step with a slightly open mouth.

"Hello, Sylvia," she said haltingly. "Are you alright?"

"I'm afraid I'm not entirely sure, Donna," I replied, before offering my apologies for the surprise visit, and asking to speak with Vince.

"What's going on?" he asked when he appeared in boxers and a T-shirt and ushered me inside.

"It's happening again. The dizziness—right now as I stand here, I'm spinning," I said, but he looked at me blankly. I raised my cup. "I just want to account for all possible explanations."

Vince pressed a hand to his temple. "Sylvia, what the hell are you talking about?"

"What if Joseph's putting something in the tea? Every time I've felt the dizziness come on it's been after drinking the tea that's served at the meditations. I might sound mad and I might be wrong, but I'm asking you to test it."

Vince sighed as I held the cup out to him, before finally taking it and shaking his head. "You know what this looks like, don't you?"

"Yes, I'm aware that it looks like I've lost it."

He sighed again. "I'm not promising anything. Please, go home and get some sleep."

As I lay awake in the hours that followed, I wondered what Joseph meant by telling us to heed St. John's arrival, and why he no longer seemed to believe it might be a sign of hope. Watching the comet's tail through my window, I thought of how it had been discovered around the time Christopher was killed. If I placed any credence in Joseph's theory of synchronicity between celestial bodies in space and human beings on Earth, how could I imagine such an object could lead to any good in my own life?

While Lionel purred by my feet and I finally closed my eyes, one hemisphere of my brain was watching me debate these questions with an incredulous eye—the side that wondered whether I hadn't in fact been covertly drugged via successive cups of dandelion tea; the side that had just witnessed a grief-crazed man demanding his students recite illogical mantras; the side that now feared for Sandy. Because I had begun to feel that Theo might have been right about Joseph Evans all along.

In the morning, while my head still ached and my limbs felt thick, I drove to the hospital for a blood test. The air through the window was cooler than usual and the sky was blue, and I felt calm, knowing that I was taking action. An hour later, when a harried nurse finally plunged a syringe into my arm, I felt a strange, virtuous relief, as though I were expelling not blood but my system's last vestiges of fantasy and temptation.

"We'll mail you the results," the nurse said flatly, as she slapped a Band-Aid over the injection site, and, feeling darkness nearing, I lowered my head so as not to faint.

If the test proved positive for some narcotic, I thought during the drive back, I'd know Joseph was dangerous as well as delusional, and I'd have compelling grounds for persuading Sandy to step back from his sessions. Beyond this, I'd have a means of convincing Vince, Sandy, and myself that my own perception of reality was sound.

Attempting a lightness I didn't feel, I stopped by the bakery for lamingtons before arriving at Sandy's. I'd been too tired to visit her for our usual morning tea the day before, and I wanted to see how she was, especially seeing as today was Christopher's birthday.

Ten minutes later, she met me at the door in her hot-pink gardening gloves.

"Oh, good!" she said, raising her two canvas paws. "I've just brewed coffee."

In the kitchen as I sat with the lamingtons, I listened to Sandy clatter around with the plunger and cups while Terry rested his chin on my foot.

When she brought over the coffee and sat down beside me, I asked how she was feeling.

"Oh, you know his birthday's always hard," she said, taking a lamington. "But I've been worried about you, since you left so quickly last night."

I nodded. "I was feeling dizzy," I said, scanning her face. "I don't think that tea agrees with me. Have you noticed the same?"

"Oh, I often feel a bit dreamy when Joseph delivers his talks. But his ideas can be quite stirring. Are you better now?"

"A little," I said, looking down at the souvenir cloth on the table, which showed a map of Australia surrounded by kangaroos, koalas, emus, and an abundance of bright red banksia.

"Good," she said. "Because there's a snap working bee at Joseph's starting in a bit over an hour. He announced it just after you left."

For a moment I watched her fingers drumming on the surface of the Indian Ocean, a few inches from the submerged blue form of a tiny whale.

She shrugged breezily when I asked what the working bee was for.

"Festival prep, I think. He's converting a section of the main house into accommodation so we won't all have to camp."

When I looked up at her, I watched her expression become quizzical.

"No one's going to punish you if you can't come, love," she said, patting my hand with a faltering laugh.

I sighed. "I'm having doubts about Joseph, Sandy. I don't think he's well."

She leaned back with a stricken smile. "Well, he's used to being doubted," she said quietly, after a pause. "But he has the courage of his convictions. If he's a little fragile, why should we be surprised?" She frowned at me and made a quick, incredulous motion with her hands. "You know his mother just died. But it's these tests in life that can help a person separate truth from illusion."

I winced inwardly to hear Joseph speaking through her.

When I said nothing, she gathered her hands into fists on the table and shook her head. "Oh, Sylvia, aren't you sick of being told what to think?"

"Isn't that exactly what Joseph's doing in his lectures?"

"No," she said, with a wounded look, "he's opening our eyes to the true nature of reality." She waved her hands at the ceiling. "Whether or not that includes UFOs, I don't really care. Because Joseph has shown me that death is an illusion of the physical plane, and I feel the truth of it in my heart."

She shut her eyes and took a breath, and when she looked back at me it was with a frank, unyielding gaze. "I live my days lightly now, because I know I'll see Christopher again."

With a tight mouth, she brushed crumbs from the cloth. In the silence, I could hear Terry panting under the table.

"You miss him as much as I do—I thought you'd be more open-minded," she said finally. "Didn't you see a white light after the accident?"

"That was my remembered perception afterward. I'll never know what it really means, whether it was a false memory or a hallucination or some final flare of my oxygen-starved brain."

"Well, that's a rationalist explanation," she said, shaking her head. "You're not even accounting for the possibility that the light was real." She sniffed. "Joseph says we travel to other planes during sleep, for instance. It just can't be quantified yet."

"Aren't you at least suspicious of his certainty, Sandy? Do you really think he knows these things to be true?"

"Well, that's the whole reason he emphasizes meditation, isn't it? It's a kind of primary research. A way of experiencing the true nature of consciousness for ourselves."

"But have you?"

"We're beginners, Sylvia." She shot me a weary look and spoke into her cup. "We have to be patient."

After a moment she peered back at me with a strange, defiant rapture. "I can feel it; there are whole worlds beyond this one, worlds of light! And in one of them is our Christopher."

When I said nothing, she began jiggling her foot, clearly angry.

I left soon afterward, my lamington uneaten. Hugging her at the door I could feel the tension in her shoulders, and when she raised her hand to wave goodbye, her eyes wouldn't meet mine.

Vince rang half an hour later, while I was slumped at my kitchen table, wondering whether I should force myself to the working bee.

"I can't talk for long," he said, "but I ran some checks on Joseph."

I listened as he spoke over the sounds of children shrieking, and told me that four years ago, during a stint in Melbourne, Joseph had been busted for attempting to import a Schedule 4 drug.

I scanned my body for a reaction, but felt nothing.

"The quantity was tiny, though," he added, "so he got off with a fine."

I tried to picture Joseph under police interrogation, and wondered whether his first instinct had been to lie, tell the truth, or call his mother.

"What drug was it?"

"Ketamine. It was intercepted, so he never received it. He claimed it was for personal use."

I could hear Vince deliberating through the receiver, and imagined him multitasking at the kitchen bench, cutting a child's sandwich just so with one hand, while Donna gestured wearily for him to get off the phone. It seemed to have happened instantly—his transformation from wisecracking police trainee to dependable family man.

"It's not a lot," he was saying now, "but it's not nothing, either. Look, I'll try to get your tea dregs tested next week, but I wouldn't jump to any conclusions yet, okay?"

"But do you think there could be more to the story, Vince?"

I heard him sigh. "I have no idea or way of finding out, Sylvia. And I've already said too much."

Even if I conceded he was right, it wouldn't stop me worrying. Murmuring my thanks, I left him to his Sunday.

Despite the warm air, the sky was a dull mauve when I ventured outside on my way to the library. As I entered High Street and narrowly sidestepped a dead rat on the footpath, I tried not to take it for a sign. In the carpeted quiet of the reference section, I sat like a monk over several hardback medical tomes, leafing through their tissue-thin pages until the enigma of ketamine revealed itself to me. Ketamine, I read, was a synthetic compound with anesthetic, analgesic, and hallucinogenic properties, originating in the sixties. Were a person to drink dandelion tea laced with it, it seemed they might well meet with symptoms similar to the ones I had experienced. But I told myself not to jump to conclusions.

I thought, instead, about the differences between conjecture and evidence, and about the ways fear and desire, like silkworms, spin their filaments to create substance where there is none. I thought of Sandy, becoming entrapped within the bright fibers of one person's theory of reality. My own doubts about Joseph's ideas and the sensationalism in the press seemed unable to touch her; maintaining a critical distance was a sober, uninviting proposition by comparison. I couldn't keep turning to Vince to solve my problems, that much was clear. He was busy, and fearful of seeing me spiral again over another man whose crimes might evade the reach of evidence.

As I left the library and walked to the botanical gardens, I recalled sitting there with Theo weeks before, under another restless sky. Looking out over the dun-colored lake, I thought of what he had said about comets and prophets and how people were liable to read meaning in celestial objects where none existed. Whether that meaning was hope or doom, it signaled the existence of an order greater than our human selves, and offered a more accessible means of transcending our prone bodies, our short-circuited dreams, our fears of death. It was understandable. I still felt it in myself, the need to believe in something greater.

But without some kind of limit, where did it end? I imagined Joseph right now waxing off-the-cuff about the holographic universe, while his students ferried furniture in the humid air. The fact was, all I had to wield so far in drawing Sandy out of her enchantment was an appeal to critical discernment and truth, but truth being a contested ground, I needed more. I needed the support of some higher authority—not Joseph's divine knowing, but science.

If the one scientist I knew could also lay claim to being the expert discoverer of the comet that had inspired the enchantment, that seemed to me an excellent coincidence. Beyond this, Theo was also the one person who I felt would understand my concerns about Joseph, even if he seemed to understand little else, and even if seeking his help might cost me some pride.

The sky was already darkening when, after feeding Lionel, I sped along the empty road to the observatory, with my eyes fixed on the mountains above the horizon. The air carried the strange, auric radiance that precedes certain storms, and when I reached the boom gates, I felt like the survivor of some mass devastation, seeking a holdout. I had no reason to assume Theo was there on a Sunday, of course, especially considering the viewing conditions, and my knock on the door of the telescope dome, which I reached on foot, yielded no response. It was only when, seeing a light on inside the control room, I hovered near the window like a ghost, that I finally saw him. He was frozen mid-stride, holding a manila folder and regarding me with mute incomprehension.

"Sylvia," he said with the same expression, when he opened the door.

"I'm sorry to drop by so suddenly," I began, trying to steel myself as I recalled our last encounter, and the way he had touched my hand. "I just didn't know who else to speak with."

I felt unsteady and prone as he joined me outside, and I glimpsed through the door a man in technician's overalls, fiddling with the cords attached to one of the monitors.

"I shouldn't have come. I'm interrupting."

He dismissed this with a shake of his head, and seemed briefly lost for words as I peered at the image of a woman with rainbow-colored hair on his T-shirt. "It's nice to see you," he said, and cleared his throat. "I was just picking up some papers before heading home."

I tried to smile. The woman was emerging from the sea, holding the sun, above the words, *Eclipse Hawai'i: July 11, 1991,* the year I met Christopher.

"I just wondered if we could speak about Joseph."

A wave of recognition crossed his face. "Sure, but I'd like to get home before the storm. I'm not far away, if you want to follow me."

So I tailed him down the mountain as it began to rain, wondering where he lived, what exactly I was going to say, and how it was that he always seemed to signal strange weather in my life. As I watched his rear lights, my mind wandered to the comet and its alleged companion object, and the light I'd seen in the sky above my own yard. I assumed Theo would dismiss Joseph's conspiracy theories, but I had no way of knowing what he'd think of my own.

# 17.

His house was an old bungalow in the foothills of the ranges, nestled down a steep driveway and nearly obscured by two enormous golden wattles. After walking down the gloomy hall, we arrived at a kitchen-dining area that led into a living room, with windows looking out to an overgrown yard and the dark, electric sky. The walls were devoid of photographs, and bare but for a single poster tacked above the TV in the living room, promoting the 1972 film *Solaris*, which showed a man's head below a strange, brain-like orb suspended in the darkness of space. Dishes were stacked in the sink, books and papers piled on the table alongside a jumbo packet of Corn Flakes, and in the dim light, I could see dust motes floating in the air around us.

"Sorry about the mess," he said, clearing the Corn Flakes from the table before asking if I wanted coffee or tea.

I asked for coffee and sat down, while he boiled the kettle and we settled into an odd silence. I had no intention of raising the question of what had caused him to drive off so suddenly all those weeks ago, and I was relieved to note that it seemed we were going to skip the subject entirely. Peering out at the sky, I felt grateful for the rain, rushing down now as if from the precipice of a great cataract above. The comet wasn't visible, so I surveyed the titles of Theo's books and papers instead: *The Absolute Luminosities of the Calan/Tololo Type IA Supernovae*; *The Age of the Galactic Globular Cluster System*; *Autofib Redshift Survey*.

"Not really bedtime reading, is it?" I said, pointing at the titles when he set a mug in front of me and sat down opposite.

"No," he said, with a faint smile. "But I have some colleagues who could be on the brink of a breakthrough. Turns out the universe could be accelerating, so I'm trying to keep up."

I returned his smile as he took a sip.

"I'll get to the point," I said. "I'm concerned about Joseph, and you seem to have had a sixth sense about him all along. I thought it was all quite innocuous—interesting, even—his meditation classes and thoughts about reality. I was sleeping better. But he seems to have spiraled out of control."

Theo peered up from his mug with a look of disquiet, and asked me how.

"He's fixated on that telescopic photo publicized in the papers. The one that supposedly shows a spacecraft behind the comet."

He nodded. "Which is bullshit, of course. The object is a diffracted star; that amateur guy had his software set up wrong."

I noticed that his hair had grown longer. I tried to focus, but it was strange to be near him again after so many weeks, and despite how things had ended, I had a yielding feeling, as though the air wanted me to pitch toward him. His face and figure before me, even his voice, seemed to take on a covert luminescence, a heightened clarity, like how the world presents after a fever. I noticed, too, how his eyes kept scanning my face with concern, as though he were a doctor interpreting symptoms.

"Joseph has a range of rejoinders to that explanation," I said now, squaring my shoulders to recalibrate. "The weight of eyewitness testimony is one. The vastness of the universe is another. But his favorite is that scientists for centuries ignored evidence of meteorites."

He leaned back with a solemn look, slowly spinning the base of his mug, and I noticed, not for the first time, that he wore no ring on his left hand. I wondered whether he ever had, and if so, when it was that he'd removed it. "Well," he said, "there have been many eyewitness accounts of witches and devils through history, too, but in the case of UFOs I'd also say that few of us realize how imperfect our own sight is. And sometimes ordinary things can create extraordinary apparitions."

It was impossible, he said, to list all the objects and phenomena that had been known to do this, among them birds, beacon lights, sun dogs, skyhook balloons, detached vortex rings, lenticular clouds, satellite re-entries, meteor radar echoes, radar angels, industrial detergents, planets like Venus, and often, simply, bright stars.

I watched the steam from our mugs swirling in the air between us, regarded his serious face, and wanted to say something amusing and true, something that would make him smile, but I only nodded limply. To me the list as he recited it sounded like poetry, beautiful and absurd—all the strange marvels of our world that contrive to fool us in our longing for revelation.

"And it's true that the universe is vast," he went on. "I grew up watching the desert skies in Arizona, wanting to believe we're not alone. But I've seen no proof of it yet."

"I thought I saw something myself, the other night," I said suddenly. "But I was tired, and my head was full of Joseph's talk. It was a strange, blinking light, near the comet."

He nodded, searching my face. "You probably did see a light. It's just more likely to have been any number of things other than a spaceship."

"I know," I said, feeling foolish, while a distant growl of thunder erupted as if from deep in the earth, and I noticed the strong forms of his hands at rest on the table.

"Are you managing okay, Sylvia?" he asked suddenly, in an uncertain, probing voice. "Joseph's a powerful character. It really worries me to think of you spending so much time with him."

I looked away to divert my irritation—after all, whatever connection we might have developed had been severed suddenly by him weeks before, and what right did he have now to worry about me?

"My concern is for my mother-in-law, Sandy, not myself. That's why I'm here."

With a deep breath, I refocused. "When I say it aloud, I feel silly," I went on, "but I've started to wonder what Joseph's really capable of. I've been feeling so strange lately after his sessions that I've even wondered whether the tea served at the school is spiked with something."

"Really?" He surveyed me with a startled look and frowned.

"I thought perhaps you knew something I didn't," I said. "All I know is that he's consumed with the comet conspiracy to the point of lunacy, and it's not abating."

When I added that Joseph had also made the point that the comet, Theo himself, and the prophet of the apocalypse all shared the same name, his face darkened.

"Well, he's hell-bent on me speaking at his festival, and he doesn't like being refused."

"Oh," I said, a little dazed.

He sighed. "All I know is what I saw with you that day at Memorial Hall—another lost soul seeking answers in the sky; another prophet in need of a flock."

I frowned. "I felt a kind of recognition at first. He's the only one who's seemed as affected as I've been by the comet. Besides you, of course."

As the rain hurled down, he peered at his hands. "Can't you just stop attending the classes?" he asked, looking up. "I think you should distance yourself."

"But that's the problem. I'm worried about my mother-in-law. She's very taken with Joseph, and won't listen. If I stop attending, I won't be able to keep an eye on things. And I'm the one who led her to him in the first place."

He nodded gently but said nothing. His eyes ranged around the wall behind me, as if searching.

"He might be harmless," I went on. "He might come to his senses once he's recovered from his grief at losing his mother. But shouldn't I be cautious, considering how uncritical Sandy is?"

"Yes. Neither of you should be anywhere near him."

"But she won't listen to me," I said, "so I'm wondering whether she might listen to someone else—an expert who could counter Joseph's claims with some authority—someone like you."

"Ah." He looked gloomy, glancing down at the table now with his shoulders a little slumped, as the dark sky through the window behind him rumbled and poured, and part of me wished I hadn't been so bold.

"You're a scientist," I pressed on. "You can claim to comprehend the solar system, the laws of physics, in ways Joseph never could."

With eyes averted from mine, he interjected to say that really it was a case of comprehending how much he didn't know. I only paused, not wanting to plead. But I knew his manner, if he agreed, would be just right to command Sandy's attention—unassuming yet quietly compelling, when he described reality as seen through the eyepiece of a survey telescope.

"Sandy would listen to you," I said at last. "You wouldn't have to present her with any formal refutation but rather just show her the comet, the skies, as you see them. That could be enough."

There was a silence.

He pinched his lip. "Okay," he said, and looked up. "I'll speak with her." He straightened in his chair and took a breath. "Perhaps we can discuss details over the next few days."

His tone was that of a lieutenant conferring about required actions. Though grateful, I found myself unsure of exactly why he had agreed.

"Of course," I said, conscious that it was time to leave. "I appreciate it, Theo."

He nodded with a rather tense smile as I stood.

"Do you still have my number?" he asked, avoiding my eyes as he followed me down the hall, and I had to admit that yes, I did.

At the entrance, I reached out awkwardly to shake his hand, as though we'd concluded a business meeting, and in his brief half smile, I noticed warmth and sadness at once. When he opened the door for me, the air was chill and the whole sky seemed alive. Rain was still falling in great sheets. He handed me an umbrella and returned my wave before I began down the path.

It was only when I was back in the car, waiting for the wipers to clear the windshield, that I heard a knock at the window and jolted. It was Theo, holding his own umbrella, making an urgent ushering motion.

"Come back inside, Sylvia!" he yelled over the rain.

It was strange to be towel-drying my hair moments later on Theo's couch, while the storm raged and he stood to attention like some trooper by the kitchen bench, regarding me with a grave look.

"Sorry," I said. "I'm sure the weather will clear soon. Please carry on with your work—I can read one of your books while I wait."

My voice sounded thin. Suddenly I longed for a hot shower, and a soapie on the couch with Lionel.

"You can't be driving in this," he said. "And I wasn't making much progress on the paper I'm writing, anyway." He looked down at the floor, seeming nervous somehow. "It's getting late. We should eat something."

I asked what I could do, and padded over in my socks to where he stood now by the open cupboard. The time would pass more quickly, I thought, if I was being useful.

"I could make spaghetti," I said, pointing to a packet of pasta. He nodded vaguely, scanning the cupboard's interior like an archaeologist before a tomb. On the top shelf I could see canned tomatoes.

"What about those?" I asked, reaching. I was on my tiptoes, but the shelf was too high. Theo reached the cans easily, and when he brought them down we were facing each other between the open cupboard doors. A strange, dazed look had overtaken his face, as though he were suddenly unwell, and instead of setting the cans down on the bench or handing them over, he just rested them on a lower shelf, without looking away from me. He reached out to touch my hair, then, like he had done in January, only tonight he hadn't been drinking. I just stood there, waiting for him to return to himself, wondering what had changed, wanting him to keep touching me, as he leaned forward, shook his head, and said, "Oh, Sylvia," like a prayer in my ear.

Now, when we kissed, it was different. He seemed to take on a new resolve, a focus that hadn't existed before, as though only his body were now in control, and I wanted it, too, the freedom of mindlessness, of losing myself in sensation. When he raised me onto the bench, I began to remember what it was to have a body, the urgency of desire, the way it could blot out the world. I inhaled his hair, its faint herbal smell, and took hold of his shoulders, broad and tense through his shirt, until he lifted off my top and I felt his hands on my cold skin.

In the brief moment it took for him to carry me down the hall to his dim, Spartan bedroom, I wondered whether it had been as long for him as it had for me. I knew that should anything happen to break the motion of what our bodies were doing—if one of us spoke or coughed, or if I suddenly slipped from his arms and back onto my feet—the atmosphere we'd entered would lose its blind logic, we'd question the terms of our surrender, and arrive in the room self-conscious and separate again.

So I shut out my mind. For a second as we moved down the hall, I craned my neck back toward the window, like a sailor seeking north. But I couldn't see the comet.

In the morning, I watched the dawn light seep through the cracks in the blinds, rendering distinct those shapes that last night's gloom had hidden. My eyes traveled over the gray sheets, the yellow-cream walls, the old wingback armchair behind the door draped with discarded shirts. It was Monday, 6:30 a.m. according to the clock on the nightstand, and I had to check on Lionel before work. But I refused to hurry.

Lying there, I had the strange feeling of awakening to someone else's life, a new slipstream in time. Even if it was true that I couldn't escape myself, there was a relief in being without any familiar reference point.

Theo certainly didn't seem familiar, asleep beside me, motionless and breathing softly through his nose. His brow wore an almost imperceptible frown, as if he were trying to solve a problem within a dream. When my mind summoned scenes from the previous night, it was hard to believe that we had been the actors, wordless and hungry and knowing exactly what to do, and I felt my face grow hot. I tried not to think of Christopher. At the same time, I reminded myself that nothing I'd done was out of line with my new bargain—and it wasn't like Joseph's meditations were helping anymore. What Theo and I had done was just a dance, a blind movement of limbs, a means of release, and its purpose had been served—I felt more alert, more alive than I had in months.

I wondered whether it wouldn't be best to leave while he slept, and suspected that if I did, he'd be grateful. Wouldn't sneaking off avoid the risk of awkwardness for both of us, the floundering small talk, the mute measuring of each other's signals, the obligation to form conclusions? Maybe, but I was too curious to spare either of us some kind of reckoning. We had arrived beside each other on this particular morning, and I wanted to face him before I left.

I was watching the ceiling and examining the strange, vertiginous lightness that I felt in my head and chest, when I registered his gaze and realized he was awake.

"Hello," I said, turning on my pillow toward him.

He peered at me with a veiled look. "Hi."

"That was a surprise," I added. "I didn't know spaghetti held such allure for you."

He laughed. "Neither did I." When he looked furtively away and traced my arm with his hand, I felt faint.

"I need to get home," I noted after a pause, "and you probably have plans to scan for objects that could imperil Earth."

He didn't smile. Neither of us moved. I waited for him to say something, some coy or deflective end remark, but he said nothing. As I watched his face in the morning light, I recalled the moment weeks ago in the car together, when he'd pulled himself away with the words, "I can't," and wanted to ask him what had changed. But I felt that if I did, he might stop looking at me in the way he was now. Finally, when I reached out to touch his cheek, he kept still, before in one swift motion he grabbed hold of my shoulders and pinned me beneath him, and we found each other again as the daylight brightened in tiger stripes across our bodies on the bed, and I realized I didn't care if I'd be late for work.

Theo was subdued and businesslike when we met the next evening, at the Rising Sun for drinks. Judging from the shadows under his eyes, he was also tired. He had called me at work that morning to suggest we discuss how best to approach his talk with Sandy, and when we faced each other over our beers, it seemed that this was indeed the chief, and perhaps only, reason for his invitation.

"What are your thoughts?" he asked, leaning back in our leatherette booth and peering at me.

I knew he was referring to my thoughts about his speaking with Sandy, rather than my thoughts about the sex we'd had twice just forty-eight hours prior, but I wondered at the meaning of this agenda. Surely it was the wrong way around? If our encounter had been such an aberration, why had he let it happen? Why was he so slippery?

I looked into my glass, while my skin pricked with a feeling I could only identify as misplaced shame. Since the storm, I'd felt lighter, as though in letting my body take over, a layer of grit had been blown from my mind. But now I wasn't sure it hadn't all been a mistake.

"Sandy's birthday's coming up soon, on Good Friday," I said flatly. "If you're free that evening, I thought perhaps I could tell her I've arranged for a private comet-viewing with St. John's discoverer."

He nodded. "Okay, that could work."

I made myself smile and tried to remember he was doing me a favor—especially considering the public holiday—but I suddenly wondered why he had agreed to help in the first place—had it just been to get rid of me? I sighed. He hadn't been cool like this when we were in bed. But the hesitation, the private sadness that was present now in his face and gestures, that had been there, just like on the day we first met at Bell Funerals. Considering that this sadness was one of the things that had drawn me to him, perhaps I had no basis for complaint now. Perhaps that's what it was—just grief, just guilt at sharing his body with someone else, someone alive.

"It doesn't have to mean anything, Theo," I said suddenly.

Even though he stared at me blankly, I didn't doubt he knew what I meant.

"It's not like I'm looking for another husband," I added. "But being with you was a nice escape. I thought the feeling was mutual. If not, that's fine, but don't pretend nothing happened."

He nodded slowly as I spoke, and before peering down at the table I was sure a look of pain passed over his face.

"I'm sorry, Sylvia," he said. "I'm still surprised by it. I didn't mean to pretend nothing happened."

I waited for him to say more, watching him without blinking as he sat there with his eyes flitting between me and his glass, his lips parted for speech. I wondered at the phantom words gathering on his tongue, and for an instant imagined reaching out to shake him—he hadn't been so limp and evasive when he was naked. Then I remembered our hike weeks before—when he'd said, in a frank way I'd believed, that he'd like to have met me at a different time—and as I sat there I saw that the simple truth between us was that for him, it was too soon. We were on different timelines, borne on different waves of loss. Like me, he'd let his body take over. But I had been ready, and he had not.

I offered what I hoped was a conciliatory smile, and we drained our beers.

It was only minutes later, after Theo had ordered us another round and we were discussing a time for Sandy's viewing, in which he would point out in a routine manner how the only objects near the comet were ordinary stars, that I saw a movement at the edge of my eye that made me turn. It was Angus in his uniform, holding a schooner and clearly well on the way to inebriation. After leering at me, he raised his glass to Theo.

"Gee, am I glad to see you," he said. "This little bitch needs a new fella."

Swaying slightly, Angus took a sip while I looked on in horror, and Theo bristled before speaking with a sharpness I'd not heard before.

"What the hell are you talking about? Who are you?"

Angus laughed, red-faced and delirious. "She hasn't told you about her adventures, eh? No, I suppose she wouldn't."

Now as Theo moved to stand, Angus stepped forward and pointed his finger inches from my face. "My wife's had panic attacks because of you," he spat. "Just know, I have eyes all over this town."

His own eyes widened with menace, but seeing Theo standing he stepped back. "Settle down, Romeo," he said, dismissing us both with a wave before lurching away to the corner behind the bar, where another policeman whom I didn't know sat shaking his head and sniggering.

I felt like I'd been punched. I was aware of Theo sitting back down, but didn't want to lift my head.

"Sylvia," he said, touching my hand, but he sounded far away. After a moment, I felt him beside me, stroking my hair. "What was that about? You okay? What an asshole."

I nodded. "It's fine," I said, taking a gulp of beer. "He's just a bad man who hides behind his uniform, and expects to get away with it."

From the edge of my eye I saw him peer at me while I gazed into my glass, and I knew he was searching for the reasons behind Angus's rage. But he didn't press me further, and I felt a wave of relief. "Hey, come here," he said instead, and drew me toward him. It felt good to rest my head on his shoulder.

Later, when the initial shock of our encounter with Angus had passed and we'd eaten Cornettos on the steps of the general store, Theo walked me to my car under the rising comet and the new crescent moon. I was surprised when he drew me close again for a hug and said in a low voice that he had something to tell me. As I rested my cheek against his corduroy shirt pocket, noticing his fast heart, I could feel him looking up at the sky. His face was pale when we drew apart and he frowned for a moment over my shoulder before looking back.

"My contract ends in August," he said after a pause. He sighed and peered at his boots on the road. "I just thought you should know."

I nodded, wondering at the gravity of his delivery when his instinct earlier had been to brush aside the fact that we'd ever touched. I supposed that his contract's end might be a blow to him—positions that offered the time and scope to discover comets were surely rare. But after discovering a great comet, I didn't doubt there'd be another role waiting, perhaps back home in America.

"I'm sorry to hear that, but I'm under no illusions about us," I said finally with a smile. "I'll survive you leaving town," I added, play-punching his shoulder half-comically as he nodded stiffly, told me to keep clear of "that nutjob cop," and, with a promise to call, raised a hand to wave me goodbye.

When I arrived home, I sat for a moment in the darkness of the kitchen, thinking of Angus's leering face and his claim to have eyes all over town, Danny's surely among them. Trying to push the image of them both aside, I noticed the kitchen's familiar shapes grown strange, the hum of the fridge, the ticking clock, as Lionel brushed around my calves and a feeling reared into view like the shadow of an object too large to see, the feeling of my own essential solitude as a geological fact, monolithic and unshifting. Forcing myself to the fridge, I stood in its cool blue light and dropped cold green grapes into my mouth, aware of the indecent way their skin burst when I chewed. For a moment I wondered whether it was too late to call Sandy, before deciding to phone her regardless. I wanted to hear her voice.

"Oh hi, doll," she said brightly upon answering. I heard no hint of hesitation or tension in her tone, and figured she'd made peace with our near-quarrel on Sunday.

"How was the working bee?"

"Good, darl," she said mildly, as Terry let out a yap in the background and she directed him to sit. "Sorry, he was reminding me about his palate cleanser," she laughed. "Oh yes," she went on, "the working bee went well; we had a merry old time actually—we fit more bunk beds in the old house than we thought we would, and I'd say Joseph will get a good price for some of the stuff we moved out—nice antiques—shame to part with them, but what can you do?"

I tried to keep the moroseness from my voice when I interjected to ask why exactly she had been moving bunk beds around for Joseph on her weekend.

She cleared her throat. "Like I told you, love—it's so we don't have

to rely on tents during the festival—those of us on early and late du-
ties, you know. But they'll be useful after that for meditation retreats. I
certainly didn't do any heavy lifting at the bee—it was Roy and Danny
and some others, mostly—I just made the tea and sandwiches."

For a moment I moved the receiver from my mouth so I could sigh.

"And how are you doing, love?" Sandy asked in a glassy voice. "Feeling better?"

"Yes," I heard myself say. "Much better—I must have just been
tired."

"Oh, that's a relief," she said. I could hear her smiling. "It's a shame
you couldn't come to the bee—Joseph asked after you."

"I hope you gave him my apologies."

"Oh yes, he understands people are busy. Will you be joining us
this Thursday?"

"I hope so," I lied, "but it will depend on whether my sleep im-
proves."

"You poor pet. I'll have to make you some broth."

"I'll be okay. Actually, Sandy, I'm calling about a surprise for your
birthday."

"Oh, truly?" She laughed. I could see her fluffing her hair in delight.

"Yes—you'll love it, so keep your birthday evening clear, okay?"

"How mysterious! Well, my catch-up with the girls is at noon so
something in the evening is perfect. I'll look forward to it, sweetie."

After we said goodbye, I collapsed on the couch, exhausted from the
effort of affecting a breezy tone of voice, guilty at deceiving Sandy, and
worried at the prospect that she was starting to censor what she told
me. For an instant, twisting my rings around on my finger, I thought
of the comet, alight in the sky above the yard outside, and saw it for
the warning it was. Without it, I'd never have attended Joseph's meeting, and never have led Sandy to Joseph's door. If I was responsible for
getting her into Joseph's orbit, it was my task now to draw her out of it.

## 18.

SANDY'S BIRTHDAY, COINCIDING WITH THE START OF EASTER, FELL on the last Friday of March, a warm, windless day. In my mind, the date had become a limit beyond which none of us would have to travel. When I imagined Sandy bringing her eye to the telescope to see the comet close up, the facts as Theo spoke them would work like incantations to break Joseph's spell. But running like a current beneath my hope was doubt, and the fear that this was fantasy.

It was with a breathless, live-wire feeling that I drove us that evening, down the dark road to the observatory. The comet had risen above the horizon and was bright overhead, not far from the moon, as the mountains formed a black mass in the distance. As Sandy chattered I watched them, trying to deflect the slippery feeling of deception.

"I feel quite virtuous, declining that fried ice cream. Are you absolutely stuffed, too, Sylv?"

She sighed happily and peered out the window as I agreed that dinner, at one of the few restaurants that had remained open for the public holiday, had been delicious.

"Aren't you a lady of mystery?" she added. "I don't have a clue where we're headed." She leaned back, checking her coral-colored nails with a sigh. "But who doesn't love a birthday surprise!"

Theo, who had left the boom gates open for us, was waiting outside the dome when we arrived. I could see his glowing cigarette.

"The observatory?" Sandy exclaimed as we got out of the car. "Oh, Sylvia!"

As we neared, Theo straightened, stamped out his cigarette, and smiled. "Evening, Sandy," he said, shaking her hand. "Happy birthday. I'm Theo."

"Theo St. John," I said, with a pointed look at her as we stepped inside.

"No!" she said, wide-eyed. "The comet's discoverer? What magic has Sylvia worked to arrange this? Oh, wait until I tell Joseph!"

I sighed inwardly as Theo rested his hands in his pockets. In the second before he smiled, I noticed a private shadow pass over his face and wondered what had caused it.

"I'm glad you're pleased," he said. "We have decent conditions tonight. Can I make you some tea or coffee before the viewing?"

"Oh, aren't you a man after my own heart? I'd love a tea."

"You Aussies are mad about tea," he said warmly from over his shoulder as we followed him into the control room. "I'm more of a coffee guy myself."

When I suggested that with the hours astronomers often had to keep, this was hardly surprising, he nodded and looked pointedly at Sandy.

"It's true," he said, while the kettle boiled. "Sometimes at dawn, I feel like a vampire ready to rest in his coffin!"

When Sandy joked that he should seek a discount from me for a premium model, I didn't mention he'd already received the full tour. I watched as she munched a shortbread and asked Theo where in the US he was from, content as a child who had won a prize, and only hoped her good humor would last.

Ten minutes later, I was leaning against the dome's back wall with Sandy's handbag on one arm, watching as she stepped onto the ladder and brought her eye to the finderscope lens to view the comet.

"Oh, isn't it marvelous!" she said to Theo after a pause. "And seemingly so near!"

With shining eyes, she turned from the lens to look at him. "Did you realize it would be so bright, when you discovered it? Are you on the hunt for a new comet? How do you know Sylvia?"

"Sandy," I said, "Theo agreed to give you a viewing, not an interview."

But he waved away her apologies. "We never really know exactly how bright a comet will be at its nearest point until the time comes, but we can guess," he explained. "I did think it would be bright, if only because it's so large. And really, the comet found me. I was just stargazing with a portable telescope in my own yard, at the time. Usually when I'm here, I'm surveying for near-Earth asteroids."

"Oh, truly? That sounds exciting!" Sandy waited to hear more.

"It can be," Theo shrugged. "But mostly, survey astronomy is ninety-nine percent watching, and one percent action. Actually, my grandfather used to say the same about his time navigating US Navy salvage ships during the war. He used to say that most collisions at sea only happened because no one was looking out the window."

He smiled. "I guess sometimes," he added, "I feel like I'm the only one looking out the window."

Sandy peered up at the dome's opening overhead. "And your ocean," she said wistfully, "is the sky!"

"The southern sky," he nodded, before adjusting the telescope with the remote, and, with a veiled glance at me, inviting her to look again.

"I thought you might be interested in the region of space the comet's passing through," he said. "It's about to cross from Libra into Scorpius, now. You'll see it very near the moon, tonight—a great time to take photos. St. John's closest neighbors are changing all the time."

When Theo asked Sandy to step aside so he could adjust the lens again, she shot me a coy look and winked, motioning her head in Theo's direction, and I sensed that she was perhaps enjoying the viewing for the wrong reasons.

"Look again," he said now. "This is the region of Libra the comet was in last month, when the telescopic photo was taken. The star you see in the center of the lens is called Alpha Librae, a spectroscopic binary star, the second brightest in the constellation. Usually, only the brightest star in a constellation is assigned the name Alpha, but this is a variable star, so its magnitude changes. Anyway, Alpha Librae happens to be the star that was diffracted in the amateur photo, giving a saucer-like appearance."

Sandy gave a philosophical sigh and drew her eye back from the lens. "I see," she said, looking narrowly at me before smiling at Theo. "It's a beautiful star."

I waited for her to remark on the absence of any alien spacecraft, but instead she peered archly at Theo and asked, "Did you hear about the Phoenix Lights, a few weeks ago? How do you explain hundreds of people seeing the same thing?"

Theo nodded, and gave her a careful look. "I don't doubt they saw something. My sister lives in Phoenix and she witnessed the lights, too. It's just that those lights could have been caused by a host of things other than alien craft."

"Well, the explanations about military flares don't seem very convincing," she said, stepping down from the ladder. "Joseph says that another explanation for UFOs, aside from aliens, is that we ourselves—humans from the future—have found a way to travel back in time, without disrupting the course of history. Doesn't it make your mind boggle?"

"It's a pretty wild idea."

Sandy gave a listless shrug. "So was flying to the moon, until we discovered how to do it—that's if the landing wasn't staged."

"Well, we have the moon rocks to prove it," he said gently, before noting how multiple space programs, including Apollo, had left metal reflector plates on the moon that, with the right laser device, could still reflect light back to us on Earth as a means of measuring our distance.

"Anyway," he continued, "I'm not saying that aliens or even time travel are impossible. Like most astronomers, my bet is that extraterrestrial life exists somewhere. But generally, if we're guided by the principle of Occam's razor, we'd hypothesize that given multiple possible explanations for any single event—like an amateur capturing an unusual shape in space—the one requiring the fewest assumptions is most likely to be correct."

Sandy made a doubtful sound and fiddled with one peacock earring, unwilling to concede. Then she peered at Theo with a bold, bemused look, and in a tone that signaled a change of topic, declared that she could tell he was a bit of a dark horse, while she winked at me, and I recalled my misgivings about the birthday champagne.

"You two are similar—noses to the grindstone," she went on. "With her, it's all about funerals. With you, it's all about space."

She made a perplexed zigzag motion with her forefinger now while darting mirthful looks at us both. "These days most of the new people my dear Sylvia encounters are already embalmed, so tell me, how and when did you two meet?"

When I interjected to suggest we'd met at Joseph's Memorial Hall talk, she nodded happily.

"That's Joseph, always bringing people together in divine timing," she said. "But really, Sylvia—fancy not telling me about meeting St. John himself!"

At some point during the drive home—between Sandy's urging that I acknowledge what a dish Theo was ("Oh, Sylvia, are you blind? He's like a rough-hewn Gregory Peck!"), and her insistence that the entire cohort of Kingdom Come might attend a special viewing one night to attune more readily to cosmic energies—I began to see how spectacularly my plan had failed.

"Don't you think it's interesting," I said as we neared town, "that even through the telescope, there was nothing to see near the comet but ordinary stars? Don't you think it's interesting that Theo, with all his expertise, doesn't believe in Joseph's UFO theory?"

From the edge of my vision, I saw her shoulders lurch in a sigh, before she leaned back in her seat and looked at me.

"Let's not disagree on my birthday, sweetie. Given the eyewitness literature, it wouldn't seem impossible for a UFO to be able to appear and disappear quickly. Anyway, I told you, it's neither here nor there to me, whether there are green men in the sky or not."

We were silent as we reached the intersection, and waited for the lights to change.

"But doesn't it matter to you," I asked, when we continued on, "whether Joseph's feeding everyone a lie?"

"He doesn't think it is a lie," she said, "and I'm not convinced, either, frankly. Who really knows? And governments can be so sneaky. Anyway, Sylvia, I can see what all this was about. Theo was sweet to agree to it, your plan to pull the wool from my eyes—he must like you."

I sighed. It was as though a puncture had opened in my skin; I could almost hear the hiss of my spirit escaping.

"You know no one can replace Christopher," I said finally.

"Maybe not, but you can't keep living on rations, Sylvia. And stop worrying about me—I've never felt better."

After we said goodbye and I drove home alone, I saw that in a way, it was true. The question of whether the view through Theo's telescope showed spacecraft or ordinary stars was peripheral to the fact that through Joseph's eyes, Sandy saw a world in which Christopher's spirit had somewhere survived—and that was not a version of reality she would easily surrender.

When, the next morning, Vince called to confirm that in addition to there being no progress to report on Christopher's case—the results from his test on the tea dregs were inconclusive—the limp, hopeless feeling I'd risen with spread out from me like rays. The results from my blood test had been the same, leaving me without hard evidence for driving Sandy away from Joseph, and without proof that my recent dreamlike episodes were chemical rather than psychological.

"Really, Sylv," Vince said, with a note of impatience before ringing off, "I'm not saying your suspicions are wrong, but we have no proof. So let it rest now. You've stopped attending the sessions, that's the main thing."

I didn't bother to say that, as I saw it now, sparing myself from the sessions seemed tantamount to sacrificing Sandy. He wouldn't want to hear it. I felt him spinning away from me in space, propelled toward other constellations by the breathless orbits of work and family life, like the Sydney friends I never saw, like my mother, while for all my efforts to move forward, I stood still.

The only person I really wanted to speak to was Theo. I needed to thank him, and earlier that morning, he had called to suggest we debrief at a café in town. The thought of seeing him helped to moderate my disappointment about the news from Vince, and I found myself putting on a sundress, brushing my hair, and dabbing color on my lips, like a dealer might polish a piece of reclaimed silver. As I wandered toward High Street under a glaring white sky, I thought about how, where Theo was concerned, I still felt at sea. In the days since our meeting at the pub, we had spoken on the phone and, the previous Saturday, shared dinner before ending the night in my bed. But sometimes I felt it was only our bodies that seemed able to broach the distance between us.

When I arrived, Theo was already seated at a streetside table, wearing a Grateful Dead T-shirt emblazoned with a skull. Seeing me, he stood, and there was something surer about the way he gripped my waist when we kissed. After we ordered coffee and he had complimented my dress, I filled him in on my conversation with Sandy in the car the previous night.

"Not really the reaction we'd hoped for, was it?" he said finally.

"No," I said, noticing the brightness of his eyes and thinking of how rarely I'd seen him in daylight. "But we shouldn't be surprised. I've been naive. Perhaps I just have to let her be—brainwashing isn't a crime. Anyway, thanks for the viewing."

"No problem," he said, as our coffees arrived. "I'm sorry it didn't work."

We both looked into our cups. I didn't know what else to say. I had a sudden vision of him taking charge, like some renegade hero in a frontier film. "Stay here," I imagined him saying from his mount on a steed, as I looked up from my footing on a dusty street. "I'll be back by nightfall," he added with a steely resolve, before bolting for the hinterlands to confront our blue villain while I waited in a rocker by the hearth.

He sighed now and looked out at the street, before explaining that he wanted to help. "I know what it's like," he said, "to see someone you love drifting away due to someone else's powers of control."

At my probing look, he peered glumly at the table and told me about how his older sister had once been lured into a nutritional supplement pyramid scheme. "After a year and a half, she was almost bankrupt," he added, "with a bathtub full of Vital Youth formula she couldn't sell."

"That's awful," I said, taking a sip, before admitting that I felt like my only option now was to keep Sandy close by doing what I could not to antagonize Joseph.

Sighing, I explained how Joseph's plans for his festival had been gaining traction, from endorsement by the local council to coverage in two national newspapers—all amid rumors that he was flying in the Oracles, a folk-pop quartet known for their international 1966 hit, "Starship Woman," a development that only caused Theo to look glum and roll his eyes.

"In my more hopeful moods," I said finally, "I wonder whether this delirium of Joseph's will pass with the comet, once the festival's over."

Theo scoffed. "Well, I don't like to dispel hope, but Joseph was mad long before the comet."

His voice was dark in a way I couldn't quite place, but I supposed he was thinking of the susceptibility that had to already exist in a person, to allow their hold on reality to be so derailed by an object in the sky.

He smiled when I changed the subject and asked whether there were any galactic updates I should know about.

"Nothing too exciting. Unless speculation about upcoming conditions for Leonid meteor storms is your cup of tea."

"Oh well," I said, "for all we know, you could discover another great comet next week."

He looked at his hands. "I'm not sure that's something any of us need."

The end of his sentence was drowned out by a sudden noise, and we looked up to see an elderly man in a tattered cardigan yelling hoarsely, swaggering toward us from the direction of the Rising Sun. He tottered on his feet for a moment before steadying, and raised his bleary eyes up at the clouded sky. A groan came then, as though from deep within him, and he squinted as if watching an eclipse. "We're out of time!" he hollered suddenly, shaking his head and raising a hand to his temple as though to contain the pressure in his brain. As my eyes moved past him to a young couple who avoided his gaze as they walked by holding ice creams, I caught sight of a figure standing motionless on the other side of the street. It was Danny, looking right at me. His usually impassive face was alert, fixated, while his backpack dangled from one limp hand and his feet stood planted a pace apart, beside his shiny new car.

"Who's that?" I heard Theo ask, but the entire span of my attention had contracted to the single point of Danny's face lifting into a sly, confounding smile.

Feeling as though my attention was feeding him somehow, I forced my eyes away and drew a deep breath to steady myself. Recalling Theo's question, I shook my head. "It's no one—no one I want to think about, anyway," I said, and tried to quell Theo's perturbed look with a weak smile.

But even as I leaned back and asked Theo what he'd do once his contract expired in August, all I could think about was Danny and what that strange, slippery smile of his had meant.

Theo, deliberating over my question, looked lost for a moment. I could almost see the child he had once been, before he answered in a glum, distant voice.

"Probably look for another program that'll pay me to scan for objects with close to zero likelihood of impacting Earth, on the basis that if one of them does, the devastation could be infinite."

"So you're the insurance policy?"

He nodded. "The asteroid impact event over Siberia in 1908 likely wasn't more than seventy meters in diameter, but it destroyed two thousand square kilometers of forest. Imagine if that hit Sydney or New York. The odds say it's a matter of when, although admittedly it could be in a few hundred years, or a few thousand."

He looked at me as I set down my empty cup, and, looking back at the street, found that Danny had gone. "I'll probably end up back home somewhere," he added. "What about you? Will you stick around in Jericho, doing funerals?"

I told him I assumed so, considering that moving would require a clearer vision of the future than I could currently summon, although, sitting there, the idea of it made me feel as though a huge wave were slowly coming to drown me.

Before he left, we made a date for the Sunday-night screening at the Theatre Royal. When we kissed for a long while at the door, and the lightness of desire returned to fade my fearful thoughts, I recalled again why it was that I'd finally let myself be pulled toward him. The opium of intimacy, albeit with a man as ambivalent about the future as I was and whose days in town were numbered, did provide a kind of pain relief. It was, I felt as I waved him goodbye, a relief far stronger than any I'd found in meditations with Joseph.

As I ate a sandwich on the porch, I tried to summon the will to steer myself toward Bakers Road that night to resume my observations of Joseph and the group, for Sandy's sake. But at the thought of seeing Danny, I couldn't face it.

When the doorbell rang later that afternoon, I'd just returned from the local pool, where I'd swum for the first time in years. Despite the screaming children and stink of chlorine, the steady motion of laps in water had induced in me a cavernous, calm feeling. But the feeling drained as soon as I opened the door to find Sandy on the step, holding Terry and her house keys. She seemed breathless and harried, as she faced me with a tight smile.

"Sweetie, I need you to tend to my garden for a spell," she said, as I stood there frowning. "Not for long, I don't think," she added, looking anxious.

When I asked why, she glanced away and sighed. "I'm needed at

Bakers Road, and there's just so much to organize that it's best if I assist on-site for now."

"Sandy, this is ridiculous," I said. "In what universe are you needed around the clock at Bakers Road to help prepare for a one-day regional festival that's months away?"

She held out the keys. "Sylvia, please. Can you look after my garden while I'm gone? Instructions are on the kitchen bench."

Because I couldn't bear to hear her beg, I found myself nodding against all reason, and felt the sour turn of my mouth.

As she thanked me and promised to be in touch, I had the sensation of the world inverting: while I had decided to face life and reality by Sandy's side, she was escaping, or so it seemed to me.

I could barely believe it, seconds later, when I stood there watching her drive away with Terry, leaving me and her tea roses behind, in her blind devotion to a man I no longer pitied. Now when I heard Joseph's name in my mind, I felt only bitterness.

For a while, I drank wine on the couch with Lionel draped over my shoulder. As the sun sank down, I imagined Sandy arriving with Terry and her luggage at Bakers Road like a starry-eyed girl at scout camp, only to be put to work in the kitchen. She was the second person I loved to end up at the mercy of a man who did what he wanted while I looked on, powerless despite my efforts. Yet even Vince now looked at me as though I were the mad one, simply for not giving up.

Regardless, as I sat there, winded and cold on the couch, I saw that I could no more stop Sandy in her quest to follow Joseph than I could stop the moon from rising.

I had to let her go.

But when night fell I couldn't sleep, or stop thinking about Danny and the reprobate who'd bought his silence, and without admitting to myself what I was doing, I found myself enacting an old ritual, a ritual I told myself was discreet enough to be harmless. And so with the slow motions of a sleepwalker I rose from bed, pulled on my coat, and slipped out the door, only to coast without headlights all the way to Jubilee Street. I sat parked there, a few doors from Angus's house under the shadow of a peppercorn tree, watching his windows with a mind suddenly drained of thought. I couldn't have stopped there for more than five minutes before returning to my senses, and driving away.

On Sunday morning I woke late, with Lionel sleeping on my head. Feeling sick about Sandy, I tried and failed to lose myself in New York's Gilded Age with Edith Wharton, before deciding to drive to Theo's. It was hours before we'd planned to meet at the Theatre Royal, but I hoped that sharing my worry with him, and perhaps taking a walk together, might lighten the sense of dread that had settled inside me overnight like a chill. I gripped the wheel too tightly, and kept sighing to relieve the tightness in my chest as I drove, and had a brief fantasy of myself as a mole, burrowing deep into the rich, dark, silent earth and never again needing to raise my head aboveground in this lifetime or any other.

When I knocked several times to no response, I felt bereft, and irritated at myself for not calling first. Limply, I sank down on his step to gather strength for the drive back home. It was only then that I noticed the corner of paper poking out from under the door. Moved by curiosity and boredom, I pulled it out to find a note written by hand on a folded A4 sheet. The first time I read it, I felt slow and dumb; the words had no effect. The second time, a wave of heat moved through me.

IT WOULD BE A SHAME TO LOSE HER, the note said. I knew it could only be from one person. It was just the kind of crude, brutish threat I imagined a man like Angus might make, and I remembered how he had taken notice of Theo at the Rising Sun. Clearly, he had decided he might have more luck getting to me via my lover, and he was right. I stuffed the note in my pocket, deciding that Theo couldn't know. If I told him about the note, he'd want the full story of what I'd done to enrage Angus—my vigilante drive-bys, my fit of rage with the porch light, my personal violence order—and then whatever existed between us would surely shrivel back into nothing.

I recalled what Angus had said at the Rising Sun, that he'd be watching me, and clearly he'd been telling the truth. I wasn't sure now that it hadn't been at Angus's express instruction that Danny had materialized at just the right time yesterday, to surveil and spook me in the middle of High Street. Trudging back to the car, I cursed myself for pulling up at Jubilee Street again last night, when I could have simply stayed at home. Evidently, Angus had seen me: I had not, as I'd fancied, melted into the night.

Driving away, I tried to tell myself that while I'd been stupid to go there again and unlucky to be caught, it had been a momentary lapse, a mistake. As long as it didn't happen again, the threats would cease and he'd stay away. I longed to believe this as the gray sky pressed down and I drove, trying to breathe, trying not to imagine Angus loitering outside my own house, looking to frighten or possibly silence me forever.

# 19.

As St. John moved from Libra, the scales, into Scorpius, the creature with the venomous sting, I lost the ability to walk alone at night without looking perpetually over my shoulder. Sometimes, lying in bed, when the floorboards creaked or branches brushed my window or a car idled outside, I would jolt upright in fear for my life. I'd told Vince about Angus's note, but as with Joseph's tea and Danny's obstruction of justice, I was met with the same impediment: insufficient evidence.

Meanwhile, as the leaves of the trees in my street reddened and fell, I felt Sandy, who remained at Bakers Road, slipping further away. As promised, she called now and then, and was always at pains to say she was well. This seemed true enough, but now in the false brightness of her voice and the trepidation of her pauses, I felt the distance between us.

If this were an old film, the footage might jump now to the pages of a calendar turning, or to autumn leaves scuttling across a cold street. The point is, time quickened for a while, and when I peer back, I see it was because those days were the ebb of a tide going out, gathering force before the flood.

In a quiet, furtive way, as the comet continued to brighten into April and May, Theo and I settled into a routine of seeing each other once or twice a week. We'd share dinner and see a movie, or hike in the mountains near the observatory, and when we spent the night together I'd escape the fears that assailed me when I slept alone. Although we were each aware of its inevitability, we spoke little now of his return to America. For the meantime we each had companionship amid our solitude, and while it lasted, it seemed to suit us both well. Often, when

I visited him on weekends and it grew late, we'd sit in deck chairs on his porch and watch the dark skies of Jericho, and during these times with him amid the brightness of space, I'd feel lighter, forgetting Angus and my worries about Sandy. He would point out details I missed, and beside him in the cool air I'd be reminded of the nights I spent over star maps with my father.

Theo seemed to hold such maps in his head, and sometimes in his explanations—of the Blinking Eye Nebula, of supernova remnants and elliptical galaxies—he would lose me entirely. All the while, his namesake in the sky returned our gaze. One night in May, as we sat in sweaters on his porch, after I'd been quizzing him on the stars over wine, he had joked that I would make a terrible astronomer, given that I was more interested in the poetry of names and symbols and myths than I was in mathematics or physics. I agreed heartily, and told him to remind me again of what constellations the comet was heading for next as it reared closer to our planet on its way to its brightest appearance in August. Obliging me, he spoke the words in my ear, his voice soft and amused: "*Ophiuchus, Sagittarius, Microscopium.*"

With closed eyes, I heard these constellations as a prayer, a prophecy, a rosary to remember. Not because the comet would never pass through those regions again while we were alive, but because its passage through them in the months to come also marked the time Theo and I had left together. Already the comet, still skirting the ecliptic, was blazing above us from sunset every day, arriving high in the sky by midnight to remain conspicuous until dawn, a blue-green beacon with tails already twenty degrees long. And every night it rose higher, reached closer, grew brighter in preparation for its peak in August, for which the whole world was waiting. But whenever I saw St. John now, I recalled the end of Theo's contract.

The woman I was back then could never have foreseen what was coming, and I can't reach back into the past to warn her. Because even though I locked my door at night when Theo wasn't with me—and though I scanned the world with an alertness that lent cars and shadows and ordinary objects a pulsing significance they'd never owned—I still couldn't have guessed that nearly three years after my first death, I would die again. The shadow of my death hovered over me already, like a dark sun above my body, or the wing of an angel who had long marked me, and it was drawing closer each day.

At the end of May, when St. John was en route for the brightest reaches of our galaxy, I received a phone call that left me shaken. It was late on a Sunday after an evening with Theo, and I was still thinking of a star called Betelgeuse, growing huge and luminous before its moment of reckoning, likely thousands of years hence, when we ourselves, and everyone we knew, would be gone. Hours earlier, just after sunset, over pizza on his porch as St. John was rising with Scorpius in the northeast, Theo had pointed out Betelgeuse in the constellation of Orion. It was a red supergiant, he'd explained—an old star running low on fuel, at risk of burning out, in danger of collapsing on itself even as it expanded.

"The question for all red supergiants," he'd said, as I stood to crane my neck, "is when they will explode into supernovae, before fading out as nebulae. We likely won't be around long enough to see Betelgeuse do either, but if we are, it will be quite a show, better even than St. John, and as bright as the full moon during the day." Then suddenly he was standing behind me with his arms around my middle and his chin on my crown while we peered together at the moon. He did such things now, although sometimes it still surprised me.

Later, as I entered my dark house, the sound of the phone jolted me out of my dreamy state. When I reached it, I was breathless, and fearful that because of the late hour it was somehow Angus, delivering a new threat. But it was Sandy I heard through the receiver, her voice low and hushed.

"Sylvia," she said, "I just wanted to say good night."

There was a delay when I asked if she was okay.

"Oh, yes. Keeping busy. We built a firepit last week to usher in the dark part of the year."

Haltingly, she went on to explain how she had sung a song for Christopher. "A lullaby, really. 'All the Pretty Little Horses.' I'm sure I sounded ridiculous, but I sang it to him when he was little. I thought—I hoped—he might hear me. Through the veil between worlds."

She took a tremulous breath and spoke again, suddenly on the verge of tears. "I wanted him to send me a sign. Just something! I've been so patient." She trailed off, before uttering, like a plea, "Oh, my son!"

"I'm so sorry, Sandy," I said, and continued after a pause. "Can you tell me what else is going on? What's happening at Bakers Road?"

She sighed. "It's Joseph," she said eventually. "I don't think he's sleeping much. He's become quite short-tempered."

I waited for more, but could hear only her shallow breathing.

When she spoke again her voice sounded muffled. "I don't mean to worry you, love. It's just that over the last few weeks, I've felt so tired, and I've started to wonder now what—"

But I could make out nothing more. A rush of static entered my ear, before the disconnect tone began its dull beep. Again and again, I returned the call, but each time it rang out. And so, I was left alone in my living room as the clock ticked toward 10 p.m., wondering what she had meant to say.


By the next afternoon, I was unable to quell my sense that something was wrong. All morning in my spare moments at work I'd peered out at the white sky, telling myself that if Sandy needed help, she would ask me. As for why she hadn't yet called me back at home or work, to at least conclude last night's conversation, I supposed it was for the same reason we'd been cut off in the first place—some sudden issue with Joseph's telephone connection. But I couldn't stop thinking about how unlike herself Sandy had sounded, how fragile and flat. And I couldn't help wondering whether she had in fact called in fear of something or someone, needing help but unable to ask for it in time.

When the afternoon chapel service began, I was greeting mourners like a puppet, focused as I was on rolling visions of terrible things—

Joseph in an insomniac rage, a home invasion by crazed youths seeking drug money, Sandy collapsing from a stroke or aneurysm with no one awake to call for an ambulance. These scenarios, too, I reasoned, could explain our rudely disconnected call—and yet here I was, presiding over an event of no mortal danger to anyone, handing out booklets. By the time the recessional hymn began, I was clammy and breathless, and returned to my desk as fast as I could without running. On a whim I called Theo at home, where he'd been napping before his observatory shift. After apologizing for waking him, I detailed the scope of my misgivings in a frenzied rush until he agreed to meet me on High Street in thirty minutes' time.

He looked weary when he arrived in his Holden and I jumped in beside him, although he squeezed my shoulder and tried to offer a bolstering smile.

"I'm sure she's fine," he said. "It'll be alright."

As we drove down the highway out of town, I was glad of his calm presence, glad that I was wasting no more time.

The sun had lowered in the sky when we arrived. Even before we were out of the car, I was scanning for signs of some kind of disaster. But the property looked much the same—the faded flag still flapped in the breeze above the raised schoolhouse, and the larger farmhouse stood innocuously beyond, its windows yellow with light. Here and there were signs of industry related to the festival—posts erected near the road for some kind of awning and what looked like a platform built into a natural rise behind the main house, but to these I paid little attention.

Theo and I ascended the stairs of the schoolhouse quickly, to find ourselves alone in the late-afternoon gloom, breathing in the smell of old sandalwood incense. I sounded a tentative hello, but no one came, and we found Joseph's office empty. Before we left, I noticed a new addition to the main room, a cryptic homemade poster stuck above one of the windows. A-TEAM, it said, in bright curly letters, inside the crude shape of a rocket. Theo and I peered at it together before catching our reflections at the same time in the nearby mirror, looking shadowed and gaunt like figures in a dystopian comic book.

Moments later as we walked up the path to the main house where a half-dozen cars were parked, my eye caught a flash of brightness, like a spot fire in the fields beyond. Only when we drew closer did I recognize it as Joseph's mother's shrine, wreathed now in the marigolds of traditional Indian weddings. At the door I felt a vague desire to say a silent prayer, but only pressed the buzzer, which was mounted inside the grinning mouth of a brass frog.

It was Danny who answered. He held a Sprite in one hand and kept the door ajar with the other, regarding us blankly. I drew a deep breath—it was the first time I'd seen him at close range since the morning on High Street when he'd branded me with his awful smile, but he showed me only indolent disinterest now, before glancing at Theo as though recognizing his image from the papers.

"It's Sylvia and Theo!" he yelled out.

An instant later Danny slid away and Joseph appeared, wearing a fringed rainbow poncho and a tense look.

"Sylvia. To what do we owe the pleasure?" he asked, opening the door a few inches wider and offering a faint smile, before looking pointedly at Theo. "And you've brought Mr. Theo St. John. What an honor."

"We've come to see Sandy," I said.

Stepping aside for us to finally enter, Joseph began apologizing for being unprepared for such esteemed company, and issued orders for Zara to prepare a round of Russian apple tea. As Joseph led us over to sit at a long dining table and tried to engage Theo in conversation, I scanned the space and wondered what kind of a reception I'd have been met with had I come alone.

Danny was now slouched in an adjacent sitting room a few yards beyond, watching *Star Trek* on a flounced floral sofa. Roy sat by a computer at a Victorian credenza along the opposite wall, eyeing us sidelong from his swivel chair and fiddling with a video camera. Behind us through an open door, I glimpsed a kitchen bench arrayed with the products of industrial-scale cooking—whole pumpkins sat beside pallets of rice and lentils, while a twenty-liter pot of something smelling of beans heated on the stove.

All around, a multitude of fringed and stained glass lamps cast shadows, while a female voice wailed softly from a cassette player in the kitchen. I couldn't see Sandy anywhere. Joseph, despite his efforts, was failing to draw from Theo more than monosyllabic answers to his flurry of questions. "I have to ask, Theo," he was saying now, with a hint of tension, "whether you've given any further thought to speaking at the festival?"

"Joseph," I interrupted, refusing his delays, "I'm here to see Sandy— where is she?"

He let out a puff of air and eyed me with a miffed look. "I'll give you the tour after our tea," he said breezily.

Before I could object, Theo spoke. "Sylvia, why don't you go on ahead and find Sandy? I'll stay here and discuss the festival with Joseph."

As Joseph exclaimed with delight and refocused on Theo, I took my chance, sailing away down the hall without looking back.

I found her in a small bedroom near the back door, in a carved rocking chair facing a window to the garden and pastures beyond, with Terry on her lap. She was sitting so still that I thought she might be asleep, but when I moved in the doorway, she turned around.

"Sylvia," she said with a strange smile, as though she'd long been expecting me, "do you see those roses?" She shifted toward me as I stepped inside to sit on the edge of the bed beside her.

Despite all I wished to ask and say, instinct told me to tread gently, as I nodded at the magenta-colored flowers clustered just outside the windowpane. "I saved them," she added. "They were failing before I arrived, but they're happy now."

Leaning forward, I brushed a strand of hair from her eye and took in the ashen pallor of her face while she looked out at the flowers and the darkening sky, where the comet hung like a silver firebird above the gibbous moon.

"I've been worried about you," I said.

She turned back toward me and tapped my knee. "I'm sorry. I didn't call you back, did I? I've just been so tired today. Joseph said I fainted."

For a moment I didn't speak, shocked as I was not just by her words but by her low, breathy voice, her sunken shoulders, the general transformation of her energy and countenance. When I asked whether she meant that she had fainted last night, in the middle of our phone call, she nodded blithely and looked into her lap, where a thick red hardback sat unopened. I tried to contain my rage at Joseph, neglecting to tell me about Sandy fainting, yet happy to crow about his festival to St. John's discoverer.

"I'm a fool," she said finally, pursing her lips even as her chin quivered.

Unsure of her meaning, I only reached for her hand, and looked out with her at the sky until she spoke again in a shaky voice.

"I tell you, Sylvia—I curse that comet your friend found." She peered through the window with a narrow, wincing look, as her eyes welled up and the edge of her mouth hardened and I scanned the obtuse title of the book in her lap: *Isis Unveiled*, it declared, in small black print.

"It's all a blasted lie," she muttered now, wiping at her eyes with her cardigan sleeve before bowing her head. There was a pause as we sat together, in a silence marked only by Terry's snuffling and the low rustle of some creature in the wall behind us. I wasn't yet sure how to interpret her meaning, or what exactly to say. But when she spoke next, the words rang in my ears like cathedral bells.

"I want to go home."

As the warmth of relief spread through me, perched there on the bed holding her cold hand, my eye fell on a small amber dropper bottle on the sideboard. HOLISTIC ANTIBACTERIAL IMMUNE SUPPORT: VIBRANT LIFE COLLOIDAL SILVER, it read.

We packed quietly and without hurry, despite the flutter in my stomach. I thanked heaven for Theo's presence, keeping Joseph and his ego absorbed a hundred meters away. Each time Sandy paused, opening a drawer or glancing out the dark window, my heart lurched at the prospect that she might have changed her mind. As I folded dresses and sweaters into her suitcase, I maintained a light chatter that sounded, to my rational self, mildly insane, like the self-soothing way Tania spoke in the basement. It was, I supposed, a way of bridging space—the space between us, and the space between being there in Joseph's house and being at last outside it.

"There we are, just about done!" I said, when she had handed me her last pair of socks and I drew the zipper closed. "Do you want to pop on your shoes?" I added brightly, as if to a child.

While she pulled on her loafers and tied back her hair, I slipped the bottle of colloidal silver into my pocket and hauled the suitcase toward the door, hardly breathing as we entered the hall with Terry.

Joseph and Theo were still at the table when we approached, and for the seconds that passed before they noticed us, I took in the way Theo was talking, while Joseph sat rigid with focus as he cradled a china teacup. From Theo's halting speech and flat tone and from the stiff way he held his shoulders, I could tell that he was loathing every moment, and the fact of our situation struck me afresh as I peered. On a Monday evening before scanning the skies, Theo was submitting to the exertion and indignity of a stage act to humor and decoy a man he disliked, for no reason other than to help me. Something surged in my chest, for it struck me as evidence I could not refute. However alone I might have been, it seemed I was not so alone anymore.

Their eyes were upon us now, their chatter broken off. Sandy and I drew still a few paces away with the wheeled suitcase between us. I couldn't read Joseph's face and tried not to look at Theo's, which was frozen with concern. Joseph, with his slightly open mouth and eyes darting from me to Sandy, looked momentarily like someone following the final play in a tennis match.

"We're heading off," I heard myself say, my tone curt and perfunctory. I set my right foot forward in readiness to keep striding, waiting for Theo to rise and hoping Sandy would follow along.

I stood there as Joseph's face broke into a perplexed smile. He craned his neck at the suitcase, and at Sandy, who stood silently beside it.

"An outing, ladies?"

"I'm taking Sandy home, Joseph," I said, as Theo slid from his seat. "She's been here too long already."

I waited for the sharp words, the angry eruption—any number of land mines could reveal themselves, I thought, in the time it took to venture from the dining area to the front door. But he met me with a cool gaze, before standing as we all began moving toward the door. Danny, Zara, and Roy all peered in silence from their stations around the wide room, as though watching a stage, while I discerned the warped opening strains of "Running Up That Hill" floating from the stereo, a sound at once uplifting and absurd as we arrived to cluster woodenly at the entrance.

"Well, this is a surprise," Joseph said as we blinked at each other. He looked at the three of us in turn with a wounded sharpness before patting Sandy's shoulder and speaking to her in a soft, rueful tone. "Did you think I'd stop you?"

I saw Sandy shake her head with a pained smile, as she scooped Terry up and he told her to keep in touch and take care. For an instant it seemed she was about to speak, but no words came. "You're getting your color back," he said instead, patting her shoulder again before standing aside as I opened the door.

"I'm sorry, Joseph," I heard her say, hesitating for a moment as we all stepped outside, but I didn't hear what he said in reply. When I looked back to make sure she was following behind us down the path, I saw him in the light of the doorway, small and rigid and still, with a stricken, dour look as he watched us, like a figure in a Greek icon.

# 20.

As the days grew colder, I felt lighter. Sandy was home, although she wasn't the same. She did not, like me, seem lighter. Rather, she seemed to be waiting for the days to leave her behind, while she sat with Terry under a tartan rug in the cane chair by her kitchen window, watching the weeds in her garden grow higher as Enya's *Watermark* played on repeat. It reminded me of how she had been in the immediate aftermath of Christopher's death. It was, to look at her, as though he had died again.

"For all Joseph's talk of signs, Sylvia, I never got a single one," she said from her chair on the first Saturday of her return, as I handed her a mug of tea. "I had hope, at least, but the waiting, the searching only to find nothing, made life harder than it was before. I saw Chris's face once, during a meditation, but what does that prove? Only that I have an imagination, like everyone else."

She sipped her tea with bleak resignation, and had no appetite for anything sweet.

"I'm sorry I worried you so much," she added, resting her mug on the side table. "No mother can bury her son without risking madness, I suppose. And what about that bastard Angus, still patrolling town for the public good?" She made a scoffing sound and peered into her lap.

I longed to tell her there had been progress on his case, but to do so I would have had to lie. Instead, I reached for her free hand from my seat beside her.

Shaking her head at the thought of Angus, she looked at me darkly. "He's proof enough there's no benevolent higher intelligence in this world, isn't he? No, Sylvia, I surrender to your side of the fence. We're most certainly alone in space."

I'd never have been able to imagine, previously, that I might live to regret Sandy coming so solidly down to earth, but at moments like these, I wished she hadn't lost all hope that signs, sent mysteriously by a process we couldn't yet understand, did sometimes arrive to comfort us. My own hope was that as time passed and she returned, with my support, to her old friends and routines, she would also return to herself again, as she had done before ever meeting Joseph. Already, as he'd said, her color was returning—likely owing to her having ceased taking the colloidal silver he himself had given her as a health tonic.

"He's well-meaning," she would say when I raised the subject of Joseph and her time at the property with his other residential students. A note of impatience often crept into her voice. "He's finding his way like everyone else, and trying to help people while struggling with grief," she'd continue. "He doesn't ask to be idolized. Anyway, I'm home now. Let it be."

And she'd return her gaze to the window, as though already waiting for the comet to rise, and I'd notice the look that would pass over her face, as though she was being reminded of everything we had no hope of transcending in our lives here on Earth.

Each day, St. John grew brighter directly over our heads as it neared its peak brightness in August, the point in its orbit nearest the sun. It was impossible to ignore.

Already in June, the comet was visible to the naked eye from Singapore to Freetown and as far north as Miami. I tried not to think of the fact that, the closer it came, the sooner Theo would arrive at the end of his contract, and so himself depart for new skies, along with the comet he had named.

But even in early June, the imminence of August wasn't easy to forget. There was talk in town of travelers, from interstate and overseas, booking out the Fairview Motor Inn, Whispering Elms Lodge, and Starlight B&B in the town center, for the festival weekend. Bookings were already spilling over, or so Tania had heard from her hairdresser, into the tiny trailer park by the gardens, and into motels two towns away.

In the windows of shops and municipal offices, at the football oval, and along the road out of town, posters and signboards had appeared announcing Joseph's festival. They all bore the official festival logo, commissioned by none other than the local council, which depicted the sunburst lightning flash of a cartoon comet. Beneath it, the words exclaimed:

OUT OF THIS WORLD!

ST. JOHN COMET NEAR-EARTH FESTIVAL: SUNDAY, AUGUST 3, 1997

A ONCE-IN-SEVERAL-LIFETIMES EVENT!

WHERE WILL *YOU* BE?

Joseph's address at the farm followed, along with the various emblems of the organizations lending support, listed like the production credits for a film—the council, the community bank, Safeway, and a nearby brewing company. Below them all was the psychedelic rock–styled insignia of Kingdom Come. When we saw the posters and signs in our outings together, Theo would invariably say something dry about having to prostitute his knowledge at a clown show, because not long after Sandy came home, he'd been instructed by his university to present a talk at the festival, just as Joseph had wanted. When he mentioned it, we were driving back from a hike, taking turns to sip hot chocolate from a flask as forest gave way to farmland through the windows.

"My head of department said it was a chance to raise awareness about the observatory," he grumbled, keeping his eyes on the road. I made sympathetic noises, but selfishly I was pleased to have an excuse to attend the festival together. While I didn't relish the prospect of returning to Bakers Road, the festival had become larger than Joseph, now. It would at once be a welcome and a farewell, the salute of an entire town to a majestic stranger. I wanted to be there, raising my hat to the heavens with everyone else, and especially with Theo.

I was still contemplating the festival when we passed by a new plywood sign affixed to the fence of the mechanics on the outskirts of town. I didn't overthink it in the moment, but in the days to come, the feeling it induced in me would intensify. It was the jittery, vertiginous feeling of being assailed by too many competing signals at once. The text, printed above a phone number, read: BUNKER INSTALLATIONS— QUICK & SECURE. CALL CARL.

On the third Saturday in June, six weeks before the festival, Theo was due to turn thirty-seven. For this Saturday, which coincided with the longest night of the year and a full moon in Sagittarius, I had planned a dinner. I wanted to thank him for the support and comfort he'd brought to my recent days, and to celebrate the beginning of what I hoped—with Sandy back and my nerves now steady—was a new cease-fire with at least one source of turmoil in my life. During that long, dark night before the days again began to lengthen, I wanted the chance to be close with him and to speak more intimately than we had done before. I told him to arrive at 7 p.m., and smiled at the sound he made through the phone: gruff, pleased.

Flitting around the house as Maria Callas sang, I made a Keith Floyd baked trout dish, roast potatoes, herb salad, and a chocolate hazelnut cake. I set out champagne flutes I hadn't used since an Easter picnic three years before, and lit the old candelabrum I'd bought at a Paddington market when I was seventeen. I built a fire in the dusty hearth. Amid it all, I noticed how rather than feeling haunted by the times when I had done such things for Christopher, I felt the newness of doing it for someone else. The window I had opened in inviting Theo into my life, however briefly, was helping me to breathe.

When he arrived, the moon was a white coin above the yard. It shone through the window, dimming the usual brightness of St. John high above us in the otherwise dark sky. He was dressed more smartly than usual, in black jeans and a blue linen shirt. As we kissed hello and he handed me a bottle of wine, I sensed something buoyant about him that a simple dinner with me did not quite explain. Inside, he exclaimed at the candlelit table, the fire, and our ready view of the moon, before I asked what was behind his air of excitement.

He offered a coy shrug and waved his hand about the room. "Isn't this enough?"

When I gave him an appraising look, he raised his eyes to the ceiling and conceded that he'd made a discovery.

"It's really a rediscovery," he went on, as I handed him a champagne and we moved to the couch.

"Wonderful," I said, waiting for more as I clinked my glass to his and wished him a happy birthday. As he spoke on with glinting eyes, I peered into the fire and noted with irritation the way an errant spark of hope had flared in my chest only to disappear. Some part of me had thought that perhaps his excitement concerned an extension of his contract, but it was nothing of the kind. Instead, Theo had found a near-Earth asteroid, lost since its first discovery in 1950. He spoke of it in the way sea captains and sailors used to speak of their ships, as a kind of woman.

"Her name is Lethe. I've been searching for her for years." The asteroid, he explained, was an Earth-crossing object of the Apollo group. There were thousands of them, but Lethe was one of the most potentially hazardous. "A hit from her could obliterate us."

"But now we know where she is?"

He nodded.

When I asked what the odds of collision were, he said that based on initial orbital calculations they were probably one in three hundred, at most, for around St. Patrick's Day in March 2880.

"So we have some time left. And what does she look like?" I asked archly, as though jealous.

"Blurry and rather gray in the pictures," he said, playing along as he sank back on the couch. "I doubt she'd pose a threat to any human woman."

But my levity was half-affected. I suddenly felt bereft as I sat there listening to him, without quite knowing why. It was when we shifted to the table, to sit facing each other, that I realized what it was. Theo had set up Nina Simone on the stereo and poured more champagne, and I had served the fish and salad and potatoes. Between sips, he told me that Lethe was the name of the Greek goddess of oblivion, as well as a river in the underworld, the river of forgetting.

"Dead souls would drink from Lethe to erase their previous lives before being reborn."

It was only upon seeing his dreamy expression and hearing his voice, which had become wistful and soft as he spoke, that I sensed how much of himself he had been holding apart from me. As he continued on without any of my usual prompting, I realized that he was sharing with me now in just the way I'd hoped he might. But the details he was sharing pertained to a long-lost piece of intergalactic silicate, instead of the real woman he had lost.

He paused from talking about Lethe to praise the potatoes, of which he was now eating a second serve. I smiled and set down my fork.

"If the river of forgetting were real," I said suddenly, "if it were right there behind us in the yard, would you drink from it?"

He looked at me directly, focused and sober at last. "What do you mean?"

I shrugged. "If you had the chance to forget the past, to forge ahead without the weight of your memories, would you take it or not?"

He followed my gaze over his shoulder to the moonlit yard as though the river were there, waiting for us to dip our cups.

Turning back around, he shook his head. "It's an impossible question. There are too many unknowns. Which memories would be erased, from how far back in time, and at what cost to cognition, not to mention identity? And in erasing one type of memory—say, episodic memory of a certain person or event or time period—what might that do to semantic and procedural memory? If I erased all memory of fights with my father when I was eighteen, for instance, would I still remember what I learned in Advanced Calculus?"

I felt like rolling my eyes. "Okay, let's say you could choose to erase select memories without risk to other abilities and functions—what then?"

He shrugged and looked at me humorously. "I wouldn't mind deleting my memory of being stood up by Cindy Thomas on the night of junior prom."

I sighed at his deflection. "Well," I said, "I often think I'd do it, given the chance. There's logic to myth. How are you free to live a new life when the old one won't let you go? Total retrograde amnesia would be one solution."

I sipped champagne, while he muttered something about chaos theory and the butterfly effect and how even the tiniest retrospective change would alter the present conditions of space-time, the very conditions that had led to us having dinner together at my table on his birthday in Jericho, Australia, in the year 1997, with a comet overhead.

"You know what I'm talking about, don't you?" I asked abruptly. "All I have left of my husband is his memory, but surviving him would be easier if I'd lost that, too."

Theo only looked into his glass as though searching for his reflection, as Lionel sprang up to take the empty seat beside him.

I shook my head. "Aren't you ever going to confide in me? Why are you happy to tell me about a distant space rock, but not the person you lost? I've wondered about her so often. I've waited for you to trust me with even the tiniest thing." I heard my voice growing shrill, felt the sting of tears building, and noted vaguely that I'd drunk too much.

He was slumped over the table now, his hands in fists, his voice cool. "What are you talking about, Sylvia?"

"The person who died, Theo. The reason you came to Bell Funerals that day in January." I flung my hand out incredulously.

He pressed at his eyes. "If you must know," he said after a long silence, "it wasn't my wife or lover, as you seem to think."

"Who, then?"

There was a pause as he looked at the bowl of salad between us. "An aunt. On my father's side. She moved here years ago. I was trying to help but her husband's family took over the planning, which was fine by me."

He gulped the rest of his champagne and glared into the darkness of the yard behind me.

"Oh," I said, peering at my hands, aware that the atmosphere we'd entered was exactly the opposite of what I'd had in mind. "So you weren't close?"

He shook his head.

"I see I've jumped to conclusions. I'm sorry. I'd supposed that grief was the reason for your sadness."

"My sadness?"

I nodded.

"Well, there are lots of reasons for that," he said, "genetic as well as empirical, but none I feel like discussing over birthday champagne."

As he averted his eyes to uncork the wine he'd brought, I waited to see which way the night would turn; whether or not there was a path of redemption. I was still considering what to say when he leaned forward and spoke again, while his face, despite his hopeful words, betrayed the sadness he wouldn't discuss.

"I'm not mourning some imaginary woman," he said. "I'm glad to be here with you. Can't we just have cake and watch the moon?"

And so we did, into the small hours, as the woman I'd imagined haunting Theo's dreams faded with the night, and I confronted the extent of my mental projections. Later, as we lay in bed, I decided that in speaking frankly, we had moved forward. The fact was that I understood more about Theo now, at the evening's end, than I had at the start, and the rest he would tell me in his own time, I was sure.

In the early morning while it was still dark, he reached for me blindly in sleep, enfolding me in his arms as naturally as if we had shared a bed for years, as though my body were a waymark in a landscape long known, a polestar. As we lay there pressed together, I tried not to project into the future, or draw up my equations about what it meant, or trust the way a part of me wanted to yield completely, like a lost soul landed at last in a safe harbor.

# 21.

ST. JOHN SPED INTO OPHIUCHUS, THE SERPENT-BEARER, AND ONE day as the sun set, Sandy and I walked into town through the botanical gardens to meet Theo, Vince, and Donna at the Rising Sun. The Sun was hosting a space-themed happy hour for the broadcast of the *Pathfinder* space probe, as it landed at last in the ancient river delta of Ares Vallis on Mars.

Along the avenue of poplars by the lake, Sandy braced my arm and nodded in the direction of the resident geese that were congregating some meters away at the water's edge, their white forms in the amber light like daubs in an oil painting.

"Look," she said in a hushed tone, "they have a leader, you know. Now that the sun's going down, he's ushering them toward the island where they roost at night."

We watched as one by one they braved the water, attending to each other's cues and flapping their wings before sailing out for the high rushes of their sanctuary in the lake's center. Sandy stood with rapt attention, her face open and tender in a way I had forgotten, and I felt as though spring had arrived even in the deepest winter. For some moments before the geese all crossed and the light faded, their cries rang out in the cold air, urgent peals of command and jubilation, the quickening sound, I thought, of life itself. When I looked at her again she was smiling, and before we walked on she reached out to squeeze my hand. The air between us seemed lighter, as though an ice crust had quietly lifted, and I longed for the change to last.

Outside the pub under the light of the comet, we had to pass by a man and woman flanking the entrance like mute suffragettes in office wear, each standing behind a sandwich board with a proclamation. Despite steering Sandy to the door without pause, the words echoed in my mind afterward like clues. THE LIGHT KEEPS GETTING BRIGHTER, and MAKE THE TRUTH YOUR OWN, they read.

"It's so good to see you," Donna said, with real directness and warmth when we found her and the others inside. I was startled to register the emotion that assailed me when we hugged as we'd used to, even as I wondered what had caused the change. Vince, too, seemed less strained than I'd seen him for months, and in the ad breaks while Donna and Sandy quizzed Theo on the ultimate aims of the *Pathfinder* mission, we spoke candidly about the cold and the latest showings at the Theatre Royal and his youngest son's newly lost tooth, all without mention of Angus or the case. When, like a roach through a crack, the thought slid in that it could be relief that accounted for their sudden ease—relief at seeing me with another man, a man they might suppose could replace Christopher, even erase my rage and grief—I pushed it aside, for their sake and mine.

On the screens now, we watched engineers at mission control in California high-fiving each other and being congratulated by the vice president, while animations showed the rover *Sojourner* coasting off over red sands to search for signs of ancient life. It was Independence Day in America, a timing engineered by the patriots at NASA, who deployed dozens of rockets to fire up into Martian skies during *Pathfinder*'s descent. There were celebrations closer to home, too—Theo had a friend at a tracking station outside Canberra who had partnered on the project, who was right now attending a celebratory ball.

We drank Martian Cocktails and craned our necks. There were cheers in the bar as the first grainy satellite images came in on the screens, showing the planet's rocky desolation. Theo raised his glass to mine and smiled, but my feelings were mixed. Our species seemed too destructive to deserve custodianship of another planet. Besides, I loved other planets for their strangeness, a strangeness that seemed to depend on the fact of our own absence across all their millions of silent miles. But I smiled anyway and he kissed my cheek. We were together, among friends, and Sandy, I saw, was gazing up at the screens with the same rapt attention as she had given the geese. The wheel of fate was turning in my favor, it seemed, and amid the clinking of glasses and the press of bodies as I found Theo's free hand, I felt almost as hopeful as everyone else.

It was only in the half hour before we left, once the crowd had thinned and the noise had lessened, that I discerned the particular shrieking of a table at the back, a maniacal sound, with an edge that made me uneasy even before I turned to look. When I did, I saw Zara with her head thrown back, her hair loose, her eyes oddly glazed as she laughed, and beside her, two identical dark-haired, middle-aged women, who appeared seized with the same secret delirium.

There seemed a hollow, stunned edge to them as I peered, an aura I did not want to be near, and I thought of the mythical gorgons. At my cue, Theo steered Sandy outside on a pretext while she was still distracted by the TVs, and before I followed, I mentioned to the barman that the table at the back had perhaps had enough to drink. But he threw me a wry look. "They've been on soft drink all night," he said, to which I could think of no reply.

As July pressed on, the atmosphere in town grew taut, and at times I wondered whether insects and bats could hear what I could only feel, the hum of a new frequency just out of range. The feeling couldn't be traced to any one thing, but rather an accumulation of happenings, a convergence no one could understand.

Rumors had been circulating that five teenagers from Jericho High School had spent a recent Saturday hiking in the national park, only to return that evening as a group of just three—before the remaining two were picked up along the road the next morning, pale from shock, with glazed eyes and a muteness that lasted for days, which they would not afterward explain. Days later, a hundred sulphur-crested cockatoos fell from the sky along the road out of town, for no reason that anyone could agree on. Meanwhile, the Department of Primary Industries had issued a warning to the district's citrus growers about a risk of unseasonal plague levels of bronze orange stink bugs, whose nymphs were now appearing in the orchards to threaten the winter harvest. And twice in a fortnight, there had been widespread blackouts in town from around dinnertime until dawn, for which the only explanation offered was that of a technical fault at the power station. On these nights, we would stream out of the sudden medieval darkness of our homes and onto the streets, to nod at our neighbors before craning our necks to the sky. Mars was a red star in the northwest and Jupiter glimmered in the east, but brighter than them both, high in the north, was St. John. Outshone only by Venus and the waxing moon, the comet had already beaten all predictions to drag visible twin tails of forty-five degrees, and its spotlight now presided over everything that happened in Jericho below.

On the night of the second blackout, Theo and I had been trying to catch sight of the Southern Delta Aquariids meteor shower in deck chairs from his porch, like fishermen looking in the wrong direction. Inside, we salvaged a cold dinner of antipasto and ate by candlelight. Drawing courage from the darkness, I asked him whether he thought it strange—the rumors, the blackouts, the apparent pressure system in the air.

He threw me a gloomy look. "You want it to be strange," he said, before suggesting that we might observe Jupiter's moons after dinner, and taking the hint, I didn't ask again.

St. John extended its global reach to share its light with latitudes still further north, from Tokyo and Algiers, to Denver and New York. On the Web, professional astronomers, amateurs, and those who had never before touched a telescope posted photos of the comet, often taken with simple Kodaks. In the photos, its flaring form—blue-green, golden, or white—streaked through the skies of six continents, over deserts and mountains at dusk, over beaches at twilight, even over the light-polluted atmospheres of cities at midnight. With reverent excitement and a spirit of international fellowship, these pictures—like the candid snapshots of a precocious and beloved global child—were shared on websites with occasionally pseudo-religious, punning titles like "St. John's Revelations" and "The Knights of St. John." A web page recently launched by NASA's Jet Propulsion Laboratory, to provide details about the comet gleaned from the Hubble Space Telescope, crashed on its first weekend after attracting over a million hits a day. At the same time, newspapers continued to track the comet's progress, making a meal of each headline, with one statewide broadsheet having run an updates column in St. John's honor since May, titled "Chronicles of a Comet."

In late July, as St. John passed swiftly from Ophiuchus into Sagittarius, the sign of the archer, near the Galactic Center, those who wished to see it at its best vantage from Earth—*the pilgrims*, we locals called them—began to arrive in Jericho. Cars and campers and four-wheel drives with interstate plates appeared outside the campgrounds and motels, and zipped at all hours in and out of Safeway. Their owners, when they materialized on High Street, were mostly a sprightly, robust-looking tribe of men and women with a smattering of children, all in sensible shoes. They could be seen eating sausage rolls outside the bakery in weatherproof parkas, procuring maps from the tourist information booth in the town hall, and seeking directions in varied accents from passersby to nearby walking trails and attractions, including the observatory, which offered group tours some afternoons.

But now and then, watching the pilgrims, I'd observe some detail that would give me pause: a woman in a leather outback hat, with a cardboard sign around her neck that read, TIME FOR A NEW SOCIETY: INTERGALACTIC FELLOWSHIP NOW! Or the denizens of a touring motorcycle club—not the Comancheros, I noted—careening in their leathers through High Street at night under the comet and the moon, like a band of grinning skeletons in their skull-patterned neck gaiters. Or young men wandering around town wearing the costume helmets of medieval knights, a reference to the chivalric order of internet citizens who were tracking St. John's progress in the skies.

The presence of the pilgrims seemed to act as a looking glass, magnifying the town's rising sense of excitement and self-importance. Even Clarence, who had nothing financially to gain from the visitors, seemed tickled. "Well, Sylvia," he said one afternoon, "here we are in out-of-the-way Jericho, with front-row seats for the main show and the tourists coming to us!"

Yet there was also strain, and everyone dealt with it differently. Vince had to issue a nuisance warning to the principal of the local primary school, who had taken to releasing rockets at night with his eight-year-old son, from the grandstand of the football oval. More than once, I observed my neighbor unloading huge quantities of potatoes and rice from the back of his station wagon under the eye of his nervous wife. On the way home from work one day, I crossed paths with an elderly woman seized by the vision of St. John in the sky. "It knows!" she cried, stricken, before her harried daughter emerged from the noodle shop to steer her away.

Queuing for pizza with Theo the next evening, in a grumbling line that spilled onto the street, we witnessed a brawl erupt outside the Empress between a cashier from the liquor store and one of the pilgrim knights, about nothing specific that we could discern. Through it all, just meters away, a busker I'd never seen before, dressed in a green alien costume replete with feelers, strummed Europe's "The Final Countdown" on his Stratocaster, until an otherwise respectable-looking retiree walking his dachshund on the other side of the street roared at him to shut up. At times like these, St. John's flare above us looked more like a distress signal than a celestial guest.

Soon the comet's blazing, winged image, after featuring on the cover of *National Geographic* back in June, peered candidly from none other than *Time* magazine, while rumors suggested that Comet St. John—alongside the Princess of Wales—was even in the running for Person of the Year—a prospect Theo seemed reluctant to discuss. Meanwhile, at least one prominent rock band had already released a single inspired by St. John, a wistful lo-fi number featuring guitar feedback, strings, and a chorus in which the comet was compared to an unavailable lover, a melody I often found myself humming after hearing it drifting from stereos all over town.

Eventually it felt like the whole world was waiting for St. John to near the sun, in the same way a crowd waits for a woman to be lifted in a ballroom dance, so they can applaud and exhale.

Looking back, I think a part of me knew, even then, that just as St. John's appearance in January had helped dispel my drive for self-destruction that night alone on my knees in the yard, with my blue pills and my last testament waiting, so would it mark me again before it left. I did not believe St. John was yet done with me. This was the reverberation of a knowing beyond reason that I heard, the kind of knowing Theo called superstition, and which I could not tell him about even at the end, when I'd been proven right, although not in the way I'd imagined.

As a child, I had awaited birthdays and graduations and New Year's fireworks with a trembling, portentous anticipation, aware that each new year, each initiation, entailed a reckoning with who I had been, in order to make way for the person I'd become. But I had never before felt an anticipation like this.

As the comet brightened, something within me was building. Strength, perhaps, or at least the readiness for change; for a new version of myself, a person glimmering just beyond the horizon, whom I couldn't quite yet see. Now, despite all the demons I had so far failed to vanquish, and in the midst of winter, the cold ground within me had begun to break, giving way to hope.

And so I imagined meeting the comet's brightest appearance in August with a light heart, by Theo's side, surrounded by the whole town and beyond, as a band played. I imagined a distraction from Theo's impending departure, a high point before the end. In my mind, I saw us rising into the sky together in the basket of Joseph's promised hot-air balloon, looking out over town in a moment of perfect stillness, a moment in which I finally felt the dawn of clarity, a clarity delivered as the comet's parting gift.

But I couldn't have known, then, how right Joseph would prove in claiming St. John was a test. My life even now retains a quality of aftermath. The daily glories of creation still catch my breath—a spider's gossamer web; a cloud shot with light; the face of a sunlit dahlia. But it's the vision of St. John that still waits behind my eyes: blue-white and ablaze, streaming in the darkness like a cathedral veil. I had my hopes for what its brightest point might bring, but I never guessed it would become a key, revealing the truth to me at last, reversing my blindness, my instinct for grievance and self-punishment and in the heat of re-birth, pointing the way to an unlikely freedom.

# ARRIVAL

# 22.

On the Sunday of the festival, when St. John had commenced its fleeting three-day tour of Microscopium, I watched dawn break over the cold yard as the comet finally faded into the daylight, and thought of Theo. I was excited at the prospect of hearing his talk, even if he was less than thrilled at having to deliver it. I imagined him cheering up when it was over and agreeing, since we were there, to walk the rounds with me from tent to tent, surveying the spectacle of humans drawn together in excitement. As the sky darkened, we would await the main event together, as lovers await the stroke of midnight that marks the end of the year. Laying out my warmest clothes, I heard the weather reporter on the radio declare a low chance of showers, and only mild winds. Against all odds, conditions seemed right, the stage set for St. John's grandest performance.

At noon, Theo and I met Sandy outside her house and rode off in his car together. Considering her recent experience at Bakers Road, we hadn't expected her to want to attend the festival, but she wouldn't hear of missing it. The whole town was going, including her craft group, and so was she. By then, St. John's brightness above us was veiled not just by the sun but by clouds, a development we all dearly hoped we'd be rid of by dusk. For now, the comet seemed to me like a bride concealed before the crucial moment. It did feel vaguely as though we were headed to a wedding—after all, it was true that we were about to celebrate the closeness of two bodies in space and time. Theo was dressed more smartly than usual, in a tailored jacket with moleskin trousers and black brogues; Sandy and I wore dresses beneath our coats. She clapped her hands in the back seat.

"Ooh," she said, with a thrilled sigh. "This is a rare day!"

"I'm amazed it's not raining," Theo said at the wheel.

I smiled at the road, trying to contain my concern at the prospect that Sandy might soon run into Joseph. The fact was, she was much improved, and had planned to meet up with a friend for lunch at one of the stalls. Besides, the potency of any encounter with him would surely be offset by the un-mystical presence of half the chattering district.

Cars and vans were banked up all along the verge outside Bakers Road when we arrived, eventually found a parking spot, and joined the crowd queuing for entry. Many had prepared as if for a pleasant siege, holding rolled rugs and canvas ground covers, baskets with thermoses and lunch boxes, coolers and endless folding chairs. Some, the pilgrims among them, also stood with appurtenances of greater seriousness— lightweight tents and sleeping swags, small telescopes and high-grade cameras. Stooped there burdened by these effects, stoic in quilted vests and polar fleece and the odd knight's helmet, the visitors looked momentarily like exiles from a war-torn city.

When, at last, it was our turn to pass through the gates, we met with Zara and Danny, who wore gum boots and hi-vis jackets and expressions of dutiful forbearance. They nodded at us as though we were the disappointing agents of an affiliate firm, as I slipped a banknote into one of the donation tins and heard Danny say in his high, flat voice to Theo, "You didn't have to wait, Joseph would've let you come 'round the back." But Theo only shrugged and strode forward into the crowd.

"Oh," Sandy exclaimed, casting her eyes around as we stood at the entrance between two enormous festival flags, as a triple row of silver star-shaped bunting shuddered in the breeze above our heads. "This reminds me of going to the Allandale Show when I was a kid!"

For a while we moved like sleepwalkers over the grass, taking in the sights as the crowd grew. At the foot of the schoolhouse, a pair of teenagers issued jam donuts and hot chips from the window of a pink mobile home. Further on, a huge peaked circus tent, filled with wooden crates and scatter cushions, offered FREE TEA, COFFEE, AND CELESTIAL TUNES. Lined up adjacent to the main house was a double row of white gazebos, representing all manner of local businesses and groups, from the Chinese restaurant on High Street selling Szechuan noodles to the Country Women's Association selling red velvet cupcakes.

In one stall, a sinuous man in an Akubra hoped to redeem the underdressed with a range of winter ponchos and aviator hats. Beside him, a defeated-looking psychic in a leopard-print sweater sat slumped over her tarot deck with a cigarette. Opposite, staff from the local library offered children's face painting and comet-themed coloring-in kits. The district Astronomical Society, near the end of the row, offered a twenty percent discount on annual memberships for new recruits, and FREE STAR-CHATS! Elsewhere, an employee of the local National Geographic franchise plied the unprepared with a range of compact binoculars.

In their own well-organized gazebo, council officers in orange vests handed out site maps to adults and free star-shaped pinwheels to children, while across the way beneath an elm tree, the first-aiders were stationed with their van, a vehicle marked—in an instance of synchronicity that must have delighted Joseph—with the words, ST. JOHN AMBULANCE AUSTRALIA. At the end of this row of stalls was a large signboard, announcing the order of the day with arrows pointing north and south.

Above it, someone had stuck a large digital clock in countdown mode. Alongside directives regarding portaloos, first aid, and lost children, the signboard read:

WELCOME, ST. JOHN!

ACTIVITIES & EVENTS

*STAGE AREA:*

12 P.M.—DRUMMING CIRCLE

1:30 P.M.—CELESTIAL MEDITATION

2:30 P.M.—THE ORACLES LIVE!

6 P.M.—COMET'S DISCOVERER THEO ST. JOHN SPEAKS!

**7:47 P.M.—CLOSEST APPROACH OF ST. JOHN COMET!**

*VIEWING ARENA/CAMPGROUND:*

BALLOON RIDES TILL SUNSET—BOOK BEHIND STAGE

FROM 6 P.M.—TELESCOPE VIEWINGS WITH JERICHO ASTRONOMICAL SOCIETY

Beyond this board was open pasture, the distant shape of Patricia's shrine, and, rising slowly over a low hill as drumming began, the rainbow stripes of a huge balloon. As we stopped walking to watch it float into the white sky above our heads, I wondered whether even Queen Elizabeth had been granted such a welcome, when she last visited our region during her coronation tour in 1954.

Over the hill, throughout the so-called viewing arena—five acres of pasture from which sheep had been cleared—people were already hunkering down, pitching deck chairs and small tents, declaring their positions under the sky. Some had brought portable camping radiators, others night-vision lamps that would glow with an unearthly red light when darkness fell. A few were setting up small kerosene stoves in order to make tea. Several were studiously assembling mounted telescopes, adjusting the angles at which they pointed to the heavens like rifles ready to fire.

A band of ribald children, a Spider-Man and Snow White among them, were chasing each other through the crowd, holding half-eaten sandwiches in their fists. Running along the arena's eastern side was the stage, now complete beneath a tin awning in case of rain, where a group of mostly middle-aged men and a few women sat drumming on a Persian carpet, nodding their heads and intermittently closing their eyes as though in a trance. The hollow, pattering beats reverberated as if from within the earth, like a question calling for response.

Gradually I began to notice familiar faces, out of context here. I saw Tania, sitting on a rug with a couple and their teenaged sons, pouring lemonade into red cups. I saw Clarence, prevaricating over his order of noodles at the Chinese stall beside his wheelchair-bound wife. I saw a librarian who had issued me my comet books months ago, tenderly tracing the whiskers of a cat across a young boy's cheek. Scattered throughout, I saw the hi-vis vests of Joseph's faithful, the ones who had not deserted. Among them were those I'd counted on seeing—Zara and Danny roving around, Roy in the tea tent, in addition to a few nonresidential students whom I'd long assumed had fled for other harbors. And

I was not surprised to see the dark-haired twins from the Rising Sun, carrying AV equipment toward the stage from the direction of the main house. But whenever I scanned the crowd, the figure waiting always in my mind's eye to darken my path was Angus, and I wondered whether he would appear.

We were still standing at the foot of the hill when I heard Theo take a breath and sigh. "Oh, Christ, here comes the meditation," he said, as I followed his eye to the grass below the stage where Joseph and Danny had appeared. Joseph, in a ski suit and a felted beret—an outfit he'd never have worn a few months ago—was conferring about something with Danny, looking perturbed. In a gesture of sudden emphasis, he shook his head and sliced his right hand vertically through the air, while Danny raised his palms in deference and nodded.

The way they were behaving unsettled me, and I wanted to know what they were saying. Watching them, I thought again of my as-yet thwarted efforts to find answers about the dandelion tea, and about Danny's knowledge of the accident. Peering at him, I thought of the absurdity of a baby-faced video store assistant being the point in common between the two men who plagued me.

Thinking to get it over with in the open air, I asked Sandy with great reluctance whether she wanted to greet Joseph and the others, and she turned to me with a wistful smile. "Later," she said, heading off to meet her friend. Despite the fact that we'd agreed to meet by the stage before the start of Theo's talk, I felt uneasy watching her wander away and merge with the crowd.

Seeking distraction, I took Theo's hand. We wove through the tents, and as we neared the stage, I could see the large paddock behind it, where a few figures presided over the deflated shape of a second balloon on its side. They were breathing air into it with some kind of instrument, as though the balloon were the body of a rare, ailing, technicolor creature. But before we reached it, I changed course. We stopped a few paces behind Joseph and Danny, who were still talking. I compelled myself to smile when he turned to us.

"Hello, Joseph, Danny," I said, nodding to each while Theo held himself apart.

With good humor they greeted us in turn, although in Joseph I sensed a guarded vigilance. Theo raised a stiff hand in greeting.

"Well," I said, casting my eyes around after a pause, "I just wanted to say congratulations on the event. It's quite an occasion."

Joseph touched his chest with a courteous smile. "You're too kind, Sylvia. This has been a collective effort, but I'm pleased to have planted the seed." He let out a joyful sigh and squinted upward at the sky, which had begun to clear and show a pale seam of blue. "My dear mother taught me that the manner in which a guest is received and sent off is in the end a reflection of the host. And with such a guest, we really did have to make today unforgettable—music, food, even flight! All the things one loves of life."

As Theo and I stood there, Joseph swept out his arm like a showman in the direction of the balloon. "Go take a ride, I insist!"

"This is a proposition I can support," Theo said in a low voice, watching the balloon with an expression close to rapture. At last it rose from its side, dragging the passenger basket upright as the pilot, a spiky-haired woman, moved in to light the burner's propane flame before ushering us, along with a few other waiting passengers, aboard.

Our ascent happened faster than I could measure. My heart was a fish in my chest. Theo reached for my hand. Over the wicker edge, as the hot air within the balloon roared in our ears, we peered at a world grown strange. People on the grass receded until they were brush tips on a vast canvas, along with the stage, the tents, the sheep in the fields. We floated over the trees, seeing them as the birds did, and we sailed over Bakers Road, where cars lay in wait like millipedes, until the town revealed itself in miniature—High Street, the sports ground, the botanical gardens, the cemetery where Christopher was buried, the mountains beyond the observatory.

As I looked over it all, the universe of my recent life, I felt the thrill of death rush through me. I felt how little separates a live heart from a dead one—just an accident of perspective, a collision with a power line, a few thousand feet. I felt, from this height, that perhaps it was possible to transcend it all, to see one's own life as a comet might, with the coolness of celestial distance. Other passengers were talking, but I didn't hear them, because by some strange enchantment, the moment was unfolding just as I'd imagined. While my mind was taking flight, I was aware of Theo's firm, warm hand in mine, his clear eyes and straight spine.

"What are you thinking?" I asked, and he took my face in his hands, smiling in a way I'd rarely seen, holding nothing in reserve. When he drew me closer, there was brightness and resolve in his arms and hands, as though he, too, suddenly felt the force of life hidden in our bodies and in the day, and as we kissed I felt sure that the thread that joined our paths had more length to run than the simple end of a university employment contract.

His words, when he spoke, were muffled by my duffle collar: "I could never have predicted you."

That was when I began to hold on to the minutes before we returned to ground, while we held hands and I watched the balloon's teardrop shadow below track our path over houses and backyards. The truth seemed easier to reach from up there.

We returned to ground as the band began to play. The crowd had grown since our departure. On the outskirts of the arena, media vans stood by while cold-looking men and women recorded footage for the evening news. People in deck chairs drinking champagne peered through binoculars and opera glasses intended for viewing the comet, while onstage an aging flower child in a red dress shook a tambourine. Theo and I watched from the grass. She was flanked by a trio of gray-haired dandies—two on guitar and one on a double bass, all wearing jeans and red velvet jackets. In dulcet folk harmonies, they sang Pete Seeger's "Turn! Turn! Turn!" reprising a verse from Ecclesiastes that I knew well from funerals.

It was during the second song, a bubblegum number about pink sunsets, that the dancing began. Children claimed the grass below the stage first, whimsical and free as a tiny troop of Isadora Duncans. During the next song, Theo deferred to the need to keep warm, and to my great surprise dragged me up to join the dancers. For a while we spun and swayed, holding on to each other's shoulders and caring little for how we looked. I kept one incredulous eye on him the whole time, so as not to forget this vision of him being frivolous and foolish, as the cold sky obscured the comet overhead.

Later, as the light faded, St. John finally appeared, on cue for the band's last song, while we stood eating black bean noodles from boxes, and Sandy made her way back to rejoin us. As people in the crowd gradually noticed it, a wave of hushed, enraptured sounds broke out. Some clapped, others threw back their heads and opened their arms as though to bathe in its light. Children pointed, and were raised onto the shoulders of their parents. Reporters issued directions to cameramen. Serious pilgrims peered through telescopes.

Everyone knew it was the same comet they had been able to see clearly yesterday, but now it was empirically bigger, brighter, closer than it would ever be again. Clear of the clouds now in the dark, moonless sky, it gleamed huge above us, its white and blue-green tails long and electric, directly overhead. In under two hours it would reach its maximum apparent magnitude, nudging the sun, and then its official departure would slowly begin, a fact that went some way toward explaining why the atmosphere in the arena with the band was like that of a farewell tour.

When Theo finally took the stage, he oscillated for a while in my mind between seeming familiar, as he had now become, and strange again, as he had seemed for so long after our awkward tour of the casket showroom in summer. Smiling, he gripped the microphone and greeted the crowd without any of the sourness which the talk had privately inspired. Like a conductor before a star soloist, he swept an arm toward the comet, where it hung in the northwest above the ghost gum trees behind us.

"As happens sometimes with great things in life," he began, looking directly at me, "I found St. John by surprise, while searching for something else—a supernova within the Virgo constellation. But there it was, a bright star that didn't make sense—a comet no one alive today had seen, making its way back to our neighborhood at last."

As he spoke, eloquently and without reference notes, I stood in the crowd and felt the fact of my feet in my boots on the ground, the cold air on my face and hands, the pulse in my temple. I listened to the voice I'd heard so often in my own ear, and watched the face whose expressions I'd long labored to decode. Before telescopes and astronomical survey methods, which is to say for most of human history, he explained now, comets would simply appear in the sky without warning, leaving those below to wonder why, and turn to God.

Watching him onstage, I felt the truth of my own nerves and cells, betraying my illusions of casual feeling. We had crossed a line some time ago, Theo and I, whatever our original intentions had been. We were in a wilderness of our own making now, and there we'd remain until one of us declared ourselves. I saw this as irrefutably as I saw the comet in the sky, while his voice echoed on, merging with the sound of my own mind.

"Today," he said, "we know that comets are icy objects the size of towns, nomads composed of remnants from the birth of the universe, that warm and brighten as they near the sun."

From my place in the crowd, I watched him with an electric, proprietorial feeling beyond my rational control, a feeling I couldn't deny was rooted in a sense of the future. As he continued, I considered how much had happened, and how much was forgone despite my plans. Reality had transfigured itself without my consent, and no mental mathematics, no retrospective squaring-up of mine could change it now.

"Comets are the ultimate revenants," he continued. "They come back, not from the dead but from remote regions of space. Halley's Comet is known for returning to our skies every seventy-six years, so that a person might see it twice. St. John will also return, but not even the great-great-grandchildren of the children here tonight will be around to see it. And so comets also teach us about time, the kind that's cosmic rather than human."

All around, night-vision lamps had lit up like embers. Feeling light-headed, I left Sandy by the stage and wandered off to lie down on the grass at the edge of the crowd. As I watched the comet return my gaze and Theo's voice echoed on in my mind, I anticipated the words I'd have to find when we were alone again. I wasn't sure how long had passed when finally I heard applause and felt people stirring and stood to find him making his way back to me through the crowd.

He smiled. "It's almost time," he said. "I'm helping with the telescope viewings soon, but I wanted to ring in the brightest point with you."

Once we had edged a few meters from the crowd so as to hear each other better, I congratulated him on his talk. Having resolved to confront the question of whether we had a future together, my heart had begun to race, and I thought that there would never be a better time to speak frankly than in that field below the comet at its closest, in the darkness of night. It was only when Theo took my hand in a tender way, and raised his eyes to mine that I realized he was going to speak before I could.

But all he managed to say was my name, before I became aware of a movement to the side of my eye, and turned to see Vince. He was making an urgent, beckoning motion and looked far more excited than I'd imagined he'd be on the occasion of St. John's peak.

"I knew you'd be here somewhere. I didn't want to wait," he said, nodding at Theo, who followed, bewildered as Vince steered me further from the crowd. By a wire fence in the shadow of the windmill, Vince gripped my shoulder as though to bolster me, while I stared into his intent, shining eyes and wondered whether he'd been drinking.

"Angus has been arrested," he said, grinning.

At first I felt the numbness common to such moments in life, when longed-for revelations are at last delivered. Before relief rushed through me, like water through a spillway, I asked him how.

"Attendant at the Shell along the highway still remembers him paying for fuel," he said. "Angus made an impression—apparently he reeked of alcohol."

As to the timing, Vince said the attendant's recollection was that Angus appeared just before the change of shift, meaning about twenty minutes before the accident. "The attendant said his memory of that shift was sharp," Vince added, "because his wife had left him a few hours before. He thought Angus looked about as crap as he felt himself."

When I asked, Vince confirmed that the CCTV footage was long gone. "But Angus is being detained for questioning," he said, "on the basis of our eyewitness."

I looked at my hands through the dark, at the still forms of the sheep beyond, and began to nod. I looked at Vince and then at Theo, who watched me with anxious inquiry from a few paces away. I hadn't yet explained to him my history with Angus, or my ambitions for justice—I'd worried that doing so would cause me to spiral again. But I didn't doubt he guessed which crime it was that concerned us now.

"I knew it," I said, with a surge of adrenaline. "He thought he was home free, too!"

I began to breathe in great gusts, worried I might fall over. When Vince patted my shoulder I looked down and noticed my hands shaking. It was strange, I thought as the sound of drums resumed, to find that the nearest approach of the comet had brought the beginning of the end for Angus. Like Nero, he would fall now, and I would be free.

I refocused on Vince as he began to issue cautions and qualifications—there was much more to do, details to corroborate and evidence to gather before we could hope for a trial—but only half hearing, I flung my arms around him. Vince, the friend who had remained by my side, through tears and drunken ravings, through harassment charges and doorstep supplications.

"We can discuss this tomorrow," I said when we parted. "Let me savor our victory tonight."

While Vince headed off to find Donna and the kids at the other end of the arena, I turned back to the crowd. I looked for Theo through the dark but couldn't see him. He had, I supposed, wanted to give me and Vince space, and was probably needed now for the telescope viewings with the Astronomical Society behind the stage. Some people had already begun to leave for the warmth of home and dinner, but the true faithful hunkered down by their tents, no doubt longing for the crowd to thin, to be alone with the sky.

Joseph's voice rang out from the stage now, announcing the time over the drums with the smooth drawl of a radio presenter. "And it's 7:47 p.m. on the clock, folks!"

We all looked up, then, taking snapshots, mental or physical, of the moment we'd waited for: St. John would never be brighter. When I peered back at the stage, I saw Joseph with open arms and closed eyes, craning his neck back in what appeared to be a state of transcendent bliss, like the frontman of a psychedelic rock band. How, I wondered, would he ever recover from the comet's departure? St. John would remain visible for some time yet, but at the prospect of its eventual disappearance I, too, felt bereft, as though the comet were a person, remote yet dear, on whose Delphic counsel I'd come to depend. Like some older, foreign cousin, prone to silence and pledged to an ancient Masonic league, St. John was bending down to kiss my cheek, before voyaging on without looking back, in the way of born travelers.

I wanted to be still, but I had to find Theo—I needed to be honest with him before I lost my courage; I needed to tell him I didn't want him to return home to the other side of the world. Barely aware of my feet, I sailed through the arena, searching, until I arrived behind the stage, where a half-dozen telescopes were angled at the sky like long-beaked waterbirds. Members of the Astronomical Society clustered around in orange tennis caps, guiding the adults and children who were peering through the lenses, but Theo was not among them.

* * *

In the hours that followed, I went through the motions people do when they find themselves to have lost, apparently without reason, a precious thing. I searched. I imagined that each time I turned a corner Theo would be there. I questioned myself, thinking that perhaps I'd been distracted when he had at some point explained where he needed to be, or where and when we were meant to meet. But as it grew later, my mind turned to other possibilities. Eventually Sandy and I secured a lift with some revelers, declining their invitation to drinks at the pub in favor of our homes.

Walking into the living room with a tight chest, I checked my answering machine to no avail. Briefly, I imagined Theo trapped back at Bakers Road, having fallen out of sight into a ditch. I even considered the outlandish possibility that Angus, cunning in the dark, had somehow escaped police custody, just in time to smuggle Theo away as a means of hurting me. As I fed Lionel, I wanted to tell myself that I was simply catastrophizing after hours of excitement, but like a broadcasting tower, my body was receiving a signal of dread.

For a moment, I sank back on the couch. My stomach turned as though I were caught in a swell, and when I closed my eyes it was a balm to see darkness. Fatigue overtook me, slumped there in silence, and I discerned an old feeling, the feeling of falling from the inside. I wanted to let sleep take me, to forget the night and all my questions. But slowly, like heat radiating from my center, anger brought me to my feet.

For whatever reason, on an evening of divine light and celebration, on the verge of laying my true feelings like a garland at his feet, Theo had left me, without farewell, to make my way home alone. So I dragged my coat back on, gulped down a half glass of wine, and forced myself out to find him. As I drove, I tried to disregard the slithering sense that his sudden disappearance was intentional.

# 23.

GRIPPING THE WHEEL, I THOUGHT OF THEO'S EXUBERANCE AND AF-
fection at the festival, the way he seemed to have cast off a burden, settled
something within himself. I wondered now whether that burden had
been me. Had he felt obliged to humor me all this time? Was he worried that admitting his disinterest in any real attachment might nudge
me back to the edge where he'd found me, the night we'd first kissed?
Perhaps, with his contract ending, he had grown tired of pretending.

I was clammy; invisible pins pricked my skin as I watched my own
headlights in the dark and considered whether our moment in the balloon basket had been his way of saying goodbye. It was possible he was
setting his house in order, placing his bags in the hall even now as I
sped toward him.

I hadn't picked Theo for the kind of man who leaves his door unlocked, but it nudged open at my touch. I knew immediately he wasn't
home—his car wasn't in the drive and the rooms were dim, although
the light above the kitchen table was still on. I stood blinking by the
sink, feeling my empty hands, wondering why I was still there. A half-
dozen amber beer bottles eyed me through the gloom from the kitchen
bench. A plastic wall clock I hadn't noticed before sounded its dull tick.
Like an actor onstage, I said his name out loud, to no response but the
shuffling of a creature outside.

When I turned on the main light, the house grew tame again, its
objects and sounds resigned to their proper stations, and I saw no reason why I shouldn't stay a while. Theo's clothes were spread around
the bedroom, his shoes were in the hall, his books and papers on the
table—there was nothing to suggest he wouldn't be back at any mo-

ment with an explanation that would make perfect sense. Until then, I'd remain calm and wait.

In the living room, I turned on the TV news and watched the footage and headlines without sound: arrests over suicide bombings in Israel; the death of the writer William Burroughs in Kansas; cleanup after the landslide in Thredbo. When the coverage finally switched to the comet, I watched as film of the festival appeared—showing the crowd in the fields, the Oracles onstage, the balloon overhead, and the comet in the sky at nightfall. It was strange to see on-screen what I had lived only hours before and a few kilometers away, contrasted with the events of remote lands, and for a while after I switched off the TV I felt disembodied, as though I were watching myself from an otherworldly distance.

Supposing hunger to be the culprit, I forced myself to eat a banana from Theo's bench as I paced around. It was only then that I noticed the disarray of his kitchen table, which aside from the usual coffee mugs and astronomy journals, was littered with messages on pale blue paper, written in spidery script. *In case of dissension, never dare to judge till you've heard the other side*, one read, a quotation from Euripides, as I learned later. Along with this message was a tarot card, taped to the note like a verdict: JUDGMENT, it proclaimed.

Hardly breathing in a kind of trance, I cast my eye over the other notes, each bearing their own cards—THE HERMIT, THE FOOL. Below each was a message that read half like a riddle, and half like a threat. On the first card, a tall, cloaked figure held a lantern emitting a star-shaped glow. On the second, a young traveler strode out under the blazing sun, apparently unaware his feet were inches from a precipice. Next I read the words:

In the darkness, along a barren path, a guide appears bearing a beacon of light. The beacon is nothing less than a star from the sky. The Hermit says: Heed the light to remember who you are, or else be lost.

At the beginning and the end we find the Fool, blindly arrived at the edge of infinity. Keep striding at your peril. Watch your step.

The notes were unsigned, but I knew of only one person who would compose cryptograms inspired by the Major Arcana. It was then, as I gazed stupidly at the disarray of the table, which I now saw included a half-empty bottle of Irish malt whisky, that I noticed the notepad that bore Theo's own handwriting, and put the question of Joseph aside. In my trancelike state, I found myself taking in the words before my conscience raised the question of what I was doing, and by then it was too late.

"Dear Sylvia," the text began. Over the course of three consecutive pages, this notepad bore the evidence of a fretful and aborted effort to write a letter to me. A prickly heat assailed me, to find myself reading Theo's words uninvited, but I couldn't make myself stop.

*Dear Sylvia,*

*I'm not sure where I'll be by the time you finish reading this, or whether you will—*

*Dear Sylvia,*

*I don't suppose it means anything now to claim that the words contained in this letter are words I have been on the brink of—*

*Dear Sylvia,*

*At times over the last few months, I've been able to imagine a different reality, a life that seems to run just beneath this one. What I mean to say is that part of my madness has been my indulgence in the illusion that the life that might almost have been, really was. I extended the terms of my agreement with myself, first for one day, then a week—*

The windowpane to the side of the table gleamed with condensation. The ashtray beside the notepad was full, like a nest of slugs. I sat down.

However I looked at it, Theo had been trying to say goodbye. From what I could tell, he was also on the brink of leaving town, and as I reread his words I wondered whether he had commitments back home that he'd been hiding, even another woman waiting.

But as the clock ticked and I grew cold, I conceived of another possibility, which made sense the more I thought of it: Theo was seriously ill, and for a host of reasons, had failed to tell me. He had wanted to extend the illusion that he had more time, "first for one day, then a week." His sadness, his frequent reticence to speak frankly, the way he had at times seemed on the brink of revealing something grave—it all began to make sense as I sat there alone in his house.

I began to wander then, as my eyes streamed in the silence. I knew that some found emotions, and scenes of farewell, more difficult than others. But when had he decided not to tell me the truth in person? He had underestimated me, and himself, I thought, as I stood over the sideboard in the living room where his phone sat in its cradle, beside his six-inch telescope and his appointment book and a scattering of old bills. I opened his appointment book, finding only a reference to the festival talk, but as I flipped the pages to next week, a news clipping fell out.

It was a photocopy of Christopher's obituary. I blinked to stop the words from blurring:

Christopher is survived by his wife, Sylvia, and mother, Sandy.

I didn't read the rest, the sentiments of love, the details of the funeral Clarence had arranged. I set the book down. With an odd, crawling feeling I looked over his bills, wondering whether any of them were medical. One by one, I cast them aside, learning nothing but the names of the companies that oversaw his rental property, his superannuation, his electricity.

I don't know what caused me to look twice at the last bill, an overdue car registration invoice. Perhaps it was the bright orange logo, or the date from over two years ago: March 1995. It was then that I noticed how the car described in the bill was not the green Holden that Theo now drove. The words as I read them seemed to stare back at me:

**Make:** Ford
**Model:** Falcon Sedan
**Color:** Navy

For a while after I sank to the floor, my mind was blank. I was a scientist, waiting for crystals to form on a watch glass. My body registered the truth before my mind did, and even then, it was a truth that defied all logical understanding. But facts began to assert themselves now in new patterns, and each time I told myself the direction of my thinking had become absurd, some new aspect would impress itself in a way that fit, until I found myself looking out from inside a new structure.

I'd assumed that Angus's threats were further evidence of his guilt. But I asked myself why a man harassed and stalked for months, over a crime for which he was innocent, wouldn't eventually respond with threats. And Danny, whose silence I'd been sure was bought by Angus, might have been behaving strangely not because of guilt, but because of my own ignorant crusade.

There was the stricken look on Theo's face when he'd first appeared before me at Bell Funerals. The way that on the few occasions we'd driven out of town, he'd always used a side route, a route that saved no time but that avoided Horseshoe Road.

There were the moments when he'd seemed about to tell me something more serious than what his lips would ultimately deliver. And the way that a person haunted by a terrible secret might be mistaken easily enough for a person in mourning.

I recalled the moment we first kissed, on the night the comet first appeared to the naked eye. The kiss had seemed illicit to me even back then, for its suddenness, for the way it seemed to heedlessly declare such things were possible after Christopher. But now I saw it for the crime it was, the crime Theo had always known our relationship to be. *You deserve to be happy*, he'd dared to say.

Other words he had spoken returned to me now, disclosing at last their true dimensions: *I was worried I took advantage of the state you were in*; *I'd like to have met you at a different time*; *I could never have predicted you.*

As I began to shiver there on my knees, all the ways I'd been mistaken began to dawn. I had stalked a man who had now been arrested. I had suspected Danny of accepting a bribe to lie, and Senior Sergeant Douglas of collusion. I thought of all the energy I had expended in interrogating the apparent wrongs of other men—Angus, Danny, Douglas, Joseph—all while sleeping beside the only man who truly deserved my hatred and rage: none other than Theo St. John.

When I noticed the light of the comet through the trees in the yard, I cursed the comet as Sandy had cursed it, for all it had delivered and revealed. And I had to press a hand to my chest, because suddenly it seemed like I couldn't breathe.

For a long while I stayed huddled on Theo's living room floor, shivering in my coat, wondering what to do. I knew it was shock, but I felt as though I'd caught a deadly flu. As I tried to disregard my own dim reflection in the TV screen, I waited in vain for some crucial detail to emerge, a detail that showed the conclusion I'd come to in the previous hours to be nothing but an awful illusion. Instead, every thread of my life since the accident continued to reveal itself as different—strange yet coherent, as Earth appears from the moon.

But so much remained in shadow. Why had Theo turned up at Bell Funerals on that day in January? It was a mystery I couldn't answer. Neither could I understand why there was suddenly an eyewitness whose testimony had given the police grounds to arrest Angus, if in fact he was innocent. And what had Theo done with that navy Ford Falcon, the car that I now suspected had killed Christopher? For a moment I recalled the words I'd almost considered for Christopher's headstone, in case the driver, reckless with remorse, ever visited: *In due time their foot will slip.* I wondered now whether the man I'd seen in the distance that day at the cemetery months ago had been Angus at all. And I thought of Theo in the costume of the tarot's Fool, poised at the edge of oblivion.

It was only when my chest grew tight that I realized I'd stopped breathing, and gasped. On the carpet around me, the paraphernalia from the sideboard and table was spread out like runes—the obituary, the car registration invoice, the envelopes from Joseph, the notepad. Again I heard Theo's words in my ears: *I could never have predicted you.*

I closed my eyes and imagined Angus being questioned by his own colleagues at the station, Angus pleading his innocence to blank faces, Angus being led to a holding cell, where he would curse my name. How could I forgive myself for condemning an innocent man, and betraying Christopher so supremely? How could I trust myself again, knowing how far my own instincts had led me astray?

As the feeling of falling returned, I eyed the scotch on the table. How easy it would be, I thought, to drink it all, to raid Theo's medicine cabinet, to seek oblivion as I'd long planned, and let my lover be his own judge.

Instead, I drank some water at the sink and tried to shutter my mind. But I was like a horse half-blinkered—from one vantage point, I felt I could finally see clearly; from the other, I knew I remained somehow blind. The reality of Theo's deception kept assailing me from new directions, even as I gathered the papers into my bag, for evidence, and made for the hall. I saw his three faces at once, like the vision of a hydra—Theo as first a reticent American stranger, and then as my mournful astronomer lover, was now betrayed as the monster from my own mythology: the speeding driver who fled the scene of my husband's needless death. The least that Theo owed me was a confrontation face-to-face, wherever it was I found him.

It was only now, paused like a thief in the dark hall, that I registered a sound breaking the silence, the sound of an engine idling outside. It was about to happen, I realized—the reckoning I could never have predicted, in just a second, and before I was ready. Sure enough, I heard a slam, followed by the patter of footsteps. But no one turned a key, and when I opened the front door at the sound of the bell, it wasn't Theo who stood there.

It took me a moment to process the fact of Danny and Zara on Theo's step at 10 p.m., regarding me with brisk attention. Briefly I considered apologizing to Danny right then, but knew it wasn't yet time. They must have been dropping off equipment Theo had lent them for the festival, I thought, as I forced a smile in the doorway.

"If you're looking for Theo, he's not here."

"We know," said Danny, a little sourly.

Beside him on the step, Zara met me with her intent, unblinking gaze and spoke before I could. "He's back at Bakers Road," she said, "with Joseph."

A weak, rubbery feeling assailed me as I stared at her and shook my head. I didn't want to believe it. "What?"

As the signals in my brain sent out their searchlights, my eyes rested on the amber pendant around Zara's neck in which an insect's wing was caught. When I spoke again, my voice was high-pitched. "What do you mean?"

"Move aside, Sylvia," she said.

I felt my mouth hinge open as Zara and Danny, single-minded as soldiers, pushed past me into Theo's house.

"What the hell are you doing?" I asked, louder now. It was as though I was speaking to myself. I watched as they loped around the dining area and living room, sizing things up like salvage pickers and gathering into their arms an assortment of Theo's work papers and books, including a box file of floppy discs. Leaning against the kitchen bench, I watched Danny pick up a hardback titled *Supernovae in Color,* while Zara folded Theo's six-inch telescope under one arm and nodded at him in a cue to leave.

As they filed past me in and out of the house with Theo's things and spoke in murmurs outside, I pressed at my eyes. Moments later, I quietly picked up the phone and called Vince's number, but before he could answer I felt myself wrenched away. With Zara and Danny each gripping one of my arms, we lurched out of the house. I tried to throw them off, but Zara tightened her grip.

"It's best if you don't fight us," she said, but she needn't have worried. As my mind strained to account for the new rifts in reality, my body had grown weak.

They steered me into their van's back seat, which was piled with Theo's things, and when I tried the back doors in the moments before they got in, I found them already locked. As though it mattered, I strapped my seat belt on, and noticed the sound of my own breathing.

I had the feeling of leaving the whole known world behind. Passing houses and fields rendered indistinct by darkness, I tried to steel myself, to gather strength, to assume a warrior's resolve. But my nervous system was still setting off new reactions. My body felt like it was welting from the inside, and I longed for the release of tears that wouldn't come. In my mind's eye I saw the blue fog gathering, only it was more insistent, more global now—the blue-gray haze of the world as seen through a glaucoma.

There were some things I wanted the haze to obscure. There was, for instance, the question of my own shame and guilt. And the way that, against my own will, my body seemed to harbor two contrary truths at once, even though the second should have surely extinguished the first forever. But if my care and hate for Theo flickered together, perhaps it was a fitting punishment for my part in things. The emotion I felt was primitive, unanswerable to the rational self that looked on aghast, knowing that my grief was not only for Christopher and my own disgrace, but also for the loss of Theo and the future I'd dared to hope for. The lump in my throat was a tumor I felt would never leave.

They drove in silence through the night under the gaze of the comet above, and the road became a river obscured by mist, a Styx of my own underworld. Here and there through the mist, visions appeared—Theo watching me from inside the balloon, Angus alone in a cell, Sandy cursing the sky, Christopher on our wedding day, my own figure kneeling over his casket. Between them, pages and knights and kings and queens from the tarot flashed in and out of view, regarding me with solemn purpose from their horses and thrones, as if to test me as I passed.

When Joseph appeared as the Hermit holding a star, hovering like a hologram on the water, I met the question of what he wanted from me, and felt the cold heat of fear. My notion of being free of him, of having the luxury to be magnanimous now that Sandy was home, had been another fiction.

As we turned into Bakers Road, I saw everything that had led me here: my grief and guilt and rage, my need for control, my crusade for Angus to be convicted, my obsession with the comet, my early admiration of Joseph, my delusions about Theo. None of them had been who I'd believed them to be. At last, I had left the realm of fantasy.

Now I longed for the road to lengthen, to have the luxury of more time. But already I could see the ghost gum trees by the schoolhouse, the dark paddocks beyond the farmhouse, the domed tents and night-vision lamps of the pilgrims who remained, and the windmill behind slowly turning against the sky. It was the same place I'd been just hours before, yet to my eyes now it looked transformed, as though I were seeing it for the very first and very last time.

# 24.

JOSEPH RECEIVED ME IN THE ENTRANCE WITH A GRACIOUS AIR, AS though I'd been invited.

"Sylvia," he said, lifting and lowering his arms like a bat disinclined to take flight. With a glance over my shoulder to the others as they followed behind, he closed the door and ushered me into the dining area. Near the table, a radiator glowed beneath a mantelpiece laden with old books, and the air was thick with the resinous, earthy smells of incense and baking. Roy, clad in his Kingdom Come T-shirt, was regarding me with careful attention from the sofa in the adjacent room.

I frowned. "Where's Theo?"

"Ah," Joseph said, clasping his hands with an indulgent smile. "Theo will be here any moment now. He's our guest of honor, after all."

Danny, settling into a chair by the entrance, said nothing, while Zara continued wordlessly on her way to the kitchen. Except for the low, whirring sound of the oven, the house was silent.

Joseph's calm eyes searched mine. "We're about to have a celebration."

For a moment I said nothing. He'd changed his clothes since the festival, and stood before me now in trousers, a blue silk shirt with a mandarin collar, and an ornate silk smoking jacket belonging to another time. Around his neck hung a string of mala beads, which in that moment I couldn't resist assessing as a potential garrote.

"Why was I forced to come here? And what's going on between you and Theo? I've seen all those cryptic notes and tarot cards you've been sending him—why?"

He smiled warmly, and invited me to sit by him at the laid dining table, where votive candles puttered beside a vase of peach-colored roses on a pristine white cloth.

"I was simply offering guidance, Sylvia, as I once did for you." He sighed and smoothed back a strand of hair. "I sensed energetically that Theo was going through a difficult time, a battle, if you like, between the lower self and the higher self, as we all do at times in life. As for our celebration—it's for the comet, of course! Naturally Theo, its discoverer, the soul chosen to alert us of its light, must be here."

For a moment he looked at me with a strangely tender smile, and even through his blue-gray pallor, there was a radiance I'd not noticed before. As he checked his watch, I considered the fact that none of what he said explained why Theo would have viewed his communications as anything less than harassment, why Theo would want to attend the party of a man he found tiresome and deranged, or why I'd been dragged there against my will.

"There's never been real cause for this divide between us, Sylvia," he continued, as I fixed my eyes on the door. "I've always seen you as one of us—few have come closer to sharing my own affinity for the comet as a celestial sign. It's others who have sown in you the seeds of doubt and suspicion."

I sighed. "If by 'others' you mean Theo, I can assure you I'm perfectly capable of being doubtful and suspicious on my own."

He squinted philosophically at the candles. "It's one of the diseases of this late time in history, to ridicule all possibilities that evade scientific proof. Who can wonder at the prevalence of depression, when our modern condition is to be exiled from our own souls' knowing, exiled from our human instinct to seek the Divine?"

As he spoke on, mesmerized by the sound of his own voice, I wondered how long to wait.

"We've only replaced our earlier ignorance of material reality with a contemporary ignorance of spiritual reality. How long must we languish until the two are understood as corresponding parts of the same ingenious creation?"

Clearly this was a rhetorical question, but still he looked to me as if for an answer.

"I see it in you, Sylvia," he said, before I could respond. "I see the rift between the rational and the spiritual; the logical and the mad. You long to connect with something more because you know it's there, but you're too afraid to trust it."

Fatigue swelled in me as I replied. "What I'm afraid of is accepting illusion in the place of truth, something I've found myself doing too much of lately."

Before he could say more, I rose from my seat and moved toward the kitchen, and he didn't try to stop me. By the stove, Zara was pouring batter into a large tin with her back to me. At the bench in front of her, the dark-haired twins looked up from their work to smile.

"Welcome, Sylvia," they said in near-unison, while chopping herbs with a strange, almost rapturous calm. As Zara turned around only to avoid my gaze, I wondered why the women were cooking dinner, while Danny and Roy, not to mention Joseph himself, did nothing at all. I wondered, too, what their own path toward Joseph had been, and why they were all so willing to serve. I thought of the seemingly whimsical prospect of six adults in a house, preparing for themselves a midnight feast. Amid the rustling sounds of the house, with its air of quiet anticipation as the women cooked and Danny lounged by the entrance and Joseph in the next room began to hum, I felt I'd entered the sphere of an enchantment that eluded only me.

Determined for answers, I peered back at Zara, who was scooping sugar into a cup.

"Where's Theo?"

"He's coming."

"So, you lied. Why?"

She looked up with a weary expression. "All things are as they should be."

When, seconds later, the doorbell rang, she met me with an arch, knowing stare, and I knew that Theo had arrived.

"At last!" Joseph crowed. "Our astronomer is here!"

"Where is she?" I heard Theo ask in response.

When I reached the entrance, I saw Theo stooped inside the doorway, staring straight at me. His mouth was tense, his hair disheveled, his eyes red-rimmed. Heavily, he moved forward, like a man approaching the gibbet, as Danny shut the door behind him and Joseph clapped.

"Wonderful, wonderful—we have a quorum!"

But Theo looked only at me. "Sylvia," he said, "you shouldn't be here. You need to leave now."

I couldn't understand why he had come, and was still registering the fact of his presence when I spoke: "We need to talk."

Joseph, ignoring me, threw up his arms. "Why would Sylvia want to leave before a festive supper among friends?"

Theo was watching me motionless, his eyes wide and fixed, his face a mask.

Joseph, seeing him, let out a bemused hoot. "Speak now, Theo. I don't think much will change as a result."

For a moment there was silence as we stood before each other. Seconds later, after Joseph left for the kitchen, I sank into a green velvet armchair, disinclined to accept any delays, as Theo in his leaden way took the adjacent seat. Danny, just out of earshot, remained slouched over a comic by the door, while Roy, still on the sofa in the adjacent room, scrawled in a notebook. I watched as Theo leaned elbows over knees and wiped his hands down his face as though removing an invisible film. When his eyes met mine, I saw that he was sober despite his smell of liquor. Barely blinking, I measured his mournful face, while the image of the man I'd known at the festival was overlaid with that of the man I knew now.

"When you disappeared tonight, I went to your house," I said.

I paused as he hung his head.

"Look at me."

When he did, it was with damp eyes and a grim mouth.

"I found Christopher's obituary in your appointment book, and the registration invoice for your old navy Ford, dated 1995."

As I leaned toward him, he drew a shaky breath.

"Tell me you weren't the other driver."

He shook his head. "I can't."

I closed my eyes before he spoke again in a low, tense voice.

"I'd planned to tell you everything tonight. But right now, we need to leave."

When I sat still, narrowing my eyes, he leaned closer. "I planned to tell you the truth so many times; to hand myself in. But by the time Danny remembered my face, I'd lost my courage; we were together."

He rested his head in his hands for an instant before steadying himself and looking back at me. "There's more to say but no time, Sylvia. We have to go."

I looked at him incredulously, amazed that he expected me to trust him.

As he implored me again to listen, his words grew faint. I didn't understand why he had mentioned Danny; all I could register was the absurd fact that he, Theo, was the man I'd been looking for all along. In his presence, I'd expected to fight the urge for violence, but instead I felt a void open in my mind. Here at last was the miracle of the Platonic solid, obviating my hypotheses, my mental specters, my need to surveil the world through the lens of my life's greatest loss. As the specters fell away, I continued to stare. This was the man whose car had appeared as if from nowhere that January night, the man whose shadow entered my life the instant my husband left it, the man who'd chosen to flee as Christopher sat dying, the man whose fate—no matter how much silence, or how many thousands of miles separated us—would always be tied to mine. As if none of this were enough, there was also the fact that having done these things, he had chosen to seek me out, to masquerade as a mourner, to stroke my cheek, to share my bed.

"Sylvia, please," he said now in the same low voice, with one eye on the kitchen. "The first thing we have to do is get out of here. You need to take my lead."

Even if there was something broken and defeated in his face and bearing, his voice when he spoke was urgent and afraid. But before I could respond, Joseph reappeared with a bottle of champagne and placed a record on the turntable in the corner.

"Let us dine," he said, with a gesture that demanded we rise, as Neil Young began to sing "Tell Me Why."

Darting a look at me, Theo faced him. "We actually have to get going."

Joseph met him with a cool gaze, gripping the bottleneck with both hands. "For an astronomer," he said, his voice now terse and growing louder, "for someone whose job it is to watch and see, you are astoundingly blind, blind to all the signs. You're both here for a reason, and you'll thank me in the end for the trouble I've taken."

"Let's go," Theo said, nodding at me, and before I could think, we were making for the door.

"Get back," Danny said robotically at the entrance, throwing down his comic and rising to stand.

Roy lumbered over now, thrusting his hands into his trouser pockets with an apologetic shrug. "We didn't want it to come to this. It's just really important that you stay."

"Roy," Theo said, drawing back to face him, "let us go."

"Can't. I'm sorry." He sighed, raising his hands as if to plead his innocence while Theo cursed and slammed his weight against the deadlocked door.

Danny's voice, suddenly savage, commanded him to stop, but Theo didn't. And then things changed again.

"STOP!" Danny bellowed.

In that instant, I looked back to see him holding, in his right hand, a silver gun. At my touch, Theo followed my gaze and at last stepped away from the door.

The gun was as compact as a joke shop toy and not yet pointed toward us, but in Danny's hand, it looked real enough.

I held my breath. Space, for an instant, seemed to warp around me.

Gently, I nudged Theo's shoulder again and inclined my head toward the table behind us.

"Sylvia has the right idea. Totally unnecessary, to taint our evening with this vulgarity," said Joseph from his place at the head of the table, where he had remained as if to avoid contamination.

I was relieved when Theo found his voice again.

"This is insane," he said, following me back and throwing a glance at Danny, who was standing by with a wide stance and a raised chin, like a cherubic soldier.

"Nice job with your disciples, Joseph," he added when we reached the table. "They're clearly doing God's work."

"And yet they are," Joseph replied. "Now, if you're quite finished, we'd like to start our supper. I've prepared a speech."

"Fantastic," said Theo, nodding and taking a seat beside me at one end of the table while I tried to process the fact of Danny's gun.

As Zara and the twins brought food to the table, I considered the discordance between the music's warmth and the way I felt, sitting there captive; the discordance between the evening I'd imagined and the evening that had arrived. The dishes were loaded on the table now—lasagna, roast potatoes and parsnips, creamed spinach, rice salad—as the first plaintive chords of "After the Gold Rush" began.

While the women, Danny, and Roy took their seats, Joseph, still standing, tapped a spoon to his glass. No one, hearing him speak, would have imagined that any of us were there under threat of violence. As I stared at my plate, stupid with shock and fatigue, his voice came to me as if from a great distance.

"At last," he began, "the comet's closest point has come, and while most have been happy simply to admire its brightness before it disappears, its signal flare has not been lost on me." Smiling, he glanced at Theo, while I noticed an almost imperceptible tremor in his right hand that grew worse as he spoke on: "The truth is, even those honored with a role in its arrival have required some help to recognize their responsibility. It takes clear eyes and courage to know when one has been chosen."

"You're mad," Theo interjected in a sour, dark voice, shaking his head.

"Yes," Joseph said, "you think I'm mad. For you, reality only exists to the extent of what your mind and your philosophy can comprehend. You don't see that, to reach wisdom, one must relinquish knowledge."

He clasped his hands together now with a look of absurd glee. "The truth is, we are all psychotic! If psychosis entails a loss of contact with external reality, then the ordinary human being is as much afflicted as the mystic, don't you see? One has lost touch with the invisible dimensions beyond the surface of material reality; the other is ever in danger of losing touch with material reality as he inches closer to the Divine. I myself have had only one foot here on Earth for some time."

He gazed into the middle distance beyond us all with a look of transformation, as though at the revelation of a holy landscape only he could see. Zara and the twins sat poised before their plates, regarding him with hopeful expectation. Roy and Danny were already eating with a quiet respect. Only then did I realize that all of them were showing, as Sandy had, the faint early signs of Joseph's own blue-gray pallor, like the subjects of a daguerreotype whose faces had been hand-tinted. I supposed this impression was merely an outward effect of a more insidious, internal malaise, a malaise Sandy had only just escaped. In another time and place, I'd have discussed it with Theo, and he'd have said something cynical and true. Now he was hunched over his plate, raking the tines of his fork over a mound of potato one of the twins had served him, in the Zen symbol for stasis.

I watched his hand as it moved, thinking of how I had held that hand and kissed it, the same hand that had held the wheel of the car that killed Christopher. But as Joseph kept talking and Neil Young kept singing and the feast on the table steamed between us, I almost wanted to laugh. Who was going to reveal the joke? I pinched my own hand, yet remained rooted there in Joseph's house.

"It was only when I saw the reports about the object behind St. John, and began receiving messages from my mother in dreams," Joseph continued, "that I realized why she had departed. From the spirit world she could orchestrate synchronicities more readily, syn-chronicities that could not be denied."

He was still speaking as if to himself, with a radiant, glaze-eyed rapture that made him unreachable. And as I listened, I felt my skin growing cold. It was then, in the midst of his dead mother's messages, Joseph explained—his voice growing strangely loud—that he began to see how the comet was not merely, like the planets, a means of timing certain influences and events on Earth. Nor was it only, as he'd first thought, an opportunity for celestial meditation.

"Friends," he exclaimed, lifting his palms. "For those who recognize its call, Comet St. John has arrived as a means of spiritual transport, a conduit for ascension!"

There in my seat, I held still while something plunged in my chest, as though at the cutting of a cable. My skin prickled; I could feel my pulse in my stomach and throat; my body knew that nothing about being trapped in Joseph's house was a joke, and as I held my breath I felt Theo reach under the table for my hand. As he did, I registered the framed photo above the mantelpiece, encircled with a garland of dried roses, that showed Patricia Evans as a bright-eyed young woman. Looking at her image, I recalled Vince remarking that she'd been a powerful lady. But who could have guessed she'd retain such power in death?

"Of course, there are no real endings," Joseph said serenely, as my palm rested inside Theo's and I tried to concentrate. "Lifetimes don't matter to the eternal soul. But to be born in a mortal body is to be born wounded, and for those of us here tonight it is simply time to leave our bodies behind."

As I grew aware of my own heartbeat, Joseph turned to me. "Per-haps, this time in the light, Sylvia, you'll finally see Christopher again."

25.

Joseph's voice had faded. I'd let go of Theo's hand. Even as my pupils fixed on the knife by my plate, I had left the room. I could feel the steering wheel under my palms, hear the engine in my ears as I drove that night beside Christopher, and I was trying to catch sight of his face. When I closed my eyes, he was still a blur of shifting form and color, a phantom; I could no longer see him. But as I drove on, I saw Danny. Standing by the road next to his Sigma, apple in hand. Now in my mind's eye, he smiled, just as he had done months ago when I'd sat with Theo at the café table on High Street. It was a smile of icy recognition, and slowly Theo's words from earlier began to make sense: *By the time Danny remembered my face, I'd lost my courage; we were together.*

I recalled the note I'd found at Theo's, the note that said, "It would be a shame to lose her," and knew that of course it hadn't been from Angus at all. I realized now that it wasn't Danny who had been coerced, but Theo. I looked back at Joseph, presiding over us all in the manner of a priest, imperious with purpose as he droned on. Danny, I felt sure, had provided the means for him to blackmail Theo to speak at the festival and to do whatever else he wanted. Otherwise, Danny would tell the police that he remembered Theo as the driver, and I would learn the truth.

The horizon line of the night hardened into focus at last. It was as though I could see the true curve of Earth, the shape of my life, the landscape that had led, perhaps inevitably, to this moment.

"And so," Joseph continued, looking finally at Theo, "I have been called upon to recognize what you can't—that in discovering the St. John Comet you have been called, Theo—called to join us tonight in our spiritual ascension of this physical plane, as we leave Earth behind while the comet is still close. We couldn't have let you betray your own soul—Mother was clear about that. You'll thank me on the other side."

There was the sound of glasses clinking. Neil Young was singing "Birds." Joseph's face glowed with wonder and pride. Theo reached for my hand again as though to steady me, and I let him. I peered at everyone as if through a fun-house mirror, finding only distortion.

Joseph passed the champagne, the twins served the lasagna, and Danny held up a potato on his fork to make a joke, all while I gripped Theo's hand and my mind's eye was eclipsed by a new reality. The intention alive behind Joseph's words couldn't possibly be true and yet I knew it was; it was likewise unthinkable that I could touch Theo now and still feel comfort, but in that moment I did.

At Danny's answer to why potatoes make good detectives—"They keep their eyes peeled"—Roy collapsed into laughter.

Peering at Danny, I wanted to choke him. Had he possessed a shred of moral sense, he'd never have offered his memory of a crime as a bargaining chip, or allowed Angus, a man he knew was innocent, to take the blame. But he was under Joseph's control, as we all were now.

Theo's plate, like mine, had been heaped without his asking, and as he stared at his food without eating, I knew that he, too, was in shock. Despite our ignorance of the practical details, we both sensed that the departure Joseph spoke of had nothing to do with meditation. Now, as I closed my eyes to escape the room, I recalled the woozy way I'd felt at so many of Joseph's sessions, and thought back to Vince's reference to ketamine, and the glazed eyes of Zara and the twins back at the Rising Sun, and knew that I hadn't imagined any of it.

"Thanks to our chefs for this delicious feast," Joseph said with sudden zeal, conferring with the twins about the excellence nutmeg lends to béchamel, before turning to Theo and me. "Leave room for dessert!" he urged, his eyes shining and huge. "There will be pudding!"

At last Theo looked up. "Strangely, I don't seem to have an appetite tonight, not even for pudding," he said, as Joseph fixed him with a tight smile.

Under the table he released my hand, but didn't look at me.

I rested my eyes on the comet through the window above Roy's head, an icy exclamation uninterested in transporting anyone. I wondered now whether I would ever have the chance to hear the whole truth from Theo, or whether it mattered anymore, now that we were trapped at an armed dinner party as our companions anticipated a comet's rapture.

The others were still eating when Theo raised himself to his feet and faced Joseph, who did the same at the other end of the table.

Theo's voice when he spoke was calm. "Joseph, I have a proposal. Let Sylvia go, and I'll give you my blessing for whatever your aspirations are tonight. I'll consent to participating in your plans."

For an instant Joseph glanced away, closing his eyes as though pained before looking back. "If you weren't so stubborn," he said, "I'd already have your blessing and your consent, and I certainly wouldn't have had to deploy my students to keep an eye on you, or appeal to your higher instincts with hand-delivered notes, or descend to the baseness of guns! You're too detached from your true self to recognize your own destiny when it's right here, the destiny your soul has already accepted. That's why I've had to behave like the enemy you always believed me to be."

As Theo opened his mouth to respond, Joseph sighed and raised his palm to signal that he wasn't yet finished, before continuing on in a weary voice. "When the lower self is too committed to the divisions of polarity to see that love and hate, life and death, heaven and hell are all prisms of the same totality—all mirrors through which the small self imagines it's separate from the One—it is impossible to awaken. Yet here I am, trying to help you."

During a pause in which Joseph stared at him without blinking, Theo said, "All that aside, I'm offering you a deal."

Joseph let out an incredulous hoot. "True consent can't be bought!"

"Isn't any consent better than none?" Theo turned his head in an odd, incredulous motion. "Weren't you about to make me hitch a ride to heaven with you against my will? What are the spiritual ethics of that?"

Joseph squinted at the table for a while. "The fact is," he said finally, "I thought you'd have seen reason by now. I thought the comet's truth would have reached you. My mother told me that's how it would be."

"Well, your mother was wrong."

In the pause before Joseph spoke again, I regarded the others along each side of the table: Zara picking at a thumbnail, the twins looking primly through the window beyond, Roy licking his fingers, Danny staring at his own fist, curled tight by his plate.

"It's my duty to ensure you come with us, Theo," Joseph said at last, louder now and with a strange note of supplication. "You've been chosen to depart with us at this precise time before the comet leaves. We have divine work to do on the higher planes," he went on, raising his shoulders in emphasis, "and I can't imagine what might happen if we left you behind. I'd prefer to have your conscious consent, but that's out of my hands, and I'm told that I already have the consent of your soul."

When Joseph turned to me and sighed, I felt my whole consciousness reduced to the beating of my heart.

"As for dear Sylvia," he said, eyeing me with a rueful smile, "she's a kindred soul at her core and here with us for a reason. She'd prefer the astral plane, and I'd prefer we were a party of eight, the number of infinity. But it's also true that the universe won't implode if she doesn't depart with us tonight. If she wishes to persist on this plane, to have other adventures, I can perhaps make a concession."

While Joseph proposed a sojourn in his cellar before the authorities arrived to find me, I imagined, behind the house, the blue-green beam of St. John's tail reaching down from the sky, a spotlight for the chosen, illuminating the roses in Joseph's mother's garden as a silver disc, softly chirring in the comet's haze, finally lowered itself to ground.

And I saw myself, meters below the earth, bound without fresh air, consoled by the knowledge that I'd soon be free of them all forever. I was hardly afraid of a night spent sitting in a chair, unable to sleep—I longed for the peace of solitude and silence, even in the cellar of Joseph's house. And yet I sat motionless, barely breathing, because I knew that accepting his terms would not grant me peace.

"If you won't release us both," I said, "then I'll have to stay here."

The calm of my voice surprised me. Watching Joseph's blue eyes widen, I recalled how I had once looked to those eyes for answers, for truth, for an absolution he could never give.

Suddenly Theo was turned toward me, holding my shoulders, scanning my face. "No," he said. "What are you doing?"

But I heard him as if from behind a pane of glass.

"Well," said Joseph, "if you're sure, my dear. I won't say I'm not pleased." He held up a finger like someone measuring the wind. "But we can't have any more distractions tonight. I'll hold you to your decision, Sylvia—not least because it's really a reflection of your soul assenting to join us."

Beside me, Theo shook his head and turned back to face the table, his body limp and motionless.

As Zara and the others began clearing plates and Neil Young began "I Believe in You," I tried to measure the chemistry of my decision, to isolate the central elements responsible. The need to preserve what was left of my own honor, if I was ever to reach a truce with myself, should have been reason enough not to walk away. But when I stared down the final molecule in my chain of reasoning, the intractable fact, for which I loathed myself, was that it was also out of love that I couldn't bear to leave Theo behind.

With heavy limbs we sat beside each other, staring ahead at the dark fields and the comet through the glass while the others moved around us, animated and tense with purpose. A part of me looked on from above, marveling at how it had come to this, as the bright object I'd taken for a beacon so crudely became a sign of death. While shock chilled my body, I tried to prepare myself. Because for all Joseph's rhetoric about departures and celestial homecomings, we were yet to learn how exactly it was all supposedly to happen.

Joseph, satisfied that the discord had been settled in his favor, was sailing around with a clipboard and pen, ticking things off a list, checking his watch and conferring in low tones with the others in the kitchen and living room.

"Not long till dessert!" he exclaimed when he passed on his way down the hall, as if to cheer us.

The women had returned to the kitchen, Danny and Roy had retreated to the adjacent room to huddle over a computer, and Theo and I were at last essentially alone.

I willed myself to think clearly, and without facing him directly, spoke softly: "We have to do something while they're distracted."

Theo turned to me. "You should have taken the deal. What point are you proving?" He sighed into his hands. "I don't want you to die here."

In my bitterness, I couldn't help but smile. "You'll understand why it's hard to believe my well-being is your prime concern."

He gave me a searching, crumpled look as I watched him, thinking it was the first time he had seemed pathetic to me. He nodded as the trees swayed through the window and silverware tinkled in the kitchen.

"Sylvia, you have to believe I'm sorry."

"Why weren't you sorry two years ago? You disappeared as I watched my husband die. Wasn't that enough? Why did you have to show up at Bell's, too?"

His eyes were wet. I wanted to shake him. He seemed to be searching for words, but as I waited I heard the commotion of glasses and dishes being set on trays.

"They're coming back," I said. "Listen, we're not martyring ourselves for Joseph. While I go to the bathroom and look for an exit, you need to distract them."

There wasn't time to say more. He nodded, and nudged me under the table just before the others began to reappear. Swiftly, despite doubting it would be of much use, I took the pocketknife he held out and tucked it up under my sleeve.

As Joseph began to speak and the absurd sweetness of toffee filled the air, I listened to the voice in my head. The words it had been repeating were predictable enough, the words that erupt when the landscapes of nightmare and fantasy and TV melodrama happen to present, without warning, as reality. *This isn't happening; this isn't real.* So went my refrain, a vain wish that recalled how the deepest root of language is incantatory. But beneath it was a knowing I tried to trust.

If I had survived losing Christopher, if I had survived my own longing for death, I could survive Joseph's madness, too.

On the other side of the night, I imagined a new life waiting, a life free of the men who had led me here.

# 26.

As everyone else took their seats, Joseph set a tray of crystal goblets on the table.

"Madeira wine," he said dreamily, raising a dusty, dark-colored bottle in one hand and casting his gaze over us all. "A wine befitting the occasion, wouldn't you say? This wine was bottled in 1910, the year my mother came to Earth."

With ceremonial glee, he unscrewed the cork and began to fill the goblets.

"When the grapes of this vintage were green on the vine," he went on, "the *Titanic* was being built. The Romanovs ruled Russia. Mary Baker Eddy was still alive, cinema was silent, and Pluto hadn't yet been discovered! But the year my mother was born was also a good year for comets. First we were visited by the Great January Comet, and then we passed through Halley's glorious tail. And so it was that when St. John appeared, my mother's soul knew it was her time to return home."

He raised his glass and sipped, before directing an impish look at Theo. "Theo, soon your own soul will remember why you were guided to discover the comet, and to have this experience with us here on Earth. Let us raise a toast." He beckoned for us to take our goblets. "To St. John. To the lowering of the great veil. To going home!"

Too overwhelmed to question him, I peered at the dark amber wine in my own glass, wondering whether a sweet liquor from 1910 was to be the agent of my undoing. I wondered at the long-dead men and women who had picked the grapes and crushed them under the Portuguese sun, a sun that had yet to look upon a world war. Everyone was drinking except for Theo and me. Even if it wasn't laced with some chemical medium for our so-called departure, we needed to keep our heads clear. In caution I raised the goblet to my lips as if to sip, but Joseph wasn't paying attention anyway. He was scanning his clipboard.

"It's nearly time. According to the schedule Mother dictated, Danny will take the pudding first, followed by the twins. Sylvia can go next, then in swift succession, Zara, Roy, Theo, and me. You know what to do so it's orderly. I'm told we should all have taken the pudding by twelve minutes past twelve, precisely."

To take the pudding; to swallow the medicine. On some level, I'd sensed that Joseph's method would be chemical, and now I knew its vehicle was to be not a wine but the most bathetic option imaginable, a sticky toffee dessert. Now, confronting the idea of poisoned pudding from a prophet guided by his deceased mother and a comet, a small, mad part of me wanted to clap my hands together and laugh. What a fabulously strange expression of human fervor; what a story to tell.

Danny was helping the others in the kitchen and Roy was on his second wine, moments later, when I nudged Theo's foot as a prompt.

Theo straightened in his chair and spoke, in a tone cunningly free of hostility. "Joseph," he said, "can Sylvia depart this world at the same time as me?"

"Oh," he said, still absorbed by his notes, "yes, I'd say that could be allowed."

A frail stream of relief entered me. This change to the schedule, which placed Theo and me together just before Joseph, represented a small victory in this grim new world, but I tried not to show it.

"I need to go to the bathroom," I said mildly now, as though I were a student in class.

Joseph nodded vaguely at my words, still glancing at his schedule.

I made for the hall, but Danny, with his gun in hand, was not far behind.

"It's two doors down to the left," he said.

Outside the bathroom, I turned to him. His face was blank, as though he were out on a stroll, as though he hadn't known I'd been dating the driver who caused my husband's death.

"So this is where it ends, hey, Danny? Who'd have thought our quest for peace would lead to this?"

He shook his head. It was the first time I'd seen unguarded warmth in his face. "This is the beginning. Soon we'll all be out of here."

I squinted at him. "It feels more like an ending to me." I knew it was hardly the time, but as we faced each other and I recalled his awful smile on High Street, I couldn't help it; I wanted to hear him admit it.

"How could you, Danny? How could you know Theo was the driver and not tell me? How could you let Joseph use your memory of the accident for his own purposes?"

He regarded me with a glum, stubborn look. "Joseph said the end justified the means. Anyway, none of it matters now."

As I shook my head and nudged open the bathroom door, I realized he was going to wait there in the hall.

"Danny, all I want to do is use the bathroom and gather my thoughts. I'll be back in a minute, okay?"

He bit his lip and shrugged. "I'm meant to wait outside."

"Please," I said. "To be honest, I'd hoped to have a quick cry alone."

He shook his head. "There's no need to cry."

"I'll be the judge of that."

I forced myself to smile, willing him to disappear until finally, in the first instance he had ever shown me mercy, he nodded and walked back toward the dining room.

There wasn't much time. I knew the need for escape was urgent, even if a part of my mind was lagging, incredulous that I'd found myself so rudely dropped into the action sequence of a film I'd surely seen before, featuring a lonely farmhouse and a mad villain and the knowledge that only my wits might save me.

The window in the bathroom was narrow, its pane thick and fixed. To keep quiet, I slipped off my tennis shoes and ventured down the hall in my socks. In Sandy's old bedroom, the window was locked, Theo's small knife useless as a lever. I imagined smashing the glass using the heavy vintage iron currently employed as a doorstop, but despaired at the noise it would cause.

Breathless, I surveyed another two bedrooms, immaculately neat with bunk beds, and a master that must have been Joseph's, replete with red velvet curtains and a sleigh bed—but I saw that their windows would require the same loud destruction. The back door, too, was firmly locked, and it was only when I entered the laundry, an old lean-to, that I felt any hope. Above the washing machine was a small ventilation window with an internal latch, the kind of window that might permit a quiet escape.

Seconds later, I was standing on top of the machine and trying to disregard the sudden twinging in my spine. I pushed the glass pane as far back as its rusted hinges would allow, far enough to poke my face out and smell the evening air, the earth and grass. Now as I strained to force the glass back far enough for a body to pass through, I knew that the best thing I could do for Theo and myself was to escape while I could and run for help. There was, after all, a small army of mostly rational people camping just a stroll away under the same sky, and I figured that one of them might have a mobile phone.

I didn't hear the door inch open. It was the shadow at the edge of my eye that caused me to turn, still poised by the half-open window like a burglar. My heart issued its silent throb before I registered who it was, and when I did, my primary feeling was of relief: it wasn't Joseph, but Danny standing there.

He closed the door behind us and sighed as I climbed down.

"I thought you were going to the bathroom," he said, frowning.

"I did. Forgive me, Danny. I needed some air—it helps when I panic."

He eyed me narrowly. "I'll walk you back," he said, ushering me into the hall, and drawing a key from his pocket. "This door should have been locked."

"Please don't lock it, Danny," I said under my breath, unable to help myself.

When he paused, as if considering my request, I held my breath. But then he was shaking his head, his resolve restored. "I'm locking it for your own good."

In his stolid, dutiful way, he bolted the laundry door behind us, and with it, that small porthole to freedom.

I felt the knife inside my sleeve, imagined sinking it cleanly into his soft, pale neck and taking the key. But as he returned the key to his pocket and squared his shoulders, all I did was stand there paralyzed, wondering where I might have been now had there been time enough for Vince to answer my call.

"We won't tell Joseph," Danny said, with a conciliatory look as we moved down the hall, and I realized that this small favor derived from what remained of his conscience.

But I registered no relief, feeling only the weight of my limbs and the invisible chains that held me there, in a house just a few hundred meters from a field of wholesome citizen astronomers, warm in their tents, whose appreciation of the comet had nothing to do with spiritual transport, and nothing to do with death.

Theo's face when he saw me returning with Danny was ashen. Joseph, in the midst of telling Danny to hurry up and serve himself from the tray of pudding now on the table, barely noticed us. As I stood speechless beside Theo, feeling my limp, useless hands, watching the steam ribbon into the air above us and noticing that the pudding had been served replete with toffee sauce and double cream—I saw that everyone, including Theo, was now wearing a Kingdom Come T-shirt, like the members of a tribute band. When Joseph said something I didn't hear and held out a T-shirt for me to take, I realized that the record had changed. It was Chopin's *Nocturnes* on piano, flowing through my ears like the voice of a friend, curious and plaintive and gentle at once, but powerless to deliver me. My father's quartet had played it, at some golden backyard barbecue in the recesses of my childhood.

I pressed the T-shirt to my eyes, but the tears came anyway. It was only seconds later that I heard the piano begin to distort into a warbling sound, and reopened my eyes to the sudden darkness of another blackout.

"Not fucking now!" cried Joseph. It was the first time I'd ever heard him swear. His face was a mask of concern as he called for Roy to follow him outside, while torch beams lit up and the music stopped.

Through the gloom, Theo seized my hand. For an instant we watched each other, knowing the sudden outage, the darkness and disorientation, had to be worth some kind of risk. We turned at the same time to follow Joseph and Roy, poised to run as soon as they unlocked the front door. But before we could even try, Danny, ever ready to dispel hope, appeared before us. With an insouciant glance, he gave Theo a torch before taking my arm with one hand and holding the gun in the other.

"You two, come with me," he said. "We don't want any surprises before the lights come back on."

As Theo lit the way, Danny steered us through the kitchen and down a set of stairs leading to a small cellar that smelled of lime. I thought of Persephone, descending with Hades to the underworld to dwell among the shades. A part of me marveled to find circumstance now conveying me to a cellar, the bardo of so many dark fairy tales, on a day when I had reached such heights.

"Our backup generator'll bring back the lights, so keep your clothes on," Danny said before bolting the door.

When he left, it was silent but for our breathing. After handing me the torch, Theo tried kicking down the door, but it was old and solid and wouldn't give. Sighing, he returned down the stairs and entered the pool of torchlight to face me.

"I found an exit in the laundry, by the way," I said flatly, "but Danny locked that, too."

Theo nodded at the floor before looking back at me.

"At least we're last before Joseph on the list. By the time it's our turn, he'll have fewer defenses. I'll detain him so you can get out."

Leaning against the cold wall, I considered this. I searched his eyes, remembering doing the same that afternoon, in the balloon basket hundreds of meters above the ground. He, in that moment as we sailed over this very house, had dared to speak of the impossibility of prediction. But I was the one who had stood there, seized with the audacity of hope, dreaming of a future and rooted in a version of the past that he, alone, knew did not exist.

"Would that make you feel better?" I asked finally. "To save me so I can return to my empty house and my blue fog and my job selling coffins?"

Against the wall, I sank to my knees. His face was ghoulish in the torchlight.

"I can't change what I did, but I can try to explain it," he said, and sat down beside me.

"I should never have been in the car that night," he began, turning his eyes from me to the dusty wine rack above us. "I was medicated and sleep-deprived and thinking of only one thing. I wanted to report my discovery."

He made a soft sound and shook his head. "I'd found a new great comet, and didn't want to share the find with anyone else. I'd been home all day on cold and flu tablets but couldn't sleep, so I'd sat up late, peering at the region around the Virgo star of Porrima, looking for a supernova. And there it was, thanks to the clear sky, a comet no one had named, one that I knew would be bright. I checked and rechecked my star maps before I knew for sure it was true. When I set out for the observatory, I felt like a king. I'd discovered something the world would soon be talking about, and I'd never have to compete for a research post again."

For a second he paused, and when he continued I heard his voice tremble. I felt numb as he explained how, approaching the bend in Horseshoe Road, he was blinded by the parked Sigma's headlights. He was moving too fast to stop or edge around me, caught as I was in the middle of overtaking Danny's car, and nudging into the oncoming lane.

"I almost didn't believe it, when I crashed into your side and kept going," he went on, speaking to the floor. "It was like I left my body. Once the car stopped skidding and I regained control, I told myself I was about to turn back. Then I told myself it hadn't been a serious impact, that it was a scratch, that whoever was inside would be okay, like I seemed to be."

As he spoke on, I saw it all: Theo, turning a reckless accident into a crime, driving on in the darkness down the back roads to the observatory; Theo, sitting at his desk, drinking a glass of whisky from the bottle left over from the Christmas party, trying not to tremble, trying not to think of the car he'd hit and left behind. I saw him, despite everything, finding the focus to email through his find to the Central Bureau for Astronomical Telegrams, noting the coordinates, and signing off with a salutation. And I saw him lying awake later at home, consoling himself before dawn with the thought that if he was relatively unscathed from the accident, so, likely, was everyone else.

While he sighed into his hands, I recalled myself in the moment after impact in the car, turning to Christopher and wishing I'd died, too, before doing so not long later on the ambulance stretcher. I recalled learning how, at the scene while I was blacked out, Danny had fled as soon as a passing truck driver slowed down, leaving him to arrange an ambulance alone, via CB radio. And I felt the days and years I'd lived since, stored as they were within me like stagnant water in a well—months and years of watching for dark cars, months and years of hating Angus and seeing the world through the phantoms in my head.

It was the sound of the phone that woke Theo, in the late morning: someone from Harvard, speaking in the warm tones of congratulation, confirming his discovery and asking to confer with him about assigning it his own name.

"I felt like the comet was my personal devil," he said.

I considered the truth of it: Theo had made his own bargain. The comet which had been a magnet for his hubris had become a sign of his secret shame. At last, I understood why his tone and expression would always darken so strangely, whenever he discussed the comet—except, perhaps, for the occasion only hours before, when he had given his talk on Joseph's stage.

"Even so," he continued, grimacing at the floor, "I still felt the thrill of being confirmed as first discoverer. It only faded a few hours later, when I heard on the radio about the man who'd died in an accident on Horseshoe Road, and the woman who was in a critical condition."

As he spoke, I saw him driving six kilometers out of town late that night, to the decommissioned water authority reservoir where families swam on hot days. It was easy, he said, to push the car in, to let the water take it, even if he couldn't quite believe what he was doing. He walked home along the back roads, cold with shock, collapsing in bed only to relive what had happened again and again, as colleagues from both hemispheres left congratulatory messages on his answering machine about his once-in-a-century great comet discovery.

"I never had the luxury of doubting what I was really made of, after that," he said. "And if I forgot, St. John reminded me."

I peered at our legs stretched out parallel on the terra-cotta floor, my feet still in socks, his scuffed boots in the beam of the torch, and for a moment I imagined us petrifying there and being found thousands of years hence, like the cowering residents of Pompeii after Vesuvius erupted.

How right Sandy had been, I thought, to curse the comet whose very discovery, it seemed, had cost us Christopher. Perhaps it was even in the spirit of some kind of cosmic justice that Theo and I found ourselves where we were tonight.

Theo turned to search my face. "Do you remember that day at the café when Danny was staring at us so weirdly? I didn't recognize him as the witness, but that was the moment he recognized me as the driver. It was perfect timing; that's why he smiled. Joseph wanted to blackmail me and now Danny could help him do it."

I nodded. "That was the real reason you spoke at the festival, wasn't it?"

"The festival was just the beginning," he said, sighing. "Every week

Joseph bombarded me with notes and calls. Danny would often park on my street."

Theo's voice was low and constricted, as he shook his head. "Joseph wanted me to see the light and join him. I should have reported him for harassment, but I was weak. I didn't want him to tell you the truth. I didn't want to let you go."

I felt his eyes but refused to meet them. Numb, I cast my eye over the bottles nestled in the rack like urns in a columbarium, and wondered where Danny was.

"As soon as I woke after dumping the car that January," he said now, "I regretted everything."

In my mind as he spoke, I saw him curse, cry, clutch his own head—unable to fathom what had possessed him to do anything but stop the car, try to help, face whatever was to happen. Remembering what he'd done instead, he'd tried to summon the courage to simply surrender himself, but thinking of conviction and disgrace and the end of the life he'd known, it was a courage he couldn't find.

"I didn't realize, then, that it was already the end of the life I'd known."

Turning away, I tried to imagine it: the hours, the days, becoming weeks and months, waiting for the crucial phone call or knock at the door, ever alert to the end in the midst of maintaining the motions of ordinary life—shopping for groceries, phoning family, surveying the night sky for distant threats—all as the world anticipated the symbol of your private horror. For over two years, I thought, he had been waiting to be found out. It must have been like living within an interval that simply kept expanding, without end—the interval between the crime and the conviction. I could understand why some offenders left clues, or eventually simply confessed. The pressure simply grew too great.

I faced him on my knees. "It wasn't a coincidence that you turned up at Bell's that day, was it?"

He shook his head. "I'd planned to visit for a long time, not because any aunt of mine had died, but because I'd found out you worked there.

I wanted to see if you were okay. And when there was the chance to give you a lift, I took it."

"Did you have any intention of telling me the truth?"

"I'd been a coward too long," he said, holding my gaze. "I'd told myself I wanted to check you were alright, but really it was to make myself feel better."

I recalled how Theo had returned to thank me for the note I'd sent, and I'd asked him to show me the comet. I recalled how, amid the fireworks outside the observatory, he had peered at my scar and I had reached for him, only to find him looking at me not in fear, as I'd then supposed, but in shame.

"But I was ready to tell you so many times after that first day, Sylvia," I heard him say now. "Do you remember the night the comet first appeared, when I came to your house? The only reason I didn't tell you was because I could see what your own plans had been—the note, the pills."

He'd known he couldn't have chosen a worse time to tell me something so shattering. And then, he said, he'd lost his nerve.

I remembered the alcohol on his breath that night, and the way I had been so ready to explain his hesitation, his haunted look, and to offer myself as a grief counselor before reaching for him again, feeling, as I always had, that we were somehow kindred.

Now he was telling me about the moment we'd faced each other outside my car, months later on the evening after sleeping together, when we had met at the Rising Sun. Dimly, I recalled him telling me he had something to say, before delivering the news about his contract expiring in August.

"But you never did tell me. Not then, not even this morning." I hauled myself up from the floor and looked down at him. "You let me fall for you instead. You let me begin to imagine a future."

Rising to face me, he reached for my hands, but I held them up in warning.

"Sylvia, I fell in love with you, too. But I hate myself for what I've done."

His words entered my ears like the vacant lyrics of a song I'd already heard.

"You saw the letters. I was going to deliver you the finished one tonight."

I shook my head, not wanting to hear his pleading voice.

Stepping back, he drew an envelope from his pocket. "I have it here. The version I decided on."

Limply, I took it, but no arrangement of words could change the truth.

He braced his hands over his head and looked at me. "It was when I began to love you that I tried to hope there was another way. I wanted it, too, the future you imagined."

As he spoke on, I rested my head against the stone wall and closed my eyes.

I thought of the eruption of Mount Tambora in 1815, an eruption so violent that it had blocked the sun and left the world without a summer. I thought of the monster I'd imagined, who didn't exist. There was only this: a man holding back tears in a cellar, a man whose cowardice and self-interest and dishonesty existed—like an equation that would never balance—alongside all the things I'd come to love him for: his generosity and self-insight, his commitment to reason, his reverence for the universe.

"By the time the festival began," Theo was saying now, "I'd begun to believe it might be enough to love you, to try to make you happy. I'd begun to believe I could live with myself. I just needed a way to appease Joseph."

As he paused, I heard him make a soft, collapsing sound.

"Then I overheard Vince telling you a man had been arrested for my own hit-and-run. That's when I knew I had to tell you the truth, like I should have done from the start."

He went on explaining, while I pieced together the surreal logic of the previous hours, like footage from a warped dream. He'd initially fled the festival to gather his courage at home, he said, before heading to my place to find me without success, and steeling himself with a bourbon at the Empress. By that point, of course, I was already sifting through the debris on his own kitchen table, and for all I knew, we might have passed each other on the highway. When he finally returned to his house, I was gone again, but without my knowledge, before we'd driven off, Danny and Zara had left him a note.

"The note told me where you were," he said, "and considering how Joseph had been acting, I was worried."

At last, I understood. Theo was not here of his own accord either. Zara and Danny had lied about Theo already being at the farm in hope of luring me there more easily, and had used me as bait to draw Theo there out of concern, and so satisfy Joseph's desire for his presence. As for why they took his things, I supposed that was either a ruse for my benefit, or a means of coercing him should I not serve the intended purpose.

I stuffed the letter in my pocket and slid back down to the floor, wanting to descend miles further beneath it, down into blue silence in the core of the Earth. Despite my fear, something inside me had at last grown still. Whatever happened now, at least I knew the truth.

A moment later, at the sound of footsteps in the house above, I looked up at Theo and spoke. "We'll delay as long as possible, but when it's our turn for the pudding, we might just have to eat it."

He frowned. "I told you, once it's only Joseph left I can distract him while you get out."

"I'm not saving my own life at the cost of yours," I said, drawing up my knees. "I need to be able to live with myself. Surely you understand that?"

He glanced at his boots and sighed. "If we have to eat it, chew for as long as you can and try not to swallow."

When I suggested we should line our stomachs with something, he gave me a hopeless look. "This isn't some frat party, Sylvia. If Joseph's serious, so is his poison."

When I heard the turn of the key and the cellar door opened into light as Danny's pale face appeared, I was almost relieved.

I wanted to reach the end, and I knew what I had to do.

# 27.

THE HANDS OF THE CLOCK OVER JOSEPH'S HEAD POINTED AT TEN TO twelve. With pressed palms and a solemn look, he stood behind his chair at the table, and observed that the electrical disruption we had experienced was likely due to the high spiritual frequencies now gathered within the house.

"We might be running late according to our schedule," he added, "but to get to where we're going, it's always the right time."

Nodding serenely at Zara, he waited as she brought to the table a thick candle in a red glass. Standing limply in a loose circle around it, we watched as she lit the wick before ambling away toward the kitchen.

He smiled. "Friends, no sacred departure should proceed without a few preliminary words. First, Plotinus."

From the table he took a tattered notebook, and read from his favorite Neoplatonist as if conducting Mass: "'Our task, then, is to work for our liberation from this sphere, severing ourselves from all that has gathered about us . . .'"

His voice, over the music, which had resumed, drifted in and out of my awareness as I stood beside Theo. In my mind's eye was the vanishing point we were nearing, the end of the night, the dawn I might not see.

"'There is another life, emancipated,'" he read now, "'whose quality is progression towards the higher realm, towards the good and divine . . .'"

I watched the others listening, their faces attentive and calm, as though following this reflection we would wander back out together into an ordinary day.

After reading the Orphic Hymn to the Stars ("With holy voice I call the stars on high," it began), Joseph fell silent. Finally, like a conductor in perfect command of his sections, he nodded to Zara, who had reappeared with a tray of cups.

"It's time for tea," he said, and I knew exactly which kind.

Like everyone else, Theo and I took our cups. The liquid was the same tan color as the tea from the meditations, with the same earthy, roasted smell, and we were both careful to only appear to drink it. As the others sipped, I discerned a faint lull, as though a calming vapor had entered the room, affecting everyone but us.

I wasn't sure how much time had passed when Joseph spoke again.

"Danny, you will now be served," he said, as Zara stepped forward, proffering in both hands a bowl of pudding.

As he took the bowl, the muscles in Danny's jaw stiffened, and he peered at Joseph with a sober, probing look.

"Repeat after me, everyone, to recall why we're here," said Joseph, raising his hands. "'The Soul of each one of us is sent, that the universe may be complete.'"

At the echo of response from everyone but Theo and me, he smiled and spoke again: "'I am striving to give back the Divine in myself to the Divine in the All.'"

When the room was again silent, he returned his gaze to Danny.

Here it was, I thought—the test of faith that always arrived for the followers of a man like Joseph. For an instant, I imagined Danny refusing. I imagined all of us converging around Joseph, forcing him to kneel as we filed out silently into the night. It was almost mundane when Danny instead began to eat, slowly and without expression. The spoon clinked and scraped against the bowl. I noticed his smooth young hand. I wanted to stop him; I wanted to cry out to everyone that the only guarantee in following Joseph now was death. Instead, thinking of being forced to go next, I looked away, while Theo clenched his fists beside me.

It was only moments later when Joseph called for Roy, who reached calmly for Danny's arm and, like a latter-day psychopomp, escorted him down the hall.

Joseph glanced at his clipboard.

Zara served pudding into a line of bowls on the table.

Roy returned holding his arms at his back, as composed as an imperial soldier.

The twins, leaning by the mantelpiece, looked into each other's eyes.

I wanted to scream. I thought of Sandy being left to wonder whether I'd followed Joseph willingly. I thought of Vince and Lionel. Angus in a cell. I thought of Theo and myself, arrived in some liminal place, like the judgment hall of Anubis, waiting for our hearts to be weighed against the feather of truth, waiting to see how the scales fell.

I thought of Christopher, willing me to live. And I felt the possibility of my future, the future I'd so long denied, like a glimmering wave held in suspension. But the situation playing out before me was not one I could control.

It wasn't that I was giving up—in the cellar, I'd resolved that once the others had taken their turns and weakened, I'd try to take the laundry key from Danny's pocket, wherever he had laid himself down for ascension. My hope was that, if Theo could distract Joseph, I might force open the window and alert him in time. But it was hardly a foolproof plan.

Swiftly and without further ceremony, the twins took their turns to eat, while I sat back down in my chair. Now they wandered with Roy down the hall, their faces as tranquil as priestesses. When Roy returned looking unsettled but resolute, Zara carried out the same motions, and I thought of her parents asleep in bed somewhere, oblivious to their daughter's terrible enchantment. My heart was beating so violently now that I imagined it must, on some level, be transmitting a sound, a sonar alarm capable of being heard by someone with the right instruments.

As my breathing grew loud, Theo, still standing, took my hand again and I let him. Glancing up at his pale, pinched face, I knew that like me, he was simply waiting.

When Roy returned again, Joseph met him in the doorway with a glass of wine. Gratefully, he took it, while Joseph laid upon his shoulder a steadying hand. A little breathlessly, Roy announced that everything was in order. No sound came from the hall. Theo and I were alone together at the table. As Roy sipped and Joseph stood tall before him, I pictured mouths being wiped, eyelids closed, limbs straightened on beds as the passengers awaited their vessel in stasis. While I didn't fully understand the mechanics of what exactly Joseph expected to happen, it seemed to me that instead of a physical departure via the comet's companion craft, what the group anticipated was more of a spiritual merging at the comet's brightest point, beyond the body, beyond death—a merging with the supposed energies of the comet, as a conduit for ascension to realms we could barely dream of on Earth.

Pointlessly, my mind summoned the memory of Joseph, months ago, noting that his mother was "just a body, now." Feeling light-headed, I turned my gaze to the sideboard next to Roy. On it, a blown-glass vase stood filled with yet more roses, these ones white and wilting.

Now it was Roy's turn to eat the pudding.

I was still peering at the roses, gathering my strength, when Joseph spoke again.

"These two next," he said, fixing his eyes on us, as Theo tensed beside me and my plan dissolved.

When Theo spoke, I could hear the rage in his voice. "Why are you changing the schedule we agreed to?"

Joseph scoffed. "Why do you think?"

There was silence. On the table, four bowls remained.

Releasing Theo's hand, I spoke in a sudden burst. "Aren't you even going to tell us what's in the pudding, Joseph?"

"None of that's important," he said, stepping forward with a searching, rather soft look. "And there's certainly no cause for all this fear."

Absurdly, in the cold heat of panic, aware that every exit was locked, I felt myself trying to believe him.

"For God's sake," Theo said in a low voice, "let her go, and I'll take my serve now."

"It's far too late for all that," he said brusquely, before nodding at Roy. A moment later, the bowls were in our hands.

Joseph eased himself into an armchair a few paces away, and rested his eyes on us with a dreamy expression.

"'Man is a microcosm, or a little world,'" he said, "'because he is an extract from all the stars!' And to the stars we return." He smiled and gestured to St. John in the window behind us. "Isn't she a beauty? We're attuning to her frequency now."

Theo, standing beside me with his bowl like a votive statue, was silent.

I straightened in my chair and looked at Roy and Joseph, each in turn. "You can't force us to eat this."

Joseph raised his eyes to the ceiling. "Why fight to stay on this dreadful material plane? Density doesn't seem to have done either of you any favors—you both always look miserable."

He sighed. I felt the edge of the knife up my sleeve.

"But we don't have time for debate," Joseph went on. "You'll see reason soon enough."

Standing, Joseph nodded at Roy. Now, in a faltering motion and without meeting our eyes, Roy drew Danny's handgun from his pocket and pointed it at Theo's heart.

Sitting in my chair, I hardly breathed, hearing my own pulse in my ears in the seconds before I spoke.

"You won't shoot," I said.

Roy's eyes flashed in anger, before, with a sudden resolve, he turned the gun at me. "You're right," he said, with a frightened frown. "I'd shoot you first. Sorry, Sylvia."

At the sight of the gun's muzzle, I closed my eyes.

"Shoot, then," I said, holding my breath as I heard Theo pleading.

In my mind's darkness, I heard the click of Roy's thumb on the hammer, and suddenly, there came the roar of a bullet releasing and the sound of Joseph cursing.

Blinking my eyes open, I looked for an exit wound on my own body before following Roy's gaze to the window behind us, now broken, while Theo seized me by the shoulders, as if his grip alone could keep me intact.

Roy looked at us in warning. "Now!" he said, retraining the gun on me and suddenly red with rage.

At least, I thought, we had agreed to eat the pudding slowly. There was always the hope of our captors at some point dropping their guard. In Joseph's bearing and voice, I sensed the woozy fatigue of the tainted tea that only Theo and I had abstained from drinking.

But Roy remained alert, and when I turned to Theo with my spoon aloft to signal my intent, he answered me with a gray, defeated look.

In the end it was almost banal. We took our first spoonfuls at the same time, seated together now, facing the others. The toffee sauce was laced with brandy, and bitter despite the sugar.

Eating it, I began to simply hope that the pudding's effect would be painless, a gradual descent into sleep. I focused on the spongy bottom of the bowl in an effort to avoid the sauce, aware even then of the absurdity of it all. They watched us all the while, and in my exhaustion, a part of me was almost relieved the battle was over, my fate in the hands of the universe. We had entered into silence.

Joseph was smiling now. Roy had lowered the gun. The roses on the sideboard seemed to peer back at me as I watched them, their open petals ready to fall and glimmering strangely, and I thought of the book I had read about fractal geometry. As an odd warmth entered my chest, I thought of the grandeur of the world, and of all I would miss, including the small things I had failed to cherish while there had been time. Sitting there, I felt as though my mind were divorcing from the substance of bone and flesh, and heard Joseph crooning at us to finish as if from a vast distance.

When, between mouthfuls, I glanced through the window at the luminous comet, it seemed to dilate, as though to signal something I should by now have understood. I supposed that the effects of whatever venom I'd ingested had begun—visions, alongside a slowed rate of breath and a strange collapse of time. Now, after what felt like only moments, Joseph was standing over us like a prophet in robes, speaking of someone called Madame Blavatsky as though she were a friend we all knew. If astronomers could not explain how cosmic matter aggregates into worlds, he was saying, then who could tell what mystic influences may not be darting through space, and affecting the issues of life upon this planet and others?

As I moved my spoon, I gazed at his jacket's Japanese landscape of pagodas and volcanoes and winding paths, and for an instant felt myself there upon that other ground, far from here.

Under our captors' watch, we swallowed everything until our bowls were clean, then at last Roy led us down the hall, and by some act of mercy or grace we found ourselves removed from the others, in the small bedroom Sandy had used. Roy stood in the doorway as Theo and I lay down together on a lilac-patterned quilt, but after a minute Joseph called him, and finally we were left alone in the silence of the room, which smelled of stored linens and lavender.

"Try to throw up," Theo murmured sleepily, raising himself onto one elbow as I did the same. Bent away from each other to either side of the bed, we tried to retch as the world spun and I thought dimly that ours really was a pathetic end.

"Don't close your eyes," he said, moments later when we had given up what we could and surrendered our heads to the featherdown pillows.

Taking his hand in mine, I looked for some target to peer at out the window, but from where I lay, all was black; I couldn't even see the comet. Instead I began to count my blinks, while listening for any sound. Then, so gradually that I didn't notice it at first, I began to see a spiraling haze of light, not through the window but above me in the room. The light wasn't blue, but pink, and it moved before me like an aurora, or a dawn that had come for me alone. I gazed at the light as though it were the face of a friend, but I knew it wasn't real. If radiant projections at death were a power of the mind, I wondered why I couldn't instead see Christopher and my father. I was still looking for them inside the light when Theo's voice roused me.

"Forgive me, Sylvia."

It was the last time either of us spoke, before the sirens.

# DEPARTURES

*Dear Sylvia,*

*I've written many versions of this letter, each of them longer than the last, because on some level I've been trying to find a way to minimize the magnitude of what I've done, in your eyes and in mine.*

*The truth is, what I need to say can be said in very few words. I was the driver of the car that hit yours on Horseshoe Road in January 1995. I was speeding, and failed to swerve in time. Instead of stopping to help, I chose to keep driving. Hours later, I dumped the car, hoping to escape the consequences I deserved.*

*When I learned that a man had been instantly killed and his wife injured, I did all the usual things cowards who can't live with themselves do to escape. I drank too much, lost myself in work, and slept through the weekend. I did everything except confess to the truth, the one thing that would have freed me. As the months passed, I couldn't stop thinking of the man who had died and the woman left behind. I wondered what he'd been like. I wondered how she was coping. My mistake was tracking down the obituary last year, reading your words of grief, knowing your name. Sylvia Knight became a ghost in my mind. Eventually I began to think that if I saw you, if I could convince myself you were okay or even help you in some way, I'd feel better. That's why I turned up at Bell Funerals that afternoon. But meeting you made everything worse. I could tell you weren't okay.*

*It was at the end of the night that I showed you the comet, the night when you cut yourself during the fireworks, that I knew I was going to have to tell you the truth, and I lived the next few days in shock. It wasn't just the shock of deciding I was going to have to face justice, if I ever wanted to be able to forgive myself or escape the prison my life had become. It was the shock of feeling as though the universe, by accident or design, had conspired to make me love a woman to whom I could only be an enemy. Life grew stranger, after that. It was no longer just a matter of finding the courage to face the punishment of the law. It was also a question of finding the courage to face your judgment, and to surrender my own desire for a shared future, the kind of future I know we could have had in a slightly different life.*

*Several times, I planned to tell you and failed. Leaving it until now, after all that's happened, is its own crime. If I admit that on some level I can't regret it, it's not because I want to diminish the wrong of it, the deception, or the pain it will cause—but only because I can't regret having known and loved you.*

*With all that's good in me, I hope you can find happiness, Sylvia.*

*Theo*

28.

PEOPLE WERE SURPRISED TO HEAR THAT I WAS CONDUCTING THE funeral. Clarence hadn't expected it, either, although he seemed grateful for the help. It was hardly usual in Jericho to have so many deaths in one night, and the extra workload had driven him into a panic. Hours before I was released from hospital on the first day of spring, his allergic rhinitis was already raging, and considering the pileup of paperwork and the media attention and my own absence—not to mention dealing with the Coroner's Court, and the numerous next of kin—he was more ready than ever to retire to the coast.

"What a month it's been," he said, sniffling into a handkerchief by my hospital bed before lamenting the sudden loss of Princess Diana. "I will say, I think her service will be a reminder of what our profession can achieve. A reminder that every funeral is a kind of ritual theater that can only be performed once."

From my propped-up position against the pillows, I watched him sigh, adjust a stem of baby's breath on my nightstand, and peer through the window beside my bed, as though playing for time. It was not the first occasion since my resuscitation that he'd avoided my eye. Now, beside my overbed table, he began to pour our tea.

"Well," he said finally, setting down my cup and patting my hand, before sinking back into the vinyl visitor's chair, "what a trial you've endured, dear Sylvia, what a business. But I knew, when the first madness began with that comet back in January, I knew it wouldn't come to any good."

At first, I'd thought it was out of politeness that he'd never asked me what had really happened on the night of the suicides. But now, hearing the wavering note in his voice, I sensed the true reason was fear.

As the sun cast us both in a prism of light, I met him with a calm smile until he looked back at me, his eyes wide, with a faint gleam of alarm.

"I've decided on the program for the funeral, Clarence," I said, taking my cup from him and getting down to business. "Have the coffins been confirmed . . . ?"

After I had been moved from the ICU to the main ward, various visitors drifted in and out, bringing cards and flowers and bolstering words. Sandy presented me with the first pink tulip to appear in her garden, and left for company her favorite fairy figurine, a wry-looking waif reposing inside the curve of a crescent moon. Vince and Donna brought daffodils and a golden get-well balloon.

Tania, squinting at me over a tin of Quality Street bonbons, had asked the question my other visitors had only implied: "What was it like, to come so close to death?"

I simply told her it had been terrifying until, at last, I'd let go. She looked puzzled, but I wasn't sure what else to say. The truth was, my brush with extinction this time had been nothing like the first. I'd gleaned details from the doctors, details which formed the milestones of a road I'd walked in sleep: a cardiac arrest before leaving Joseph's house, followed in the hospital by hypothermia, an absent brain stem response, and a five-day coma; an ordeal induced by the pudding's lethal levels of pentobarbital, a barbiturate capable of euthanizing humans and horses alike.

During the cardiac arrest, before CPR restarted my heart, I had, in the clinical sense, died for the second time in my life. But this time, apart from my hallucinations in Joseph's spare room, I recalled no aurorae, no white light, no cosmic embrace. During the coma, apart from the mechanical functions that kept my body alive, it seemed as though my consciousness had been held in suspension, until at last it was restored, and I had no way of knowing where I had wandered, or why I'd returned.

For the entire length of my hospital stay, the TV news programs had recycled footage of the scene outside the Bakers Road farmhouse from the hours following the tragedy, when detectives and forensic investigators in hazmat suits trudged around in the gloom as the sun rose. Some reporters arriving on the scene early had interviewed the few pilgrims who still remained, standing by their tents in thermal wear, looking dazed.

"We were woken by the gunshot. We thought it was a car backfiring," said a man with a Chevron mustache. "But then the cops stormed in."

At night in my hospital bed, as other patients moaned softly in sleep and the sneakers of nurses pattered relentlessly on the lino, I'd recall the moment in Joseph's house before the gunshot, when I'd made my last play for life. The moment had reared into view like the accumulation of all the high-dive platforms I'd never yet, at any age, been brave enough to jump from. As Roy drew out the gun, a region of my body that held deep conviction had told me it might all be for show. It told me that if I knew Joseph at all, he'd never compromise on the crucial details of his own vision of departure from the earthly plane. Having one of us shot, I'd wagered, would derail his plans for everyone's orderly exit via the correct chemical medium, in accordance with Patricia's instructions, quite apart from risking undue attention. But if I could goad Roy into firing a warning shot regardless, I knew someone outside would likely hear it. Even if we were out of time, even if I was wrong and taking the risk killed me, at least I'd have tried. So I'd closed my eyes, stepped off the edge, and told Roy to shoot. But when he did and I found myself alive, I measured his wild look, measured the gun still trained at me, and didn't trust that I could take the same risk twice by refusing the pudding. That one gunshot had been my prayer for life, fired off into the dark sky through the glass beyond us, and I'd had no way of knowing where it would land.

* * *

On the same day that I phoned through a bulk order of coffins from my hospital ward—intent, for a reason yet to crystallize, that no one else should handle the details—reports broke of the ketamine shipment discovered by police inside a fenced-off woolshed in one of the back paddocks at Bakers Road. Not only Joseph but also Danny, it emerged, had been charged with possession in the past, although they each appeared to have escaped ever being charged with supply. Regardless, reporters now referred to Joseph using the epithet "drug-dealing cult leader," which did little to dim the fascination he seemed to inspire.

As it turned out, Kingdom Come had anticipated the public interest in its celestial departure, and had prepared for it in almost the manner of a PR company hoping to capitalize on a big launch. So it was that instead of having to make do with the usual paltry photograph or two, journalists had the luxury of a VHS videotape recording from each member, speaking directly to the future from which they planned to disappear. The tapes had been mailed to the *Sydney Morning Herald*, the *Australian*, and ABC. Inside each package, according to reports, was a note announcing Kingdom Come's successful arrival in the fifth dimension, the same announcement that had now replaced the website's weekly meditation schedule. In clips from the videos on the news, they all had the same intent, shining eyes, the same ardent intensity, like seers returned from the edge of knowing to bestow a last blessing.

"It's simply time to go home," Joseph said at the end of his own languorous reflection, before breaking into a radiant smile and pressing his palms together as if to pray.

"Mother Patricia awaits us, and we're ready to rise," concluded the twins in unison.

"The new dawn is here," said Roy, with a bashful grin.

Danny, less radiant and effusive than the rest, simply stared impassively at the camera and declared, "Joseph says it's time," before nodding like a boxer ready for the ring.

In light of what had transpired, the videos were oddly hypnotic, seeming to bear a weight of testament and prophecy that eclipsed any words that were spoken.

Because of the strangeness of the tragedy and because of the videos, which animated the public perception of people who would otherwise have existed only as thumbnail photographs in the collective imagination, interest in Joseph and the incident persisted long beyond the initial news bulletins. Local teenagers, lured by its aura of the tragic and forbidden and perhaps by the prospect of a remnant store of narcotics, began to trespass at Bakers Road so often that the council had to order the installation of a chain-link fence.

In cyberspace, strangers from around the world met in the chat-rooms of UFO-themed websites to discuss "what really happened" on the night of the suicides, why Joseph was really blue, and whether authorities had covered up the supposed fact that the "real bodies" had disappeared. In queues at the bakery, people would shake their heads and share scraps of information received thirdhand with beady-eyed fixation, intent on staking their claim.

"My cousin knew Patricia Evans," I heard a woman in a velvet bucket hat say one Saturday. "Strong lady, she was. Had to be, farming alone after her husband died. Proud, too. And to think of what's been done in her name!"

My own grainy image had featured, without my consent, in papers as far away as London: AUSSIE FUNERAL ATTENDANT SURVIVES COMET CULT was a typical headline.

The attention appalled me, but it was true: I had survived attempted murder at the hands of a charismatic blue fanatic, and people like survivors. It was a strange kind of violence, in the days and weeks after my release from hospital, to be pulled from the privacy of my own thoughts by near or total strangers looking for sound bites. In the history section of the library, in the slow lane at the pool, in the bread aisle at Safeway, and at my desk at work when I returned, I would be recognized as the woman who had survived Joseph Evans.

Their voices formed a chorus in my head, playing the same notes in different patterns: *Aren't you a brave one! That blue guy, what a fruit loop! How did you stay strong, when you thought it was the end?*

In the days leading up to the funeral, TV news programs, talk-back radio shows, and opinion columns picked over the facts until the facts gave way to myth. A TV reporter, on location outside the chain-link fence, concluded dryly that "Kingdom Come was right about one thing: Comet St. John will not be easily forgotten—at least, not on this planet." A Jungian analyst suggested Joseph was likely suffering from unhealthy maternal attachment, leading to a dissociative split following Patricia's death. A prominent journalist, taking a loftier approach, argued Joseph's longing to leave our planet was symptomatic of our present culture—as we teetered on the edge of a new millennium, already at the intersection of innumerable self-made disasters, was it any wonder that some among us were drawn to ask, "What if reality itself is a conspiracy?"

But because I refused all requests for interviews, none of the news reports described what it had been like to hear the song of the sirens and to realize they were real, before finding myself drifting in and out of consciousness as brisk, shadowy figures with soothing voices laid their hands on my body and removed me at last from that house. None of the reports explained what it was like to open my eyes and find myself moving on my back through the cool night, with the ghost gum trees looming above in the blue haze of the ambulance headlights, before the comet branded me with its bright eye and the world again dropped out. And none of the reports explained what it had been like to wake from a coma five days later, having survived.

I hardly knew how to explain it myself, except to say that I had woken with a clarity that felt new, and no longer had the appetite for recrimination or revenge. Even so, watching Tania from a distance in the mortuary, as she ministered to the bodies of the people I'd known, I couldn't help but ponder the question of cosmic justice, or divine retribution, or karma—whatever we call the prospect that none of us escapes the consequences of our actions in the end.

It was on the first Friday in spring, the same day Mother Teresa died in Calcutta, that I stood at the entrance of the Serenity Chapel holding a tray of white roses. I had only been discharged for a few days, and it was strange to be back in my polyester pantsuit, looking down at my orthopedic pumps on the brand-new mint-colored carpet.

Exacting in their plans to the last, Joseph and the others had left behind wills to be executed by the same solicitor, which—along with making provision for their website to be maintained in perpetuity—declared their desire for identical coffins, a shared service, and cremation, with ashes to be dispersed around Patricia's shrine. Throughout the weeks of delays—due first to the autopsies and then the difficulty of locating certain next of kin—the many family members who objected to these instructions had to be informed that the executor was legally bound to heed them.

Everything was ready. A refreshment station stood in the hall. Six oak-veneer coffins had, with some effort, been maneuvered onto the chapel platform. There was to be no formal order of service, no hymn or eulogy unless someone chose to speak. To avoid attracting undue attention, we had distributed service details to immediate family only, although all of the families had already elected to hold private memorials, to reclaim some degree of agency over their own goodbyes. As I waited in the doorway, wondering whether anyone was going to come, I craned my neck at the stained glass window above the altar behind me and saw it as if for the first time. It was a tree, with many branches stretching into a blue sky, while its roots, in a mirror image, extended downward into the earth.

I was still alone in the hall. Somewhere outside, a magpie lark was singing. When I'd given up waiting for anyone to appear, I turned into the chapel to lay the roses on the coffins myself, thinking, as I did, of who was inside.

The twins, whose names I only learned from the papers and who had returned to Jericho recently to care for their late father—women who had seemed girlish even in middle age, whose eyes had shone with hope for the celestial future they were promised.

Roy, who in his other life had apparently been both a computer technician and a volunteer football coach, and who had initially looked so incongruous and apologetic holding a gun.

Zara, with her flutelike voice and her decades ahead, ruthless with purpose in her devotion to a man too lost himself to claim authority over the truth.

Danny, motherless, I'd learned, and barely out of adolescence, who in his search for direction had sought Angus's advice on entering the police academy, a prospect which in the end could not compete with a one-way ticket to intergalactic paradise.

And Joseph, who in the end had ventured too far into the reaches of his own internal universe to ever find his way back to this one.

Stepping up to the lectern, I replaced the classical music playing on the stereo with a CD I'd held in reserve. Now I let Buffy Sainte-Marie sing "Moonshot" as I stood there, feeling momentarily as though the floor beneath me were pitching. When the song ended and I was feeling steady, I pulled a note from my pocket and read my chosen words out loud to the empty room: *I have always found that mercy bears richer fruits than strict justice.*

That was all. I stepped down, finding in my final glance that all I hoped for was that Joseph and the others had found themselves where they wanted to be, if they were anywhere at all. It was only then, before I left and consigned the coffins to Tania, that I knew why I'd really conducted the service. Clarence was right about rituals. If you don't formally mark the end of something, when is it over? And how else do you begin again?

On the evening of the funeral, I arrived at Vince and Donna's for dinner with a bottle of wine. It was a kind of homecoming, to kiss them both at the door, to be ushered into the glow of the hall, and to hug their two pajama-clad boys, four and five—so much taller than I remembered—before they were tucked into bed.

Ben, the youngest, looked at me with wide nocturnal eyes from his bedroom doorway and asked, "Did you die?"

"In a way," I said, nodding.

Faced with his look of incomprehension, I only smiled and added, "But I'm here now."

The words sounded glib, spurious, in view of the mortal magic trick I was laying claim to.

Sensing this, Jin, the oldest, posed a logical question: "How do we know you're not a ghost?"

As best I could, I explained how medical science had returned me to life—how well-timed maneuvers, medications, and machines could help hearts to restart, lungs to breathe, bodies to survive the otherwise deadly consequences of awful accidents. When I finished, their up-turned faces looked grave and impressed.

While Donna read bedtime stories, Vince and I sat together on the living room couch, eating Bombay mix and olives.

"Glad you're not a ghost, Sylv," he said, filling my glass.

I smiled. "If I'm not, it's thanks to you."

"But *you* seemed to know back in March that Joseph was danger-ous," he said, leaning back. "And your suspicion about the ketamine tea kept you alert for longer."

As I took my glass, I thought of the tenuous threads of circumstance that had spared me that night. Vince, on a hunch months ago after telling me of Joseph's historical ketamine charge, had begun to track deliveries at the farm, planning to tell me nothing until he had proof. On the night of the festival, the plainclothes junior officer Vince had stationed outside the farm called Vince for backup when Roy fired the gun—the shot that had saved my life.

"I never dreamed Joseph was murderous," I said now, looking back at Vince. "Then again, neither did he. Joseph believed he was saving us. But no one was able to save him."

For a moment we were silent, before, feeling my chest grow tight, I excused myself to step out onto the porch behind us. Leaning against a post, surrounded by bright-colored children's toys, I tried to breathe. The garden was dark. The moon was thin. Resting my eyes on the silver frame of the Hills Hoist, I recalled Sandy's visit to my bedside in the ICU, after I'd woken from my coma but was still intubated, unable to speak. Holding my hand, she'd spoken instead. Between tears and exclamations of regret, she anticipated my own silent question.

"At least Theo is alive," she said, leaning forward in her chair, her eyes glassy and astounded. "That's one mercy in all this, isn't it?"

Staring at me in the silence, she shook her head and gasped. "Oh, Sylvia, I'm so sorry!" she finally cried, wiping at her eyes.

Only later could I tell her, as she had once told me, that none of what had happened was her fault.

# 29.

IN THE MORNING, I WALKED THROUGH THE BOTANICAL GARDENS TO the cemetery alone, carrying a luminous spray of poppies in my arms like a child, thinking of the comet.

St. John had now entered the constellation of Cetus. Day by day, it was heading toward the celestial northwest, to the delight of Europe and the US. As a result, it had slowly begun to fade from our southern skies, and the pilgrims had packed up. There were no news crews, no American or German accents at the bakery, no gift shop displays anymore, and neither was there the prior sense of a collective breath withheld. With the passing of the comet's nearest brush with the sun, an event now infamous due to the suicides, we had entered an atmosphere of aftermath, despite the spring weather. At the tail end of the festival, the comet had become the sign of death some had always believed it to be. Because of it, whatever happened in the future, Theo, Joseph, and I would always now be tied.

I looked up at the poplars in leaf, felt the new softness to the breeze on my face, and smelled daphne blooming somewhere I couldn't see. Through the trees and at the edges of my eyes, the sunlight glimmered, while the geese marched with purpose past me on their way out the gates, and I recalled the strange, permeable feeling from childhood, of being separate from nothing.

At the cemetery, I replaced the lilies that Sandy had last left on Christopher's grave with the poppies, and lit a tea light candle. It was the day of our fifth wedding anniversary, after all. Thinking of him, I watched the red petals on the stone, and the flame as it quivered. I felt the sun on my hands and squinted at the blue sky while king parrots called. It was the first time I had knelt there and felt anything approaching peace, if acceptance at long last can be called peace.

The simple truth was that I was grateful to be alive.

Following my visit to the cemetery that afternoon, I sat beside Lionel on the porch holding the letter from Theo. Like skin kept clean around a wound, I'd wanted to cultivate a margin of separation between myself and all that concerned him. It seemed the only way to heal, the only way to learn how it was that I really felt in the aftermath of everything. I read the words, but the letter contained nothing that I hadn't already heard, and as I sat there I had the strange sense of holding myself in suspension, as if waiting for a new planet to show itself.

I thought of everyone who had died. I thought of how narrowly I'd escaped the end of my own life. I thought of Angus. He'd been dropped as a suspect while I was still in a coma, after the Shell attendant was deemed to be nursing a grudge against him, following a pub brawl arrest months earlier. Meanwhile, Sandy had flown to Queensland for a vacation as a way of moving on, and I pictured her now, by a resort pool somewhere, holding a spritz. But mostly, I thought of the strange relief I'd felt in my hospital bed weeks before, upon hearing her tell me Theo was alive. It was a feeling my mind had no control over, a chemical reaction, a sense of oxygen in my blood, and there on the porch I realized I felt it still.

Hours later when I finally sought him out in his cold backyard, I found myself gripping his body as though it were a keeling ship's mast. When I began to shake, he drew back and searched my face.

"I'd hoped you'd come," he said. "I've been waiting."

After I met his eyes, he pressed my head to his chest and spoke again, words that I could feel him address to the sky.

"I needed to say goodbye, first."

I knew what he meant, even as I frowned and pulled away, breathing in hard, ugly gasps while a force I couldn't name reached through the gloom, to gather in my chest and stomach and behind my eyes, but words still failed me. Standing before him on the lawn, waiting for my vision to refocus, I recalled Lethe, the river of forgetting, whose waters cleared the way for a soul's next life. And I realized that I didn't have to forget, in order to let go.

In an electric rush, there amid the sighing trees as the light fell, I saw that I was now free. I was free to choose my path in the life that had been returned to me. I was free to choose my own terms with the universe, when it came to questions of justice. Beyond the shadows of Theo's garden, I saw a glimmering point within reach, a second chance.

But he intuited none of it. He was speaking in a trembling voice about the statement he was ready to make, now that he'd been able to see me one last time.

"I'll go to Vince in the morning," he said. "I'll tell the truth, and it will be done."

I'd already sunk back in a deck chair by then, waiting for my heart to slow and throwing my head back to the stars, to Venus, to the silver glyph in the southwest that watched us still.

For once, I didn't need to think. I would bring about my own revolution, be my own judge. The words, in the end, spoke themselves.

"No, Theo. We have all been through enough."

The comet was still visible unaided for months, although it was no longer brighter than the stars. But as time passed, it retreated even further into the northern celestial hemisphere, venturing from Pisces into Aries, and began to sink and fade from view. As its distance from us increased, St. John became a ghost low in the southern sky, before at last we couldn't see it in Jericho with the naked eye at all. Later, as St. John's distance began to evade the capacities of amateur telescopes, and updates were issued to the public from observatories around the world, I would read it described in the manner of some international recluse being tracked, a celestial Lord Lucan, a luminary on the run. But to me, even back in September, the comet was already gone.

Sometimes in the course of ordinary life, I look at the tender side of Theo's neck that I like to kiss, or at his hands that reach for mine so often I could cast their shape from memory alone, and recall how for years I'd believed happiness had left me forever. I look into his green-blue eyes, the eyes that—wherever in the world we are—scan the skies each night for distant, dangerous, wonderful things, focused always on bright objects beyond here. And I think of how I could never have accepted, before—in my self-righteousness and rage—how emphatically two things can be true at once. And I realize that in love and justice alike, no law is absolute.

In the quiet of certain afternoons or at times on the edge of sleep, I still hear the sirens. The tritone sound drifts through my mind, gently insistent, like a voice. It calls me back to the fact of being here on this planet, eight light-minutes from the sun. It reminds me that death spared me not once, but twice. And because I chose to claim my life, the new continent I'd only glimpsed before is solid now, the winds are fair, and my gaze is on the future. It's summer again. Lionel's purring in my lap. And today the sky is blue.

Now, before Theo joins me in our garden, I imagine the comet's eye upon us, an eye before which the grandest and most grievous scenes of human life become fleeting and small. And I wonder what the Earth might look like in another four thousand years, when St. John returns. But the truth is that I don't know, and I'm not sorry I won't be here to find out.

# AUTHOR'S NOTE AND ACKNOWLEDGMENTS

In writing this book, I've drawn upon various sources related to the cultural, religious, and scientific history of human beings responding not only to comets but to the possibility of hidden or higher orders of reality in this universe. In particular, I wish to acknowledge the following: *Atlas of Great Comets* by Ronald Stoyan (Cambridge University Press, 2015); *UFOs: A Scientific Debate,* edited by Carl Sagan and Thornton Page (Cornell University Press, 1972), especially the article "Historical Perspectives: Photos of UFOs" by William K. Hartmann (drawn from chapter 17); *Knowledge of the Higher Worlds and Its Attainment* by Rudolf Steiner (Anthroposophic Press, 1947 ed.); "Man's Relation to the World of the Stars," a 1922 lecture by Steiner (accessed via the Steiner Online Library); *The Six Enneads* by Plotinus (trans. Stephen Mackenna and B. S. Page, accessed via the Internet Classics Archive); *Isis Unveiled* by Helena Blavatsky (Theosophy Company, 1982 ed.).

The titles of the two newspaper articles referenced in chapter 1 were inspired by two real article titles. The first is "Holy Comets, Here Comes Hale-Bopp" by Alan Samson, published in the *Dominion Post*, April 29, 1997, p. 7. The second is "Close Encounters of the Comet Kind" by Alan Hale, published in *Astronomy* 25, no. 3, March 1997, p. 56.

Sylvia's note to Theo in chapter 1 quotes the nineteenth-century rabbi Samuel David Luzzatto, drawn from *Words of the Wise: Anthology of Proverbs and Practical Axioms* (ed. Reuben Alcalay, Massada Press, 1970).

The quotation in chapter 9 referencing the Zodiac Killer is drawn from an encoded letter sent to the *Vallejo Times-Herald* in 1969.

Joseph's dialogue line in chapter 12 that begins "We belong not just to Earth" paraphrases the first line of Rudolf Steiner's abovementioned 1922 lecture.

Joseph's quotation in chapter 27 that begins "Man is a microcosm" is attributed to Paracelsus. His consequent reference in the same chapter that begins "If astronomers could not explain how cosmic matter aggregates into worlds" paraphrases Helena Blavatsky in the abovementioned *Isis Unveiled.*

Unless otherwise indicated, remaining quotations recited by Joseph, appearing within single quotation marks, derive from Plotinus.

All tarot cards described refer to the renowned Waite-Smith deck from 1909 by Pamela Colman Smith.

The fictional asteroid Lethe was inspired by a real asteroid called 1950 DA.

Finally, the quotation Sylvia reads at the funeral in chapter 28 is attributed to Abraham Lincoln by Joseph Gillespie in a letter to the *Herald and Torch Light* in 1876.

To the small galaxy of talented and dedicated people across two hemispheres who have helped bring this book to life, I now have the pleasure of giving thanks.

First, to my fabulous agent, Janet Silver, whose editorial insight, faith in this book, and steadfast support sustained me long before I knew it would be published.

To the team at Allen & Unwin, particularly Jane Palfreyman and Genevieve Buzo, for their commitment to this project. Special mention to Genevieve, my wonderful Australian editor, whose understanding of this story was clear from the start, and whose insight, care, and grace have imparted so much to this work. Also to production editor Christa Munns for all-round organizational excellence, Australian cover designer Alissa Dinallo for her considerable artistry, Jessica Friedmann for thoughtful copyedits, Pamela Dunne for her eagle eye, Rosie Scanlan and Isabelle O'Brien for publicity, and Sarah Barrett for marketing.

To the team at Simon & Schuster US, especially Tim O'Connell, my brilliant American editor, whose tireless edits, efforts on behalf of this novel, and generosity of spirit have been such a benediction. To US cover designer Natalia Olbinski, for sharing her great and intuitive gifts with this book, as well as Maria Mendez and Anna Hauser for always-gracious behind-the-scenes support. Also to Julia Prosser, Danielle Prielipp, Maggie Southard, Jonathan Evans, and Rob Sternitzky.

To Oliver Gallmeister and the team at Éditions Gallmeister, for their support of this book.

To the three amazing astronomers with whom I was privileged to consult on this project and who shared their expertise with such kindness: Dr. Davide Farnocchia, who charted a hypothetically possible orbit for the fictional Comet St. John; Dr. Brad Tucker, who assisted with my many queries in a series of delightful chats; and Dr. Donna Burton, who graciously shared her knowledge with this astronomy novice during visits to Siding Spring Observatory and Milroy Observatory in New South Wales. (Any inconsistencies remaining, that aren't the result of creative liberties taken for the sake of the story, are of course my own.)

To Erin Files, Kayla Grogan, and colleagues at ACM, for expertise and advocacy in foreign and film/TV rights, and Ryan Wilson from Anonymous Content, for believing in this book.

To the judges and organizers of the 2023 Victorian Premier's Prize for an Unpublished Manuscript, for which an earlier version of this book was short-listed. To the staff and stewards of the Wheeler Centre and the Readings Foundation, for a Hot Desk Fellowship gratefully received during edits to this book in 2023.

To the organizers of the 2019 *Ploughshares* Emerging Writer's Contest, and especially to fiction category judge Ottessa Moshfegh, for the precious encouragement of a prize win during a low ebb in my life.

To my dear friend Antonia Pont, for believing in me for so many years; to my beloved bookworm family; and to Brad P., the brightest point in my own sky.

*Bright Objects* was written primarily on the unceded lands of the Wurundjeri Woi Wurrung and Bunurong peoples of the Kulin Nation. I pay my respects to their elders, past, present, and emerging, and to the Indigenous Australians who were Australia's first astronomers.

# ABOUT THE AUTHOR

RUBY TODD is a Melbourne-based writer with a PhD in writing and literature. She is the recipient of the 2019 *Ploughshares* Emerging Writer's Contest award for fiction and the inaugural 2020 Furphy Literary Award, among others. Her work has appeared in *Ploughshares*, *Crazyhorse*, *Overland*, and elsewhere. Short-listed for the 2023 Victorian Premier's Unpublished Manuscript Award, *Bright Objects* is her debut novel.

ruby-todd.com

# ABOUT THE TYPE

The body of this text is set in Adobe Garamond Pro, designed by Robert Slimbach and released in 1989 for use across Adobe systems. A digital interpretation of a roman typeface by Claude Garamond and an italic typeface by Robert Granjon, this Adobe Originals font is a historical revival that achieves the maturity and balance of the original Garamond. Its elegance and contemporary efficiency make it a popular and enduring choice for desktop typography and design.